About the Author

Ian McClellan spent the last ten years of his career working in the video game industry, giving him first-hand experience of pop culture. He grew up on the Wirral, in the 1980s and 1990s. *Number Nine* is his first novel and draws from a lifetime of being uncool, in an increasingly cool world. He lives in North Yorkshire, with his wife, Emma.

Dedication

For everyone who is trying to find their calm place, in
the storm.
And especially for Emma, where I found mine.

Ian McClellan

NUMBER NINE

AUSTIN MACAULEY
PUBLISHERS LTD.

A CIP catalogue record for this title is available from the British Library.

ISBN 9781786124296 (Paperback)
ISBN 9781786124302 (Hardback)
ISBN 9781786124319 (E-Book)

www.austinmacauley.com

First Published (2016)
Austin Macauley Publishers Ltd.
25 Canada Square
Canary Wharf
London
E14 5LQ

Part One

2004-2005

Chapter One

Miles' Story

November 14, 2004.

It always struck Miles as ironic that his parents had called him just that, because he felt so often as if he lived his life a few steps behind everyone else.

Growing up, it was even as if they reminded him of this feeling often, although always with a twinkle in their eye. Miles' father enjoyed telling stories and he always picked the audience to make sure of maximum embarrassment for Miles. But Miles endured it, because both he and his father knew, in turn, that his mother loved them and they both loved to hear her low, staccato laughter. The best ones would make her cry, with the happiness and sadness of watching a son grow up with all the imperfections that made him perfect. The sad ones would make her cry, the tears of a job unfinished, a rough diamond that she didn't know quite how to polish. The ones she liked hearing the most, whether they were happy or sad, always centred on family outings or family Christmases. But, her absolute favourite took place many winters before and Miles would recognise it coming, like the opening bars to a nostalgic, childhood song.

The story started with Miles and his friends, bundled up in coats and mittens, taking turns at elaborate knee-slides on the slick surface of a frozen pond in a local park. In the story, Miles, as usual, was on the outside of the group, with his hat pulled down so far, he could barely see where he was going, or hear anything through the double layer of scarf and beanie. Of course, he kept getting it wrong and was working himself up with effort and frustration. Each time he got it wrong, he would slump further and further into his shoulders, his reddening face and shiny nose disappearing under a pile of damp wool. It wasn't as if he wasn't trying – in fact, he was attempting more and more advanced moves, as a kind of over-compensation for his under-performance. Of course, this combination of impaired vision and frustrated elaboration, meant that he didn't hear the ice cracking as he tried to execute a particularly ambitious breakdance move he had seen in a Beastie Boys video. He thought it was all part of the game, when the children scattered, abandoning loose knitwear and abandoning Miles.

In the story, he was fully committed to the caterpillar element of the move, when the ice opened up in front of him. Two huge pieces drifted apart from each other, creating an icy cavern and resulting in Miles disappearing headfirst and up to his waist in the frozen water. His wellies pointing almost vertically in the air, in some kind of homage to the Titanic as he disappeared under the surface. If this ignominy was not enough, in his panic and efforts to free himself, all he could think of doing was madly thrash his legs. Which on reflection, is exactly what might happen when you are eight years old and think you might actually be dying a full seven decades before you are supposed to. There is no rational thought; you rely solely on the instinct to struggle, as if held in the unwanted embrace of an elderly relative.

He was very young and so his memory was a haze of dark colours and muted sounds as the water closed around him. Water that was razor sharp with cold and metallic in taste. His eyes, under the water, were wide open with terror and although not being old enough for life to truly flash before them, he did remember dark thoughts, on how his favourite teddy bear might react to his passing. Or how the family cat might doze in confused grief on the bedspread, wondering where her warm bundle of pillow had gone so suddenly. Thoughts that you don't expect to have so young, and thoughts without the faculty of perspective to fully understand.

After what felt like an eternity, he felt the firm and secure hands of an adult on his ankles, his parents as it turned out, pulling him to safety, legs first. Soon he was free and gasping for air on the grassy bank of the pond. According to them, he was babbling incoherently, which he didn't remember clearly. All he remembered, through his tears of terror and embarrassment, was looking up into the faces and hearing the ringing laughter of his friends, who spent the rest of the afternoon doing handstands and trying to imitate him, upside-down in the cold green water. Something traumatic to him, had become a game that afternoon and then, over time, a family fable of which no one ever got weary.

The punchline to his near-death experience, because of course there was always a punchline, was delivered with a pause for effect. The punchline for this terror fuelled and tear-stained afternoon, was how he earned the nickname that would stay with him for over twenty years, well after he had grown up and moved away. From then on, even to those who were not there on the day, he was Duck-Head, or Waddles. Laughter from all; eye-roll from Miles.

But then there would always be an arm around his shoulder, a strong arm and the same words from his father. Life is a storm, he would say. You step into my house, you step into our arms and you are always stepping into the shelter.

The reason this particular story is important is because, despite the happy ending, this experience of childhood had stayed with Miles ever since. Firstly in the form of graphic nightmares – of suffocation, of fish eating his eyeballs, weeds growing in his ears, or pretty much any imaginative event that could occur when you are trapped headfirst in shallow water. Then, over the years the dreams faded, but the echo remained in a very specific feeling of dread. It became faceless, but always crept up from inside him at moments of stress or depression – the "exam worries", the "Sunday night blues", the "end of month skint", the "drunken memory loss". When he first moved to London, he would often get triple-whammies that would leave him sleepless, with a gnawing anxiety that lasted for days.

Fast forward, from the pond to present day 2004, and we find Miles, once more, stuck in that two-second phase between waking and thinking, where he was feeling distinctly uneasy about something that he had either said or done, but was not yet awake or conscious enough to remember what it was. This particular angst had been with him for some weeks and was always the same, with the same moment of realisation – the realisation he was waking up in a motorway services hotel in Surrey and not on the comfortable mattress that, until a month ago, had been where he thought he would spend most nights, for the rest of his life.

He gave the same groan that he had given every morning, a groan that resonated with the same broken, gravelly quality. A groan that had the same stale, lager taste that he had become accustomed to. Too many beers, too many hung-over mornings. All since making "The Decision".

"The Decision" of course, was something that was no surprise to his friends, and in fact, since it happened, everyone claimed to have predicted it at some point or other. If these premonitions were true, he wished that perhaps they could have said something earlier. He even called out one of his friends on that point and the sad answer was that no one thought he had the guts to go through with it. Then, like a hammer blow, he explained that far from this being just him, he told Miles that it was actually the general opinion.

To be honest, he didn't think he had the guts either. It had been spontaneous and reckless and it wasn't until the words had formed in the air around him, after several weeks of false attempts, that it had become real. Sometimes it's that way with big decisions, Miles always thought – the harder the decision, the harder the words, and then the faster the crashing sense of reality, and reality of carnage afterwards. Miles was a planner in life and had a very carefully constructed plan of what steps and moments one should take. He even called it "The Plan". Perhaps he could trace it all the way back to the moment in the pond. Control the outcome and you are less likely to get the dread.

But "The Decision" had ended all this and thrown Miles' value system into the air. He was in unchartered territory, off "The Plan" and because of that, Miles liked to stop thinking about the past, because it stressed him out very much. The smallest reflection would throw him into a panic and the trauma was so heightened, that it seemed to have erased some of the finer details in his memory of how things had got to this point. The last seven years were now just strokes of colour; red and angry, blue and sad. This was apart from one vivid story, which appeared to be the only one he could fully bring to mind when people asked. It had become his explanation for the whole episode, but to be honest, it wasn't one that really ever gave a convincing justification of calling off a wedding, three months before the big day.

The story centred on the kitchen bins, which wasn't a great place to start a story of any kind, so he could understand its unconvincing tone. It was also a very simple narrative and it started like this: every time he got settled down to watch sports on TV or his favourite documentaries, the latter usually presented by David Attenborough, his ex-fiancée would ask him to take out the bins. Guaranteed. Every time.

When you said it out loud, just that preface, he had to admit it sounded petty and ridiculous. So as well as implausible, for this to be some kind of crushing blow to what was supposed to be a lifetime together, was dramatic to say the least.

But Miles tended to think about this, more as a metaphor for what was a mismatch in their fates. He was convinced that you don't have a mental list of everything that goes wrong in a relationship, instead you just remember that last moment. That small thing, which on its own was petty and ridiculous, but when added to a crushing weight of other petty and ridiculous things, became a crashing tower of pettiness and ridiculousness.

The romantic in Miles, a romantic that he had barely realised existed until that moment, tormented over how it came to be. If fate was doing its job properly, he would love taking out the bins, or at least he would get something in return after the bin task that made the chore worthwhile. Perhaps on the way back in from the bins, one day he would bump into actual David Attenborough and then every week David and Miles would watch reruns of *Planet Earth* together. David would pause the TV at the end of each episode, take a sip of his single malt and give the real inside track of how they managed to get so close to penguins in the wild.

Given the immediate reaction to the bin story from almost everyone, Miles soon came to a conclusion. He concluded, not long after he had received what felt like his two-thousandth disappointed look, that instead of focusing on the scabs of their relationship, he would forge ahead with the help of lager, and endure the daily suffering of the dreads. It was his punishment, just like the fact that he was the one 'between flats' and had needed to take the pity of friends and the offer of a few nights at their houses. But soon, a deep sense of embarrassment meant he preferred to be alone and had moved into the hotel, although not a particularly good hotel.

That morning in the hotel, however, the final stages of waking up were interrupted in the most surprising fashion.

He heard a little cough, one of those half intentional, half self-conscious 'ahems', and it was unmistakeably female. The walls were thin at the hotel, but that sounded like it was coming from somewhere much closer than the next room, or the ice machine that was inconveniently located outside of his room. He didn't exactly remember getting back to his room and falling asleep the previous night, so instinctively his hand fell to the bed beside him to check for another person, as his mind raced to try and catch up.

'As if, loser.'

This time the voice had more confidence and also an edge of sarcasm that brought events back into full clarity. He had met "that girl" and "that girl" was currently lounging under a blanket on the multi-coloured 2-seater in the room. Her frame fitting perfectly to the small sofa, one slim, bare leg trailing outside, pale in contrast to the dark grey woollen material of the blanket she had slept beneath. Miles smiled – the previous night had been a big night, even by his recent standards.

The reason for the big night was that, after all the weeks of wallowing, he was actually taking the chance to go out and have fun. His favourite band, The Killers, had come to town again and were headlining at Shepherds Bush Empire. He went alone, but that was no change to the usual routine. Because of some of the choices he was making prior to "The Decision", he was often going to things like that alone. It was very simple, being in his relationship had led to a gentle but gradual untangling of his own social life. Some of the people who he had known for many years, and shared many late-night meals with in shop doorways in Covent Garden, fell away to no more than the occasional text on a birthday, or a cup final. He had yet to repair the relationships he had lost, plus he was still furtively avoiding anyone who reminded him of the past and therefore risk sending him backwards, into the abyss. He did not need that tonight.

It was a cold Friday night and he got to the Empire early, to secure a spot. Miles had two simple factors that dictated where he stood when he was at a gig alone, and that was to have both an uninterrupted view of the stage and an uninterrupted path to the bar. The Empire was good for both of these criteria. If you positioned yourself correctly, you could stand with your back to most people and have a terrific view of the stage, almost directly underneath one of the old theatre boxes that harked back to the venue's heritage. The bar staff tended to read books whilst the performance was on, so you didn't need to engage with the public or staff, until you wanted a beer.

However, with a bit of a thirst that night, he also encountered the challenge of being in an establishment that serves alcohol, alone. He really needed the toilet and it was getting close to gig-time.

He figured that he had enough time to pop there and back, before it got so busy where he was settled, that he would lose his spot, as most people were concerning themselves with getting as close to the front of the arena as possible. It was a trick he had learned before from this venue, that in the end, the people who collected close to the back of the venue, were generally similar types to Miles and therefore, considered trustworthy. So he left his drink on the bar, nodded to the guy next to him to indicate his intentions and received a nod back. Anyway, the guy next to him did not seem to be going anywhere, given that he was only sipping water. The moments passed and Miles returned, feeling much more comfortable and excited for the night ahead. But there were two surprises when he came out of the bathroom.

The first was, that it felt like the world had changed. In the time he had been in the bathroom, a couple of Underground trains had arrived from the east of London and brought with them a fresh army of Killers fans. The atmosphere crackled with anticipation that was making Miles nervous, but also exhilarated. It lifted him and amongst all that energy, to his surprise, he felt a rush of hope for his life again. The air was intoxicating and he felt maybe things would be OK, he could re-build and re-invent his life from the desolate place he had found himself. Besides, this was the first step in re-discovering his love for music and his identity. So he decided that he would head back to his quiet spot, have his beer, and maybe another; but then, perhaps he would be reckless again. Perhaps attempt the lower level of the stalls, and even throw a few shapes.

But that was the second surprise, which immediately took away this renewed hope in life. As he headed back to his spot, to his dismay he did not recognise anyone from before, even the guy drinking water had disappeared. In his place there was a girl and she was clearly holding his beer. He had left for five minutes and this person had taken it upon herself to mine-sweep off the bar. Not even off a table, or a ledge at the side of the venue, but the bar itself, where people do not just abandon their drinks half-finished. It wasn't even nine o'clock yet. He wasn't sure exactly what time it became fine to mine-sweep, but he was pretty sure that this was too early.

It took a few seconds for him to register all this, by which time he had taken the last few steps and was standing in the girl's personal space.

'Way to get into my personal space,' she said.

That was all it took and even in that fleeting moment when he caught her glance, Miles knew it. He was about to step into a storm.

Chapter Two

Sophie's Story

November 13, 2004.

The evening had started badly for Sophie. She was supposed to be meeting her boyfriend, Smooth, for dinner, ahead of The Killers gig.

Smooth wasn't his real name – his real name was Neil, but just about everyone called him Smooth. It was how he introduced himself to her in the VIP area at the festival where they had met the previous year and therefore, it was what she had always known him as.

Actually, Smooth was not in the VIP area. Sophie was in the VIP area, by virtue of a work contact who had a spare ticket, but Smooth was in the V-VIP area. Both were separate areas to the regular festival, defined by a high temporary wall and wide, temporary bouncers. The subtle differences between the two areas included the V-VIP area having free alcohol and a larger quota of wood-chips on the ground than the VIP area. Wood-chips were important on the ground at festivals, as they soaked up any mud or other fluids that might spill, over the course of the weekend. So the idea was that, the more important you were as a VIP, the more wood-chips you received and therefore you were able to almost walk around the V-VIP area in regular shoes, or even high heels. This was something that regular festival visitors would never dream of, as they generally received no wood-chips at all. Not that this stopped the V-VIPs still wearing designer wellies.

Smooth had just sauntered up to Sophie holding a black wristband and asked if she wanted to accompany him to some acoustic sessions.

Sophie was new to the festival environment, and so initially had no idea what Smooth was talking about. She had not yet learned about access rights at festivals, the different levels of access and the fact that each area worked on coloured wristbands. She had no idea that they were literally the most important item of your outfit for the day, and how much Smooth was drawing looks, because of his multiple array of wristbands. The door, or gap in the fencing, between each class of area at a festival was controlled by extremely hard-looking festival security, who had gaffer taped to the wall, or fence, for their use, a handy chart of all the coloured wristbands and whether their particular wristband was allowed through that particular doorway. It was as simple as that. If your wristband colour on the chart had a circle around it, then great. If it had a line through it, then hard cheese. The security guard had the plausible deniability of not needing to know 'who you are', or even if your 'name was down'. If you didn't have the appropriate colour then you were just 'not coming in'. This is how it worked, from standard admission all the way through to VIP, V-VIP, production and artists.

Although Sophie had no idea about this, she was getting a bit bored where she was anyway. The friends she had visited with, were all off in the bar area and were all working in the media industry and thus, were feigning 'work'. She was beginning to wonder when she would hear any actual music. The VIP area was a good half-hour walk from the main stage, so they had not yet ventured over there, which meant she had already missed four of the afternoon artists, all of which she was looking forward to hearing. So when this guy sauntered up and offered the chance to hear actual artists play actual music live, she thought that it would certainly be better than hanging out in, what could effectively be, the terrace of a posh pub in London, except it was a bit muddier. Sophie was bored and feeling a bit rebellious. She accepted the wristband and with an unacknowledged wave to her friends, she followed Smooth through the unmarked fence and into the V-VIP area.

She was slightly relieved that his promise of acoustic sessions was not some kind of festival-related euphemism; it did actually mean acoustic sessions. The artists, as part of their appearance, were contractually obliged to perform in a small, converted London bus after their performance on the main stage.

Despite the weather being pretty good and the access to the campsite being a short stroll along a temporary walkway, all of the audience were dressed impeccably in a weird combination of shiny wellingtons, denim hot-pants and beanie hats. Sophie wondered what kind of weather would demand this kind of attire. The beanie would mean they were expecting it to be cold, but without long trousers or sleeves the beanie would be rendered pretty useless. The wellies would indicate some kind of aggressive downpour, which would render the beanie a bit useless, as damp wool is no good to anyone and could even bring the onset of a chill. There might be some waterproofs secreted somewhere on any of the individuals, but she doubted it, as one could never get them in the diamante-adorned clutch that most of them also had. You could not fault the style or the quality of everything that was being worn, in isolation, but from a practical standpoint, none of it worked together in her opinion.

As much as it was Sophie's first experience of this environment, Smooth (real name: Neil), fit right in. He was busy identifying all the labels to Sophie, which rather than impressing her just had the impact of making her feel dramatically un-cool. She was pretty, but liked to dress it down. She was also just starting out in her life in London, so relied on being able to spend a fiver on a t-shirt or a tenner on a dress, rather than spending money on expensive fashion that didn't seem much different. When t-shirts only cost a fiver, it doesn't matter that they may only last one wash, because you can just go out and buy another one the next time you need it. It also had the added benefit, that Sophie always managed to sport the right colour and right style, at the right moment. If there was a new slogan, or a new logo, or a new high street collection by the latest supermodel, then she generally had it.

For someone who relied on natural beauty, a hair bobble and a trusty can of dry shampoo, the V-VIP area can be a very stressful experience. No one here appeared to subscribe to the concept of a time-saving short-cut to their grooming, which meant they could squeeze out another 10 minutes in bed on the cold side of the pillow. Sophie felt the first pangs of self-consciousness and anxiously checked what t-shirt she was wearing.

Generally, it was whatever was on the floor next to the bed and today was no exception. Oh well, she thought, if Smooth had noticed, then he had shown no sign of it, perhaps she was pulling it off as 'shabby chic'.

Smooth, himself, on the other hand, was basically dressed like a girl. They could have swapped clothes and he would probably have been as comfortable in hers, if not more so. He was wearing a deep-v t-shirt, made of that clingy material that means if you have a single hair on your body, or even one per cent body-fat, then you look like a clod of damp, grassy soil in a plastic bag. Smooth had neither of these things, so she had to basically accept that he looked great. He was wearing skinny jeans in an aggressive bright colour that she didn't even know the name of, and biker boots. A perfect choice for a festival, although, just like with the rest of the crowd, she was a bit confused where he would have been able to plug in his iron, hair straighteners and beard trimmer at a festival, because she couldn't see one hair out of place. He obviously saw her looking, raised an eyebrow and playfully draped an arm around her shoulders to lead her through the crowd to the bar.

'Very smooth,' she said.

Then she realised what she had said, and blushed the same colour as his skinny jeans.

So, that was how it had been – it was the start of Sophie and Smooth. They had continued to see each other once the festival was over and they were back in London. So far it had seemed, well, easy. They both had busy jobs and a typical London-length commute, so had got into a regular rhythm of seeing each other once during the work week and then spending weekends together, at each other's flats. Sophie was independent at heart and the weekdays gave her a chance to catch up with friends. Smooth also had an active social life and an ability to score tickets to almost anything, so when they saw each other in the week, it was generally in the hospitality section of the next hip electronic artist. She soon got used to this lifestyle and it made her feel good. Being with him also made her feel good. He was handsome and popular and she had met some amazing people through him.

He was literally out every night, but never seemed to look tired or out of sorts, or at least, not after he had applied half a pharmacy of lotions and balms in the morning and conducted his routine of about a thousand press-ups and other exercises. They would joke that, if they moved in together, they would need two additional rooms – one for her wardrobe of cut-price clothing and one for his toiletries, with completely mirrored walls. Sometimes she feared that when he was older, he would literally have no skin left, just layers and layer of expensive moisturiser, night-balm and eye-creams. A bit like when the windows are so old, all that keeps them together are the layers of paint that have been applied over the years.

That night though, they were in the middle of an argument, over whether or not Smooth would come with her to the Killers gig. He was claiming that he was too busy, whereas she argued that he was always too busy to come to things that she wanted to do, but never too busy for his own arrangements. The argument was probably a few months in the making, but had only just manifested from bickering, into full on confrontation. Sophie could not confirm for definite, but it might have been their first proper argument. Like a snowball on a hill, it had gathered in size and momentum, and neither of them were backing down.

She understood, for example, that he was very busy in the week networking and that, sometimes, a lot of his business was done after 8 o'clock. In a bar. Not the kind of business she was used to, that included spread sheets and graphs, but the kind of business where shared experiences and shared fun leads to a kind of mutual appreciation. Then the mutual appreciation turns into a mutual understanding, to find a way to continue the mutual fun, and the best way to continue the mutual fun, is to make sure that you can fund the mutual fun through pretending it was work. It was a bit of a 'club', in her opinion, but he would define it as making sure he was up to date on the latest trends and fashions, and that it was important for his job. So he would say it's not mutual fun, but an earnest swapping of information and experience of fashion and trends in real life.

That would have been fine for Sophie, except Sophie had to admit that she knew of a few grey areas in the concept of his partying being essential to his work; especially as he was simply a data analyst for a large consumer goods company, not a cutting-edge innovator or member of fashion royalty. It just so happened, that the consumer goods companies had defined youth marketing as, basically, spending as much money as possible sponsoring musicians, artists and events. With these agreements came free tickets and back-stage perks, so the incentive was, therefore, to continue sponsoring the best and newest acts and network with the right people, so that the supply of free tickets to hot events did not dry up.

It felt a bit of a stretch, but she could understand how it became a self-fulfilling pressure. Once you are hooked on the "new" in the world and define yourself through it, then perpetuating the life becomes a basic need. It was dizzying listening to conversations about it sometimes, and although she could see why people had entire jobs dedicated to spotting what is new and appealing, she sometimes wondered what had happened to the world. Sometimes, she felt a desperate urge to escape from some of the parties they went to – just walk out, go home and make a nice cup of tea.

Not this night though. The thing that had irritated Sophie, was that going to see The Killers was something that she had instigated and had actually bought the tickets herself. Smooth could probably have "sourced" them, but she wanted to feel like a proper fan. So much so, that she might even buy a t-shirt and break her £10-per-item maximum spend for clothing. She was really in the mood for a party and wanted Smooth here to keep her company and party with her. Recently, it was starting to feel like, more and more when it was something that she wanted to do, Smooth immediately de-prioritised it, or at least was inflexible to his own agenda. It had happened the previous month when she wanted to go to the theatre and although Smooth did make a good point in that most plays these days ended in depression and suicide, it was important to her and so she expected it to be to him, too. The same thing had happened again tonight. They had planned to meet for a quick dinner, at a restaurant that had featured highly in the Good Curry Awards, before heading over, with hopefully enough room for some beers and a late hot dog. To Sophie, that was a perfect night.

But Smooth had gradually re-set her expectations through the day, and not even by calling her. He had, basically, starting sending texts about ten o'clock in the morning; firstly, to say that he would meet her at the restaurant instead of the pre-drinks bar, then the venue itself, and finally that he would get there just in time for The Killers to come on.

Texting was pretty new and so she could understand him embracing it, even if she preferred a good old-fashioned call. What was irritating however, was that for someone who was supposedly embracing new technology, he wasn't very good at it. Not the mechanics of texting, he was fine with that, it was more that he seemed to take efficiency of communication to the extreme. Granted, you had limited space to save spilling your message onto two texts, but he seemed to think that you paid by the letter. Everything was abbreviated and you needed some kind of special lexicon to understand what was going on. Vowels were especially something that he focused his abbreviating obsession on, and Smooth had almost altogether stopped using them – to the point that she had once asked him if his "e" key was broken. That was when she had just received six letters and it took her over ten minutes to figure out that PLSCLL was PLEASE CALL. Who texts someone to ask them to call, anyway?

Finally, after waiting for twenty minutes past his LTST UPDTE arrival time, she realised that she had waited for at least two underground trains after the one he promised to be on, and the crowds were starting to move inside with more of a purpose. It was also cold and getting colder, so Sophie decided to just teach him a lesson. She took a deep breath and did her first rebellious thing since the festival where they met and sold his ticket to a tout. She got a good price, and resolved to spend the entire profit on beer. And probably then text him later to tell him that she spent it all on BR.

She switched her phone off and headed inside. It was a relief to get out of the cold, but once inside and mingling with the crowds and in the noise, Sophie realised that she wasn't used to going to places like this alone. She had maybe spent a sum total of an hour on her own in bars and restaurants, if you counted all the occasions and waiting time she had ever spent in her life, waiting for friends. But actually spending a full evening on her own, at a music concert, was something brand new. It probably required some kind of etiquette to be here alone, she thought, so she headed over to the bar to take a bit of time to inspect what was going on and formulate a plan – and especially to decide, where best to hang out when you were on your own and didn't want to be hassled.

After standing there for a while, at the largest of the bars, she realised that standing in the middle of the queue, at the middle bar of the venue was probably not the best idea. She spotted another bar over on the far back wall of the venue, where she thought she might be less in the way. It seemed, at first glance, to be where all the losers were, so there was probably a risk of getting hit on. But on the other hand, all she could see was knitted sweaters and coats and not a neon colour in sight, so perhaps it was a safe zone. Sophie decided that getting a beer was a priority. Embracing the new situation she found herself in, she soon found herself at the head of the queue, with one hand on the bar and a clear path to a drink.

Or at least she thought she was at the head of the queue (and was silently celebrating), but as she settled in and tried to catch the eye of the staff, it seemed there were a few people stubbornly taking spots at the bar, who were clearly not drinking and were blocking everyone else's chances of getting a drink. Next to her, for example, was a chap who was not only taking up bar space, but appeared to have just a bottle of water, that he probably picked up in a grocery store, not even at the bar. She tapped him politely on the shoulder, which he ignored, so she gave it a little shake – like you would wake someone up on the train.

'Excuse me,' said Sophie, 'would you mind if I got to the bar, please?'

For some reason, this seemed to offend the water drinker, who shouted something about being there first, which she thought was totally obvious, apart from the fact he was drinking shop-bought water and didn't seem to have any intention of ordering a beer.

'Yes, I know!' She shouted back, adding a smile for reassurance. 'But it's my turn now.'

This didn't work and this time she actually thought that the man might cry. In taking an aggressive step towards her, he had left a small gap, so Sophie instinctively dodged past him to the bar. For a moment, they were involved in a dance-come-jostle, where she tried to swivel her hips to avoid touching him on all accounts, but in the end it appeared that rather than trying to assault her, he was just reaching past her and picking up a beer off the bar.

'Excuse me!' She said to the disappearing man, trying to give the impression that the last thing she wanted to do was excuse herself, but feeling slightly bad that actually he had a beer after all, even if he had chosen to put it a good yard or so along the bar from where he was standing.

With that, the guy lurched off and she was left in peace to get a drink, which she promptly did and took a large, satisfying slug. The next job was to plan her next move, which did not involve staying anywhere near this particular bar. It was a pretty good view, but much too far from the action and her first impression had been right. It was entirely grid-locked with odd-looking people, who were either drinking water, or sipping on one beer for the night, rather than trying to order more.

She was turning to leave, when she almost barrelled into another guy, who was a similar age to her, but seemed to be dressed as a middle-aged man. This one didn't have a drink, but the fact that he had worked his way past the queue, seemed to indicate that he wasn't interested in getting one. Maybe he had a fruit juice or something hidden about his person, or was very rude and thought he was above waiting in line like everyone else. He was also glancing in quite an aggressive fashion at her drink. Perhaps he couldn't even afford one himself, thought Sophie, and defensively she took another sip of her drink, to show ownership. He continued to stare, so she tried to think of something to say to break the ice, or at least make them feel less uncomfortable. But instead, she heard herself speak and immediately regretted it.

'Way to get into my personal space,' she said.

Chapter Three

The First Morning

November 14, 2004

'As if, loser,' said Sophie from her makeshift sofa-bed.

If there was one thing that being in a destructive relationship for so long had created in Miles, it was an aura of over-sensitivity. But somehow, Sophie called him a "loser" in a way that made him feel nothing like a loser. As he lay there, he found himself unconsciously smiling for the first time in a long time. For the first time in a long time, his initial feeling of dread had almost completely disappeared and he felt almost calm, almost contented.

He remembered them meeting by the bar, in the most clumsy of fashion, and then it was all a bit patchy. Apart from the fact that he distinctly remembered that nothing bad had happened and that there was a lot of dancing, a lot of drinking and a lot of laughing. In fact, he can't remember the last time he did two out of those three things, so all in all, it had been a great night.

There was of course his lack of memory, however and anything bad could have happened in the fuzzy period, but he didn't think it had. Sure, he didn't quite remember everything that had happened the previous night, after about mid-way through the gig, but that was what usually happened when you leave a warm place after too many beers and step into the cold, fresh air. They had definitely been flirting and they definitely had a snack on the way home, from one of the ubiquitous chicken shops, because he could still taste it. Then they had chatted, lying on their backs, side-by-side on the bed for a while. He couldn't even remember exactly what they had talked about, but the conversation had flowed in a way that was completely comfortable, easy and therefore, unnatural to him. But after that, he had no memory until he had woken up. He was pretty sure there had been no kissing, which gave him a twinge of disappointment, but he did remember their fingers touching as they lay together and that had given him a feeling of connection with this person, who, to all intents, was a complete stranger.

He had also noticed, that on waking up this morning, he was in the bed, under the duvet and she was on the sofa, under a scratchy blanket, which completely went against all of Miles' principles of chivalry. So there must be only one simple explanation: he had fallen asleep. Dammit.

'Oh my, I have such jerk chicken breath', said Sophie.

She then cursed herself, silently. So far, she was on fire with the comments. This was always the way it was, when she was feeling a bit uncomfortable. She just became all banter and jokes, all sarcastic comments. It wasn't that she was shy, but it was just her way of coping in difficult situations – especially where boys were involved. It was born out of a lifetime of being pestered on nights out by over-amorous guys, or guys that tried to be her friend, but then later started to over-compensate with their emotions and talk about love, as if falling in love with her was something that happened in a cheap bar over a couple of pints of lager.

Last night had been different, though. To be honest, she didn't remember much, which was a success, as she had started out intent on getting drunk. But she did remember almost immediately meeting Miles as she walked in, and that Miles had seemed to be intent on the same. They were on the same path that night and it had been fun. At the end of the night she didn't want it to end and so had made a half-excuse about weirdos on the night-bus, so that she could extend his company a bit longer. She was only half-joking about the night bus, but then, she was also not exactly soothed at her choice to skip going back to the safety of home, when she found out Miles was living out of a suitcase at a motorway hotel. But as time went on, her regrets faded and they had enjoyed chatting, until he had passed out next to her. Plus, she loved fried chicken and around the Empire there was just the most stunning selection of fried chicken outlets that, basically, catered to any format, flavour or processed nuance that you could imagine. So when he suggested a post-concert chicken snack, she couldn't resist and by the time they had finished their snack, all options of other transport, apart from an expensive cab, were probably out the window anyway.

She had also felt comfortable from the start, that he wasn't going to make any kind of move at all, so perhaps that had helped her relax in his company. A small part of her wished he had tried something on, maybe to give her a confidence boost, but also because she really felt a connection. She was fairly certain she would have responded had he tried, or at least let him kiss her; but in the harsh light of morning it was probably best that the night had passed without any awkward touching or difficult conversations. Her mixed emotions included the fact that, despite carrying a little bit of extra weight and his appalling dress-sense, she actually found him quite handsome. He had honest eyes and a kind of vulnerability that she felt was born out of situation, rather than part of his in-built personality. She sussed it out properly after about the fourth time that Miles had talked about 'we' and then corrected himself. He was clearly coming out of a long-term relationship of some kind, and it must have been pretty sudden and serious, to warrant taking up in the temporary accommodation he had chosen.

The details he wanted to share were brief and therefore, the conversation on the topic was the same. All she could learn was that he had, basically, been all-but left at the altar, because all girls are controlling and manipulative. The conversation felt fine to be left there, despite her not feeling he had been completely honest and also, despite her not really volunteering that she, actually, did have a boyfriend. She just grabbed a chip and then moved the conversation onto how the gravy that you got in fried chicken outlets, was the greatest gravy of all. There was no disagreement from Miles there.

There was, of course, also one discomfort from the previous night. She had not thought about Smooth at all. In fact, the morning was the first time she had even thought about Smooth since she switched her phone off, just before the concert. But instead of wanting to call him, or feeling stressed at what he might think, she just thought about him disapproving of the calorie count of the chicken, the complex carbohydrate nature of the chips and perhaps the fact, that no gravy should be the colour of that particular gravy. She started to feel the first pangs of guilt and checked the screen of her phone, and it confirmed what she thought – she hadn't even switched it back on. As she powered it up, she started to dread the beeps, as the texts and voice-mails came through, and started to try and formulate some kind of explanation and apology as to what had happened, that left out the part about spending the night in a sleazy hotel with a stranger. No matter how she tried to explain that, it would never go down well.

But, when she had waited an appropriate length of time, she realised that the beeps were not going to come. She even called the voice mail a few times to be sure. But there was nothing. It seemed Smooth had not even tried to contact her in any way. No text even, to say that he had arrived and where was she? No voicemail, with a frantic Smooth wondering where she was and if something terrible had happened to her on the London streets. Nothing. It made her feel a bit sick, but at the same time, it meant that she was right about the night before – he was putting himself first.

'So, that was fun. You can certainly put it away,' said Miles and interrupted Sophie's thoughts.

He meant the chicken, but it could also have easily referred to the drinks as well. He had never quite seen such ability on such a small frame. He had no idea where she put it, unless she was secretly homeless, and had mugged a passer-by that night to pay for her first sustenance for several weeks. Or, as his mother liked to say, she had hollow legs.

He was also amazed that she managed to eat like she did and in Miles' opinion, look so perfect. He could tell the previous night that he was not the only one to think so, especially as every time he took a few steps to the bar he would come back and there would be some guy or other talking loudly into her ear. But she always made direct eye contact with him, as soon as she saw him coming back and gave him the slight cross-eyed "come and save me" face. Even when he saw her first, before she saw him, all she saw was an expression of patience – the kind of patience and slow nodding that comes from many years of practice. Miles enjoyed being the protector, handing over the drink each time solemnly to Sophie and waiting for the guy to either step back into the crowd, or step forward and punch him in the face. Happily, his face made it through the concert with only a small scratch from the glancing blow of a plastic pint glass, being thrown arbitrarily from the mosh pit, rather than a deliberate fist of another suitor.

She also wore jeans in a way that he had never seen before. It took a special type of person to throw on a t-shirt and jeans and look as good as Sophie did. It was something about her swagger, but also underneath all that, he sensed that she was a sweet girl. She had declined his dare to climb into one of the communal gardens, which are scattered around the London neighbourhoods, to eat their late night snack on a quiet park bench, for example.

He was day-dreaming about that as he lay there, slowly waking up in the hotel. But it was also at that moment, when he realised that sometime soon, he was also going to have to get out of bed, and although he was still wearing his jeans, he had wriggled out of his t-shirt in the night and he had no idea where it was. Several recent weeks of binge-drinking and take-aways, had given his physique a doughy quality. He couldn't remember the last time he had been to the gym and although he had vowed to get back into shape, he had not yet managed it. Damn procrastination, he thought, and damn all this time not caring about making the best of what he had. He used to be proud of what he looked like, when had that changed? When had he become someone who was satisfied with a potbelly and love handles? From now on he was going to exercise more, stop drinking and put himself in the position to be found attractive by girls like Sophie.

Nearby, Sophie was thinking something similar. Not about wobbly body parts, but more that she was desperate for a wee, wearing just a thong, and had to pass by Miles' bed to get to the bathroom. He didn't seem in any hurry to move, so she was going to have to make a bolt for it.

'So Miles, I'm starving,' she said.

'You're starving?' asked Miles. 'After what was probably your own body weight in low-grade chicken pieces?'

Sophie smiled. 'Everyone knows that anything you eat after midnight doesn't count. It was technically breakfast, so all I am asking for is an early lunch.'

'They do say that it's five o'clock somewhere,' said Miles. 'So maybe we should just skip food and go for Bloody Marys.'

'I like your style. So, it's a kind of jet lag. Let's call it food lag.'

Sophie paused, there was no way around the issue, she just had to face it head-on.

'But before we do anything,' she said, 'I need to skip past you and get dressed, so I would appreciate it if you covered your eyes like the gentleman I know you are.'

'Cheeseburgers!' said Miles, because the prospect of seeing nearly-naked Sophie was confusing him a bit too much.

Sophie had no idea what he was talking about, but if it meant he found her tasty, then she was happy about that. So she grabbed her clothes and shot from the sofa to the bathroom, slamming the door behind her.

They headed round the corner to a chain restaurant to eat, which was the only option, given Miles' current abode. Miles had something called the "Fat Boy" breakfast, with an additional side order of black pudding, plus he added fried eggs to the portion of scrambled eggs that were included in the meal. When you have a hangover, he thought, breakfast was one of those meals where the idea of eating, is much better than the experience itself. Ordering breakfast with a hangover always leads to over-compensation of some kind. Either you go too large with the fried meat, or you end up ordering a strange concoction of all the things that seem appetising in your head, but end up being a strange and gut-churning combination, that you spend the day regretting.

Sophie ordered muesli, a fruit plate, onion rings, and fished a pack of processed cheese squares out of her handbag.

'Strong combination,' said Miles, waving his fork in the general direction of Sophie's random plate of food.

'You can talk, egg boy,' replied Sophie. Then, changing the subject, 'So, tell me your full story and leave nothing out. Living out of that hotel room means you are either a really bad rock star, or there is a story.'

So Miles did and he surprised himself by leaving nothing out.

He told Sophie about "The Decision" and about how it made him feel. He told her about how he had "The Plan" and how he had been so focused on "The Plan", that he became the definition of "The Plan", rather than "The Plan" being defined by him. They had lost control of their life and their love for each other. He told her how it was convenient, for example, for them to move in together to save on rent in such an expensive city as London. Then getting engaged was convenient, because it gave them a new target to set and project in their lives, to occupy their time. But that was it, all the conversations were about convenience rather than love. He told her that he now realised that you lived forwards, but life only makes sense backwards. It only made sense, as well, when you took a step back and asked yourself, if you have been truly happy today, this week, this month, perhaps even this year.

If this sounded like regret, or the words of a victim, he didn't see it that way anymore. Life was just a collection of moments and you learn more in the bad moments than the good ones, and try to make sure you never repeat them. In these situations, victims are not real victims who cannot help their situations, rather they are their own victims who accept their own fate.

In the end, he told her, accepting not being happy will creep up on you and inject slow poison into any relationship. It will eat away at it, until in the end, you don't care about yourself and worse, you don't really care about the person you chose to be with. You will end up wondering when it happened, that instead of becoming bigger than the sum of two people, you had become two people who just found it easier and more convenient to be together. Small signals, like the relief, for example, that she worked late, or the embarrassment on the nights when you sit in silence watching a TV show and would prefer to be doing something else, shouldn't be ignored. By burying the problem, you are probably being more selfish, than making a difficult decision.

He surprised himself, by explaining what he had been thinking recently, that people deserve love, and love stays alive because you keep it alive, by trying with every sinew to make the other person happy, not yourself, and you expect the same in return. The love you receive by sharing the last chip, is much bigger than the enjoyment you get from the taste of the last chip. To get a quarter of the last chip back, is one of the most wonderful things in the world. He knew that now and he felt that he had a second chance in life. He wanted to share that last chip, to love emptying the dishwasher and to love putting the bins out. He might be living in a hotel room now, but soon he would be back on his feet and taking a look at every part of his life, to make sure he never went down this path again.

What he didn't tell Sophie, was that 24 hours earlier he didn't feel like this. He just wanted to get drunk 24 hours ago, that was the sum of his "big night". But something had changed, and maybe it would change back again, but he felt happy. Happy and connected.

Sophie listened to all this, although admittedly she got a bit lost around the bit about the bins. It was a story with surprisingly more depth than she had expected, and also one that she felt more emotion towards than she expected. She subconsciously glanced again at her mobile phone, a phone yet to ring or beep. Part of her felt terrible that she had not said it out loud yet; that she had a boyfriend. Sure, they had an argument last night, but now, with her head clearing, she realised that she was probably a bit unreasonable to insist that he came to watch a band that he didn't know much about. The Killers were new and hyped, but at the mainstream end and so did not fit into the mould of edgy, not-yet-discovered-by-NME vibe, that did not appeal to Sophie as much, but did appeal to Smooth. Maybe she was being selfish, expecting him to drop his busy life and perhaps fall behind in the new trends and styles.

She had to find a way to break this to Miles. She wanted to be kind, because she did have a good time the previous night and she wanted to keep in touch. But in front of her was someone who was clearly in the midst of a minor breakdown. If he ever recovered, and she doubted that it would be soon, it would not be easy being with someone as damaged as that. Smooth, on the other hand, was handsome and carefree. He got her humour and they didn't need to talk about feelings in such a deep and emotional way as Miles. The currency of their love was traded banter and insults all evening, with a smile, because that was their thing.

'Listen, Miles…' She began, but at the same moment her phone beeped and it broke her concentration.

'It's OK, Sophie,' said Miles, 'if the answer you are about to tell me is you have a boyfriend. To be honest, I did wonder last night, but assumed that you must have. Anyone that looks as great as you, is bound to have a boyfriend.'

There was a pause, whilst Sophie found her phone amongst the debris of sweet wrappers and make-up in her bag. 'Not that I didn't love hanging out, because I did,' he added unnecessarily.

'That's very understanding, thank you,' said Sophie, but she was suddenly distracted. 'I had a lovely time last night, as well. We're buddies and that's what buddies do. Thank you again, for being a gentleman.'

Buddies, thought Miles. That was always a sign that you were being firmly placed into the "friend" category and so, he had to try and recover that. 'Not that much of a gentleman, actually,' said Miles. 'I might have looked like I did, but I didn't cover my eyes when you skipped past me to the bathroom this morning.'

For a moment, their gaze met and a spark passed through Sophie's eyes. Just for a moment, a spark of fire. Then it was gone, as she looked down at her phone.

MVE IN WTH ME, read the text.

It was going to be a while before Miles and Sophie saw each other again.

Chapter Four

Resolution

January 25, 2005.

Miles hated Tuesdays. It was traditional to hate Mondays, but in Miles' opinion, the trouble with hating Mondays is that everyone else did, which gave Monday-hatred an air of camaraderie, that took the edge off it.

No, he hated Tuesdays. Tuesdays just felt like a bit of a non-day. It was still the beginning of the week and although it might be trying to fool you that it isn't Monday, it might as well be Monday - Part Two, as there was still more of the week left to work than you had worked already. On Monday, you can also waste parts of the day talking about what you did at the weekend. You can easily add ten minutes onto the usual morning coffee discussing the weekend, add ten minutes to the first meeting of the day and send a few emails to friends reminiscing about Saturday night. So that could actually give you a whole hour on Monday, of non-work conversations and excuses not to work.

On Tuesday though, there was none of that. No one would ask you, 'Hey, what did you get up to on Monday night?' and expect any kind of interesting story, or for it to take more than thirty seconds of skiving time. Then by Wednesday, you could start to talk about what you might be doing the following weekend, because you were "almost half-way there" and it was "Hump Day". Tuesday still felt like there was a slog to go to the weekend and although most people seemed to get into the swing of the week by Tuesday, Miles had never found that. And so, he felt like a Tuesday just defined how out of step he was with the world, and he hated it.

This was the thought that was running through Miles' head, as he sat in one of the regular meetings that his work tended to hold on a Tuesday morning. To be honest, this probably added to Miles' general disdain for Tuesdays. Not just the meeting itself, but even the décor of the meeting room, that this particular meeting was taking place in, made this, in Miles' opinion, the perfect place to be if you were looking for things to be depressed about. He had been in the room for about an hour already, and had probably absorbed about three per cent of what was said. He wondered if anyone could possibly absorb anything in a room that was just so grey. The walls were grey. The carpet was grey, albeit with an attempt at some kind of pattern – which was off-grey. Even the table was topped with grey Formica – which actually he should probably applaud, as it could not have been easy to find a boardroom table that was quite so uninspired. When you grew up in the suburbs, this kind of table just reminds you of old church halls and stirred a memory of being forced into conversations, of tea stains and biscuit crumbs.

Perhaps grey should be another thing he should give up, along with Mondays, he thought. He had made several resolutions of this kind over the previous months and it had been going well. Giving things up and moving on had practically become a new hobby.

It had started the day after The Killers concert in November; he had made appointments and visited about 20 flats. He had selected one on the spur of the moment and had checked out of the hotel with a spring in his step (and a lingering bruise from a loose spring in the hotel bed that had been consistently digging in for the past few months). He had moved into a small, ground floor flat in a more central, but cheaper area of London, that the estate agent described as "gentrifying". Until then, he had probably lived exclusively over a two-page range of an A-Z, and in the kind of neighbourhoods where you were no more than 50 metres at any point from a caramel latte, or a shop that sold heart-shaped trinkets. So with that, he had given up an entire borough of the one of the largest capital cities in the World, and it had felt good.

His new place was scruffy, but it was perfect for him. A place where he could just shut the door and know that the outside world could not get to him, as he dragged himself out of his relationship-induced funk. It was a place that you didn't appreciate as a haven, until you were truly in a dark place. If the phone rang, he could ignore it. If he wanted to sob uncontrollably, or shout his troubles at a daddy-long-legs, then he could. Now, he was allowed to play whatever music he wanted, he could turn it up as loud as he wanted, which along with allowing some cathartic singing, had the added benefit of drowning out the engine whine and rumble of the 219 bus that passed about a foot from his bedroom window, every 20 minutes from just after six in the morning, until just after nine pm. Of course, there was no way of getting away from the associated rattle of the window frames, he could put up with that because it was home. Especially in London, a place which teaches you to find somewhere you are mainly happy and to put up with a few other things that make the city unique. So having bus passengers see him in his pants, three times an hour, if he forgot to close the curtains, was balanced out by the peace, and by having somewhere he could call his own.

The local shop was open from five in the morning until midnight, and at any time during these hours you could get home-made lamb samosas or hot onion bhajis, the size of your head. At weekends there were fresh cheese dosas, made to order in what looked like a broom cupboard, but managed to house an oven, a full cooking range and a deep fat fryer. Curry for breakfast was another pinnacle of luxury in Miles' new life and he'll take a bit of window rattling, just for that.

Perhaps the only irony to Miles' new culinary opportunities, was that he had also resolved to give up beige food for a while. The idea had come to him one day just after he moved in, as he was unloading another baking tray of crispy pancakes and potato waffles from the oven. His diet was delicious and convenient, and everything he ate always went well with gravy. But it did strike Miles, that as well as eliminating things from his life, the introduction of a few other colours into his diet – especially green – might help him get back into the shape that he had promised himself.

It was a small change, but it was working. He was looking visibly younger and had even forced himself to huff and puff around the local park a few times. Jeans that he had been wearing for five years had started to get loose and he could definitely notice less back-sweat when he made a jog for the train or was late to the pub.

Before he knew it, he had broken the cycle of a nightly six-pack of lager, which made him look at so many areas of his life differently, with a new-found excitement to be ruthless with anything that he didn't love.

Right now, at work, he looked around the table and realised that he was falling out of love with his chosen career. That said, there was not too far to fall, if Miles was totally honest with himself. There was not really too much to be in love with in the first place. The black and white assessment of the situation, was that he was a low-ranking member of "tech support" at a large consumer goods company that specialised in canned products. As if that was not unglamorous enough, the office was attached to, and above, one of the main canning factories on an anonymous industrial estate on the edge of the city, and so at any moment the office would smell like what they were canning that particular day. Because they served a lot of the major supermarkets, the array of smells was fairly wide – but there was a good chance that the office, above the factory, in the middle of a grey industrial estate, would smell of cabbage.

In fact, one of the stairwells in the building had been re-named "Fart Stairs", simply because it smelled of farts for an awful lot of the time. The smell would linger for days, which actually made Miles suspect that when people needed to release some wind, but could not be bothered to go all the way to the office bathrooms, they would sneak out there and let go. He would sometimes tiptoe after people, as his desk was very near "Fart Stairs", to try and catch someone mid-fart, or perhaps catch the look of guilt on a fellow employee's face as they climbed back up to the offices, shaking their trouser leg or wafting a pleated skirt.

The only upside Miles could think of, was that he supposed that his job was safe and during his new-found health kick phase, fairly convenient as he could get lots of canned vegetables from the lavishly stocked (and equally smelly) staff shop. But all the same, he felt that he was starting to make too many compromises in life. He wondered if that tended to happen when you make a big decision and successfully start to change one part of your life. Now that one part of his value-system had changed, he was feeling like others were now out of place. For example, he now felt that, when he hung out in the local pubs, he was a bit embarrassed to admit who he worked for and what he did. He would embellish and make his current job, which was basically asking people to switch their computers off and back on again, sound like he was re-programming the space shuttle and had actually described it as 'a bit like a roadie' on more than one occasion. He would then have to beat a hasty retreat, before the person in question probed too hard, or just give a questioning 'hmmm?' to any challenging questions, raise an eyebrow and move the conversation on.

Alternatively, sometimes he would just out-and-out lie about his profession and was always surprised with what he came up with on the spur of the moment. He kept away from the very unbelievable and preferred to stick to invented careers that you could also invent fairly believable back-stories to. Along that vein, his favourite was the chocolate biscuit designer. That had so many directions you could go, from bringing a modern twist to the trusted malted milk, to leading the analysis of the optimal thickness of icing in a new bourbon cream biscuit. He had only come unstuck once, when a girl with a weirdly encyclopaedic knowledge of biscuits called him out, on his claim to have invented the jammie dodger.

The problem, however, was that Miles was starting to realise that if he didn't do something brave soon in his current job, then he would continue on this long road to the middle and be there forever. By holding on too tight to a poor relationship, Miles had realised that holding onto anything too tight and for the wrong reasons, is a very destructive thing. Although in a safe career, he did not aspire to be anyone around him. The talk was all about what car they were planning to buy next, or the house extension they were planning to build in the near future. That could have been Miles until recently, but now, he had decided to give it all up, he didn't feel like he belonged any more.

That is how it seemed to start, in Miles' opinion. Everyone just seemed to be in such a damn hurry these days. There was always the next thing to buy, or the next rung on the ladder. You start by pushing yourself to buy a house that is just within your range, by convincing yourself that you can compromise on other things to afford the mortgage. Then you need a car to go with the house, because you can't put your beat-up old Ford outside the new house, without giving away the fact that you might not be quite the achiever you want everyone to think you are. The next thing is, that you end up needing your job rather than wanting it, to be able to afford everything you're stacking up around yourself.

He knew he was over-compensating a bit in his attitude, but for him it was kind of the chocolate biscuit designer argument in reverse. Whilst he needed the social currency that having a cooler job brought, although it was a fantasy, at least this was a fantasy that he could step away from when it went too far. You could run away from a hot girl who had just disproven the timeline of jammie dodger invention, but it was harder to step away from a real-life stage that you tried to push too hard, or too fast. He had experienced part of this through "The Plan" and had stepped away from it at just the right moment. He had made the resolution that he would never rush into anything again; he had just shaken loose of one set of shackles, had just cast adrift one anchor, and he had developed a taste for it.

So here he was, at a grey table, thinking about boycotting grey as well as beige, and also finding himself getting irritated by the generous plate of cookies that was on display in the centre of the table. He could smell them but, due to their beige colour he couldn't eat them and right now they were the only thing he could think of that might brighten up his day. If only they had chosen pink wafers, then he could have munched a couple on a technicality. Maybe pink wafers are the dream of the biscuit world, thought Miles – they are the biscuit that dares to be different.

It was lucky for Miles that he was only half-distracted by the cookies, as just at that moment he sensed a 'we need to' coming in his direction.

A 'we need to' was something that was coming his way so often these days, that he had felt the need to name it and imagined it in speech-marks and sometimes, even in capital letters. Basically, he had realised that every time his boss started a sentence with 'we need to', it generally meant that he was the last person that was going to do it. Most likely, it would come in Miles' direction. Miles had got more and more used to this, but honestly, he couldn't quite figure out what it was that his boss was doing, that was either more important, or keeping him so busy. Also, recently Miles felt that the 'we need to' comments were starting to be passive-aggressive and although they were comments generally about the company, he couldn't help but have the feeling that his boss had it in for him.

He had to admit that he'd had a rough few months and had probably been hung-over quite a lot during the weeks he spent in the hotel. He also suspected that his new-found taste of freedom, meant that he didn't approach resolving tech issues with the same vigour as he had a few months earlier, when he believed that he should make a career and have a steady job as part of "The Plan". His general meltdown was no secret in the company, but actually, during that turmoil, he had tried harder and used work as a refuge to distract him from the general horribleness of the hotel room and the chaos that came with "The Decision".

Of course, there was the generally fuzzy memory he had of that period, but from his recollection, he had made more of an effort. In fact, he remembered more than a handful of times, he actually spent longer than he needed to, checking in with each job afterwards. Granted, this was mainly because, on the bad days, he sometimes got distracted and needed to tweak or fix something he had recommended or implemented, once the fog had cleared and he had realised that he had probably made quite a fist of it. However, he had not given it much of a thought, given that it never seemed to bother anyone who seemed to genuinely enjoy these new visits and the chance to chat – several times during this period he was told with admiration that he was putting on a brave face.

'We need to speed up the time we take resolving staff tech issues and generally improve the standard of the service and attitude in this area.' Miles' boss said, being unusually specific this time, as Miles was the only person in the room and at the company, who resolved staff tech issues. 'Miles, can we please have a quick catch up after the meeting?'

Miles didn't say what he thought, he decided that it wasn't the time just yet to be revealing all of his inner-most thoughts and that he should stick to the small things, like giving up beige food, for now.

But on a hated Tuesday, Miles was starting to dream.

Chapter Five

You Can Do Anything

March 8, 2005.

'That escalated quickly,' thought Miles, as he sat in his local pub, sipping a mid-strength lager. It was five weeks since the unusual Tuesday meeting, when his boss moved from being passive-aggressive to just downright aggressive. He wasn't sure if the events of the previous weeks were karma catching up with him, or if he had just been handed the biggest opportunity of his life.

That day, he was called back into the main boardroom after everyone had left. He had picked up the fairly obvious indications that it was not going to be a pleasant meeting and expected that he would get the usual speech about ensuring standards, and earnest advice to let him know that, should he want to progress in the organisation, then he had to raise his profile in the correct way. His boss had already mentioned a few times that there was some 'talk' about his general attitude and attire – the expected uniform of shirt and trousers was starting to slip, and occasionally he was even seen in jeans in the workplace. He thought this was a bit of a strange argument, given that it didn't affect his ability to fix computers. He could imagine if he started coming into the office in flip-flops, then maybe his boss could argue that his feet were a health and safety hazard should a keyboard or heavy piece of office equipment, like a hole-punch, fall on them. But jeans? Seriously?

Miles thought that, if that was the theme of the meeting, he was steeled for it and resolved that he would make the case that, actually, he found being a bit more relaxed about his dress made him feel like he was more of an individual in the office and better at his job. Wasn't he customer facing, with everyone in the organisation a potential client? Everyone with broken computers, they were his customers, so giving them a relaxed and happy experience was a good thing, in Miles' opinion.

This would have been a great plan, except it wasn't just his boss in there this time, but pretty much a who's who of the HR and security organisation. People that you only saw talking quietly into their phones behind closed office doors, or hulking around when you worked late of an evening, checking doors, were now sat in the room, in a foreboding line on one side of the boardroom table. It was a bit like a modern version of the Village People – one in a sharp suit, one in a military-style uniform, and one in a more humanistic, Oxford check shirt and chinos. It just needed, perhaps, one of the office handy-men, with a belt of screwdrivers and Miles thought you would have the full ensemble. As he sat down, with this running through his mind, he did actually start to reflect that perhaps he wasn't approaching this particular half-hour of his life with the best attitude.

There was a pregnant pause and Miles subconsciously tugged down the sleeves of his t-shirt, as if that would somehow fool the room into thinking it was actually a regulation button-down shirt. Rather than a t-shirt bearing the video game iconic phrase, and rather apt slogan for the meeting: GAME OVER.

The summary of the meeting, which was led mainly by his boss, was that they had a very clear choice for Miles. The organisation had been pondering what to do with him for some time now. They delicately explained that they understood he had some changes in his personal life and although they were sensitive to that, they also had to separate the two things. Personal life was just that, they expected that it would be left at the door when coming to work and that employees would maintain a positive and productive attitude. There were also counselling options available for individuals who were going through personal difficulties, they carefully reminded Miles. Although they had already explored this option, they understood that Miles had chosen not to take this offer on board when it was offered.

At this point, Miles felt a wave of indignation, he didn't remember getting this counselling offer that they were now using as a weapon against him. He opened his mouth to interrupt. However, in his moment of hesitation, he also felt a memory stir, a memory that was triggered by Miles catching the eye of the HR representative, who was fixing him with a glare. It was a glare that stirred a memory. He started to vaguely recall this person approaching him at the Christmas party a few months earlier and asking him if he would like to step outside the main function room and have a quick chat about some options available to him, in this difficult time in his life. It was one of those Christmas dinners held in a four star hotel in the neighbourhood of the office, with table plans designed to introduce employees to people in the organisation that they might not usually speak to. So for Miles, a particularly stressful night and moment in his slow rehabilitation, because the answers to many of the polite questions and conversation that might be had at the dinner, would generally cause him to break down in tears.

His response was, therefore, to explain that the only options he was interested in - and he was pretty sure he used more colourful language than this - was between the free red wine that was being offered on the tables and the free white wine. He seemed to recall being given the reasoned response, that it was only 7.15 in the evening and perhaps stealing wine off the tables of the gala dinner before it was even started, was not appropriate behaviour. A fair point, he had conceded and as a compromise, had simply taken the glass of pre-dinner Cava from the said unsuspecting HR representative's hand, drained it in one gulp and then handed it back to him. He then didn't really remember the rest of the night, but did remember waking up the next morning with lots of unexplained bruises and scratches, that were consistent with close contact with the kind of dense and well-groomed ornamental hedge that grew in those kind of hotels. So he thought it best to stay quiet.

Back in the conference room, his boss was beginning to sum up the choices he had been building to. There was a bit of pre-amble about having his best interests at heart, and something about a clean-break, but the summary was this: he could either go onto what they called a "development plan", which to him sounded like a bit of a detention, with restricted duties and a daily interview about his performance and attitude. Or he could take what they called a "compromise agreement". The latter seemed to be some kind of agreement where he received a sum of money that was equivalent to about six months' salary, tax-free. In return, all he had to do was promise to leave the company and never come back or complain about how or why he left the company.

At this point, Miles was told he would be given 24 hours to think about it. To the delight of everyone in the room, he needed 24 seconds and a contract was quickly whisked in front of him, as if by magic, from a slim folder. He signed with a flourish and with a spring in his non-regulation Converse, Miles took another step away from the life that had so spectacularly imploded, in the space of three months.

So here he was on a Tuesday, the very day that he had previously hated, having a rather good time and a few drinks in his local pub. Now that a few weeks had passed, Miles guessed that he had to start making some choices about what to do next. But thanks to a swelled bank balance, he still had a bit of time. Thanks to his own sensibilities when re-locating, his new and gentrifying neighbourhood had the advantage of being a little easier on the rental pocket than he was used to in his co-habited previous life. The only people who had been upset following his exit from the company were his parents, who despite being understanding, he suspected were just becoming less and less surprised about the things that were happening to him at the moment. They were still fielding questions from the more distant parts of the family, about what exactly had happened a few months earlier, so losing his job was just another piece of news to add to the family gossip columns.

He had spent the weeks doing what anyone does, who suddenly finds themself single and jobless, for the first time in a decade. He went running in the mornings and then spent the days watching sci-fi movies, playing video games and napping through re-runs of sports shows. He would, on average, eat three packs of Monster Munch per day without a care in the world and then decide in the evening whether to open one of the stash of canned vegetables, or go to the local take-away. He would then usually head down to his local pub in the evening and found himself being able to start conversations about his life with some elements of the actual truth – that he was in-between jobs and currently deciding which direction his dreams would take him next. Of course, he was usually either non-specific of what jobs he was in-between, or the nature of the in-between-ness. If pushed, he would specifically claim to have just sold one of his software companies and was trying to decide what venture to turn his considerable talents to next. In short, he was free. He felt a little bit out of control, but he was embracing it.

The next thing to do was to actually make a choice, or in other words, figure out exactly what his dream was. The traditional path on these occasions would be to go 'travelling'. This was appealing, except that Miles was locked into his flat rental contract for a while yet. Perhaps hippy-dom was an option at some point, but Miles wanted to aim higher. It wasn't that he wanted to take a break from reality, the fact was, that he believed his reality was destined to be bigger and better than it had been up to this point in his life. It had only taken one big decision from him, one piece of bravery and his whole existence fell apart. He was sure it was going to be hard to construct another life, one that was built to last. But that was the thing about dreams, Miles thought, they shouldn't come and go that easily. If you build them, then you build them to last. From now on, he was not going to be in a hurry and would only make decisions for love. Love that he believed would last.

No, what he needed wasn't travelling. What he needed was an idea. With his technology knowledge and experience with computers, and his personal interest in video games and pop culture, there must be something he can do. He didn't want to take any short cuts, but wanted to build something through graft and talent. Miles could feel his hope and excitement building with this thought and decided that he deserved another beer, a bag of Scampi Fries and perhaps a decent tune on the jukebox whilst he planned his next move.

It was perhaps the combination of beer and music that cast his mind back a few months to Sophie and he smiled to himself. That was a really great night. She had gone a bit weird at breakfast the next morning and excused herself far too quickly for his liking. Sadly, that made him suspect he was just a bit of fun to her. She was probably in a relationship with a painfully handsome chap and the only reason she had been there alone is because he had a gig himself. As the first rock star to play a previously inaccessible communist nation, or Amazonian jungle venue or something. She had probably been late to meet him from his private jet, or get back to their place in some trendy East London warehouse, where they lived together and stockpiled Banksy artworks.

To be honest, if that was true, he thought he would be happy for her. They had only spent one evening chatting together, but they had a connection. He should stop speculating, he thought. He hadn't even asked what she did for a living, or at least didn't remember asking and so shouldn't really presume to knowing her at all. But that itself, he thought, showed how they had got on. None of the predictable topics had been covered and he had basically poured out his heart and soul to her the next morning. He was full of hung-over emotion, but at the same time he had told her things that he had not even said out loud to his parents, during that time. He felt like they had spent time existing together and he thought she also felt it during that evening. They had rolled out of the Empire, smiled against the cold air and staggered down the road, singing out-of-tune renditions from the night, with her playfully punching him in the arm when he went into falsetto and tried to imitate her.

He had also remembered wondering as she left, what would happen from there. In his mind, he was hoping she felt the same and was waiting, maybe for him to make the first move and text. If so, she had not had to wait long, as Miles was not great at texting politics and had texted her almost immediately, to let her know what a great night he'd had. She was probably not even back on the Underground and he regretted that a little bit, but the speed that she left had made him over-compensate. He had babbled over breakfast, but despite that, and once she had left and he could finally put his thoughts in order, he realised he wanted to talk some more with her. Talk more about life and destiny and dreams. She had responded to his texts, but he had to settle for a bit of back and forth that day and in the next few weeks. It always seemed like Miles had sent the last text and was always the one waiting for a response. He noticed that sometimes she left a kiss on the texts and sometimes did not. He always did and was quite deliberate about that.

Once he had even forgotten to put a kiss on and had sent a new text to apologise for that, with a witty comment that he didn't really recall and the missing kiss. Anyway, that didn't even get a response – not even a LOL. By the time it was close to Christmas, they were only really texting once a week and the one that Miles sent on Christmas Day was still unanswered.

Against all this evidence, Miles decided he would text her right now – that would be his first piece of forward momentum in his new approach to life. He was sure that she was probably just going to ignore it and was probably hanging out in a cool bar drinking some kind of sophisticated cocktail and talking about the latest foreign film. But he wanted to make contact and wanted her to know that he was thinking of her. Anyway, Reading Festival was coming up that summer and the rumour was, that The Killers were playing one of the days, so that could be his excuse. He had been thinking of buying a ticket and a few guys from the bar were going, so that again was an opportunity to act. Another piece of karma in his new-found lust for life. So with one elbow on the bar and one eye closed to make it easier to focus on the screen, he composed the following:

HEY HOT SOPHIE. INFORMATION BOMB – I HAVE QUIT MY JOB AND AM GOING TO TAKE OVER THE WORLD. FANCY A RE-RUN OF THE BEST NIGHT EVER? KILLERS - READING FESTIVAL. I HEAR THEY DO GOOD CHICKEN XXX.

Satisfied with the balance of drama and mystery, and with a subtle signal that he enjoyed her company, he hit send, ordered his next drink and wandered over to the jukebox. It was one of the really old-fashioned ones, which had CD inner sleeves clipped to a rotating board and you used a large round button to rotate the albums. You then had to select a five-digit code that corresponded to the album and the track number and if you put your ear to the machine, you could hear the clicks and clunks of the internal mechanism as it selected your song. Miles found this comforting and selecting songs had become a ritual, even though usually the bar had closed before his song got a chance to play. He didn't really understand why, but it seemed to happen every night. It was as if there was someone following him there, who was feeding £20 into the jukebox every night and selecting exclusively Britpop songs. Granted the volume was never that high on the music, but sometimes, hearing a few bars from one of your favourite songs drifting through the bar can be a very soothing thing. Although he now had a certain fondness for Champagne Supernova, variety would also have been a nice thing.

It was whilst he was standing there, trying to figure out if there was anything new on there, that he noticed the sign that had been taped to the machine. Just a plain piece of A4 paper, which was probably printed out in the back of the pub, although on quite a nice laser printer judging by the typeface and depth of colour, Miles noted, helpless to the echoes of his former career:

HELP WANTED!

That is how Miles decided that working at the bar at the end of the street was a good first step to "taking over the world".

Chapter Six

Little Things

March 8, 2005

Texting can sometimes get a bad rap, thought Sophie. The fact was, it is definitely easier to text someone than call these days and in some ways, it does take an awful lot of pressure off chatting people up. There is less need to have a one-liner ready, or think on your feet for a bit of banter or a particularly effective put-down. You can be in a taxi, miles away from the person who you are flirting with, and give them such a clear indication of your interest that it had become a bit of a flirting version of a nuclear bomb. It had made it less fun to watch people crash and burn in real-life, bar chatting-up moments, but at the same time, meant that the playing field was starting to get better for those who are naturally shy, or are lacking the cocky streak that it takes to make an instant impression on complete strangers. She could deal with that, although she hoped that it didn't ever replace the effort that guys put into dancing. Because in Sophie's opinion, if you could dance, then all bets were off, anyway.

On the other hand, perhaps because of the opportunities that texting had, it also raised the stakes of flirting. The very fact that something is written down, means it can be re-read several times in the cold light of day and also, you can interpret so many layers into texts that might not even be there – based on the time it was sent, the number of kisses or even, whether or not there are kisses at all. You know, for example, that a text sent close to or after midnight was probably sent drunk, clinging onto the bar and a crush, so if you know them well it can be taken with a pinch of salt. But if you don't know them well, it can give you a bit of insight into their feelings and can be fifteen or twenty words that you can agonise over for days. Searching for the meaning that they found at the bottom of a vodka bottle, or even composing a response that could be equally misunderstood. Usually, those conversations end when someone is brave enough to respond: we need to talk.

So yes, texts get a bad rap. However, despite all the ways that they can complicate your life and how many hours you can waste composing text responses, sometimes a text has one advantage that is as beautifully simple as a line from a song or a thought from a loved book. Sometimes, a text can just make you smile and there is nothing better or more enjoyable in your day, thought Sophie, than a text that just makes you smile.

When she received this text from Miles, she smiled:

HEY HOT SOPHIE. INFORMATION BOMB – I HAVE QUIT MY JOB AND AM GOING TO TAKE OVER THE WORLD. FANCY A RE-RUN OF THE BEST NIGHT EVER? KILLERS - READING FESTIVAL. I HEAR THEY DO GOOD CHICKEN XXX.

Now, you could definitely have a field day with those 36 words, and not just because it was approaching 11 o'clock in the evening and so definitely fell into the 'drunk' category. It was clearly the thoughts of a slightly manic person and clearly showed that Miles was still a bit broken, but was going through his own kind of personal awakening. She could picture him, as he was that night they first met, with intense eyes, but a vulnerability that you either run towards, or away from. Usually, she would have no time for such a thing, but for some reason she felt drawn to Miles. His text was a machine gun of thoughts, in both content and subtlety, but she thought he was so funny, and so raw and honest with everything he said, that you had to respect him. But three kisses, Miles, really?

Of course, for Sophie, that also put Miles into a category that she had to very careful with. He had basically told her, in just that one text, that he thought she was hot, he enjoyed her company and that he wanted to see her again. All alarm bells, unless you are also willing to put yourself out there. For a girl, there is a point in a friendship with a guy, when you have to decide to be the responsible one, take control and take the relationship in the direction that you want it to go. She could respond in kind and give Miles false hope that she felt the same, or she could be very clear in the other direction and make sure she left no doubt that they were just friends. Or in Miles' case, they were two people who had met once, got drunk together and then parted ways the next morning. It was a moment in time and nothing had happened between them, she had only really given him her number because she was probably still a bit drunk and a bit giddy the next morning.

Sophie thought about this for a while and then sighed. She admitted to herself, that there was a third way and that was what was bothering her. The third way was to simply not respond at all and that was the approach that Sophie had been taking so far. They'd had a few text chats over the months that followed The Killers gig. Every time they had ended up with a bit of flirting and every time, Sophie had to leave the conversation, because she felt that she was starting to lead Miles on. Better to say nothing at all, she thought, than something that would make things complicated. During those moments, she would stare at the screen of her phone, in a small but significant personal turmoil about what to do next. But in the end, she would always leave it and not respond, rather than just cutting him loose, because she enjoyed getting his texts. They made her feel good and actually, she cared that he was OK and what was happening in his life. Which clearly, at this moment, was quite momentous if he had quit his job and was going to "take over the world".

That was the other thing she liked – his flair for the dramatic. Not an empty flair, or insincere poetry said for effect. No, when Miles said something, she actually believed him and knew that he believed himself. It seemed that he had stripped himself bare of any pretention and that every day was like a new adventure. They were at an age, an exact moment in their lives, where everyone else seemed to be doing the opposite. Everyone else she knew, seemed to be entering that part of their lives where they started to take less risks, go home earlier, wear more V-necks.

Not that this applied to her of course, she thought. At that moment she was in the garden of a bar called Cargo, in East London, looking at the Banksy artwork that had been painted on one of the walls a few years before, when Banksy seemed to enjoy a special relationship with the venue. It was now protected behind plexi-glass as his fame, or infamy, grew. She was sipping an imported beer straight from the bottle, a bottle that was wrapped in a napkin and she couldn't help thinking that life was pretty good. Shoreditch suited her, it was cool, but in the kind of way that bare wood could be cool, and since her and Smooth had moved in together there, life had been on an even keel.

He was still going out a lot and staying on top of his relentless search for the newest, coolest thing. But these days he was happier with her coming along with him and that was part of the reason that they were at Cargo. Smooth was trying to get a new job to match his new Shoreditch image. It had started a few weeks before, when Sophie started noticing that Smooth would come home in a completely different outfit than the one that he was wearing when he left in the morning.

At first, it was subtle things. He would arrive home wearing his smart shirt and trousers, but with some kind of chunky knit sweater on top, or strangely mismatched trainers to his chain-store brand trousers. She initially put it down to perhaps him being cold, or needing to walk quickly to the station, but in the end, when he had turned up at home wearing his work outfit, but with a cravat, she had to ask.

It was then that he revealed that he actually got changed in the toilets, when he switched tubes at Bank. In the morning, he would leave in his regular conservative work outfit of shirt and trousers, complete with ironed crease in the front. He felt comfortable in the morning, as most of 'his sort of person' were still in bed, but he said that he felt very conscious in the evenings that he wasn't giving the other passengers a true representation of himself in his normal work clothes. What if he saw someone he knew, he told Sophie, they would wonder why he was dressed in such a 'mainstream outfit'. He thought maybe he could pretend that he was on his way to a fancy dress, he could claim some kind of ironic geek theme. But he thought that would only maybe succeed once. Generally, he thought action was required and so he had taken to packing additional clothes that he believed more truly reflected him as a person. Then, he would change part-way and take the remainder of his journey in a more comfortable frame of mind.

Sophie had initially found this hilarious, on so many levels. Firstly, for anyone to even use the term 'mainstream clothes' in a decade that wasn't the eighties was just brilliant – as if everyone else was dressing up like Boy George. These days, the walls of individualism were falling and really, there was becoming less of a definition of 'mainstream' as long as you were happy. Then secondly, for him to even think that anyone around him even cared what he looked like, showed the scale of ego that Smooth had. (Although to be fair, he still insisted on her calling him 'Smooth' even though they were living together and had been going out for getting on for two years.) Then, to basically make the effort each morning to pack two outfits, one of them specifically for the last 30 minutes of his commuting time, was just priceless.

Of course, she didn't mention any of this, as it would not go down well and she had learned to stay away from topics that involved Smooth's self-image. She had wanted to suggest to him that the reality was, that he was an analyst for a large consumer goods company and that the change of clothes was really the fancy dress, but the last time she had given him a reality check he had sulked for pretty much the whole of an Anthony and the Johnsons concert. Having to go through something like that again, alone, was something she was keen to avoid. So here they were, as Smooth was trying to penetrate some of the circles that hung out at Cargo and re-invent himself, so she had decided to support him in that.

This evening, however, it wasn't going too well and that's why they had decided to head outside. They wanted to give the impression that they were enjoying the fresh air and street art, rather than having very little in common with the clientele and therefore, no one to talk to, because neither of them owned a creative media agency or was a musician.

Also, Sophie was realising, it was absolutely, nipples-that-could-cut-glass freezing. Winter had continued well into the new year. Smooth was OK, as he had taken to wearing Ugg boots at all times, because he had been told by someone that there were the "next big thing", even though Sophie was pretty sure they were for girls. But for Sophie, she hadn't really wanted, or needed, to change her image and had been so busy at work that she hadn't the chance or desire to succumb to the same trend. The downside of course, was that if there was something that Ugg Boots did, it was keep your feet warm.

It was also not helping Smooth's ego that Sophie's job was going well. You could have called the company she worked for a DOT COM at some point (the dream of an artist), but was, for now, a reasonably established Internet hub for aspiring and established artists to showcase and sell their work. She had fallen into it after leaving university as an aspiring journalist and soon felt at home, in what was an extended family of other journalists and artists, with just the right amount of crazy to make it interesting. Her job was, ostensibly, to write the 'blurb' that accompanied each artist, or each piece of work on the site. It was something that she really enjoyed, as it exposed her to some brilliant and some downright weird, creations from the minds of the creative. Of course, as a journalist, she still harboured a desire to have something of her own, that went beyond two-hundred words of gushing on the potential of someone she had maybe met once or twice; she longed to have an opinion that made people sit up and listen.

But in the meantime, work life was good and they were starting to gain a good profile with some of the more influential artists and taste-makers in London. She had also been experimenting with the growing online video sharing services, to record little snippets of observations about life, fashion, music, anything really, that felt interesting. As a little girl, she had loved keeping a diary and this was just an extension of that – something to look back on each year and have a laugh. Smooth made fun of it whenever he could and called it her 'daily brain fart', which considering she had never seen or smelled him fart was quite ironic.

So, it was just at the moment when the wind was starting to cut her in two and Smooth's mood was also getting a bit frosty, that Sophie got Miles' text, and smiled.

'Banksy's not even any good, Soph, everything he does looks like it was done with a stencil kit,' said Smooth.

'I think that might be the point, Smooth,' said Sophie. 'He's actually doing quite well at the moment. I think it's more about the message, and he doesn't exactly have lots of time to put his art up onto his chosen canvas, given graffiti is illegal.'

'Whatever, save it for your brain farts,' responded Smooth, also not a master of hidden meanings, in his own special way. 'Who was that texting, another one of your admirers?'

This was a new twist in their relationship. Because of her video blogging, Sophie now had a handful of people who regularly commented on her pieces from all over the world. It was generally just a few words and from all continents, as video sharing spread slowly and globally. It was mainly supportive and definitely authentic – given the vocabulary that was used, especially from those who were getting their thoughts across in, perhaps, their second or third language. She was also still pretty in awe of the whole thing – how someone who might be several tens-of-thousand miles away, had found something that she created interesting.

She dealt with art every day, with physical items that inspired that feeling of inspiration in people, but a video just felt a bit different. She considered it a piece of art and was very proud of the efforts and the content that she put into each piece, but it was not like you could hang it on your wall, or take a picture of it and show your friends. But for Sophie, it showed that people were listening. She wasn't sure if she was purely driven by this, or just that she had so many words inside her that she wanted to get out and this seemed to be the best way. She just loved it when she saw a message pop up like: THIS IS SUPER-LOLZ. She had no illusions that this was not something that would ever pay the rent, but it was fun to experiment with the new ways you had to talk to people these days, without even leaving the lounge in their little flat in Shoreditch.

Perhaps this is also why Miles' text had resonated with her. The fact that he was starting to dream about taking over the world, was something Sophie found very worthy and attractive, even if this was something that she hoped was a metaphor, rather than harboured ambitions of tyranny and dictatorship.

For some reason, this small collection of fans that Sophie had picked up, seemed to irritate Smooth. She was constantly reassuring him and explaining that they may, or probably did, all live in a lunatic asylum, for all they knew. She often felt that this was cheapening her work, but to avoid having to spend the evenings dealing with Smooth in a sulk, it was a small price. It was as if every time she had some affirmation, it reminded him that he was falling short of his own personal targets and she could see that look in his eyes right now. Sophie just wished he would look around himself and enjoy what they had together. They were living in a place where most of the planet would envy and although she was getting a bit older these days, she was still pretty sure that she could class herself as a hottie on the good days and pretty good arm candy to have.

Sophie had suggested that perhaps he could try a few new things to break the cycle. But, it was as if everything had always come easily to him and he expected just donning a pair of trendy glasses would trigger a momentous change in fortunes. As if some creative mogul would stroll up and say: 'I believe you have no experience in the creative industries, but can knock up a mean spreadsheet and hell, you're a handsome lad too, so why don't you come and work for me?'

No, all the stories now were about people who had used what was around them to create something new and worked hard to get it. You didn't need to invent the car any more, or come up with the next new breakfast cereal. These days you could make so much more happen just from your bedroom by having a good idea. But Smooth seemed intent on being discovered for something he basically wasn't and without working for it, and beyond looking good, she wasn't even sure what he was good at.

Sophie felt a shudder of guilt and told herself off. She should stop being a bad person and thinking such thoughts like this, about the person she loved. Perhaps she should give up the videos, she thought, at least until Smooth had something of his own and had his confidence back. It would definitely be easier and with her normal job and the evenings with Smooth, it was not like she didn't have a full schedule. But at the same time the thought of it made her a bit sad and she already had a couple of new ideas for her next entries. Surely they should be a team, so anything that she did that made her happy, he should also be happy, because it was all for the good for the pair of them, for Team Smooth (that is probably what it would be called). A good compromise would perhaps be, that she just started doing them in private, in the bedroom instead, and to stop talking about it or reading out any of the nonsensical notes of support. Then, when the moment was right, she would have a chat with Smooth and let him know how she felt about things and the support she needed from him.

She will have a think about how she approached that tomorrow, she thought, there must be a way of making him understand, without triggering an argument or awkwardness. So before she knew it, in her half-distracted and slightly irritated state, she had fallen into the trap of another half-truth about Miles, 'Oh, just a work colleague,' she lied.

She just wasn't ready to give Miles up yet and was keen on seeing The Killers again. And so, she might just respond to this one.

Chapter Seven

Contact

March 27, 2005.

Sometimes, the best things happen when you are not thinking.

Miles, however, felt like he had spent the last six months of his life doing nothing but thinking. But something as spontaneous as applying for a vacant bar-staff position at his local pub, seemed to have given him his groove back at last, for the first time, he could remember, in a long, long time; in such a short life.

The interview process, he had to admit, had been a bit weird. The bar manager, with whom, as a customer, Miles had only a courteous relationship, turned out to be called Tim and was about ten years older than Miles.

The best way to describe Tim would be a walking contradiction. His bar was impeccably clean and well stocked, but this sense of order and organisation seemed to fail when it came to his appearance. He moved about the bar area with the grace of a sportsman, but had the build of a barrel. He fixed you with a flint-like gaze when he spoke to you, but his eyes were peeping out of a week or more of thick, greying stubble. He seemed to have a telepathic knowledge of the order that customers needed to be served, but for the entire conversation seemed to insist on calling him Merv, despite him correcting him at least three times during the exchange.

The first thing that Tim asked Miles to do when he enquired about the job, leaning across the bar a few weeks earlier, was to write his name and number on the HELP WANTED sign that was taped to the jukebox, where he also hoped other candidates would apply. Miles wanted to be polite, as he was in a position where he wanted something from Tim, but gave a mild resistance to this based on the fact that writing his name and number on the juke box seemed to be one step above writing his telephone number on the gent's toilet wall. At this, Tim seemed to just stare at him with a puzzled expression, but at the same time produced a yellow sticky note from thin air as an alternative. They then organised to meet the following lunchtime at the pub and Miles was inexplicably asked to bring with him cheese and tuna sandwiches. When he asked Tim why he should bring along a sandwich, Tim gave him the same baffled expression and explained it was because they didn't do food during the day. This was how their relationship started.

The next day, Miles arrived at the pub a few minutes early for the interview. He had agonised for a long time that morning on what to wear for an interview in a pub. His initial thoughts might be that a shirt and tie combination might give the impression of experience, but perhaps was a bit keen. At the other end of the spectrum, as the bar was frequented by a fairly fashionable crew, he wondered if he should go for the hipster look. He thought better of that, in case he was asked for a demonstration of pint-pulling. He had briefly worked behind a bar before and didn't want to ruin a nice shirt by spraying beer all over it. So he went for the option of black shirt and blue jeans, to give the right balance of a casual look, but with a smart and classic palette.

Tim appeared to wear the same outfit as the night before, and also looked like he had slept in it.

The interview turned out to be a bit of a one-way process and Miles barely got a word in over the whole duration of their meeting. Tim began by giving a non-abridged version of how and why he took over the bar a few years previously. It turned out that he was an actor and playwright, and had made a bit of money in Los Angeles a few years earlier by starring as an extra in various sitcoms. Usually, he said, he took the part of 'Brit #1' and because there were not many European actors in LA at that time, he had a fairly consistent supply of work. His lack of talent, he explained, meant that he never quite made it beyond the extras crew and then in the end, he had to return home as casting directors were starting to recognise him and felt it was getting a bit confusing for viewers, that almost every minor British part in day-time soaps was acted by the same person.

So he returned home and planned to use the bar as a way of working in the evening, freeing up his days for writing screenplays, to send back to the same directors and give him his "big break". He felt that he was more suited to a life behind the lens. But sadly, apparently the prejudice of the film-making community was a barrier to this plan, as they prioritised US-based screenwriters.

Although Miles suspected from the few plots Tim elaborated on, that the real issue was that the lead character in all his shows was a middle-aged, slightly out of shape, but adorable male, preferably with a British accent.

Despite this, Miles found himself warming to Tim and the two of them bonded over a love for sci-fi movies, video games and an intangible chemistry. That was that; without Miles having to explain why he was right for the position and without any evidence of ever having done it before, Miles got the job. He was to start that evening, as apparently the previous incumbent took too long to get used to the alphabetised spirit shelf, and kept getting Aftershock Red and Aftershock Blue the wrong way round. Don't even get him started on Smirnoff Ice on the rainbow-categorised shelf in the fridge, Tim explained abruptly, before just as abruptly jumping up and giving Miles a hasty handshake, sweeping up his untouched sandwich and bustling off, leaving Miles feeling excited and a bit like he had been mugged. He collected himself and felt his stomach flip with excitement and nerves about the evening. As he left, he caught a glimpse of Tim furiously feeding the jukebox with pound coins and jabbing the numbers of songs either at random or from memory. The volume was low, but Miles could hear Oasis drifting quietly through the bar. So that explained one thing.

The weeks that followed were amongst some of the most enjoyable he could remember. When you are on the working side of the bar, you become the guy that everyone wants to know. The customers he half-knew from his times in there as a regular customer, were now full of conversation and keen to show that they knew him with winks and high-fives. The ones that didn't know him, soon got to know and like him. If you were to ask him, Miles would say he was actually pretty good at the job and had found a passion in something for the first time in many years. The simple joy you could get in giving people a good night out, a good drink, even a quick one-liner or a bit of playful banter, was almost like a drug to Miles.

He found himself working harder and putting more effort into being a barman than he had into anything else before. He had always had a good work ethic, but generally it had been a selfish work ethic – aimed at getting further in a company, or striving for a pay rise. Now, he just enjoyed the simple pleasure of working for a smile, which in the end meant that he also did pretty well in tips and that he drank his fair share of free beers after his shift had finished. Plus, because of this attitude, he could see that Tim also liked him, they had an easy interaction that not only served as light entertainment to the customers, it also added fuel to their relationship and buzz to the bar. A few weeks into the job, Tim asked Miles if he wanted to hang out together at a friend's bar in London on Easter Sunday. His pub was going to close early, as generally, Easter Sunday was a family day. So as a traditional boozer, it was empty, but would then fill up again on Easter Monday when London took advantage of the long weekend to have one last blow-out before going back to regular life. Miles enthusiastically accepted.

So when he finished his shift after lunch on Easter Sunday and stepped onto the pavement, blinking into the spring sunshine, he felt an equal spring in his step. The clocks had been put forward overnight, and all in all, he felt it was a day that was full of hope. Then, when his phone beeped and he checked the screen and saw that

Sophie had sent him a text, he felt like he could almost burst with joy. He had completely forgotten about texting her a few weeks earlier and had accepted that perhaps he would never hear from her again, but here she was. Even better, she was saying in her text that she was also thinking of going along to Reading Festival that summer and would love to meet up, if it worked for them both; and there was a kiss! He could hardly contain himself and so, without thinking, he flipped over to the address book screen and pressed the dial button for Sophie. Let's have a chat, he thought.

If anyone was watching Miles at that very moment, this is what they would have seen. They would have seen someone duck out onto the pavement from the pub, glance at the sky and break into a broad smile. They would then see him, suddenly distracted, reach into his pocket for something, pull out his phone and actually give a shoulder-shuddering giggle. He would take a few more steps, press the call button on his phone and put it to his ear. Then, almost immediately turn grey, stop dead in his tracks and look paralysed with fear.

The reason was, that Miles really was in fact paralysed with fear. All of this took place over the course of about five seconds, but inside Miles' head his thoughts were moving at a million miles an hour. What was he thinking, calling Sophie on a whim? He hadn't rehearsed anything he was going to say, he didn't even have a list of topics to talk about, in case the conversation got awkward. He had met her in person once and since then had just traded texts and they are, by nature, messages he had put actual thought and time into. So what was he doing now, just casually calling her for a chat? Perhaps he should hang up. Nope, it was now ringing at her end and she could see he was calling.

Hopefully she wouldn't answer, he thought, and then he could just let her see the missed call and call back. In that time, he could dash home and put some proper preparation into the conversation – maybe practise some jokes as well and revise a little bit about current affairs and music on the internet.

Sophie answered on the fourth ring. 'Hey!' She said, sounding happy, but not without an edge of surprise.

'HANG UP!' Miles surprisingly heard himself say, a little too loudly. This was becoming a habit, he thought.

'Erm. I can do,' said Sophie, 'but you did just call me and so it might be a bit rude without a good reason.'

'Sorry,' said Miles, 'I was just talking to someone else.' What a terrible excuse. This was going terribly, so he decided to over-compensate.

'How are you? I must admit, I called you without thinking about what I was going to say. I was just feeling really good today and then you texted and I thought it would be good to say hi and maybe talk about meeting up in Reading. I know that's a few months away, but there's no time like the present, eh?'

So there it was, brutal honesty and transparency. Nowhere to hide and Miles could feel himself in the kind of conversation cul-de-sac that just ended in "Disappointment Cottage".

'Ah, that's nice,' said Sophie, and she meant it. 'What did you have for lunch?'

Miles then embarked on the most surreal twenty minutes of his life. Surreal because he suddenly found himself giving a full two minute summary of his lunch, giving a particularly colourful description of the sprouts. But also, because Sophie sounded genuinely interested and even laughed out loud at a few of his, more tried-and-tested, bar-staff jokes. Actually laughed, this cool girl who had almost become a myth in his mind – a myth who only hung out in the coolest places with the coolest people and knew exactly when to leave their text conversations, so that she stayed utterly in control.

Then, in turn, she gave him a run-down of the lamb lunch she had just had with family and how one of her uncles had stitched himself up with a young nephew, by claiming that lamb was a vegetable so that he didn't have to explain the farming cycle of livestock. Only to discover that they were taught a lot more and a lot younger in school than he thought, and so was in turn patronised by said nephew, who promised to take the uncle through his *'Where Does My Food Come From'* picture book at the next opportunity.

When Miles hung up the phone, he had to do a little skip. He felt like suddenly he was in some kind of movie and the backing track was probably soft-rock. He actually felt like he had been completely himself and that they had connected again, just like that first night. Why had he waited so long to call her? This was just amazing and he had about five months to prepare for the Reading Festival. He could make sure that he was looking good by continuing his exercise and with the shift patterns, even had time to get a good tan if the weather was good. The bar job and continued stash of canned vegetables, meant that he was also feeling good and was full of effervescent conversation and stories from the nights in the bar. He could even borrow a few stories from customers – after the "chocolate biscuit maker" days he was pretty good at creating an exaggerated background and history. Then he checked himself. No, he couldn't do that to Sophie, he had to be completely honest. For goodness sake, Miles, he thought to himself. Be cool.

Across the city, Sophie pressed the 'end' button on her phone and then pressed the heel of the phone to her forehead. Again, unconsciously, she was smiling. It had been a good day today, she loved hanging out with her family and Easter was a family time for her. They were a bit dysfunctional, but only in that way that families are. It is always amazing that so many people can share such an unshakable blood bond, but be so different. The red wine had been flowing and for most of the lunch everyone had been in stitches laughing, plus that thing with her uncle and the 'lamb is a vegetable' was just hilarious. She would definitely have to find something lamb-related to give to him as a gift at Christmas, to remind him of the story.

Then she felt that guilt again. It had also been easier because Smooth had not been there – on these occasions he tended to go and see his own family, who lived a long way outside of London. She also loved his family, they were great people and insisted on calling him by his proper name, so it was refreshing to see the veil drop every now and again and see him wince every time they called him Neil.

But for her, not having Smooth there, meant that she didn't have to talk down about herself and talk up about him. She didn't have to pretend that he was starting to make some good contacts and good progress in moving his life towards what he thought it should be, and what he thought he deserved. But, truth be told, he was actually just becoming a parody of that and starting to hang on just a little bit too tight. He had started spending almost every spare hour researching new bands and trying to find new musical genres that no one else had heard about, and then littering his conversation with them, arbitrarily to try and impress the guys they were meeting in Cargo and other places that she was getting sick of going.

At one point she actually heard him try and invent a new genre of music, called garunge. When asked about it, he tried to insist that it was a blend of complicated hard house beats and simple beats, made famous by grunge bands of Seattle. That just didn't make sense and when she heard it she thought he just came across as a bit of a tosser. She almost had a word at the time, but decided to leave it, as the guys they were talking to seemed to nod in some kind of agreement and although they made their excuses a few minutes later, Smooth seemed to think he had scored some kind of victory. All the way home, he was babbling away about garunge and was not even discouraged when an Internet search only seemed to confirm that it was probably a load of rubbish. He kept going on about an article he had read, but Sophie was pretty sure that someone had just accidentally misspelled 'grunge'.

There was also no respite when she tried to divert the discussion to his actual job and his actual life. In his opinion, all of his work-mates were boring and his boss didn't understand him anymore. They all just wanted to talk about the pop charts, he said, almost spitting out the words. According to Smooth, his boss didn't understand when Smooth was a few minutes late because he'd had a late night, pursuing his dream and meeting other like-minded people.

Sophie had to stand by him as she believed in dreams, but was a bit confused by this, as it seemed to her that all they did was hang around in bars and laugh at other people's jokes. A lot of the time these days, she didn't even understand half of the stuff that was being said and actually longed for someone to talk about the pop charts. She had visions of standing on her chair and screaming 'I LOVE JAMES BLUNT! HIS SONGS ARE QUITE NICE TO LISTEN TO!' Then run out, before anyone could get a clear look at her. Not that they would do anything about it. Probably just 'tut' loudly and make a sarcastic comment. She could understand if he was writing, or creating music, and would actually quite like to see him squirrelling away in the spare room, up late to finish a chapter, or a verse, and would find it quite romantic to find him under a blanket the next morning, with his chin resting on his chest and his fountain pen still in hand.

As for her, she had loved being able to talk freely about her work at the table and about her attempts at video blogging that seemed to be loved by foreign exchange students in late night Internet cafes. Her parents had got over the fact that she might get cyber-stalked, or have her identity stolen. They were now genuinely interested as well as completely baffled. Her last video post had got 300 visits and over 100 comments, which was the most she had ever received. It had been her bravest so far and was about love. Although, it was mainly about her love for cats. She had found a collection of videos, from kittens sleeping in wellingtons, to failed, but adorable, attempts of jumping across tables or over fences. Happy videos, or unexpected moments of failure that only cats can do. It was telling the story that moments such as these – simple moments – were what kept her going when she was feeling down. So it had been a relative hit with her online fans, they seemed to love the cute animal story theme, especially cats.

Then, after lunch, she was just relaxing by the river, enjoying the sun on her face and her fuzzy red-wine head, when Miles had popped into her thoughts. She had been a bit tardy with him, she had to admit. It had been a few weeks since he texted about Reading and although she wanted to go, Smooth had insisted that it had gone too mainstream and was refusing to accept any tickets for the festival on principle. But now, she was having a bit of a change in heart. She'd had a good time with Miles and he was thoughtful enough to contact her, so she should consider going. No, she would go.

She was also a little bit interested in how things were progressing during his breakdown and felt like she had an obligation to him, given that she had met him at such a big moment in his life. Perhaps it could give her some inspiration for her video blog. She could also do with a compliment or a bit of attention, so she quickly composed a response and sent it over.

To her surprise, she had not even put the phone away when it rang in her hand. To her even greater surprise, it was Miles. This was a change in approach from him. Usually, he was very responsive in his texting, but actually going old-school and calling her was unusual. She considered letting it ring and go to messages, but then thought, why not? She was a bit drunk and so could tolerate a little bit of crazy. If it got too heavy she would just gently let him know the state of play and perhaps that could be a nice way of gently breaking communications with him. So she answered.

'HANG UP!' Were his first words.

Now that was an unexpected opening. What followed was a little bit awkward at the start, but soon she found it nice to actually speak to someone in London who was genuine, warm and pleased to speak to her about boring stuff like food and what she did today. It was refreshing and she also felt that Miles sounded a bit different. As the conversation went on, he was... well, funny and happy. This was a bit different to the slightly manic Miles that she remembered from The Killers gig, a few months earlier. She liked it and even found herself flirting a bit.

She stayed away from sensitive topics such as Smooth and the fact that since they last saw each other she had moved in with him – he didn't need to know that, in his fragile state. Instead, they just chatted and in the end, agreed they would try and meet up at Reading and watch The Killers together. It was a few months away, but maybe that was a good thing, as it allowed Miles to get even more normal and he might even get a new girlfriend by then. The thought of that made her feel a little bit funny, but it would make things easier if Smooth was with her and he was with someone else. At least there would be no chance for Miles to be weird, or try too hard to impress her.

So that was that. She also resolved that she had to speak with Smooth, explain to him that he needed to think about her a bit more and be a bit more normal. She would explain that they were going to Reading, even if she had to buy the tickets in the traditional fashion. She also blamed herself a bit that it had got to this stage. She should have mentioned how she was feeling a few weeks earlier, but she just hoped that he would go back to being normal, but he had just got worse. If she could spend one day apart from him and with just that small amount of breathing space, reach that conclusion, then an intervention was definitely required. Yes, she resolved to do that.

She couldn't do it today, of course, that would ruin Easter Sunday. Then they also had Bank Holiday Monday together and she couldn't face a sulk. She would do it tomorrow night, or the absolute latest, the end of the week.

Chapter Eight

Zombies

March 27, 2005.

It should not have been a surprise to Miles that a guy who owned a bar could drink. Really, really drink.

Tim greeted Miles with a warm hug and a cold beer, made even more so from a frosted glass that stung Miles' already cold hands. He took his first pull and gave a small moan of satisfaction. Miles had been looking forward to the afternoon and the first sip and the bar did nothing to lessen his euphoria.

Miles had never seen Tim drink at his own bar, he was far too professional for that. All staff were allowed unlimited soft drinks, but it was against policy to drink alcohol on duty. This rule was as strictly enforced as the 'no glasses left behind' policy and the 'you can never wipe a bar too many times' rule. When someone had a passion for something, he respected the attention and the pride that they put into it; to Miles it showed character and he found this aspirational. Tim tended to disappear very quickly at the end of a shift and although he sometimes let the staff stay behind for a drink at the end of the night, he never participated. He always made an excuse that he had to review an order, or research a new beer. They all respected that.

What Miles did know, was that every alcopop, every rum, every ale, was personally approved by Tim. This was not a surprise of course, because as well as being meticulous in arranging his bar, he was also meticulous with what went behind the bar and therefore, into his customers. He had often heard Tim give a five minute explanation to a customer on a new type of beer, giving the history, his reasons for allowing it into the pub and the story behind when and where he was, when he tried it. This ranged from a visit to the brewery itself a few miles up the road, to a sun-kissed West Coast beach at sunset, on a particular Sunday evening, with the warm Pacific breeze in his hair and the smell of spiraea in his nostrils.

But he also explained that day, he also wanted to know what it felt like to be drunk on certain drinks, so he was better placed to explain that as well. This then explained how well-practised Tim was at drinking. He saw himself as an artist of alcohol, he explained. To him, there was no snobbery of brand or type of drink, only taste. He considered an alcopop as art of the same level as a whiskey, just for a different person. In his bar, he prided himself in his ability to talk to any of his customers about their drink, no matter who they were, or what they were drinking.

These new insights into Tim's meticulous nature also made it all that much weirder, that Tim was wearing a t-shirt marked with, what could only have been, an old curry stain, right in the middle of the chest area, above the logo for an American university.

The best way to describe the inside of the bar Tim had brought him to would be, baroque. The walls and ceilings were draped with heavy velvet, which gave the bar an air of Middle Eastern coffee shop, except that they were all edged with twinkle lights that acted as the primary light source in the main lounge area. This gave way to dark oak tables and a mixed collection of chairs, which were similar, only in that they were all re-upholstered with the same deep colours and materials as the walls and gave a forgiving sigh when you sank into them. Despite the fresh and bright day, the bar kept an air of an attractive gloom, with dark alcoves, each illuminated by single, upstanding, polished steel lamp, every one festooned in diamantes and crystal shades. It was the kind of place where time slowed down, secrets were shared and lasting friendships were made, through smiles in the dim corners.

Miles knew that a place where publicans drank would have atmosphere, but even with this expectation, he was surprised by just how far away from a traditional pub the bar was. He could see how this was the lounge-owners lounge, a place where you could take your mind away from your own noise, your own clutter. The bar was run by beautiful staff, dressed to their own style, but in tailored black and white, with a dark red carnation pinned to each suit breast or dress sleeve, which matched the upholstery. They moved around the bar with ease, each drink reviewed by at least two staff before it left the bar, with a small adjustment of a mint leaf, or a check that the levels of head were flush to the top of the glass. The service, as you would expect, was also impeccable. As soon as he drained his first beer, a slim waitress in pressed linen and a pencil skirt appeared with a fresh one and a small plate of cold meats and breads – Miles felt the prick of balsamic vinegar and roasted garlic in his nostrils.

'What do you really want to do, Miles?' Tim asked.

Tim had chosen a seat in the middle of the bar, the typical choice of a bar owner who loved the big city, loved being in the middle of things and able to see life going on all around him. It was an unexpectedly abrupt opening question in some ways. Tim had given Miles a few moments to settle into his surroundings, but was now addressing him with the same intensity in his eyes. Miles could imagine that without drinks orders to remember, tabs to add up and customers and staff to supervise, Tim still needed to keep his mind busy - collect information, collect knowledge.

It felt like, for Tim, life was always a forward motion. He had seen him watch the news on TV and he was always upright, staring unblinking and almost right through the TV. Reading the newspaper was the same, mouthing the words as he read them and then immediately turning to anyone who would listen, to repeat the story to gather an opinion or a debate. He could see this intensity now, he was not passive in his relaxation, but genuinely interested. It was as if inviting Miles to the bar was a signal of friendship, but not without Miles proving that he wasn't a distraction. That they could provide forward momentum to each other's lives together. This felt like the proper interview and made Miles smile when he remembered the half-listening meeting they had some weeks earlier, over uneaten tuna sandwiches.

Miles paused for a moment and then reached for his phone with the intention of showing Tim the texts that he had swapped with Sophie.

'Ah, sorry,' said Tim and placed a large hand over Miles', 'we don't use mobile phones in here'. He shrugged apologetically with his body, but his eyes remained fixed on Miles, questioning. 'You're going to have to tell me the story.'

'OK,' said Miles and took a deep breath. For the second time since "The Decision", he told his story to someone whom he had just met.

When he had finished, Miles realised that time had slipped by and that several beers had also slipped down. About three more beers had magically appeared like the second, of course with the accompanying snacks, which seemed to get better each time they received a new round. In the last one, there was a fresh Spanish omelette interpretation, fluffy on the outside, but with potato and cheese in the middle that oozed with every bite. In that time, Tim had not interrupted him or taken his eyes off Miles even once, apart from when he took a mouthful of beer, or a bite of snack. His eyes drank in the information and if he was thinking, then he did it in languid ease, with an expression that was hard to read, beyond the fact that it willed you to give more, to open up more.

There was a long pause and Miles unconsciously picked at an olive, wondering what was going to happen. The stereo system had the same quality as the décor and Miles could tell, even at low volume, was playing an instrumental session from the Foo Fighters. Probably taken from some of the promotional sessions ahead of the launch of the new album that was coming that summer. Even silences in this place are cool, Miles couldn't help thinking.

'That makes you sound like a victim,' said Tim, making Miles flinch. 'So I hope that it's also the intro, because it also does not really answer my question.'

Miles thought he was right. He realised that all he had done was give an historical account of the last few months, right up to the moment that he met Sophie. It did make him sound like a victim, but those days were over. It was just an introduction and made him think again, that meeting Sophie was the exact point where his life went from the dark negative to the colourful positive. The past was exactly that, it was a dark barometer for the future, a cautionary tale about a person that he no longer wanted to be. He had been explaining events, as if this would explain the future; but the trouble was he didn't really know what the events of the future were going to be and that was the beautiful fact. He realised that the future was much simpler than that. He realised that it wasn't in what he wanted to do, but how he wanted to feel and in that, the answer to Tim's question was the reason that he had reached for his phone.

'I feel like my life is a brand new jigsaw,' he began, 'and I know the exact moment that happened, because it happened when I met someone and when they text me, or talk to me, it feels like the right pieces of the jigsaw. It feels like, without trying, they have become part of my fabric, part of my jigsaw. As I put my life back together and figure out all the pieces, I want each one to feel like that, like the moment I get a text from them, or the moment that I think about them.' That was it really. He realised that it was that simple. When you found the right pieces, it, at once meant you felt excited and at once at peace.

'Now we're talking,' said Tim mischievously and made a signal to the bar; at which a glistening bottle of vodka appeared at the table, along with two glasses and a generous portion of ice in a bucket that was, of course, studded with diamantes.

'Do you know why I come here?' Tim asked, but Miles could tell that the question was mainly rhetorical, so he let Tim continue.

'Life is a constant pressure that is just increasing. It is a pressure to be outward and we are letting this outside pressure define us. The reason I bought the pub was to give people a place to step away from that pressure. Where they can relax at the end of a day, or at the weekend and forget about all that pressure. But do we really give that? Isn't it that, actually, the very place you go to relax, is becoming a place where you have to prove every moment that you are the funniest, the coolest, the most beautiful in the building? The world is changing, my friend - quiet is boring, peaceful is for the cemetery. The present and the future are converging and people no longer want to step away from it. If they have a spare moment, they reach for their phones. If it's quiet, they reach for the TV.

So, why is my pub the busiest in the neighbourhood? It's because I understand that. I understand that my customers are not me, so I give the people what they want, not what I would want. You have to decide to get on the train or not, and when I am in that bar I am on that train. You step into my bar and have a drink, it's a story. The music I play is my choice, but it's for my customers. So when you hear it on the radio, you don't remember that moment, you remember the moment you heard it in my bar and you remember the story you have about my bar. Everyone wants to be a part of that, not because they enjoy it, but because they can tell their friends – I went there and I did that. And that reminds me, I need to get some t-shirts printed.'

Tim glanced around him and vaguely waved at the surroundings. 'But when I come here, all I have to do is feel my feet on the ground, take a breath and enjoy the present. No stories, no pressures – just be inward. That is the real luxury in life for me. The place you can go where nothing else matters but the present; the person you are with, they are the real treasures and you don't need money or a postcode. They are the moments when you close your eyes and remember that yes, you were truly in the present – in a small way or a big way. I come here so I can think of that moment and I re-align myself. Then, I take my peace and put it into everything I do in my pub, in whatever way my customers want it. I have peace, so that my customers can have their chaos. For me, being in the moment is a peaceful thing, but for some, being in the moment is about providing the perfect party atmosphere.'

Tim paused and poured them both another shot from a now half-empty vodka bottle. Miles was starting to get the numb sensation that you get from ice-cold vodka shots and could feel his eyes retreating from his mind, feeling wonderfully more relaxed and detached than he had for a long time. Tim continued.

'You talked about meeting someone. I knew someone once and that moment you talked about, for me was on Santa Monica beach, with the sun setting behind the Ferris wheel on the pier and the surf soaking into the bottom of my jeans. I used to go back and sit on the beach and remember that moment, because it was perfection. Then life gets in the way. In the pressure of life you step away from that true happiness and get distracted for a moment and the opportunity goes. That person goes because of obsession with the big decisions, with goals and tangibility you can boast about. For me, it passed because I forgot about the small decisions, the smile at that sunset, the fizz of the waves and the feeling of her smile. Instead of realising that she wanted the same as me, the peace, I thought she wanted Mexican food, excitement and music. So in the end, our heartbeats did not align.

The mistake we make sometimes, is that we can only move life by making big decisions and we expect the same from others. But actually, the small ones, the ones that nudge us forward just that little bit – are just as important. Take yourself, for example. For you, it was initially a big decision that you made. But since then, you have deliberately only made small decisions and they are bringing you closer to happiness and closer to having a life that you love as much as any big decision. Without noticing, you are already half way up the hill and the path is getting more and more clear to you. More and more clear.'

Miles had to agree, but he did have one controversial point and before he knew it, he had blurted it out. 'Yes, but at some point I am going to have to get a proper job.'

Tim smiled. 'Maybe. But there you are, jumping forward several steps. Maybe working in a bar is what you need right now. That is where fulfilment comes in. If it doesn't fulfil you, then you need to make a choice. Every big and small decision in the end is a choice and they are all as hard as each other, because when you make a choice, you give something up. The key is to make that choice for the right reasons.

The pressure in the world is creating a storm and if you're not careful you'll be sucked back into the storm. So what do you do? You find the calmest place in a storm and from there, you make choices and you can be in control. The calmest place in a storm is right there in the middle, in the eye of the storm and that is your happy place. It is the place where you can see the storm raging, the cows flying, the buildings being ripped up and lives torn apart around you, but you feel in control. Stepping into that storm is losing control.

I have had future musicians, future actors, future bankers, future lawyers, all through my bar – all thinking that it wasn't a proper job. All of them looking for something, searching for their own fulfilment and I say the same to all of them. We have never before been in a world where you immediately get out what you put in. Make the job a piece of your journey, use it to be in control and find your path. You are now in control, Miles, but you have had to put yourself in that position and you should be proud of that. You have to find your own eye of the storm and if you decide to take a leap back into the storm, then that's fine, just do it for the right reasons.'

The vodka and the surprising emotion that Tim was expressing had heightened his senses and Miles was feeling no concept, or worry, of time. He was feeling that things were falling into place. Maybe he was no longer on the path that he had chosen a few months earlier, but he could also feel the world changing and moving away from the singular desire and singular goal of the new suit, or the new car. You no longer have to be an "emo" or a "metal head", because quite frankly, most bands now contained at least a keytar and a power chord. It was a world where the Internet was starting to create an environment where anyone can go from nobody to superstar, because they have good ideas and kind thoughts.

Tim drained the last of the vodka into their glasses and held his up to Miles for a last cheers. Their glasses connected noisily in the quiet of the bar and although there was a sense that the evening was drawing in, it was hard to tell through the vodka and the semi-darkness. Tim's expression changed and he laid a heavy hand on Miles' shoulder.

'The other thing that has always been there, of course, is love. The most positive and the most negative choices we make, should have love at the heart of them. Whether it is a person you love, a thing you love or a moment you love, we are encouraged to love. The trouble is, maybe love is not a choice. Maybe love is not a moment, but a journey. Let's also not forget, that love is hard and sometimes not enough. For you, maybe you have found love. Love is not just a storm. Love is a hurricane, wrapped in thunder, etched with lightning and moving at force thirteen. Finding the eye of that storm, my friend, is a miracle. It is still a wonder how we manage to ignore the other paths and the other temptations and take the path that eventually can lead to true love.'

Sometimes, drunk wisdom is the best wisdom and when you share drunk wisdom, relationships move into friendships. Miles felt that was happening on that hopeful day, where the sun shone and the even clocks had sprung forward.

'So, what is it you love?' He asked Tim. He didn't want the conversation to end. He felt like this bar was the eye of the storm for Tim in many ways. The place where choices were made.

'Zombies,' said Tim with a grin, his gaze unwavering and never leaving Miles. 'I hope you don't have plans, because I'm just getting started. Let me tell you about zombies,' and he unscrewed the cap of the second bottle of vodka, that of course, had arrived without them even noticing.

Chapter Nine

Cats are Evil

May 21, 2005.

Tim was not a zombie. That was Miles' first relief when they had talked about zombies for the first time. Not that it was likely, but after several beers and half a bottle of vodka, the mind can certainly play tricks on you.

Instead, he shared a dream with Miles. A story, in return for a story. It was a dream that had pursued him actively for the last five years, but had followed him for many years before that. It developed from a fascination that he carried with him, since watching re-runs of horror movies when he was young and not insignificantly influenced by Michael Jackson's "Thriller".

The fascination was in all things undead, but particularly zombies. Although first it was vampires, he had to admit.

The rise of zombies to be number one in Tim's mind, took place in the later years of his childhood. His initial obsession with vampires, he reasoned to Miles, was because of the glamour pull of the vampire to a young person. Vampires are very much the rock star of the undead world. The vampire is always well turned-out, in a sharp suit and a cape, and we all know how awesome it is to have a cape when you are a six-year-old boy. Plus, vampires could fly and hang upside down for long periods of time. Both things made a young Tim very jealous and something that he tried to emulate whenever possible. In fact, it was exactly this experimentation, he couldn't remember whether it was flying or hanging, that led to a nasty broken arm and one of his most vivid and earliest childhood memories. The list went on. They only came out at night, just like rock stars. Again, for a small boy with a strict bedtime, staying out late was something that got him all wide-eyed with wonder.

Then, as he got older and was allowed to watch some of the less gruesome Hammer films, he would watch Peter Cushing and Christopher Lee fighting it out over various backdrops and incarnations, and every time Peter Cushing won, he felt a small sense of loss for the vampire. He figured they were a bit misunderstood and that all they were trying to do when they bit the necks of their victims, was to get some friends that they could keep with them over the years, instead of having to see all their human friends grow old and die.

As the years went on zombies started to shade vampires, as his "all-time favourite undead". The trigger for this was a similar sense of compassion. If the vampires were misunderstood, then the zombies were even more so. They were usually really normal people, who by some trick of sorcery were brought back from the dead against their will and that's always going to make you grumpy. Plus, being buried for a few decades, with all the worms and woodlice nibbling at your bits was also not going to add to a sunny mood. He could imagine how they would give the living a nasty shock, suddenly popping up out of a grave, moaning and gurning. But then, he figured, once they were out of the ground and lurching along, they didn't look so fearsome after all. There were all these rumours that they ate human brains, but in all his research on zombies, which was extensive, there was no actual evidence of this. Rather, it was something that was made up and sensationalised by the movies. In fact, perhaps it was one of the earliest forms of modern discrimination, creating the impression that they ate brains instead of vegetables, was definitely more likely to get you persecuted.

So from this, he identified with these scruffy, misunderstood souls and whenever he had the chance to dress up in fancy dress, he would always choose zombies.

At this point in the conversation, Miles was tempted to chip in with the observation, that he didn't dress unlike a zombie these days either, but thought better of it.

This interest carried on into his older years and also, it seemed that zombie-fanbase was growing, as the Internet allowed people with common interests, like zombies, to talk to each other across the world. He was now a member of several high profile zombie fan clubs and even something called "zombie walks" was beginning to gain popularity, around the time he was working as a jobbing actor in Los Angeles. That was an awesome experience and he would attend them whenever he could. The walks were a great way to get together, but also through this community he could get tips on how to make the blood on your face look especially fresh and how to stay up long enough to actually have the dark rings under your eyes without make-up. The bloodshot eyes were easy, as the "zombie walks" often involved copious amounts of drinking and by the second or third day hanging out with other zombies, you had made friends for life, ironically.

His love and empathy for zombies had given him a thought for a screenplay, which had evolved into a stage show, and was taking shape in his spare time. It was unsurprisingly called *"Misunderstood"* and basically, put forward the tongue-in-cheek counter argument for zombies.

The plot was simple. Zombies were indeed undead, but instead of being evil, they were unwilling pawns in the political games that humans played, trying to turn the world against the vampires as the icons of the undead. The humans thought that, if they could vilify this gentle race of the underworld, then it would turn everyone against vampires as well. The government could therefore, have an excuse for continuing to persecute and murder vampires into extinction. I guess at a basic level, it was a kind of evil political movement and instead of having to spend all that time and money on wooden stakes or silver bullets, they could ask the public to do it. Also, with public support, they could create funding and experiment with quicker and cheaper extermination methods, that might not be so publicity friendly. Of course, there were cost saving benefits for the government and in modern times they could focus their investment on other weapons, for humans to kill other humans, in larger and larger numbers and more and more imaginative ways.

The core of the counter-argument to support zombies in the play was despite the fact that, some of the biological facts about zombies were true; in the sense that they were from beyond the grave and that they tended to drop limbs here and there. But, the counter-argument went, the actual "zombie purpose" was terribly misunderstood. Given their time underground, they clearly found it difficult to communicate one important fact, that had been overlooked by movie producers and the wider media, and it was this: they just wanted to be loved. Imagine, Tim argued, that you have been dug up and brought back to life, half eaten and woken from your particular afterlife. What would your first instinct be? To go home, of course and to get a great big hug. So the lurching, aimless movement of a zombie was not threatening, they were just trying to find their way home; as erratically as anyone would, after worms had eaten their brain. The reason they walked with their arms outstretched was the biggest fallacy of all. It was not, as people thought, to try and grab their victims. It was just the universal sign for a hug.

That was as far as he had got, Tim admitted to Miles, as they reached the bottom of that second bottle of vodka, and he had to admit there were some holes in his plot.

The chief one, was what the actual "zombie purpose" was. He had explored various political parallels to draw in his mind, to make it relevant to people and also to perhaps make a statement in a world that was ever-numb to oppression. But every time, he fell back on the fact, that it would mean that you would always be characterising any oppressed noble race or worthy movement as zombies and therefore, in a very negative light. Such was the strength of the Hollywood image of zombies, this would probably have the reverse effect to the one he wanted. He probably wouldn't get the show off the ground and might actually be in line for some physical harm from rightly peeved activists, who did not like being equated to brain eating, lurching, mindless creatures, when all they were trying to achieve was a world where equality conquered bigotry. It was a real head-scratcher.

Miles, perhaps because of the fact he was terribly drunk, found the whole thing both highly amusing and very exciting. Like any self-respecting video game fan, you had to have something of an affinity to zombies. They were the poster-boy for an increasing number of video games and also, as a pop culture icon, gaining momentum in Hollywood. So he could see the opportunity. He immediately offered his services as an assistant to the process and an editor, if Tim would like one, given that he did A-Level English. He also offered to use his considerable spare time to try and get a platform and some bookings for the show. They could start small, try local halls and perhaps even small video game conventions, before working up to the Edinburgh Fringe, for example.

Tim, in turn, was happy to have got the whole thing off his chest. He had been really struggling recently, he said, and had encountered something of a writer's block. It was hard to find people he trusted enough to review the show impartially, but also that he could trust not to steal the idea. He had experienced a lot of this kind of mischief on the "zombie walks" and ideas travelled fast. For example, he had been the first to discover that fake cheese made an excellent substitute for pus and you didn't have to worry about putting it near your mouth, as it also tasted delicious. The next thing, it was impossible to get canned cheese from stores anywhere in the lead up to a walk, which was fine as you could borrow some, but he never got the proper credit for that piece of innovation and he didn't want that to happen again.

Currently, Tim would work on the script for the majority of his spare time, which when you were running a bar was very late at night or very early in the morning, and he welcomed a fresh perspective and a bit of relief. They arranged to meet the following day, hangover permitting, and try and make a breakthrough together. What Miles eventually got out of it, they agreed, would depend on what he brought to the table. Or, as they said in the zombie world – they would drop the eyeball and see where it rolled.

Of course, when Miles woke up the next day, his first thought was that, ironically, he actually felt like a bit of a zombie and also wished that at least three of his limbs would fall off and save him the pain. Maybe, even worms would eat his brain and save him the pounding headache. But on top of that, with the new project and Tim's advice earlier in the evening, Miles continued to have the buzz of hope in his veins, as well as the previous evening's vodka. The evening had a profound effect on Miles and he felt invigorated. As with all hung-over bar staff, he was certainly not looking forward to his shift and the accompanying smell of alcohol, but the fact that he would get to read the *Misunderstood* script afterwards was compensation enough.

He also couldn't wait to tell Sophie and texted her that morning. Partly to apologise for calling her out of the blue the previous day, but also because he couldn't think of anyone that he wanted to share the news with more. To his surprise, this time she responded almost immediately and actually, they texted throughout the day. It felt like something had changed generally with their relationship. Instead of feeling like he had to deliver Shakespearian lines in every text, he found that they were now connected on everyday topics and just random thoughts that he might have. There was still an undertone of flirting, but he now felt less pressure and was comfortable sharing small details about his day and she always reciprocated. There was still a point where she would opt out of the conversation and sometimes Miles did push it a little bit, but he was not prepared to become just a friend... yet.

So the few weeks following the night that Tim and Miles had agreed to work together on *Misunderstood,* had been a settled and enjoyable time in the early summer sunshine and the partnership on the show had gone pretty well. Miles had some suggestions about the plot, to try and make it less of a geeks-only show and make it sound less like a political statement. This had been mainly by introducing humour and treating zombies more like the general repression of society, rather than a particular persecuted race. They had actually taken it from being a stage show, which was Tim's initial vision, to a straight play with a few songs. He thought that it might be easier to start like that, as it would be easier to introduce more music into it later, after the storyline was solid, rather than the other way around. That was a big debate, as Tim had his heart on a big number he had written called "Half a Brain, but Full of Feelings", but they agreed that this could be a closing number. A kind of theme tune, Miles had mused and Tim had warmly agreed, at the same time giving Miles validation that he was making a difference with the production. Miles had also spent some time gathering together a group of individuals who would like to take part on the first, and very rough, performance of the show. It was mainly people from the popular zombie forums, but they also had some interest from aspiring actors through friends of friends.

That was why on this particular day, he was sitting in a coffee shop in Sophie's neighbourhood. Many of the creative folk in the capital had migrated east of London and so he was meeting a few interested parties from the out-of-work acting community. He had also taken the opportunity to mention to Sophie that he would be around and she had agreed to meet for a coffee in the afternoon, if she could get out of work. It was the first time that they had seen each other since The Killers gig, although they now texted every day without fail. As Miles waited, he had the same feeling as he described to Tim, but multiplied significantly because he was actually going to see her. He had spent at least an hour in the morning perfecting a casual, yet cool look and had got a new pair of trainers especially for the occasion. Life was always better when you put your feet into a fresh pair of trainers, Miles always thought. He was glad he did, because if there was one thing that the trendier folk in London paid attention to, that no one in his neighbourhood did, it was their footwear and their sunglasses.

'Nice trainers.'

Miles looked up and there she was. It's a funny thing, when you hold on tight to people in your head. For example, there is a common acceptance that movie stars are always shorter than you think. Miles had never really met one and so he wouldn't know. But what he did know is that often, people you fancy are a bit disappointing when you meet them the second time. The first time and the period in-between, you only remember the good bits of them. Then, as time goes on, you realise that they have a wonky nose, or that their ankles are much bigger than you remember. They can also get less attractive based on their personality. There is nothing that can take a hot girl down a few points than an air of arrogance you didn't notice the first time. He was sure it was the same for guys. No one likes a big-head.

When he saw Sophie, not just in her appearance, but her teasing smile and those heavy grey eyes, it was all he could do not to jump out of his chair and grab her. She was more attractive than he ever remembered and he could also tell she was pleased to see him as well. This made the fact that he acted on the first part of his impulse and did actually leap out of his chair, almost knocking the table and his coffee flying, the more embarrassing. He also wished that he hadn't yelled, 'It's you!' a little too loudly, because now everyone in the coffee shop was looking at them.

'Hey, Miles. You're not one for a traditional hello, are you?' She said casually and gave him a hug. It wasn't awkward. It was one of those hugs where there was more than just the top half of your body touching – a proper hug. Miles could almost burst, but he managed to re-gain his composure and administer the coffee order to the waitress who had bustled up to their table, at the same time nodding, taking notes on the order, but managing to look totally disinterested.

An hour later, the coffee had gone well, from Miles' perspective. They had talked for a little while, with a light touch, about their lives and what had been going on that the texts had not covered. Sophie had also explained a bit about her video-blogging, which Miles thought was brilliant, even though he didn't really understand what it was all about. He thought that he really must make more of an effort to keep up with trends now that he was basically a playwright. He tried to ask a few intelligent questions, but kept getting the terminology wrong. More than once he got 'views' and 'watches' mixed up and she kept having to correct him, which again made Miles curse himself that he had not done his research more thoroughly.

They then moved on to the topic of the play and Miles explained where they were in the process. They had a date fixed in a few months' time, he explained, to do a private performance at the pub and he thought she should absolutely come along. Miles was thrilled that she agreed and the conversation turned to the storyline itself, where Miles was more in his comfort zone.

'So,' said Sophie, 'if I understand correctly, it's kind of a film about Orwellian oppression, but set around zombies.'

She's perfect, Miles thought, just perfect. 'Yes,' he said, 'the core of the story is about a campaign of misinformation about the zombies and of course, they are powerless to put their side of the story together, as whenever they try and wave placards for example, their arms fall off.'

'Nice,' smiled Sophie, at the image.

'They discover the humans' plot and that they are under constant surveillance. So their struggle is made worse, as humans manage to anticipate their every move. They have to try and work out how that is happening, whilst at the same time try and organise themselves in a world that they never expected to return to. The humour is then in the pitfalls. For example, in one scene, they manage to find a zombie that had more than half a brain and had a bigger vocabulary than just 'urrrrr'. But he died over a hundred years ago, before cars were invented, so before he could do anything he was run over by a lorry. We are just struggling to figure out how we explain the surveillance, without going into CCTV and making it sound like a campaign against privacy laws.'

Sophie thought for a beat. 'Well, in my opinion, it's obvious.'

'Really?' Miles asked. They had been struggling with this concept and plot line for weeks and even more vodka had not solved the problem.

'Well, I think so. It's the cats.'

'The cats?' Miles asked, but he could feel a thought forming in his mind and a rising excitement that they might have stumbled across something interesting.

'Yes.' Continued Sophie, and you could also hear that she was getting equally excited. 'In your world, everything is the wrong way round, everything is unexpected. So what do you have in every suburban street that no one would notice? Cats! The cats are spies. Cats....'

'...are evil,' they both finished together and this time Miles really did grab her.

This took Sophie a little off-guard, but she liked it. For her, the coffee had been going terribly. Well, she was thoroughly enjoying it, but that was why it was going terribly. She was completely thrown, because Miles was actually looking very good.

There was such a change in his appearance, that when she first came into the coffee shop, she had almost stepped back outside as she thought she either had the wrong place or the wrong time. It was only when she looked more closely, table-by-table, that she had realised that the handsome chap with the mop of dark hair was actually Miles and he was blending into this hip coffee shop in a way that even Smooth couldn't. He was doing it naturally. She felt a tug in her stomach and had hovered a few steps away from him, racking her brains for something to say.

'Nice trainers.'

Why had she landed on that? They were nice trainers and she had read in magazines that guys who really took care of themselves paid attention to their shoes, so it was something of a compliment. But was this really the right way to meet someone? Didn't it just give away the fact that you had given him a thorough look up-and-down, from head to shoes? Luckily, when he looked up, he had the same shy twinkle in his eye, but also she could tell that he was equally nervous and awkward, so this made her feel a bit better.

If there was anyone in the world that could out-awkward you, it was Miles, she thought. Right on cue, he got up and simultaneously almost sent the table flying and came within an inch of elbowing the waitress in the face.

When they started talking, she was also surprised how easy it was to slip into a familiarity with Miles and although she had told her work she would only be twenty minutes, she found that time had passed and they had been there for almost an hour. In that time, they had started politely, but soon she was telling him everything about her video-blogging and although she could tell he was a bit out of his depth with it, the fact that he was really trying to relate and ask her lots of questions about it was very flattering and made her feel good. He also adorably kept getting all the technical phrases wrong, so sometimes it was a bit like talking to a really keen dad about it. But he was interested and he was genuine, and rather than hearing constant put-downs and patronising comments, Miles made her feel like she should about her videos – she felt like she was doing something impressive.

In turn, she found herself being impressed by his zombie play. She had the feeling that, when it was actually performed, it would be awful. It felt like it was the inside of someone's head who had really over-estimated the importance of zombies in life and that the storyline was a bit thin. But the fact that he was embracing and doing what he loved, rather than just talking about it, was really attractive. She was also very proud that he looked properly happy when she had mentioned the cats, but it had honestly seemed so obvious to her. She could also see how her community had embraced her post about cats and so thought it might also help make the plot-line a bit less... geeky, she guessed.

As time passed, coffees cooled, were sipped, and then the empty cups went from warm to cold. She found herself feeling disappointed that she wouldn't see him again until Reading and found herself wishing he would start to step outside of the conversation and flirt a little. He had been very well-behaved, but she guessed that he didn't have the protection of a text screen to hide behind. She wanted him to say some of the things he did in his texts, because this time she would flirt back and give him some kind of signal that although she was in a relationship, she was interested in him. Not just interested in his looks, but also interested in spending more time together and talking more. She had felt better for the last hour than she had for a long time, perhaps since Easter Sunday when she had that great day with her family, without Smooth. Miles would have fit into that group perfectly, she thought and she could imagine her family getting on well with him. 'At least we can call him by his proper name,' she could hear her mum saying.

But the time passed without flirting, although they did agree that she would come along to his play and also to keep staying in touch and meet up at Reading. Maybe in the meantime she could loosen her boundaries a bit in her texts. It was always a struggle to not respond to Miles when he sent something romantic in his messages and it was getting more so. There were so many times she had written something, deleted it, written it again and deleted it, then hidden the phone in a drawer to remove the temptation for the rest of the evening. But seeing him, she was caught by surprise.

The last time she had seen him, he was a hollow shell, wrapped in a pudgy body. She knew he had got some confidence back, but she was completely taken aback by the fact he had lost a lot of weight and the handsomeness that she had a whisper of last time, was now in full voice. I mean, she thought, he has cheekbones and a chin. These were two things that he didn't have the previous time they had met, as she guessed he was drinking a lot and eating take-away food. He looked in good shape and frankly, she couldn't take her eyes off his arms. She felt like she wanted to sniff them and breathe in the smell she caught when they hugged earlier. That urge hadn't happened before with anyone, ever.

This was going to be trouble.

Chapter Ten

Cannon Fire

August 4, 2005.

Perhaps it was fate, thought Sophie, as she stood outside the pub that Miles worked in, on the night of the play. Maybe yet again, on a night that was important to her, she was waiting for Smooth and it was a sign.

Maybe the universe was telling her something about who was the reliable person to have in her life and who was not. She had started thinking about that a lot recently. Since she had last seen Miles, she had been struck by how she felt whenever he texted and she looked forward to it each day, usually staying in communication with him from the early morning through to the end of the day. Sometimes she even instigated the conversation, if it was creeping towards the time his shift started in the pub and she had not heard from him. She didn't want him to get distracted, or busy at work, as that could mean that it would be early evening before she heard from him on that particular day – or maybe even later if he got stuck into the play writing with Tim. Increasingly, she also wanted to make sure she wished him a good day at the pub, or a good day's writing with Tim on *Misunderstood*. It kept her connected to him, although she wouldn't admit that to him, in fact far from it. She would usually start the text with something like: 'I'm sure you're missing me, so thought I would say hello.' No, she would never admit it, but she needed it.

As for Smooth, this time, at least he had bothered to give an excuse, not that it was a particularly good one. He had blamed an 'important interview' and had scolded Sophie for not caring about his future and instead, was playing her 'little arty games', as he called them. He wouldn't even recognise that there was a parallel between what he was trying to do and the video blogging that she was working on. He just put them all into that category of 'silly little hobbies'. Whereas, he argued, what he was trying to do was to really involve Sophie and himself in the creative community of London and didn't she understand that? Sophie just thought that if Smooth opened his mind a little bit, maybe they could even work together, instead of feeling like they were competing against each other.

Sophie also knew for a fact that it wasn't an interview, she knew that is was just a normal Thursday night and that was when all the various small agencies in the East London area would descend on the pubs. The "New Friday" they called it. She knew that there was no arrangement with one individual, just another cycle of trying to get into conversations with anyone who would listen and hang onto any conversation that he thought sounded cool. She could see him now, jeans getting skinnier and skinnier, despite the fact that his waistline was getting wider and wider and his thighs chubbier and chubbier. The youthful playfulness had gone from his eyes and his use of facial products and hair products was increasing, as his cheekbones and hairline were decreasing. She was sure she even saw him looking online at tinted moisturiser. Perhaps the only plus side was that he was not getting noticed as much by other girls, although maybe it was her getting more confidence and therefore, not caring as much, or feeling insecure. She still loved him, but it was becoming a weary love and she wasn't sure if it was coloured by the fact that she was just used to him, and that she felt a little bit sorry for him.

Perhaps because of this, she had stopped going with him every time he went out to roam the bars. She frankly felt a bit embarrassed and pleaded with him from time-to-time to take a break and concentrate on the life that he actually had. This also added to his overall demeanour and his more persistent whining. He had started to make more obvious side comments about her videos, somehow angry that it was going well whilst his life continued to drift. She tried to explain that, since the cat themed episode of her video-blog, visits and comments had consistently picked up and so she had to spend more time planning and publishing more frequent blogs. She had even once been called a 'rising star' of the new media age on a blog, albeit it by a user called SuperSuperLove1x1x77; who in the same post had claimed that he was from another planet and that in his home city of Tokyo, he talked to the sky and the plants that whispered to him that his people were coming and hiding codes in the Internet. Nevertheless, she did feel like a bit of a rising star sometimes.

Plus, for every SuperSuperLove, as she called him for short, there were more mainstream things happening on the Internet. Sites like hers were becoming increasingly popular, especially with musicians, and this was bringing more normal people into a world that previously was the domain of geeks and the socially inhibited. There were even sensible and coherent comments starting to be left on her videos and more than once, she had been tempted to respond to them and perhaps see if that could lead to like-minded friendship or even a partnership on the videos. If Smooth could just realise it, he would see that there was no such thing as just the creative community of London any more. We were all becoming the creative community of the world and that included SuperSuperLove.

What was also getting worse, was that she actually hoped he wouldn't turn up at all for Miles' play. Then she had the excuse to pick a fight and that was not something she admired in herself. She hoped secretly that she could use his non-attendance to win a battle with him and buy herself peace and quiet to work on her blogging; without Smooth leering, in his jogging bottoms, or bursting in with a mouthful of kebab and nothing to say, expecting to be disruptive. She could tolerate his sulks these days and they were even welcome, as it meant he stayed out of her way rather than interfered. But since the last big argument, she had to review all of her videos more carefully, after she had unwittingly uploaded one to her community with a shot in the background of Smooth, naked, except for a t-shirt and socks, walking past the bedroom door.

It was only after one of her fans commented, that she noticed and thankfully took it down, before too many other people had the chance. He claimed that he was just about to get in the shower and had forgotten a towel, but she clearly remembered putting fresh towels in the bathroom that morning. She knew that it was just another way of him trying to exert some power over her. Anyway, who wanders around the flat in that state? She had yelled. She had secretly thought, that in the early stages of the relationship, she might have actually found it quite funny and attractive. She didn't say it out loud though; she didn't think his confidence could take it.

Sophie decided she had waited long enough outside the pub, turned on her heels and headed inside. She had not been to this part of London before, for no particular reason than exactly that – she had never had a particular reason. Now she was here, she quite liked it and thought it suited Miles. The area still had character, but was just a bit more open and green than where she lived. The same shops and take-aways were in abundance, but the bars were more like traditional pubs, rather than the bars that now outnumbered the ale houses in some parts of the city, and the buildings were interspersed with small parks and open areas. There were not as many floors to the buildings as well, which made it feel more suburban and open. The pub itself had a good atmosphere, although she knew that Smooth would hate it. It was a traditional pub, complete with thick patterned carpet and built-in benches, but it was impeccably maintained and the colours and tones that Tim had chosen gave it a modern feel. He had even gone as far as replacing the heavy stained-glass in the external windows with plain frames and glazing, which let in significantly more light than was probably, originally intended. Although there was still a lot of dark wood and original features in the fittings, there was also chalk-boards and granite that balanced out the heavy timbers and carpets.

As her eyes adjusted from the sunshine outside, Sophie caught sight of Miles at the far end of the pub.

He had his hand on the shoulder of a younger guy and was staring intently at him and giving some instruction. It was quite an amusing scene, as he was all serious-faced and the younger guy was made up as a zombie, complete with quite impressive, realistic looking blood and what looked like pus. It's not often you saw a zombie getting an old-fashioned talking-to, thought Sophie and smiled. In his familiar surroundings, he looked focused but relaxed and if anything, Sophie thought that he may have caught a bit more sun, which suited him. She was ready this time though and had made sure that she had stopped up the street to apply a bit of fresh make-up in a shop window. Miles turned towards her and Sophie half-waved, suddenly feeling self-conscious as she realised that this was his turf, not hers or neutral ground.

'Hey!' He shouted over the heads of the gathering audience and headed over. A normal greeting, Sophie thought. First time ever.

He even managed to make it to her without knocking anything over, or tripping over anyone. That had to be a first as well, although it wasn't hard to avoid the audience members. There was probably only about a dozen, with the pub set up to accommodate about a dozen more on hard, school-style chairs. The other half of the pub was given over to an elaborately designed and seemingly unnecessarily large stage area. It had actual carvings of human heads in it and what looked like a life-size, burned-out motorbike and side-car. Then, there were four cannons; proper cast-iron cannons, complete with wheels, pointing out from the front of the stage.

Miles hugged her warmly and Sophie got that smell again. He must have sensed her looking at the set-up, because he said, 'You like our stage? Or do you think we are overcompensating for something?'

'I can see how that might be the impression,' said Sophie. 'It kind of looks like the inside of a prog rock music video, if they were making music at the time of the French Revolution.'

Miles smiled at the analogy, he never ceased to be amazed by the things that Sophie came out with. If you looked at her, she basically looked like a product of the coolest end of pop-culture, all slogan t-shirts and skinny jeans. But her music references came from all fringes and genres and were timeless. Miles wondered if that was her parents' influence. She could imagine Sophie being from a close family, where her parents would make them cringe by putting on old CDs, but where this kind of experimentation and love opened her mind and made her the inquisitive and bold girl that she is. Her dad probably called himself 'DJ Dad'.

'Yeah, we borrowed a lot of it from a guy who drinks here. He has a band that is trying out a new electronic sound and claims that his music is the new rock opera, so hence the over-use of tassels and chiffon.'

'Are they real…?' Started Sophie, motioning to the cannons, which were currently being furiously buffed by a girl dressed as a cat.

'Confetti cannons,' confessed Miles with a smile. 'All part of the rock opera vibe.'

'How very Flaming Lips,' said Sophie, although she was genuinely impressed. There she was again, thought Miles, he laughed and unconsciously touched her arm, before realising what he was doing and quickly changing the subject.

'So, do I get to meet the famous Neil?' He said, thinking he sounded a bit too defensive with it and regretted it, especially as he realised that Smooth might be anywhere in the local vicinity. He also thought it was a bit petty, probably, to use his real name, but he honestly refused to call anyone by the name 'Smooth'. Handsome or not.

'Ah, he'll be here,' said Sophie breezily, but inside she was burning. She liked that he touched her and it made her feel even more angry and guilty about Smooth. It would be just her luck, she thought, for him to turn up now. She felt like, if that happened then she couldn't be herself and would have to put up with his comments about the set and the pub and the general South London area. But at the same time, she felt guilty that she was treating him like this and enjoying Miles' attention. Not that Miles had done anything wrong, it was just a friendly bit of touching and they hadn't done anything wrong, it was just her supporting a friend at his production of a play. But at what point did what you think, become just as bad a lie, as what you did? If Smooth and Miles met, could she really claim that things were normal between her and Miles, or even her and Smooth? She didn't want there to be any kind of atmosphere and so the best way was to just keep everything inside her until she worked out what she was doing. She certainly didn't want Miles to pick up any vibes that would put him off his big evening, so she just smiled again and allowed Miles to show her to her seat.

'This way,' said Miles, 'I have reserved you a seat.' He led her towards the front of the audience and dramatically removed one of the 'reserved' signs that was actually, no more than 'reserved' written in biro on another one of Tim's yellow sticky notes. 'Best seats in the house,' he smiled and things were normal again. She loved Miles for that.

Miles promised to introduce her to Tim afterwards, as currently he was in hair and make-up. That did make Sophie laugh, as it probably just meant he was in the gents getting changed. She settled into her seat, checked her phone one last time to see if Smooth had texted (he hadn't) and was pleasantly surprised when a zombie tapped her on the shoulder and presented her with a glass of Prosecco. She could get used to this, she thought and without thinking glanced at the seat beside her. Reserved.

The play lasted for about two hours and Sophie was pleasantly surprised by the quality. She had to admit, she didn't follow it all the way through and she was pretty sure that halfway through, one of the zombies wasn't meant to trip over the wrecked motorcycle and fall so heavily that his fake arm clattered across the stage onto the lap of a shocked member of the audience. But, all in all, she enjoyed the spectacle. The finale song was also funny and rousing and the whole production had the air of a black comedy. If she was being hyper-critical, then she would suggest that they lose the confetti cannons. As well as scaring the audience half to death, they were too close to the stage's soft furnishings and at the same time as the charge went off, the curtains also caught fire a little bit – although the same guy who received the fake arm missile, had the forethought to throw his beer on the flames and so there was no damage done.

She joined in warmly with the applause and felt privileged that she had been here to see the maiden performance of what was probably quite a labour of love from Tim, and Miles as well. They both took the applause with huge grins and gave each other a man-hug. Sophie thought she could also read Tim's lips as he hugged Miles and was pretty sure he said 'Holy cock and balls.' He then glanced over in her direction, caught her gaze and was equally unsubtle by clearly saying 'is that her?' to Miles. She hoped the two phrases were not linked, or perhaps actually she didn't care, she just felt happy for Miles and was in awe of where he had got to, from where he was the first time they met.

She had also completely forgotten about Smooth. She gave a half-wave to Miles, gave him an enthusiastic thumbs up and mouthed that she was going to the toilet and would see him in a moment. It was only when she turned that she saw Smooth, lurking at the back of the pub and her heart sank for a beat. No, she thought, pull yourself together and be happy that he made it. He deserves my support and I love him very much. She was repeating that over and again in her head as she headed over to Smooth and used it to fix her facial expression. She could not deal with starting an argument straight away.

'So, I made it to The Dive Arms, on the dark side of London,' said Smooth with a half-sneer as she kissed his cheek. She closed her eyes for a moment, took a deep breath and continued to repeat in her head: be happy, be happy, be happy.

'Oh, it's not that bad, Smooth. I'm happy you could get here. Did you have a good time at your interview?' She tried to ask it airily and didn't mean for the inflexion on the last word to be so sarcastic, but by the look of it Smooth was too drunk to notice. She could also tell that he had not had a good evening. His eyes had the glazed look that you only get from hard spirits, combined with the bitterness of someone else's success. He was also in his East London uniform, which now it was out of its radius of relevance, basically made him look like an arse.

'What was this anyway?' He asked. 'Some kind of *Rocky Horror Picture Show* tribute? All you needed was Meatloaf and you'd be convinced you'd stepped into a time machine back to 1981.'

Rocky Horror was in 1975, she felt herself thinking, but didn't say it. Instead, she asked Smooth to behave, that she was going to the bathroom and when she came back she would like to introduce him to her friends. Smooth gave an enthusiastic curtsey, that just wound Sophie up even more and she decided to go to the bathroom via the bar, where she nailed a tequila shot as a punishment for evil thoughts, as at that moment she just wanted to punch Smooth in the face.

When she got out of the toilets, she could see that Smooth and Miles were already talking. That could only go two ways, she thought and then checked herself. This could only go one way, she corrected herself and quickly headed over to intervene.

'Hey, here she is!' Miles said and gave her an overly playful punch on the arm. She smiled and realised that she had not prepared for this moment. Here was the guy she was living with, who really, she avoided talking about or acknowledge existed, whenever she was with Miles, who of course, did the same, so it didn't shatter his dreams. From the other perspective, here was Miles, meeting said "elephant in the room". She was pretty sure that the elephant was too drunk to notice any kind of atmosphere and she also hoped that he was big enough to recognise that this was important to her. He hoped that

130

Smooth would roll back the last few years and be the charming Smooth that she had met, who had charmed so many of her friends and family.

She took a deep breath, and turned to Smooth. 'Smooth,' she said, 'this is Miles, who I was telling you about.'

Smooth looked Miles as directly in the eye as he could and smiled.

'Who?' He asked.

That was how the evening ended. Well, three seconds later, when Sophie dragged Smooth by the arm the short distance from the back of the pub into the street. Smooth's head exited via the door frame, with a sickening thud on the way through, that made Sophie say 'ha!'

Even she was surprised by the way that turned out, she thought.

Chapter 11

White Lie, Dark Truth

August 26, 2005.

'It was pretty awful, wasn't it?' Miles said, as he took a long drag on the cigarette. He didn't even smoke and so that act of coolness was followed by a hacking cough. If Sophie could see his eyes, they would be bulging. All round coolness fail.

They were lying side-by-side again, on the top of a retro camper van that Sophie had hired especially for the Reading Festival. She had spent the last few weeks rewarding herself for being such a tolerant girlfriend and Smooth had been so mortified by his behaviour after the performance of *Misunderstood*, that he didn't argue. Although the mood that Sophie was in, he probably wouldn't have had the gumption anyway.

It was a fully-reconditioned, split windscreen, 1964 model, in immaculate cream and metallic blue. It was, as Miles had eloquently put, a glorious machine. It had always been a dream of hers to stay in one, so she had found an enthusiast in London who re-conditioned and hired them out, and taken it for a week. In that week, she had been to Brighton and sat on the promenade, and to Dover and parked at the cliff-tops. Basically any whimsical cliché you could imagine, as Smooth had petulantly reminded her each time she had come home, flushed and exhilarated and a little sore from the shuddering journey.

She had then driven it over to the festival site herself and felt awesome doing so, especially the last few hundred metres where she was crawling past hundreds of other festival goers and absorbing admiring looks. She was aware that a hot blonde, driving a camper van, was either extremely stereotypical of festival chic, or incredibly enviable. She knew she had one of those faces and a way of holding herself that gave the latter impression. So it was a good job no one could see she was driving it in designer wellies. She had parked it in the VIP camping, amongst the rows of more modern six and eight berth motor homes that other VIPs used whilst they pretended to slum-it at the festival. Amongst these beasts that were inspired by the likes of Sophie's model, the VW was a representation of how life used to be. It was a bit like the camper van was the original, acoustic version of a song and next to it were the future covers of the same song that had not yet been written. Complete with full orchestra, auto-tune and mixing desk technology. Beautiful in their own right, but there was nothing like the raw original.

The VIP tickets were another pay-back from Smooth, who had organised them through contacts without any argument. Sophie's only condition, to which he had agreed to eagerly, was that he didn't come and Sophie was able to take Miles as her plus one. Things had been a bit awkward with Miles in the weeks since the play, so she wanted to get it back on track and show him that she was still there for him. In all honesty, she was a bit ashamed of what had happened and although the screaming and arguing had not happened until they were home, she still felt like the memory of the evening was ruined. Now, she found it hard to discuss *Misunderstood* with Miles, because it took her back to the night and just how crushingly embarrassing Smooth's behaviour had been. As she reflected, she realised how much she valued Miles' opinion of her and tried to imagine what would have happened if they had argued and she had to take a side. This thought and internal struggle had occupied so much of her thoughts, that she had even taken a pause on her video-blogging for the week afterwards. She just could not find the creative drive to make an entertaining piece of footage and she hoped that spending the weekend apart, and in Miles' exuberant company, would help her see things more clearly.

Miles, as expected, was absolutely in his element. He was a VIP at a festival for the first time ever, and with Sophie. It had basically been another "best day of his life" and he had told her that several times. He was like a one-man entertainment system, producing beers from nowhere, conjuring up festival hats at the exact moment it started raining and sun cream when the rain stopped. He filled every moment with stories, made friends with almost everyone he met and had Sophie in stitches with his anecdotes from the bar. Since the first performance of *Misunderstood*, there had been about six more, as they honed the script and each came with its own self-depreciating set of happenings. He told her that the audiences had got slightly bigger and so they had to lose a bit of the stage area. That was no bad thing, as apparently the lead zombie had a tendency to spit and shower the front row with the fake cheese that they used for pus, in one case actually making someone in the front row dry-heave and have to be taken back-stage for a glass of water followed by a stiff drink.

As for Miles himself, the "best day ever" effect seemed to be happening a lot when he was around Sophie, he had to admit. He had just seen one of the most incredible performances by The Killers. Brandon Flowers had worn a white tuxedo jacket with black trim and they had played their biggest hit so far, Somebody Told Me, pretty much at the start of the set. Miles had pointed out that this was a brave move and definitely set the tone, given that they were not headliners or even established properly in the mainstream. It really announced the intentions of the band and also Brandon's growth, from a somewhat awkward front man in the first few tours, to one who could now command festival audiences. He would now engage with the crowd much more and direct some of his undoubted high energy levels towards them, one foot atop a monitor system at the front of the stage.

A few people around them in the crowd had enthusiastically agreed and that had spun off into shared beers and more new friends. Sophie had just told him he was a geek and needed to shut up and dance. But he could tell she was having a good time and he had decided that the ruder she was to him, the more she was enjoying his company and the more she liked him. In Miles' tortured hindsight, that also would have been a great moment to try and kiss Sophie, but he had bottled it and done as she he said. He had shut up and he had danced.

One of the other great things about the VIP area at Reading, Miles outlined, was that it was located behind the main stage and so just a hop away if you needed the toilet, or another few beers and you wouldn't miss too much of the atmosphere.

An additional irony was that, despite it being VIP, it was not really patrolled by the security staff from a contraband perspective. They were so busy maintaining the integrity of the wristband system, that you could slip in and out with as many beers as you wanted in your back-pack. The key was to make sure you looked confident and engaged in a bit of conversation with the staff on the way through. Preferably, with your face to them, so they could just see the straps of your bag and not its bulging contents. So the supposed rich and famous and crème of the festival crowd, were actually the ones who could most openly flaunt the rules and drink for free. Miles' back-pack was never empty and he had pointed this out to Sophie during her most ferocious moments of mickey-taking. Yes, he said, it was essentially the kind of bag you would take on a hike or that the nerdy kid would take to school and yes, he wore it with two-straps. But he had not seen Sophie complaining or making fun when she wanted a drink or a bit of sun-cream. End of argument.

So here they were, after an exhausting day, a great Killers set, a bit of silent disco and then a few beers on the roof where they now lay. For the first time that day, Miles had caught Sophie a bit off-guard asking about the play and Sophie had to tell a little white lie.

'It was great,' she said. 'I enjoyed it from beginning to end. Even the confetti cannons had a place in the whole thing. Definitely.'

'The confetti cannons?' Miles asked. 'You do realise that one of the neighbours called that into the police as they thought it was gunfire? They turned up at the back door, ready to bring in the armed units as they thought there was some kind of siege going on in the pub.'

Sophie couldn't resist. 'Well, there was kind of a bit of a siege, if you look at it in that way. I was trapped in there for two hours.' This time, Miles laughed so hard that he burned his hand on his lit cigarette, making him throw it in the air and fall the eight feet to the grass beside the van in a shower of sparks, with Miles almost following in any ungainly heap.

Now they were on the subject, Miles didn't really know where to go with the conversation. It was great that Sophie had enjoyed the performance, but it was obvious that something quite serious had gone down either before or after with Smooth. The way they had left and before Miles had even got a chance to introduce Sophie properly to his friends, was something that had lingered over the subsequent weeks. Miles wasn't bothered about what had happened because it was none of his business, but he was bothered that Sophie had been upset and he had been surprised by both the appearance and behaviour of Smooth. He had put him on a pedestal alongside Sophie; this handsome, trendy guy that his idea of a perfect girl had chosen. The way she talked about him, Miles could not say exactly what he had expected, but it was certain that he had expected something more. Instead, Smooth had looked like someone who had already peaked in looks and charm. He had definitely been handsome at some point, but Miles felt like he was looking at a reflection of himself a year earlier. Except that Miles never had the arrogant streak that the cool school-kid had and that had probably led to his nickname and he could see in Smooth's eyes that he was one of the bully types.

It had then taken a few days for Miles and Sophie to be back in contact and he had chosen to just not mention the situation in his texts and she had done the same. He didn't expect an apology from Sophie and he didn't expect he would get an apology from Smooth, but he wanted to know if she was OK and help if he could. He could tell that there was something on her mind, as her texts had got a little bit more reserved again, as if she had chosen to take a step back and re-align their relationship in some way, or that she wanted to sort things out her end before she took things further with him. If that was the case, he thought that was a little bit unfair, as selfishly, he had done nothing wrong. If Sophie was going to take a side, then maybe it should be his side and not Smooth's. You couldn't deny that there was a spark between them and he didn't think it was fair that she would choose Smooth completely and cut off communications with him. He would never say that so candidly to her, because of the way he felt. But he had gone so far as practising a few words that would give Sophie an excuse never to speak to him again if required, but at the same time preserve his pride.

But then she had contacted him and offered the VIP tickets for the festival. So Miles had just put that to the back of his mind and resolved just to have a great time. If anything happened, then it happened.

'I don't want to talk about it, by the way.' Sophie said suddenly, as if she had read his mind and Miles realised there had been about a fifteen second silence, the longest there had been, since they had met at the site the previous evening. 'Tell me something fun. Tell me a story, you know I love your stories.'

She had turned onto her side and had her big eyes fixed on Miles, but then she turned away again and stared at the sky. 'Tell me almost everything you're thinking.'

What came immediately to Miles' mind was the vodka night he had with Tim, the night that they first talked about zombies. Tim had his bar, his own mindful space and Miles wondered if for him, it wasn't a space, but a person.

'I was just thinking about how weird it feels sometimes, to be here, compared to where I was six months ago. But how wonderful.'

'Here?'

'Well, here we are, on top of a camper van. Here we are, two people that didn't know each other six months ago and only met by accident. I was even at The Killers gig a little bit by accident as well, so if I hadn't chosen the path I did, then maybe we would never have met.

But that's not all of it. I guess it's also that I can feel my back against the metal of the van and it even feels like it's electric blue, not just looks electric blue. I can feel the cold of the night in the air and the sun from today, with just a tiny bit of rain refreshing my face and arms. I can feel this can of lager in my hand and the rest of the lagers in my head, fuzzing around and making me want to laugh at the smallest thing. I can smell the festival, although I probably don't want to. It's a mixture of smoke, booze, mud and something indescribably disgusting, that I know my shoes will smell of for weeks. Everything is just so… loud. When I was with Tim a few weeks back, he said something to me. He said that he went to the bar across town because it gave him somewhere to enjoy the moment, to be in the moment and to shut out anything else in his life – the noise, the pressures, the texts and the emails. He said that when you get rid of that noise, then you can think and be in the moment and be happy. Because of that, when we write for the play, we switch everything else off except the music. We listen to a track, or an album that we think represents the tone of what we are trying to achieve. In the fierce bits, we actually once listened to Beyoncé, because apparently she is fierce'

'How did that go?' Sophie asked.

'Terribly. Because although Beyoncé is fierce, it just got us onto a Shakira versus Beyoncé debate and that took up a few hours actually. But anyway, why do we select when and where to enjoy the moment, and not every moment in life? Why do we not just give every little thing our undivided attention and do our best to make everything special? It's like we are always trying to get the next thing, or the next day, and not enjoying the present. So when I pull a drink now for a customer in the pub, I give the drink and the customer my full attention. I say to myself: this is going to be the best drink that this guy has had all day, at least until the next one he gets from me, which will be even better.

When we were together today, I felt like we were in every moment. I was honestly not thinking about anything else except you, the beer and the music. I could see people taking pictures of each other, on these new phones with cameras, and holding their phones up when some of the songs came on and I just thought, if you are going to do that, why didn't you just watch it on DVD, or invite that person in the first place? Maybe they were thousands of miles away, or maybe they were relatives confined to wheelchairs, but I would wager that they were not. To me it just seems to be a way to turn an inwards moment of enjoyment, into an outward moment of boasting.'

Miles felt Sophie frown. 'Maybe it is what you said though, friends can be anywhere in the world these days. So what you're saying is that you're not allowed to share something with a friend if they're not there, right now. That would be impossible.'

'Yeah, maybe,' Miles thought for a moment. 'But here's the thing. Why do you need to combine those moments? Why can't you have your time at the gig and because you are paying attention, soak in every note, every experience, every smell and taste. Then go home, wake up the next morning, and call them and tell them everything? Isn't that better than getting a strange phone call late in the evening, which when you answer, is a really loud and confusing mess of sounds. You can tell that there is something going on and you know your friend is at a gig, but all you can hear is a wall of sound, and your friend yelling incoherently and probably out of tune. If you didn't know any better, you might think your friend has been in a bad car accident and was trying to shout for help over the radio.'

'That would be a nice world to be in, Miles,' said Sophie and sighed. 'I also love that you think like you do. I admire what you are doing and I admire that you have opted out from the normal. I honestly do and you have taught me a lot about life over the last few months. I sometimes wonder how to get there myself and when I would have the opportunity to do it. But maybe we have to accept that life is a bit more complicated than that and that not everyone gets the chance to write and star in a play about pretty much their favourite thing of all time.'

'Yeah,' Miles was on a roll now. 'Except I don't feel like I have opted out. I feel like at last I have opted in. I have opted into a world where you follow what makes you happy. Imagine if we all started to follow a dream? If we make that dream central to ourselves? Imagine a world where no one followed the easy path and did what they said they would, when they were eight years old. You would still have your fair share of accountants and doctors, because some kids want to do that. But you would also have a world with way more artists, horse riders and musicians, and the right people would end up as firemen or nurses and the world would be a better place. If you think something is a good idea, then you should stand behind it and do everything to make sure you are the best you can be at that, not something else that your parents, or your school, wants you to be. If your life is complicated, then de-complicate it. Make it a little bit smaller, not constantly bigger.'

'But if everyone did what they said when they were a child, wouldn't that also mean that you had tonnes of fairies and astronauts? I'm pretty sure one of those doesn't exist and the other one would make the moon a very busy place.'

Miles was aware he had been ranting a bit and so was happy that Sophie had lightened it a bit. 'I guess what I am trying to say is that I have had the perfect day. I will always look back on today and smile – and any music from today will always remind me of right now, and just how perfect and simple my life is. I can honestly say I have never considered a single day as perfect before and so, thank you.'

She thought for a moment, because today had ranked pretty highly on that list for her as well. 'That's lovely, Miles, and thank you too,' she said, 'I guess there are loads of good days and good weeks. There are the kind where you spend the whole time giggling with your family, and there are the ones where you hang out with friends in stupid hats and drink wine. Today was a bit of the second, but also felt a bit like the other one too, it was a bit of everything good and I'm so glad I invited you Miles. You have basically been a friend and family all rolled into one. Even if you did bring cheap lager, your smuggling skills make you as good a barman in a field as you are in a pub, I am sure.'

It was strange, she hadn't really thought about it that way until now. Miles was right about the paths in life, it seemed that when you were young, it was so simple. You were either a fairy or a princess. But as you got older, the paths became more complicated and there were more of them. Of course, that meant more opportunity, but it was no longer black and white, and decisions had shades of grey. The grey areas were where the implications of your decisions lay. You could do this, but then it would mean that. You could do that, but it means this. Where you landed in the grey area might be closer to black, but also, might be closer to white. So many grey areas to navigate, with those implications lurking like little grey monsters, planting doubts.

But she put that down to responsibility; you couldn't make every decision in the moment and accept the consequences as you got older. Not every decision, but perhaps, even very few decisions. Sometimes, once you chose a path through the grey, you had to ignore other temptations, even if they were more appealing in the moment, as Miles would call it. In fact, the life that Miles described might even be bordering on irresponsible, but she understood why he was doing it, and she liked being around him, because it was so refreshing. Smooth, on the other hand, was a lurking grey gremlin and the thought of him brought her back to reality.

'You know I'll always have your back, Sophie,' said Miles. 'Always.' He touched her hand and she unconsciously curled her fingers around his.

'Oh, Miles. There is something I need to tell you.' She screwed her face up and took a deep breath. 'Smooth has proposed. He wants to marry me.'

Part Two

2006-2007

Chapter 12

Pause

December 31, 2006.

There is always a space between thinking something, and doing it. It could be a second, a minute, or never.

For Sophie, that gap was over a year. It was over a year since she last spoke to Miles. Over a year since they had any communication at all. She could track it pretty accurately, because the last time they spoke properly was the Reading Festival the summer before.

She had thought about calling him many times after that, but days passed, weeks passed, and eventually months passed. At first slowly, such as in the days after the festival, when she wondered about calling him almost every hour of every day, and even picked up her phone, practising what she might say. Then time passes more quickly, as she started to feel that it had been too long to be casual and so would seem strange to suddenly contact him. Then finally, I suppose you could say that the habit was broken and he only drifted into her head from time to time, if she ever saw anything about zombies, or if she passed through South London on the train.

Sophie had mixed feelings about who was to blame. It wasn't even as if she had the obligation to call him. She had to admit, things had changed after she had told Miles that Smooth and her were to be engaged. Or had she said that she was thinking about it, or she had accepted? She couldn't remember. But the fact was that she had no obligation to check on him and anyway, it wasn't like he had even shown any emotion about it at the time. Of course, she could tell that he was upset. His expression hadn't changed, or at least she couldn't tell in the darkness, but something had happened behind his eyes. The best way to describe it would be that a light had gone out or at least got a lot dimmer. Then, for the rest of the weekend he made excuses to see his friends from the bar and had made sure that they were not alone again. She had asked him directly if he was OK, first because she really cared, then later in the weekend, she supposed out of frustration that he wouldn't talk to her. Each time he just said yes, and that he hoped they would be happy, before moving the conversation on.

Always the same words, she thought. He didn't actually say that he was happy, that was something she definitely remembered. There was a subtle difference between someone saying they hoped you were happy, and that they themselves were happy for you. She guessed it meant that he didn't agree with her choice and she had to respect him for his honesty. Miles had been through such heartbreak, that he was always going to be against relationships for a while, and if he did like her in addition to all that, then she could understand why he would be upset. But in the end, that wasn't really her fault.

Anyway, hadn't he said that he would always put her first? Didn't he say that he would always watch her back, not two minutes before she told him about Smooth? So he could also have kept in touch, it shouldn't have mattered that she was engaged, because she was already in that relationship and so not much had changed, really. Granted, after a pause of a week or so, he had sent a few texts and left a few voicemails, but she was so busy organising her and Smooth's engagement party, and seeing friends and family to show off the ring, that she barely had time to keep up with anyone else. When you added in her work and the video-blogging, there was almost no time to relax, so eventually the calls and the texts had dried up, and Miles had ceased all contact. He had to take his share of responsibility as well, it wasn't all her. She had thought about inviting him to the engagement party, but in the end she figured that he wouldn't really want to come, as he wouldn't know anyone. So she decided it was easier to just leave him off the list, plus the last time Miles and Smooth had met it hadn't gone too well and she didn't want any kind of atmosphere to ruin her special night with Smooth.

The rest of her friends had been really happy, and Smooth's friends too, although there were probably less of them at the party than he expected. They held it at a trendy 'space' in Shoreditch, which was at one time an art gallery and another time a pop-up clothing store, probably vintage. The general opinion of everyone was that they were definitely one of the most handsome couples of the area. At the engagement party the vibe was great and everyone had made such an effort. When guests spilled onto the pavement it could very well, to passers-by, look like the opening of another venture, another dream. In some ways it was and she knew that

Smooth would really appreciate how the party looked, she really wanted to use it to help repair his self-esteem and confidence after the last few months.

Sophie had arranged most of it herself, with the help of her mum, to save on outside catering. They had long wooden benches set up and stuffed them full of bruschetta, meats, breads and salads. Along one wall, they had set up bins full of cold beers, so that everyone could help themselves to the necks of bottled beers that stood like green periscopes out of the top of the ice. Sophie had even managed to convince a few of the guys that Smooth respected in the local area to come along, in the hope that Smooth could use it as a networking opportunity. That seemed to work quite well, and she saw Smooth on several occasions deep in animated conversation with individuals from that part of the invite list. It was only later in the evening, when the autumn sun dipped below the buildings, that the crowd melted down the street and into their familiar haunts.

So a success all round, Sophie thought - it didn't even seem to matter to anyone that her mum appeared to have a nap in the corner, halfway through the evening.

She always wondered how people did that, just fall asleep like that. It was a gift. Or in this case a miracle, because the baseline that the DJ was playing was quite aggressive. That was perhaps the only contribution to the evening by Smooth, who had insisted on choosing the DJ. Also, she couldn't blame her mum for being exhausted, she had been non-stop with Sophie since the moment they had announced their engagement at their house.

On that night, Sophie's mum had squealed, held her tight and cried for a good ten minutes into her shoulder, with Sophie the same. She and her mum shared that special bond, they were a close family, so happy and sad news was shared through tears of different kinds. Sophie's dad had been a little more reserved and surprisingly so, which she thought was probably because he was more of a traditionalist and was a little bit thrown by the fact that Smooth did not ask his permission ahead of the proposal. But if that was a lingering thorn, he hid it well and had shaken Smooth warmly by the hand with his congratulations. She suspected that her dad would have preferred to see her end up with someone a bit more rugged, or more in the image of himself. Maybe a bit more hairy, or rough around the edges, someone who could wrap her in his arms, make her disappear and protect her. That was what all dads wanted, she figured. But life doesn't follow that script and Smooth did keep her safe in his own way, albeit she could probably beat him in an arm wrestle.

Since the announcement, Sophie's mum had helped choose the engagement ring, the venue for the party and helped to negotiate with various suppliers and staff to make sure that the evening was a proper celebration for her little girl. It seemed that every time they saw her parents, there was a new supply of fizz to open and fresh celebratory talk. She had never seen them so happy and they would re-live moments in Sophie's childhood and adulthood, bursting with pride with where she had come from and what she had achieved.

There were pictures produced that even Sophie had not seen, and she realised that her parents had also kept all the clippings from the local paper of all of her sports achievements. Here was Sophie collecting her under-9s badminton tournament winner's trophy. Here is Sophie with her gymnastics team; she is the one with the bowlhead haircut, third from the right. It was at once exhausting, and exhilarating and embarrassing, and made her realise how little Smooth and her had talked about the past. Sure, she knew all about him since he had finished university, and had met a lot of his friends, but she suddenly realised that she did know if Smooth had been the school champion at the javelin, or was in the school orchestra as first flute. He tended to dismiss anything like that as lame – sports were lame, orchestras were lame, school was lame. She made a mental note to make sure she asked his parents for all the embarrassing stories next time they saw them.

The fizz theme then continued with friends and the sound of popping corks across the country was something that they got very used to in the ensuing months. There was no mealtime that was out of bounds. Breakfasts with friends would start with a bucks fizz, lunches would have a glass as an aperitif, dinners would have a little something that just had to be taken with a fizzy tipple. Then there were the deliveries to the flat in half-dozen cases; one from Sophie's work, one from Smooth's parents, and even one from one of Sophie's blog fans, after she posted a video about the latest trends in wedding dresses, using celebrity weddings as examples of the best and worst of bridal-wear. At one point, their small kitchen felt like it was a storage cupboard for Champagne, Prosecco and Cava. Bottles were stacked on the floor and in the cupboards. You would go looking for a tin of beans and have to hunt amongst the gold and silver labels of most of the big Champagne houses. Of course, when it was in your face like that, you ended up cooking the beans, but then having beans on toast with a celebratory glass on the side. It was one way of clearing space for other cupboard staples, after all.

There is something about a wave of love from friends and family that can take you on a tide and make you forget about everything else. For months, that was what happened to Sophie and Smooth. They spent more time together and felt like once again they had something in common. Smooth had even stopped being so intense with his hunt for a new direction in his life, and seemed to be happy to go back to his regular analyst job. He said that he would definitely focus on it again once the wedding was out of the way, but in the meantime he had started working longer hours again. Although he still changed his attire on the way home and still liked to hang out at gigs whenever he could get the tickets, he was largely back to the Smooth that she remembered when they first met. He was even becoming more attentive to her and more considerate. For example, he was using the time when she recorded her video-blogs to work later at his office. To get that promotion, so they could afford the posh canapés at the wedding, he said.

On the video-blog side, things had also continued to develop and she now felt really comfortable in front of a camera. So much so, that her regular workload at the web company had expanded from just writing the artists' biographies, and they were now starting to give her the chance to introduce some of the artists at events. Some of the artists even knew about her blogging and in a way, she felt a bit closer to them, as they were both creating something new. In fact, at the engagement party, it was probably her, more than Smooth, that had the proper A-list connections there, with some of the artists and the fans of her site coming along. Smooth hadn't even minded when she disappeared for ten minutes to record a small entry as 'live from the engagement party'. It felt like she really had a community through her blogging and it was growing all the time. The rate it was going, she would probably have to ask her work for some time off in the week to create more entries. Or perhaps combine the two things and think more expansively about the themes. There was only so much that you could cover from your bedroom. She could see herself covering artist events through video and announcing new art pieces and exhibitions though her site, which was now getting several thousand views per episode and had a bank of entries stretching back almost two years. From rising star to veteran, she had thought with a grin.

. As the months passed, gradually their lives calmed down. A few of their other friends had also got engaged, and whereas that took the spotlight off them, it did give them a chance to celebrate with others who were joining their path in life. It meant more champagne, which meant that Sophie could re-pay the kindness and love that had been shown to her and Smooth over their engagement. She really enjoyed spending time making cards for these friends and seeing their faces as they opened them, because she remembered what it was like to feel that way. It gave her a group of people that she could discuss wedding ideas with and soon, the talk at all the parties was about venues, colours and special dances. She loved this, because it gave her lots of new ideas for their special day and several times she had to change the themes she had collected in her scrapbook for the big day, to account for something that she knew a friend loved and wanted to use as a distinctive theme at their own wedding. It didn't matter to her, as any idea she lost was quickly replaced with new touches suggested by her online friends around the world. Origami from Japan,

153

small additional customs to incorporate from all over the world.

More months passed and she couldn't remember exactly why, but suddenly she realised that they had been engaged for almost a year and not yet set a date for their wedding.

Perhaps it was the other couples around them who had got engaged at a similar time that acted as a trigger for these thoughts, or those who had now sent out invitations, or in a few cases actually had the wedding. On each of these occasions, it had prompted her to have the discussion with Smooth, who always promised to talk about it tomorrow, but tomorrow never seemed to come. It wasn't a big deal to her, as they had agreed to have a long engagement and choose the right time to get married, so she had no doubts about the relationship. They still talked fondly about their engagement parties and told each other stories that made mild fun of some of their relatives who had got too drunk and danced like, well, drunken old people. But the stall in momentum had started to make Sophie feel a bit insecure with her friends and actually, lately, a bit embarrassed when she talked to them about the wedding, as nothing concrete had happened just yet, aside from her ever-growing pile of wedding magazines and ideas.

Then, as the end of 2006 approached, she set herself and Smooth a deadline to have set the date by Christmas. It would be great, she had reasoned with Smooth, to send out Christmas cards and the wedding invites at the same time. Smooth had enthusiastically agreed, and then done nothing about it.

Whenever they discussed it, he always agreed with whatever she said, but then seemed to completely forget about it afterwards. She started to make a joke of it, saying that she would just go ahead and book it herself, but all this meant is that Smooth agreed, and actually seemed to perk up when that was mooted, even though it was meant to be a joke. The joke wore thin and Christmas came and went, with still no decision being made. Her parents were very supportive, but they were absolutely right when they said that she and Smooth had to make the big decisions, they could then fill in the gaps and help with arrangements and even funds if required. They had heard horror stories from friends whose parents had been too pushy, and driven a rift between themselves and their children that took years to heal, or perhaps never did. That said, they had emphatically and emotionally explained, they were there for them in whatever way they wanted, always.

The situation had reached its first true flashpoint on the lead-up to New Year. Sophie had suggested that they stay in for New Year's Eve and use it as an opportunity to make their own fun and make a game of the wedding planning. She suggested they get a case of fizz and re-live some of the fun they'd had when they were first engaged. Just the two of them, with some posh food and just get everything done in one night – the guest list, venue short list and date options. Then they could start 2007 with a clean slate and a head-start in the planning, and then always look back at New Year's 2006 as a special day and make a memory.

Smooth had initially agreed, again to get her off his back, Sophie suspected. But then, as New Year approached, he became increasingly irritated and kept mentioning all the parties that friends were going to and that he was being forced to stay in. This stung Sophie and she dug her heels in, as he had agreed already to her plan. But then later, she figured that it would not be a productive and happy environment, and so reached a compromise. The compromise was that Smooth went out early with some of his friends from work and then came home in good time for them to have the evening together. This had seemed like a good solution, although she still secretly couldn't understand why suddenly the friends that Smooth had once described as a 'bunch of boring morons' were suddenly so important. But she let it go. Better that, she thought, than yet again be painted as the nagging fiancée. Or heaven forbid, a Bridezilla.

The morning of New Year's Eve, things had been going well and it seemed that her compromise had built some middle ground for them. Smooth had got up early and headed to a local bakery. She woke up to the smell of fresh coffee and croissants. The croissants were in the oven, but the coffee smell was accounted for by Smooth waving a Starbucks inches away from her nose.

'Sorry,' he said, 'I wanted it to be an authentic experience, but we don't have a coffee machine and the smell wouldn't carry all the way from the kitchen.'

Sophie laughed and resisted the urge to throw a pillow at him, because she wanted to drink the coffee, not have one of them wear it.

The rest of the day carried on in the same vein of frivolity. Smooth had also bought flowers and was talking enthusiastically about the evening and how they were going to make a new scrapbook together. He had set up the lounge table with all the magazines that Sophie had accumulated, and bought a new notepad and some coloured pens and highlighters. They spent the day watching old movies – *It's a Wonderful Life*, *An Affair to Remember* and *Back to the Future II*. The last one was

Smooth's choice and Sophie really quite enjoyed it, despite the fact that the 'future' date in the movie was 2015, so they were actually closer to the future in 2006, than the day the film was made. Sophie then saw Smooth off at the station in the late afternoon, where he promised to have just a couple of drinks and Sophie headed home to put up a few banners and check the TV listings for the *Review of the Year*. He texted about a half-hour later to say that he had arrived and would let her know when he was leaving, but probably not before then as he wasn't sure if there would be much reception, given they were in an underground bar.

It got to seven o'clock and Sophie started to get a bit anxious, as Smooth was still not home. She had deliberately not set a curfew with him, but evening was evening. She was not sure what the universally accepted time for the start of the evening was, but it was dark, so that could be used as a pretty good benchmark. They didn't really have a lot of time left now to spend planning and if Smooth had been drinking since he left, it also meant he was probably drunk by now, whereas she had only had one glass of wine. She decided she would give him another half-hour and then call if he had not arrived home. At seven-thirty, Sophie dropped Smooth a text, just to make sure that he knew she was waiting. She even made a joke of it, about being the hen-packed husband and to get used to that for the years to come. She thought that had the right balance of humour, but also a reminder that she was waiting at home for him and to remind him what they were supposed to be doing.

By nine o'clock, she had texted several more times, and even called once, which had gone to voicemail. In her message, she tried to keep her voice calm, but inside she was experiencing a mixture of anger and upset. Part of her wanted to shout and scream at Smooth, and part of her felt like she was a teenager again, being humiliated by the boy that she liked in the playground. She started to wonder, how had it got to this? She accepted the argument guys were not really into weddings as a day, than girls, even if she didn't agree that it was the way it should be. She had been told several times by Smooth about how stressful the proposal was for him and that for him, the proposal was the main event, not the wedding. But even if he wasn't that excited by the wedding, the fact that they were planning a marriage, a life together – that should mean something to him. She decided that at least she was going to have some fun, so she popped the cork on one of the bottles she had bought for the night and started drinking.

By nine-thirty, she had reached the bottom of the first bottle and still not heard from Smooth. The TV was focusing that year on the weather around New Year, particularly the bad weather bringing 2007 in with a blast, they said. In Edinburgh, the Pet Shop Boys were booked to headline, but the party had to be called off because of high winds and torrential rain.

Just like my mood, Sophie thought, and that was when her mind drifted to Miles for the first time in months. She recalled, before they stopped talking, that he was planning a way to take *Misunderstood* to Edinburgh Fringe festival and she wondered if he had managed it this year, or whether they were still running the show from the pub. She also thought he would find it heart-breaking that the Pet Shop Boys had to cancel their gig. She knew he loved the Pet Shop Boys, a love that stretched all the way back to his nerdy schooldays, when it was taboo to enjoy that kind of electronic music, based only on the fact that it was a bit camp. She felt a wave of compassion when she imagined a young, cute version of Miles, struggling along. Being a nerd and liking camp music must have been a difficult combination for a teenager, sometimes kids could be so cruel.

At ten o'clock and half-way through her second bottle, she decided to call Miles, which she put down in part to that nostalgia that everyone gets at New Year. She was also feeling whimsical, as she remembered the first night at the Reading Festival, how he had managed to have the right piece of festival equipment, or entertainment, at exactly the right moment. He must have been planning it for weeks, gradually having to upgrade the size of his back-pack as the list of sun-cream, stoves and snack bars got longer. He would never have left her hanging here, on her own, at New Year. She needed a friendly voice and she knew that he was vehemently against New Year parties, or any kind of forced fun, so she was sure he would answer. At the worst, he would be with a new girlfriend, in which case she could just wish him Happy New Year, and hopefully use that to get back in touch more regularly. At best, he was on his own too and she could apologise for not talking to him for such a long time, and try to explain why Smooth and her were right for each other, to try and make him understand. Although at this moment in time, she was not coming up with a compelling argument. Perhaps they could then see the New Year in together on the phone, as it was pretty clear that Smooth was not coming home. She might even help him out with his ambition to stay out late and put the chain on the door. That might help him start to realise what life might be like without her.

She felt excited as she reached for her phone. Why had she waited this long to get back in touch with Miles?

Friends are friends and for her part in it, she would let him know that she was sorry and she was sure he would understand.

Chapter 13

Thunder

December 31, 2006.

Miles had even stopped visiting Sophie's website. Or at least stopped visiting it as often. He had convinced himself that it was because he had finally managed to put her out of his mind and move on with his life after the heart-breaking news and heart-breaking weekend of the Reading Festival. But actually, it could have been that Sophie had started to blog quite ferociously about her wedding, so as well as causing him intense sadness every time, it also acted as a constant reminder that all hope of being with her was lost. Perhaps it wasn't his own strength, but a sense of self-preservation.

The fact that they were never going to be together should not have been a surprise to him, because apart from what he thought were signals, she hadn't actually made any explicit promises or statements that they would ever end up together. He knew this, because he had re-read every text conversation they'd ever had and also had spent hours awake at night, re-evaluating conversations for responses that he had got wrong, or words that she used that he could have misunderstood as affection. In relationship terms, she basically had a water-tight argument that it was Miles who had always made the first move, or pushed things the hardest. She had been sweet and nice, but it was the look in her eyes and her tone, rather than her actual words that had made Miles think she was interested.

Deep down, he thought the best explanation for how he got it so wrong was that he was not very experienced with girls as friends. Throughout his life, he had mainly hung out with guys, so girls in his life were generally either relatives or a sparse smattering of girlfriends. This meant that in his mind, affection from a girl came from a place that led to a relationship, not a life-long friendship. He was conditioned to see girls that way, but also, with Sophie it would never have been a choice anyway. Sure, he did like hanging out with her as a friend and if he hadn't found her so attractive then maybe he could have had his first ever platonic relationship with the opposite sex. But sadly, every time she looked at him, or he saw her, or imagined her in a pair of jeans, or she looked at him whilst wearing a pair of jeans, then all bets were off.

Tim had been a great support to help Miles rationalise all this, but because he had never actually had the chance to meet Sophie after the brief, but intense, episode at the first performance of the play, he wasn't able to give a true, unbiased opinion. He had generally kept out of it altogether, but as soon as Miles had returned from the festival, he had sensed that something was not quite right and so, in his own way, had helped talk it through. His own way, was to make sure that Miles got as drunk as possible, as often as possible, and allowed him to vent for as long as he wanted, or alternatively just spend hours in silence.

The conclusion in the end was the same. An independent voice on this situation would have warned him off months ago, because it was probably very obvious to anyone else that he was getting nowhere and should give it up. So Tim promised, from that moment on, that he would make it his business to keep an eye on Miles' relationships and step in if he started going off-track. Two heartbreaks, in two years, was enough for anyone. Besides, Tim had a vested interest, as the performances of *Misunderstood* were starting to get the attention of small theatres across the country, so he needed his partner in the best emotional shape possible, given that it was a comedy. Having one of the key writers and directors sobbing through the performances was doing them no good at all.

As the weeks went by, Miles started to get some perspective and was more able to rationalise the situation. The overwhelming emotion he started to feel was stupidity. He felt stupid that he had so dramatically misread signals, and he felt stupid that he had let himself start to project forward and imagine a life together with Sophie. He had come to rely on her and that was probably the most stupid thing of all. Even though they didn't really talk about it, she was in a relationship when they met, was in a relationship for the whole time they knew each other, and was still in a relationship. So nothing had changed in their situations, except that Sophie's relationship had become an engagement. To rely on the support of someone like that was not a good judgement call and was always going to end badly, with you in second place. It had just all been such a surprise, and again, although there was no evidence, he took their

163

weekend at Reading as an indication that she was interested in him and was starting to think about a life without Smooth.

So it was only when she dropped the bombshell, that he realised how deep he was into the situation, because instead of feeling happiness for her, or anger, or sadness, he just felt nothing at all – he felt numb. He literally could not speak and wanted to run away. Although his muteness probably worked in his favour as he couldn't say anything stupid, he had tormented himself with what he should have said, over endless nights lying awake and staring at the ceiling. As for running, being on top of a vintage camper van had not helped there.

Finally, about a week after the festival, Miles steeled himself and decided to be the bigger man. He had been through one big break-up in the last two years and although this was not technically a break-up, he had learned that the last thing he should do was stew on the emotion, or ruin what they had. So he had decided to call her, as after all, he had said, just a few moments before she shattered his dreams, that he would always have her back. Tim thought this was a terrible idea and was all for zero communication, but Miles was determined. Short of being a bridesmaid, he was willing to do anything to make sure he kept the promise of looking after her and being there for her. Besides, he had reminded Tim, people who get engaged don't always get married, do they?

At this point, Tim had hidden Miles' phone for a good two days before he gave up and allowed Miles to make the call that he was sure would just deepen the disaster even further.

The last eventuality that Miles had considered in all of this, was that he would be ignored by Sophie. In fact, it was only after he had left a few voice-mails that he realised that several weeks had passed and Sophie had not returned any of his texts or calls. He initially thought she might be on holiday, or busy with work, but then he saw that she had posted a live feed from her engagement party. That was when Miles had decided that he should cut ties. He had convinced himself that she was waiting for his call and that his opinion mattered to her as a friend. But to not even invite him to her engagement party could only mean two things. Either she had feelings for him and could not face seeing him at the party for fear of calling the engagement off, or that she was angry with him for being upset at the news of her engagement. On the latter, if that was the case then she was definitely out of order, because Miles could tell from her tone that she was well aware that it was bad news that was being delivered. On the former, it was perhaps still a clinging thought, except for the fact that all her blog posts explained just how happy she was and how excited she was to be Mrs Smooth.

So Miles had doubled-down on *Misunderstood*, to the point where he was spending as much time on it as he was in shift-work at the bar. This meant that he was rarely out of the bar, or Tim's apartment above the bar, except for late evenings and early mornings. Given this lack of distractions, they had managed to develop the script and also book new venues, as the play had been gaining a cult following with sci-fi and zombie fans firstly in London, then visitors to London from other areas of the UK, and eventually abroad. They now ran a weekly evening performance of the show on a Tuesday night in the pub, a night chosen specifically by Miles to

165

cheer people up on what he said, to Tim's bemusement, was the worst day of the week. Wasn't that accepted, the world-over, as Monday, Tim had consistently argued?

But Tim didn't mind too much, as Tuesdays were a slow day in the pub and this gave a welcome boost to the revenue over the bar and a relief to Tuesday night boredom. There was then a matinee on a Saturday afternoon, this time chosen because there was a correlation between sci-fi fans and an aversion to sports. So they pitched the matinee as an antidote to football, an angle that worked pretty well.

They then took the play on the road periodically, either to conventions or comedy festivals. Initially they had started small, but then early that year they had the chance to perform at the Edinburgh Fringe Festival, which was the first stage of the dream for Miles, and something he had been working towards and lobbying since they first put on the launch show. Tim had embraced the opportunity by hiring an enormous motor home for him and Miles to share and they had taken the show on a pub tour, all the way from London to Edinburgh.

The pub was doing well enough for Tim to let hired staff run it for a period and the timing of the fringe was also during the quieter summer months, when students and young people took holidays, so it wasn't too much of a risk to allow someone else to keep the standards up. Tim knew that when he got back, it would take him days to re-categorise all the drinks, but in a perverse way that was something to look forward to.

Using contacts they had gained from the success of the show in London, they booked cities and venues that they thought would guarantee a good audience and good support from the venue. By the time they arrived in Edinburgh, they were well practised in life on tour and had even learned a few additional scenes and routines that went down well with the audience. For example, they had realised that fans visited partly to be grossed out by the pus and the spitting. So in addition, had planted a couple of fake audience members, who near the end let off old-fashioned stink bombs in the audience to give the finale the smell, as well as the sight, of rotting flesh.

Once at Edinburgh, they had quickly realised they were small fish, in a big pond, but they had a consistently full venue and a well-received run of shows. The routine that they most enjoyed would be to sit at breakfast, eating through the hangover and pouring over the previous night's reviews. To laugh about the good bits, but also hone the script and the performance, to take into account the poor reviews. They both agreed that it was an amazing experience and as performers, the camaraderie and the parties that they attended were some of the best they had ever been to. Even Tim, with his slightly awkward manner and way with people, managed to find others who were similarly socially inept, and he had even bumped into a few old colleagues from his days of acting in America. It gave them both a continued feeling that they were in the right life and as the coverage they received was low-key but largely positive, it gave Tim and Miles enough heart in the project to resolve to come back the next year with *Misunderstood 2: A Farewell to Arms*. The title was a work-in-progress.

It was whilst in Edinburgh for the Fringe, that Miles had also met someone. A girl. They had met at the wrap party of the show and she had been as impressed by his credentials as a director, as by his looks. They had started something of a long-distance relationship, as she was a resident of Edinburgh and a student at the university. The irony of this was not lost on Tim, who reminded Miles of his new role as "advisor of relationships" and as part of that he must urge that Miles try harder to meet someone that he would be able to touch once in a while. Miles took this in good humour and assured Tim that he was not taking this too seriously, but they had agreed to spend New Year together in the legendary New Year city of Edinburgh. At this point, Tim had theatrically slapped his hand to his forehead, and as Miles' barometer on these things, this told Miles that the reading was firmly pointing to 'run away'.

But she had sold a good story to him and seemed to be treating it just as casually, so he had agreed to visit even though he was generally against New Year in principle. The problem for Miles started with the fact that New Year was not a religious festival, or a day in memory of anyone or anything. On that basis, he really didn't see the point in celebrating January 1 in any other way than every day. He didn't really see how it was a new start of anything, you didn't lose points off your driving license for example, or there was no mass pardoning of any crimes or misdemeanours you had carried out the previous year. It just seemed like everyone was forcing fun and by doing that, putting far too much pressure on themselves to have a good time. So in turn, it led to mass disappointment, arguments, and statistically a much higher rate of suicide than other days in the year.

That said, he was prepared to give it a go and wondered to himself if he would get some kind of sign that might suggest that she could be a serious girlfriend and put an end to his two years of poor luck and judgement. The Pet Shop Boys were also headlining the annual New Year's bash on Princes Street and Miles was a huge fan, having spent many days of his childhood experiencing Neil Tennant through headphones in the back seat of his parent's car, and imagining that if he was a pop star, that is exactly the type of pop star he would be.

When you are looking for a sign from the heavens, the fact that the forecast for the weekend of New Year was biblical levels of wind and rain, to the extent that it had meant the cancellation of all the performances and celebrations, Miles should have read the warning signs. On arrival, when the weather was just as biblical as predicted, Miles actually felt hopeful rather than foreboding. It could be a good weekend and it could be that he at once banished his memory of Sophie and his jinx of New Year – a double win. Maybe the only problem he was going to face was having to leave at the end of the weekend, with a new relationship, a new future.

In the end though, the problem was nothing to do with weather, or forces of nature, or having too much fun. The problem, in essence, was when he stepped off the train and was met on the platform, he had a massive case of the second-time disappointment.

It was disappointment in her clothes, which at the height of the summer were a joyful and colourful combination of denim shorts and vests, and were now, well, purple and black hippie clothes. It was disappointment in her looks, which he always remembered were cherubic, but now struck him as, just, chubby. At first he thought it was just her face that disappointed him, but when he hugged her, he could tell that it was everything, she even hugged differently to how he remembered Plus, she smelled a bit funny, like damp washing. He felt shallow thinking it, but he just didn't fancy her.

He was drunk a lot over the time of the Fringe Festival, but he was pretty sure that he had a good look at her and a good sniff of her sober as well and he didn't remember it being as it was. So he couldn't put his finger on exactly why he felt this way and how his illusion of her had so dramatically mismatched reality. Worse than that, it was so unexpected, that he felt his demons creeping back in and a rising panic as his mind took him to the one place he did not want to go. Basically, she just wasn't Sophie.

She suggested that they go back to her flat, but for Miles, he had entered a damage limitation mind-set. He quickly decided that the best approach would be to make sure that there was no chance of them being alone in a room, until he could figure out a way of leaving Edinburgh and heading back to London. He was scheduled to stay for several days, but already he was thinking that he could make an excuse of weather-related transport links and make an early exit. He also knew that they were meeting her friends that evening, so if he could feign interest in Edinburgh's tourist sights for a few hours, and pretend that he hadn't already visited them all that summer, then there would be no awkward moments. In the meantime he could figure out a way of letting her down gently. So much for new starts, he thought.

He needn't have stressed too much about letting her down gently, as his body language had almost immediately given the impression that he wasn't interested. It was never Miles' strong point to keep such things hidden. He could tell that she was as awkward as he was and as the day wore on, they started to run out of conversation. He could tell that she was also looking forward to meeting up with her group of friends and not having to be alone with Miles any longer. So he gave the opportunity and suggested they meet them earlier and reserve their spot in a bar in town, before they become ticket-only. It was almost a relief when they were swallowed up by a mixed group of student friends, all of whom had ignored the weather and still chosen to dress as schoolchildren, ballerinas and Roman soldiers. So, on top of feeling alone and that he had made a huge mistake, in his jeans and sensible hoodie, Miles felt old. Old and sensible, miles from home, and miles from the New Year's *Review of the Year* on the TV.

He managed to get through a lot of the evening by drinking heavily and staying on the outside of the group. He found that, given they were several years his junior, and several times more excitable, you could actually waste quite a lot of time just listening and allowing the group to take you into their excitable banter, without ever having to give an opinion or make a comment. Thankfully, it also seemed that his supposed date for the day had found someone else to talk to and so hadn't even noticed that he was avoiding socialising with anyone. To his horror, she had changed into a velour tracksuit and had informed Miles that it was a fancy dress theme and she was dressing as a "chav" for the evening. Miles wondered why she hadn't told him before about the theme, but to be honest he probably wouldn't have embraced it anyway. The chav outfit, if anything, just made things worse in the attraction stakes, despite being at the complete opposite end of the scale to the loose frills and velvet that he had met at the station.

He slowly retreated to a corner and decided that he would move a table further away from the group each time he got a drink, so that in the end he was either at the opposite side of the bar when it got really busy, or even better, in a different bar altogether. He had experienced Edinburgh's hospitality before, there was bound to be someone, or a new group, that he could see the hours through midnight with. Then, he could re-join his original group and hope that they didn't notice he had been gone for a large portion of the evening. At least then, he had a roof over his head for the night with his date. He glanced over at the bar, where she was currently busy trying to light a shot of something and simultaneously trying to keep the material of her tracksuit away from the naked flame. Yep, definitely an opportunity to blame alcohol for her not remembering where he was all evening.

He headed outside the bar, to clear his head and try to convince himself that his situation was not as dire as it seemed. He was three hundred miles from his flat, where he could have spent a very pleasant evening watching TV and getting mildly drunk alone. He could have then wished his parents a Happy New Year at midnight and disappeared off whilst the rest of the country pretended to coo in appreciation of fireworks and make promises to each other that they would have forgotten by the end of the month.

Instead, here he was in a very beautiful city, but a city that was currently in the grip of one of the worst storms in its history, with the rain coming down harder and harder from a sky that was as black as his mood.

What he really needed now, was some advice and support, so he decided to call Tim and see what his advice would be. Tim was spending the night with some of his close friends in his favourite London bar, the same one that he and Miles had hatched their first plans for *Misunderstood* and Miles' life in general. So he wouldn't be able to answer the phone, but would hopefully see the missed call and realise that it was an emergency. He called him five times just to be sure.

Of course, whilst he was waiting for that call-back, with his phone in his hand, it rang and of course, it was Sophie. Forget the weather; if there was ever a sign, this was it.

Chapter 14

Un-Pause

December 31, 2006.

'Where are you, you sound like you're in the middle of a hurricane?'

The same old Sophie – straight into the one-liners.

'I suppose you could say so,' Miles shot back, 'both literally and metaphorically.'

Miles was trying his best to make his voice sound calm and hide the uncertainty that he was feeling when he saw Sophie's name on the phone screen. There is probably only one thing that is more hurtful to someone's pride, than the moment you realise that your love is unrequited, and that is trying to treat the situation as normal and having your attempts at normality or reconciliation both ignored and unacknowledged. He and Sophie used to talk every day, Miles thought. They were in contact every day and then suddenly nothing – for months.

At first, Miles had to also understand that he had left it a few weeks, but in the end he did call. He didn't over-compensate as he sometimes might, he just called and texted for a catch-up like a normal friend after an argument, and was very careful to keep his tone neutral and his words ambiguous. He even practised his voicemails on one of the dogs that regularly frequented the pub. One of those with a sad face, but happy eyes and ears that swivel to your voice so you know it's listening. That went well and helped him to get over his nerves, so well in fact, that the dog took to seeking him out for a chat. At least, that is what he thought, until he realised that every practice session was rewarded with a biscuit, so maybe the dog was just being patient to whatever he was saying, in the hope that the session would finish with a treat. Perhaps there was a life lesson, thought Miles. Always bring biscuits, but then he had a flash of the grey meeting room he used to spend his days in, before he quit his regular job, and gave a shudder.

His trump card was always going to be to call Sophie with a hint or a suggestion for her wedding, but that was somewhere that he decided he couldn't go and Tim would have been proud of him for that. That would have been too painful – because Sophie probably would have responded. Then, she would have talked about the wedding in return, which was horrible and that feeling would last a lot longer than the joy of hearing her voice or seeing her words in a text. No, he would not throw her that biscuit. Biscuits are just for dogs.

So when Sophie called on New Year's Eve, imagine balancing this feeling of hurt, with the uncertain excitement that someone like Miles would have, in looking for a sign and having it answered in such poetic, if a bit clichéd fashion. It was all he could do to control the high and low emotional waves and try and keep his voice from trembling. But in the end, with just that one exchange of banter, things were back to normal again.

Which Miles hated, because it just made things confusing again. Did that mean they were friends? Isn't that the greatest thing, he thought, about friendships? True friendships have the ability to put issues behind them. They have their ups-and-downs and are not perfect. Things that happen can lead to long periods of silences, but then there is a mutual understanding that the silence takes the place of any kind of discussion or argument about what had happened in the past. Once the silence is broken, the agreement is that the relationship returns to normal – whether that is a day, a month, or years. He knew there would be a time to discuss his feelings and how she had upset him, irrational as he was, or was not, but right now he was just happy to be back in touch with Sophie and also, that it was her that had made the first move; so he was sure that she felt the same. In some way, he felt it was a kind of apology in itself, getting in touch, especially on New Year's Eve when you are thinking about friends and family. It meant that she put him in one of those categories.

Miles explained his predicament and Sophie chuckled her way through it. The irony of the situation was that he was explaining his disastrous decisions and poor choices in love, to the one person who embodied that trait in him, the one person to whom he had the most experience in misreading situations to heart-breaking, rather than comedy, effect. He was secretly enjoying it.

He was enjoying it because it gave him a chance to show Sophie that he was moving on and meeting other people. It showed her that he was desirable to other girls, if not to her. He might still be making terrible decisions, but at least he could tell her there was at least one other relationship he had since the last time they saw each other. So for that, he hoped she would be a little bit jealous. But also, he was enjoying it because he had the chance to make Sophie laugh, even if it was in the most self-depreciating way. It was a story about his misfortune, but it was also a good way to re-connect with her and hear her tinkling laugh and her comments that were goading, but urging to hear more.

When he had finished the story, it felt like they spent a few seconds together over the phone, both just enjoying the silence and the companionship. For Miles, he was fighting the urge to ask where Smooth was and why she wasn't out at a dinner party or something, celebrating New Year. Surely he should be the one she is talking to and chatting with, on this, of all nights. Was he there in the background? Had he popped out somewhere? Maybe to get some take-away and she was just filling the silence, as he had suspected on the first night they met. Was he just being used as a convenient way for Sophie not to be alone?

In the end, Miles decided that none of this mattered. The fact was that she had decided to call him and sometimes you just have to embrace that and enjoy the moment that the universe has given to you. It was a moment that had taken him away from his black mood and also, had eaten up some time before he had to go back into the bar and try to implement his half-hatched plan to re-join the group. He could see them now, through the window and it seemed that everyone had started to reach that moment in the evening where they had started to swap outfits. So through the window he could see the Incredible Hulk was now in the top-half of a velour track-suit, over his ripped jeans bottom-half. Wasn't that what she was wearing, he thought and then decided he didn't want to know anything more than that. He had to do something to get out of this.

The fact was that the decision was rapidly being made for him anyway, Miles realised, as he turned and took in the street outside the bar. The niggling feeling that the previous plan for the evening might be falling apart, was now turning into a certainty, as he could see a queue forming outside of the bar and in his haste to leave, he realised that he forgot to check with the bouncers about any re-entry policies. He took a step towards the bouncers, with the intention of discussing the matter with them, but the look he was given as he approached the velvet rope from the wrong direction made him stop in his tracks. No one crosses a velvet rope without permission, he thought, especially not in Edinburgh, in the pouring rain, on New Year's Eve. At least that gave him a plausible excuse and maybe just another sign and so, he shouldn't push it too hard. She had probably forgotten about him anyhow and because they hadn't been to her flat, he had everything he needed in his backpack – again a victory for the nerdy backpack.

'Sophie,' he said, 'I think we might have a problem.'

'That's OK.' It seemed that Sophie sensed what was going on, 'I'll stay with you until you sort it.' Miles' heart melted again.

The trouble with the position that Miles now found himself, was that Miles was not one of those people who have a homing-pigeon instinct when they are drunk and under pressure. Some people you can lose at any moment in the evening and you will find them in bed the following morning. Or you find them in the kitchen, sat at the table and part-way through eating a kebab, with no recollection of what had happened or how they got there.

No – Miles was not one of these and in fact, despite his creativity with *Misunderstood*, his problem-solving ability was pretty bad in these situations. The way he saw it, he had two rather bleak options. The first was to try and catch a train. Head straight to the station, get a fresh ticket back to London and sleep on the train. It only took a second to realise he was unlikely to be successful, given the time of year and the time of night, so he dismissed it entirely. The second was to get a taxi back to London, which he admitted was probably the expensive option, but was the only other one he could think of. He could head to the taxi rank before the midnight rush and use a combination of negotiation and pleading, to get a good rate, at least to get to a cheap hotel part-way home.

'A taxi. Back to London. On New Year's Eve?' Sophie said, very slowly. The kind of slowly that makes you realise before she had finished saying it, just how ridiculous it was. 'This is how you ended up in that motel where I first met you, Miles, you need to think outside the box.'

Without even pausing for breath, Sophie reeled off four more options to him. The best one by far was also the simplest. To try and find a hotel. He had chatted to enough people on the train journey up to Edinburgh to have a mental list of the local hotels and also, to know that a lot of people had cancelled their rooms and not made the trip on account of the weather. That would surely mean there was a surplus of hotel rooms in the city. With his own knowledge of the city, garnered from the time he spent at the Fringe Festival, he thought he could definitely take a stab at finding a reasonable hotel for the night. They agreed it was the right thing to do and in addition, Sophie also logged onto the Internet to help him navigate some of the closed roads, despite Miles' insistence that he didn't need that kind of technology, that he had a photographic map of Edinburgh already logged in his mind. He didn't catch Sophie's response to that, because she was laughing so hard, but there was something in there about needless-bravado, he was sure.

It also became clear, very quickly, that she was right. He did need that kind of technology, as even on that wild night, there were enough roads closed through the weather, or the previously planned events, to make the city unrecognisable. He'd had just enough alcohol to confuse imposing landmarks and grey-stone buildings, which he had previously been certain about and he found himself following Sophie's directions more and more. She guided him over the slick cobbles through town, before they eventually reached the beating heart of the New Year's party on Princes Street, where despite the lack of organised distractions, people had still come to party in large numbers and in various brightly coloured waterproofs. You had to admire the spirit and the single-minded ambition to party. He described what was going on to Sophie, the cacophony of voices, colours, songs, much to her initial amusement, but soon this faded and Sophie suddenly went quiet. Miles, sensing something was wrong, came back to reality a little bit. They had been talking and been together on the phone now, for well over an hour and Miles almost asked again about Smooth. Why was she able to speak to him on New Year's Eve? Why was she alone? He felt the question forming when Sophie broke the silence.

'Where are you now?' She asked.

'I'm on Princes Street, near the gardens,' he yelled into the phone through the singing and the din of cheap party accessories, which were taking the place of fireworks and the Pet Shop Boys, in the gardens that night. 'Sorry, is it too difficult to hear me?'

'No, but can you just stop a minute and hold up your phone, please? I just want to hear the party a little bit. I'm not bothered about actual New Year this year, but I'd like to think about how it is up there with you. I know you don't like to do it, so I'll only make you do it for a minute.'

Miles realised now why people did it and sat down on a nearby wall with his phone in the air, with her in London and him in Edinburgh. Letting her enjoy the moment, but understanding that sometimes, that means that you have to take yourself out of the moment and share it. He supposed he knew now, sometimes it's not to boast, but just because you want to share the atmosphere and give someone else a few of the senses that you are experiencing, even if they cannot do it physically.

They were so far apart, but they were together in experiencing that New Year's Eve in 2006, and Sophie always remembered that.

It took three attempts for them to find a hotel. Sophie had one eye on the directions from back in London and one eye on the prices. The first two, who had already tripled their rates from the normal pricing, had added on another £100 because of the lateness of the hour, and probably because they had sensed Miles' desperation. Sophie had thought about offering to talk to them and make up a story about him being her slightly simple brother, who had run away from home nearby and was a bit confused. She added that it wouldn't be difficult, as he was wearing a school boy's backpack and all he would need to do is stand there and let her do the talking. But Miles didn't think that would work, because Sophie had carried on drinking since they had been talking and although to her, she was doing a passable Scottish accent to illustrate that they lived in the neighbourhood, to Miles, it sounded part-Welsh and part-Jamaican.

In the third, which was actually the most upmarket of the three, they had a stroke of luck. Miles had ducked into the bathroom in the entrance reception, whilst the doormen were busy with a reveller who had passed out in their revolving doors. He had smartened himself up, dried his hair and dug out a shirt from his overnight bag. When he approached the reception desk, they firstly saw someone who was a bit smarter than some of the guests who had been arriving, but also, he had got past the door staff who had been briefed to give a rigorous line of questioning to anyone who came in, as they had found in previous years, that their reception had turned into part campsite, part public toilet and had led to the sacking of several previous desk staff.

What also helped, was that the reception representative took quite a shine to Miles. He had been working at the hotel for just a few weeks and had been told a lot of horror stories about New Year's Eve and what he would have to deal with. He personally thought it was beyond his job description to deal with anyone who treated the hotel like a festival site, given that he had undertaken most his training at The Ritz in Paris. So he had made sure of the increased security and added a sweetener to the security staff, by personally buying them all matching beanie hats that he had personally had shipped in from his favourite ski-store in the Alps.

Warm staff are happy staff, he thought on this occasion. He had not had any issues thus far and now here was this handsome man approaching, on his own and looking distressed.

The distressed look was part of Sophie's strategy to garner sympathy, an adapted strategy after the second failure of the night. Sophie was playing the part on the other end of the phone of the girlfriend, who had been stranded at an airport, en-route to Edinburgh and was too upset to remember where she had booked to stay and had run out of battery on her phone, although she was sure it was this hotel. Miles could then in turn play the part of the patient boyfriend, whilst at the same time making apologetic faces to the reception staff, to indicate that clearly she was in no state to explain anything, so could they help him out please.

It worked a treat and before he knew it, Miles had a room for the night and therefore, an escape route for the evening. The thought of not having to see the group he had left in the bar ever again, plus if he was quick enough to catch the end of the evening's TV programming of midnights across the world, was a New Year miracle. They even had a pot of porridge on the stove downstairs in the kitchen, ready for the morning and the concierge said he would be happy to prepare a bowl for him to take up with him, with a drop of whiskey in, as was New Year's Day breakfast tradition. It looked cold out there, Miles was told and this would sort him out in no time. Of course, if he had any other needs once he was settled, then all he had to do was call down to reception and it would be no problem at all.

Miles, oblivious of the flirtatious nature of the exchange and its role in his good fortune, slumped into a chair in reception whilst the necessary keys were being fetched and porridge arrangements were being made; thinking about being able to phone his family and being able to head back to London on the train the next day and forget about the whole episode.

'Sophie, this is a New Year's miracle,' he said, 'and it was all down to you. You called me at exactly the right second and you knew exactly what to do. I'm so thankful to you tonight and now you need to spend midnight with me.'

He thought he would take the chance, as obviously something was going on with her in London. It was only fifteen minutes before the New Year and there was no explanation about where she was, or why her and Smooth were not spending the last New Year's Eve before they were married, together. There had been a lot of one-sided talk from Miles to update Sophie on this evening and then a lot of time spent sorting out the hotels and walking the streets of Edinburgh. But there was still plenty of time for Sophie to have explained what was going on. As far as he could tell, she was in their flat at home, but this did not explain the absence of Smooth. He had almost felt like she was there with him in Edinburgh and he didn't want it to end there if there was a chance she could be the last person he spoke to in 2006 and the first in 2007. That would make it the first New Year that he did believe in new beginnings.

'Oh, Miles, not this year, thank you, and I do mean thank you. This is just not a New Year that I want to remember. But you have really made my night, I really enjoyed hanging out with you. But I think it's just best for me to be on my own.' There was a sadness and pleading to Sophie's voice, for him to leave it there. But it did confirm that she was alone and again Miles felt the urge of protectiveness rise in him, so he ignored the obvious signals.

'Sophie, tell me.' Although he didn't mean it to, it sounded a bit direct, despite him speaking softly. But the situation felt urgent and Miles didn't know what else to say to make sure she knew he was there and would support her. It brought the feelings of Reading back. He couldn't open discussions about it at this time, it was the only way he could explain again, that he would always be there for her. But it also meant, that he would have to say that he was hurt for a long time, but in the end it didn't matter. As soon as he answered the phone earlier that evening he had forgotten it and was just happy to hear her voice. Her tone had told him that this would be too much information and would just break the fragile thread they had just re-built, so he couldn't push it any more than that, and just let her decide.

At the other end, he could tell she understood and she just gave a sigh, almost inaudible over the commotion outside, but to Miles it roared in his ears.

'Thank you, Miles, just not now. Not tonight. Really, thank you for being there for me tonight, it meant a lot. Such a lot. Good night, Miles, sweet dreams. I'll call you tomorrow, OK?'

Before Miles could answer, the line went dead, but Miles knew it was OK and they would speak soon. This time he knew.

Chapter 15

Not Cool

January 1, 2007.

There is a reason they say you feel emotions, because that is what happens. You don't think them, or decide them. You feel them; in your head, your stomach, your heart. Bad emotions are as involuntary as being hit with a hammer and sometimes, it feels like it hurts as much.

That was one of the things that always made Sophie wonder about being human – if they happen in your brain, why did they make you feel sick and exhausted. If they happened in your brain, then why didn't just your head hurt and why couldn't you take a headache pill and make them go away? Instead, they attacked you in the most surprising places. As she lay on the sofa, watching the fireworks at midnight, she was feeling so many emotions that it wasn't even like a hammer. She felt like she had run a marathon. Everything ached.

She also couldn't separate or decide which bit was the most exhausting. For example, should she have said sorry to Miles? Maybe that was the first thing she should

186

have said, rather than another one of those nervous jokes. She hadn't spoken to him for so long, that she panicked. But jokes were their thing, Miles and Sophie, and he had quipped back fast enough. After that, it was too late to say sorry without having to go into everything that had happened over the last year and a half. Better just to move on and try and get back to being friends. She had missed him and although she was too proud to say it out loud, she wanted him to know that. He had become an anchor in her life and in the bad times she found herself needing that anchor, needing to hear something nice about herself, which she could always rely on Miles to provide. She also needed to hear some of Miles' stories, she had really missed his stories.

Besides, if she had dragged up the last eighteen months of no contact, it wouldn't have been half as much fun as it was, to hang out with him on the phone. Miles had not disappointed and if he was annoyed with her, it hadn't come through in his behaviour. It was just like the best of the old times, with their easy banter and his ability to tell a story in a way that made her laugh so much. No one could turn misfortune into comedy like Miles and he had outdone himself tonight. She didn't even mind that it took him about twice the time of a normal person to get to the point. For most people, it was the beginning and end that you heard of a story, perhaps with a little bit of narrative in the middle. With Miles, he focused on every detail and he could tell you about one tiny part of the story with the same ferocity as the punch line. Often, even the middle parts and the tiny details were the funniest bits and at those times, she could tell why he was really good at and really enjoyed his play writing.

She thought about him, tucking into porridge in his hotel room and had the urge to be with him and watch the night fold in over Princes Street, even though she knew that wasn't right. When the mood was light, Miles was the best person in the world to be with, but he was a complicated person, with a complicated life.

Anyway, she was not sure even if she should apologise. She was in a relationship when she met him and was now going to get married. That was the way it worked and Miles knew that, from the moment they met. Or perhaps not the exact moment they met, but soon after. Plus, she had made lots of assumptions about how he felt about her, but maybe he didn't feel that way at all and she was giving herself too much credit. Perhaps he was that way with everyone and fell in love very easily – like the girl he had gone all that way to see and then left hanging in a bar that night. Sophie had genuinely called him expecting him to be at home and watching TV, like her. Either way, someone had to be the responsible one and make sure that they didn't get carried away by saying things or doing things that they would regret in the long-run. Besides, surely the universe was giving her a sign that they weren't right for each other, given that every time it seemed one of them was thinking about the other, the other person wasn't.

When she considered that, it actually sounded like Sophie herself was the one thinking too much – maybe it was her with the complicated life these days. In the end, she was the one who called him and needed him this evening. Miles was the one who was just seizing the day in Edinburgh, with half a plan and no contingencies. She thought about him again, hunched outside the bar with his backpack on, trying to avoid the gaze of a girl who, it seemed, might have swapped her tracksuit top for whatever the Incredible Hulk wore on his top half – which she was pretty sure was nothing.

Then escaping through the streets of Edinburgh and experiencing the hubbub of Princes Street; even just through Miles' phone and Miles' eyes, had been exciting. She had seen Princes Street on TV and the news had made it out to be a disastrous New Year, but it didn't seem that way at all. It seemed just like everyone was having a great time and seizing the best of a bad situation. It had been as Miles had talked about, on top of the camper van at Reading. That sometimes you had to just exist in the moment and embrace it. It felt so real to her, without even being there, and she could almost sense the party and smell the slightly stinging aroma of cheap fireworks and damp clothing. Feel the bite of the cold on her skin, combined with the warmth of the whiskey on the inside.

She was in what should be the most romantic period of her life, planning a wedding and planning a life, but the last two hours with Miles felt like the most excitement and romance she'd had for a while. She hoped that Miles got away without any trouble and she hoped that the girl didn't call overnight and make things awkward; but at the same time, Miles was at least good enough to let her know that he had found alternative accommodation, so at least she didn't worry. After all, they were kind of boyfriend and girlfriend.

That was another confusing emotion. The thought of him having a new girlfriend was a bit weird. She had never really imagined herself with Miles, beyond fleeting thoughts and half-baked romantic notions, but never in real life. Perhaps that is what made it weird. She told herself that she didn't fancy him, but at the same time, it made her happy it hadn't worked out between Miles and the new girl. Did that mean weird, but also, was she jealous? No, she dismissed it. Talking with Miles had been just the tonic she needed to cheer herself up, with everything going on with Smooth she was entitled to a bit of innocent, irresponsible fun. How ironic, that it was Miles that was giving it to her, rather than the other way round, as it had been when they first met. That was some poetic payback and she felt it again, that pang of jealousy that she was here and he was there. No, if she felt any jealousy, she was probably just jealous he was enjoying himself and she was stuck in the flat.

Which brought her back to the subject in hand. Where was Smooth?

She checked her voicemails, in case he had called whilst she was talking to Miles, but there was nothing. She had to admit, in the past he had been a bit of a loose cannon, but she thought that with the proposal, he was starting to think about her a bit more, wasn't that the whole point? Proposals were not supposed to get you past an awkward pause in conversation, or be some kind of ostentatious metaphor for a bunch of flowers when you had done something wrong, or a way of trying to inject excitement into a stale relationship. She kept going over what he had said, about the proposal being the main event for him and how stressful it was, and started getting angry. After all, a proposal is just words. The action is then in the planning of the wedding and your life and behaving like the person you proposed to is the only person in your life and that you cannot wait to stand up in public and tell them so. Proposals are done in private, so the words can become just an empty gesture without the action to back it up – and doing half a job that evening was not good enough. All the arranging of the room and buying all the scrapbooks and pens was just another empty gesture, unless it was backed up by action.

Sophie was working herself up and could feel the anxiety rising up in her, turning her exhaustion into something new – that stomach churning worry where the seconds stretch out into minutes, and where terrible impulses and implications start tumbling over each other in your head. Small things in their relationship started to bloat and inflate into huge issues. Like the fact that they still had separate bank accounts. They always said it was because they were independent people, but was it an unconscious way of making sure there was an escape route? What would happen if they were not right for each other? They had declared a lot already in front of people; they'd had an engagement party where they behaved like the perfect couple. Was that just pretending? Were they just carried away in the moment and going along with things for the sake of friends and family?

She found herself starting to panic, doubts rising and colliding with each other, and she found herself unable to hold onto a rational thought. He didn't invite many people to the engagement party because he was embarrassed. Sophie's mind was turning into a dark, pulsating and jumbled mess of voices: her own, her friends, her family, Smooth. She could vaguely hear the chimes of Big Ben on the TV and realised that this was it, this was how she was going to spend New Year 2006. Full of doubt and anxiety, rather than joy and hope. She felt like an idiot, so she did the only thing she could think of, when you need a distraction and an expression of the black mood that is slowly taking over you. She got herself another drink. Gin this time – and put on some country music. Loud.

Some of the all-time best break-up songs are country songs and some of the bleakest, most inspirational lyrics come from country songs. In their essence, they are a narrative of life and there is no one, like a country musician, who can capture the anger, or the violence, of a wronged lover with such clarity and romance. Sophie had been introduced to country music through some of the artists that passed through her office. Country musicians who were almost unknown in the UK, but could fill stadiums in North America.

One particular big client of theirs was a huge country fan and used to say that there was no one as attractive as a country musician who wrote about heartbreak. That country musicians never stayed single long, because they used the emotion of a break up, to write a beautiful song that would make more people fall in love with them, than had ever broken their heart in the past. Sophie had to agree and felt they could also work in the opposite direction and take hold of your emotions in love so much, that you want to leap up and shout 'YES!' Yes to a lyric, or a chord, that uses the right words or the right timing to illustrate perfectly the ebb and flow of the heart. But not tonight. She used the music to drown out the voices in her head and given the wine she had drunk over the evening, it was also trying to stop the nauseous feelings from rising and taking over.

She was in such a zone and the music was so loud, that she didn't hear Smooth come in. It was only when he turned the music down and said something about Sophie not caring about the neighbours, that she realised he was there. She looked up and took him in. He looked terrible and she heard herself say something about being dragged through a hedge backwards, but at the same time, caught a whiff of what seemed to be cigarettes and vomit, and it was too much. She leant forward, meaning to ask where the hell he had been, but as she opened her mouth, all that happened was that she projectile vomited on Smooth's shoes.

'Woah, woah,' slurred Smooth, 'these are suede.'

That was typical. No remorse, just empty concern for a pair of brogues.

'Suede? Suede?' Sophie realised she was shouting. 'I'll give you suede…' she said, but then couldn't think of how to follow that up. She just slumped back on the sofa, back to being exhausted. 'Where have you been?' She realised she was crying, but not with her voice, which was level and reasonable. Just with her eyes, tears of frustration and anger.

'Well,' said Smooth, 'we were having a drink and then, I just lost track of time. It's not my fault, the guys made me do shots and you know I can't do shots.'

Sophie was not sure how to respond to this pathetic excuse. Was she supposed to blame his friends? Was she supposed to forgive him because of his body's inability to process tequila, or whatever shot it was, properly? She took him in for longer now and realised that the state he was in at the performance of *Misunderstood*, where he had been snarky with Miles, was nothing compared to this. He was pale and his eyes, ringed with red, were looking anywhere but at her. His shirt was open nearly to the navel and he smelled strange. He had definitely been smoking and seemed to have some food stains on his jeans. He basically looked like he was just rolling back to a low-end bed and breakfast. The only thing missing was a half-finished cheeseburger, to finish the whole thing off with an elaborate air of onion.

'Where have you been?' She said again. 'We were supposed to be planning our wedding.'

Smooth knelt beside her, careful to avoid the pool of vomit which spread towards the sofa from his shoes. 'I'm so sorry, I'll make it up to you, it was just that one of the guys got into some trouble outside a bar, so I had to help with the police.'

'Outside a bar? I thought you said that you were just having one drink? In one place? Where have you been? I've been trying to call.' She was getting visibly more annoyed now.

This seemed to confuse Smooth and his voice rose an octave. 'Yeah, we were in one place, but then we went to this other place. Sophie, what am I supposed to do, one of the guys was in trouble, I couldn't just leave, that wouldn't have been right. I had to take him home because he couldn't get in a taxi and then I had to get the bus back.'

Sophie couldn't believe what she was hearing. He was obviously lying, but she couldn't figure out why. She hadn't nagged him into not going out, it had been Smooth's choice until recently, to stay in with her, and it was only in the last few days that he had started acting like a petulant schoolboy who wasn't allowed out. His story wasn't adding up and every time she asked again, it had changed, or there was a new piece of information. So far, she had heard that it wasn't his fault because he was rubbish at drinking shots, it wasn't his fault because one of his mates was rubbish at fighting or whatever he was doing, and it wasn't his fault because he had chosen to help out some useless lump, rather than spending New

Year's Eve with his fiancée. She had honestly hoped that there had been some kind of issue, that he had been arrested and had his phone taken off him, or that he had injured himself trying to rush home and ended up in hospital. It was a bit morbid, but at least then, she wouldn't have had to listen to his blaming of everyone apart from himself and his pathetic apology. It would explain why, at no point, had he even chosen to tell her where he was for the whole evening.

If he was unconscious, then at least she would have a proper explanation about the gaps in the evening, instead of feeling like second place to his friends. A few months ago, he was claiming that his work friends were all buffoons, but now, suddenly, they were the life and soul and you could literally get lost in their company for hours. To the extent that you forget to think about or call your fiancée, who is waiting at home and expecting you to be back. It was almost as if coming home now, was worse than not coming home at all, because it showed just how thoughtless and culpable he had been that evening. She would have been less angry if he just took responsibility for his actions, instead of all the wheedling and whining.

'What about your phone, Neil? Why didn't you call?' She deliberately used his real name, because she knew that would annoy him, and stared at him as he rummaged around in his pockets.

'Oh, I must have left it off by accident,' he said as he produced it out of his pocket, 'when I was in the first bar. There was no reception and so I thought I'd save the battery in case I needed it later.'

Sophie grabbed it off him and flipped it open. It was definitely on and there were no missed calls or texts on the screen, so he must have seen that she was trying to get in touch and just ignored it. She could see that his cogs were turning as well and he suddenly leapt up and strode over to the table where the wedding planning set-up he had made was still there, untouched.

'What's the big deal, Sophie? Let's just do it now, what do you think?' He was grinning now, like he had found the answer to time travel. 'Let's just do it now. I think you're overreacting a bit anyway.'

But Sophie wasn't listening. She was looking at Smooth's photos. He insisted on buying the latest camera phone that year and kept banging on about it having a three megapixel camera. It was just another way he was trying to prove that he was 'cutting edge', but to be honest, the photos he took were mainly of cool cars he saw in the street, so held absolutely no interest to Sophie. She didn't even mean to look at the photos, she was just trying to see if her text messages had got through, but she couldn't work out how to unlock the screen to look at his call history.

So what happened next was a total accident and she felt the rising nausea again. The latest photo, although grainy and on a small screen, clearly showed him in a bar and they were sitting down. This went against what Smooth had said about it being a spontaneous meet-up, as they must have had to reserve the table a long time in advance and pay quite a lot for it.

This deceit was bad enough, as was the photo of Smooth with his arm around a gurning guy with a beard on his right, who Sophie vaguely recognised as a work colleague of Smooth's, although the last time they had discussed him Smooth had dismissed him as 'small time', whatever that meant. There was also a third guy she didn't recognise, who had his glass raised to the camera and that is why Sophie noticed what she did. She saw that on the table in front of the guys, apart from the third guy who was giving the cheery salute, was clearly two pints of lager. On the other side of the table, it was impossible to see who the rest of the group was, as only their legs were visible and dissolved into the dark of the bar. But, as clear as the three megapixel camera could manage, in front of these seats at the table, there was clearly two expensive looking, and pink-looking cocktails and one light blue alcopop.

Sophie would probably have been well within her rights to react to that piece of evidence, but at the same time Smooth's phone beeped with a message alert and startled her. But what startled her even more was Smooth's reaction, as he suddenly leapt across the room to grab the phone, so that as she opened the message and leaned in to read it, Smooth's forehead and hers came together, causing him to lose balance, slip in the half-set vomit and end up on his back in the sticky pool. Sophie didn't even need to read the whole thing, just the bits about it being GREAT TO MEET HIM and SORRY HE HAD TO LEAVE, accompanied with kisses, alternated with little 'o' symbols for hugs. Mysteriously, the contact was just listed as 'E'.

'Bell-end,' was all Sophie could manage, as she got up, dropped his phone into her final, half-finished gin and tonic, sashayed over his prone body and slammed the bedroom door behind her.

As an exit, it didn't feel very country, but it was good enough.

Chapter 16

Wrong Foot

January 21, 2007.

'You called him an actual bell-end?' Miles asked. 'A bell-end?' This time he added a hand flourish, as if he was Aristotle, delivering great piece of wisdom.

'Stop saying it, it's gross,' said Sophie, but she was laughing so hard that she could hardly breathe.

It felt like the first time she had laughed since Miles and her had spoken over the phone on New Year's Eve. The weeks that followed had settled into an uneasy truce between her and Smooth, characterised by exhausting discussions and post-mortems about the night itself, then slow and simmering arguments about what it meant to their long-term relationship.

The arguments always started as attempts to clear the air, but Sophie's feelings were so raw that they soon deteriorated from conversations, into petty bickering, and occasionally into full-blown shouting. This was not Sophie's style, her natural tendency would be to go quiet rather than confront the issue aggressively, so these eruptions had caught her as much by surprise, as it caught the unfortunate passers-by or fellow diners in earshot by surprise also. They could happen anywhere, so were as surprising in location as they were in intensity.

On one occasion, she had yelled so suddenly and so loud in a coffee shop, that the waiting staff had to ask them to leave. This was on account of a complaint from the couple sat three tables away, who claimed that her sudden temper had caused their child to, first bite his own tongue with surprise, and then when he irritated it with a salty chip, had used the word "arse", which they maintained he did not have in his vocabulary until Sophie had unwittingly taught it to him through her rage.

For this reason, they had stopped going out as a couple, for fear of triggering a volcano of an argument either in public or with friends. In turn, this made matters worse, as it meant that they stayed almost exclusively in their flat, which could sometimes be described as a pressure cooker, sometimes a depressing fug. They had lost a bit of their connection and Sophie didn't know how to get it back, and in her opinion, Smooth wasn't even trying.

On the other hand, she was really trying to fix their relationship for her own pride's sake and getting nowhere. The problem was that every time she thought back to that night and the abject humiliation she had felt at being left alone whilst Smooth was out partying, she was consumed by such a knot in her stomach and such a mist of confusion and anger, that it made it really hard to look at Smooth in the same light. All the doubts that had been simmering, were now so near the surface that

Smooth had become unattractive and she wasn't sure if she could find him attractive again.

For example, she didn't know if he was always this irritating, or whether it was since he hurt her feelings so badly. So in this sense, she didn't know if she had entered, or was just leaving, a dream. She had always accepted him having this front, this falseness when they were out in bars, but now the front had become the man. Where she once found his skinny jeans attractive, now it made her just wonder if his legs were always that short, although he had taken to rolling them up at the ankles and that might not have helped the effect. She found his conversation was now also littered with abbreviations. Everything was 'totes' this and 'whatevs' that, and more than once she had been shot by his finger-guns. She found herself cringing and wishing he would pull his jeans up so she didn't have to constantly look at his underwear, and wear some socks as his shoes were starting to smell. In short, she felt like she was becoming the mum to a balding teenager.

During their first attempts at talking, he had first stuck to his story of it being a complete surprise that what he thought was a quick drink, was actually a pre-planned party and that someone else must have put E's number in his address book, as a joke. But in the end, and layer by layer, she got nearer the truth and in the end, she managed to cut through to the pain of the facts of the evening and to the feelings beneath. Smooth eventually admitted that the spectre of getting married was looming large and he was struggling with it, especially on big occasions when there was a lot of pressure on the situation. He was certain that she was right for him, he said, but at the same time it felt like they were still so young and had so much of their lives in front of them. So for him, staying in with her on New Year's Eve was an admission that his days of partying and enjoying himself were over.

Initially, Sophie had reacted emotionally to this. She didn't understand why guys seemed to equate getting married to the end of some kind of life. Assuming that Smooth had been faithful to her so far in their relationship, she didn't see what had changed. She didn't want things to change and for them to stop going out, and she certainly didn't think that his relationship status had changed that much really – he was already unavailable. Although, she supposed that for the girl you have many months to get used to it, as you wear a representation, the engagement ring, from the first day of the engagement. But she was proud to wear the ring and didn't care that some guys treated her differently because of it. She was a good catch, if you were going to boil it down to that, so Smooth should actually want to go out more and have her on his arm. She understood how big occasions, like birthdays and New Year's Eve, were moments that forced life into a kind of perspective, or reflective, but for her it was a chance to share the occasion and make a memory that was special to them. Why spend the night with hundreds of strangers? Taking pictures on your phone that you will never look at again.

That was not to say that her understanding stretched beyond her suspicion and she made Smooth promise that nothing had happened, that this was a girl he had met on the night and that the entry was deleted from his phone's memory. Sometimes, she realised that the only way to know if people could be trusted, was to trust them, so she decided to look past it. Also, she rationalised it through the fact that she had been talking to Miles for a large proportion of New Year's Eve, which was also technically spending the evening with the opposite sex, albeit for her it was a friend and someone who was known to Smooth. He had tried, half-heartedly, to get angry about this, until Sophie pointed out that it was his fault in the first place that she talked with Miles. Plus, if he hadn't had been so drunk months ago at the showing of *Misunderstood*, then he would have been able to speak with Miles and know he wasn't a threat to their relationship. She was aware she was going red when she said this, but hoped it passed off as anger.

Sophie was explaining this to Miles over coffee, in neutral territory along the South Bank in London. There had been intense, actual storms that January, as well as Sophie's personal storm, so it wasn't only her that had been confined indoors. It was nice for both of them to feel the breeze off the river and the chill from within the tented terrace of the coffee shop. It was one of those places that used an awning to reserve the pavement for outside seating, so that you felt cosy and almost continental, as you watched the world blur past through the PVC windows. Miles was in good spirits, but an equally reflective mood as he sipped on his thick hot chocolate and traced a finger across the pattern on the vinyl tablecloth. He had so far allowed Sophie to tell her story in almost silence. She had called Miles on New Year's Day, but had been unable to speak coherently through her emotion, apart to say thanks for the previous evening and apologies that, although she was calling as she promised, she didn't want to talk, but would call him soon. Miles had understood this and although he could tell that again there were issues between Smooth and Sophie, he was just pleased that hers was the first voice he heard in 2007.

'It's been difficult,' said Sophie, suddenly serious again. 'You know those days when you start off on the wrong foot and you can't quite get back into the swing of things? Those days when you wish you had a time-machine, to either take you back to the start of the day again, or to fast forward to the next day?'

'Yeah.' Miles knew the feeling well, in fact he had spent most of 2004 and at least the early part of 2005, wishing for a time machine.

'I feel like I've started the year off in the wrong place and I don't know how I make it a good year again.'

Miles knew how she felt, although not this year. He felt great and had a good feeling about 2007. He had done the right thing in Edinburgh and had faced the consequences of his decisions, by calling his New Year date straight after he and Sophie had got off the phone and before it got crazy after midnight. He had just left a voice mail, but with a long and truthful explanation of why he had left and apologised for wasting her time. He added that he thought it was safe to leave her in the bar, given that she looked like she was having a good time, and that he hoped she didn't catch a chill later in the evening. Perhaps she should do another swap of clothes with the chap dressed as a gorilla, seeing as it was hitting minus two outside.

Miles also backed this up with a text and a further voice mail on New Year's Day to make sure, but it was all unanswered. It didn't really matter, as he was pleased that he had been brave enough and not left it hanging over the cusp of the year. Best to start with a fresh slate. It was not until he was passing through York on the train back to London that he got a text response. It was only one word and one opinion of him through her eyes, a word he would never use and didn't think she would ever use either. But it summed up the night and his behaviour well, and also gave the clear impression that matters were closed between them, so there was no need for further correspondence. Like Sophie's recent outbursts with Smooth, he thought, sometimes just one colourful word can speak so many. Miles felt like he deserved it anyway.

'It's a really modern problem, isn't it?' Miles asked, 'I guess that the New Year always makes you think about it.' He meant the trend of texting and flirting on mobiles in secret and paused for a moment, because it was something that he had been thinking about a lot for the past few weeks, but didn't want to touch too delicate a subject. After all, he and Sophie kept in touch on their mobiles and sometimes she flirted with him. A little bit. He looked at Sophie, to try and figure out if she was expecting him to change the subject or lighten the mood. But she just turned her grey eyes to him and Miles thought how well they went with the red beret and scarf, it gave Sophie a kind of Parisian charm.

So he continued. 'Do you remember when you were a kid, if you were out of the house, then pretty much no one could contact you, unless they knew where you were. Then, when you got home, you would check the answer machine and that would let you know that someone wanted to speak to you. My parents used to say that the phone or the doorbell was just a request to talk to you and you didn't have to accept that request. But now, you have to be available, every moment. Similarly, when you were out, you had to make contingency plans for if you got lost shopping, or at a sports game. For my parents, this was usually a particularly boldly painted door of a house, or outside a very tall building or sign that you couldn't miss.'

Sophie smiled and imagined a little Miles, with his backpack on and lost in a park, or having wandered off in a busy street, lost in his own daydreams.

'These days, the scribbled yellow sticky pad replaced the longer note and that has now been replaced by the text message, and mobile phones mean you can plan days and evenings on the fly. It's certainly more convenient, but for me lacks the kind of charm and excitement you got when someone met you at the appointed place, at the appointed time that you might have arranged several weeks earlier. A feeling of wondering if they would turn up and then looking out for them over the heads of a crowd. I used to love doing that in Covent Garden, watching everyone stream out of the entrance and searching for that familiar face. It has a kind of old-fashioned romance to it.'

'True, true,' said Sophie. 'Mind you, if it wasn't for mobiles and the Internet, then I wouldn't have been able to help you escape from that sticky situation you were in and take a tour with you around Edinburgh for a hotel.'

Her eyes were twinkling and reminded Miles of another resolution he had made. He believed that the world was getting more and more chaotic and difficult to understand. The world was becoming as stormy as the weather that January, with people being blown in all directions with temptations and information; relationships were coming under increasing pressure as it had become easier to cheat and easier to keep secrets. You could now get in touch with people from your past, easily and using nothing more than a keyboard. Mobile phones meant you could keep in touch with anyone in secret, you didn't have to organise clandestine phone calls at phone boxes, or when your partner was out. Perhaps his and Sophie's relationship trod a line, but through it all, he loved her and he wanted to say he believed in love. He was worried for Sophie and resolved he was going to be there for her, no matter what his feelings and what kind of love he felt.

If he was the friend that he said he was, then he should definitely give her some strong advice, which came from his own experience of life. He knew what it felt like to take things too far and to mistake love for loyalty. Whether it's after one night in Edinburgh, or after several years, you have to make sure you acknowledge your mistakes and not ignore them. As long as you know you gave it your all, then knowing when to walk away is just part of the story of life. He had a sense this was not going to end well between Sophie and Smooth, and his resolution was to say something, to give her that advice and risk whatever it meant. For the first time since they met, the balance was shifting in their relationship and Sophie now needed him as much as he needed her. It might even shift further, especially if he was right.

That was the resolution. But, instead he just said, 'What are you going to do?'

'I honestly don't know,' said Sophie and she really didn't. She had to give Smooth another chance, she was too loyal to just take one occasion and let go of all their history. She remembered Miles' story from when they first met and she was aware how bitter things could become. But at least her and Smooth were now talking and she really thought it had been productive. She had to admit that she was concerned at first that it was all lies, but Smooth had slowly opened up and to be fair, it was the first time in their relationship that he had talked so openly about his feelings.

She knew that Miles would be thinking about his own experiences and knew that he was trying to give her signals that he would be willing to talk about it, that she just had to give the hint, and she knew the advice he would give. But because she understood that, he didn't need to say it and she didn't want to hear it, she knew he would be there for her if it went sideways and that was all she needed to know.

As far as ignoring the signals, she was probably just as guilty in that respect as well. For months, she wanted to speak to Smooth about feeling second best and that his desperation to change his life had made her feel like she had shifted from the centre of his life, where she believed your partner belonged, to the edges. She hoped that the shock of New Year, and also the fact that he seemed to be happier in his current life and work, would mean that she never had to have this specific discussion. But if she did, then she was ready. She felt that he had been honest with her and that he had learned his lesson, with true regret about how he had behaved. Besides, when someone asks you to spend the rest of their life with them, it can't all be undone by one night, one mistake, especially when nothing had happened, as Smooth had assured her. So she needed to stand by him and keep trying to move past the occasion, so they could regain the connection.

She thought perhaps she would plan something for Valentine's Day, as a surprise perhaps. It was something that would give them a change of scenery and away from the flat, which was just a constant reminder of their arguments, and still faintly smelled of vomit. They could forget about London and the stress of the wedding for a few days. She could do with the change of mind from the wedding as well, away from reminders of napkin colour schemes, or the dizzying array of personalised favours or methods of transport from church to reception. There was even new trends in sharing original things in video format from your wedding, which had been started the previous summer by an American couple, who performed a parody and choreographed first dance to Afrika Bombaataa and posted it on YouTube. So now, even that was entering the template and expectations of a wedding day.

No, they should get away. In February, places like Budapest or Prague were supposed to be magical. Gothic buildings rising from a river mist, grey stone standing against the white sky. Sophie resolved to do something and to keep it secret from Smooth, and Miles for that matter. It would be theirs and a wonderful surprise that would get the year back on track.

She didn't know how to explain this to Miles anyway, she had given him so many mixed messages recently that it was best that she just stayed vague. So she just said it again, 'I honestly don't know.'

Miles sensed a chance to lighten the mood again and happy not to hear out loud that Sophie wasn't breaking up with Smooth.

'So, it's too early to ask you out on a date then?' He asked.

Sophie laughed again and despite the fact that Miles was probably serious, it was the nicest thing anyone had said to her in the two long weeks since New Year.

'Not yet, I'm afraid,' and she looked through her fringe at Miles. 'But you can add me as a friend me on Facebook if you like?'

Chapter 17

Like

January 31, 2007.

Every year, Tim closed the bar from the end of Boxing Day, until the last day of January. It was his principles, he said.

He was open until the end of Boxing Day, because he liked to see families together on that day, traditionally one where you took your grandparents or parents out for lunch. He even had special deals – if you brought three generations to the pub on Boxing Day, then the oldest person drank for free. Or, if your group contained the oldest person in the pub, then the whole family drank for free and could also have unlimited crisps, with a maximum of one bag per round. Miles had pointed out that encouraging old people to drink and eat crisps was perhaps not a smart marketing technique, but Tim insisted that he did more good than harm. At that age, you knew how to regulate your intake, so actually, although it looked ostentatious as a deal, it was usually only one or two drinks that went for free per group. Unless you got a group of the Irish in, he said.

Then he was closed in January, because he didn't like taking people's Christmas money. He believed that your Christmas money should be spent frivolously, but not on a night out in a pub. If you wanted alcohol, you should go down to your local wine merchants and get a bottle of wine that you would never normally buy. Go and get a Chateauneuf Du Pape, he said, and drink it in front of a black and white movie.

He also recognised, that outside of Christmas money, for those general folk earning a regular pay cheque, in January you didn't need temptations like the pub. He had been strapped for cash before and he knew it was all about survival. It was also naturally quiet and so a good month to take off and Tim would often head to the wide beaches of India's West Coast, or Thailand's white coves for the month. It didn't matter to him that the rest of London capitalised on New Year's Eve, he much preferred to allow his staff to get drunk instead, but not in his establishment. If pushed, he also said that he couldn't stand strangers hugging to Auld Lang Syne. It was a beautiful song of remembrance, not an excuse to paw the person next to you. He was full of baffling, yet outstanding excuses. He would stay around until the turn of the year, but then he was gone until the end of the month.

On January 31, he always opened with a bang and an almighty party – pay day. He said that the last day of January was his New Year's Eve. He had spent his younger days, scraping together pennies through January, trying to get enough to pay for petrol to get across town in California for a casting, or a script read.

Then, on the last day of the month, he would get his pay-cheque from whatever regular job he was using to try and pay the bills. He would hit the beach during the day and then head to the Venice Boardwalk for sundown. He always had a Pilsner as his first drink and he always made sure he had an outside seat, so he could catch it when stall owners mixed with office workers on their way home, with bums and with ordinary folk, playing sports or using the boardwalk to run and roller-skate.

For Miles, it was also his first day back at work and Tim had embraced him warmly when he arrived at the bar. It seemed that Tim was in as good a mood as Miles and the familiar smell of the bar was making Miles excited for the evening ahead. He could feel that both of them had some energy they needed to expend, so they would be entertainment for the customers. Tim even looked like he had put on a clean t-shirt for the occasion, although there were what looked like moth holes in the front, or perhaps they were part of the design, it was hard to tell. It was probably the former, given that the t-shirt was adorned with a huge acid-house smiley design and was so out of fashion that it was probably coming back in again.

Miles was also feeling good about how Sophie and him had left each other, when they saw each other a few weeks earlier and had filled Tim in, on the full story from New Year onwards; to much thigh-slapping and head-clutching from Tim, but all good natured. He needed that validation from Tim, because he was feeling good about how he and Sophie were with each other, he felt more in control. When you are in love with someone like that, you always focus on how things are left when you say goodbye. Miles had spent so many days after he and Sophie had been together and parted company, cursing the fact he had pushed things too far, or that he had overcompensated in some way. But his performance over hot chocolate and then the following weeks, had been less desperate and on a more equal footing. He didn't even find himself texting her, to explain something he had said that he was afraid she might have taken out of context, or adding an additional thought to a discussion that hadn't occurred to him until the way home. Post-rationalisation, he called it, and he had to do it as it burned a hole in his head and his heart if he didn't act on it. He didn't know what she called it and tried not to think about that.

He and Tim were also talking about the small things. Tim had spent a good part of January in Goa, spending his time between the beach and in the beach shacks, drinking Kingfisher Lager until the cool sea breeze took him to bed, to fall asleep to the rhythmic sound of the ocean waves, and to start again the next day. The only company was the egrets, he said, and the occasional passing tourist who spoke English. But with his naturally scruffy appearance, deep tan and grumpy disposition, he found that he tended to be left alone and that just suited him fine.

During his time there, he had some further thoughts on *Misunderstood* and Miles agreed that he was excited to get back into it again, now they'd had the chance to step away for a few weeks. Tim had also met a video game designer in India. A guy who worked out of Los Angeles, but like Tim, spent some of the winter months relaxing on the beach. Tim explained that the guy had introduced himself as Guillaume, but he never knew if that was his real name. There was apparently a strange parallel between his glamorous Californian business and the South London pub business, in the sense that January was also a bit of a quiet month for the creative industries in the US, so a good chance to recharge their batteries and become anonymous for a while.

They had only had one night together, over fried fish on the beach, but Tim said that he was interested in helping them with their stage set-up and direction, to perhaps bring in some tricks that they used in movies and video games and give it an old-school animation feel. He was thinking along the lines of the Solomon Grundy character in the DC Comics issues of Green Lantern in the 1940s – beautiful but dark. Miles had enthusiastically agreed, and also couldn't wait to get working on the sequel either. He wondered out loud to Tim if they could use this style from the start in the sequel.

Predictably, the theme for the party that night at the pub was zombies and evil kittens and they were really pleased with the turn-out. They had only put up a few posters and mentioned it on some of the forums that they used for *Misunderstood*, but word had spread quickly and some people had made a real effort. They were also very pleased to see some familiar faces from the shows they had put on, and they knew that these guys were also responsible for helping with the promotion of the night and the size of the attendance levels. They always looked after their own and Miles and Tim had already agreed that the community was always to be drinking doubles for the price of singles and that they had a round of shots with every round of drinks they bought. Tim had even bought a few additional cases of Aftershock Red for the occasion, to give the shots a gory air. There was something about being liberal with shots early, that started a party like nothing else could, as well as the Aftershock giving the atmosphere in the bar a slightly cinnamon edge. From where he was standing he could see at least four groups going through the ritual; a sniff, a pulled face, a tipped glass, and a further pulled face, accompanied by groaning at the sting and the taste. But they always had another round.

About ten o'clock, the party had reached its peak and Tim came over and shouted something in Miles' ear, something that he never thought he would hear. So much so, that he had to ask Tim to repeat it several times. The first few because he thought he had misheard and then after that, just for dramatic comedy effect.

'I said,' shouted Tim, his forehead resting on Miles' temple as he tried to be heard over the DJ and the overall din of the bar, that was close to capacity, 'the DJ finishes at eleven o'clock, but I'm staying open until one o'clock, so I'll let you deal with the jukebox.'

This was big news and Tim pretended not to notice, but he could see the surprise and glee on Miles' face. To Miles' knowledge, no one's choices had ever played on the jukebox except Tim's, due to his diligent ritual every morning to feed it with enough coins to ensure that it only played the 1990s indie hits that Tim considered as safe pub music. A ritual that Miles, himself, had witnessed the first time he had come into the bar for his interview. Tim considered the giving of control of the jukebox away, as a pass for the staff and customers to either sully the bar with pop music, or worse, easy listening or anything that pre-dated Oasis. Of course, this meant that the first choice that Miles selected on the jukebox had to be a special one. It had to be something that would capture the attention of the party, but also annoy Tim just enough to get a reaction – which was actually going to have to be quite a lot, as he knew that Tim would try and keep his cool as much as possible.

It was such a responsibility, that Miles also didn't feel like he could take it alone. So every time one of the most hard core of the zombie-fans came to the bar, Miles would make sure that he casually dropped it into discussion for ideas. Everyone knew how uptight Tim was about the bar and the music, so soon there was a buzz around the place about what the first song might be, and more importantly what Tim's reaction might be. Generally, the most they had seen from him was a disappointed shake of the head. For example, if the DJ he had hired for the evening tried to spice things up with 2Unlimited, or calm things down with a ballad from Rod Stewart. Usually this also meant that Miles should quietly take them off the roster of DJs for future events.

But this was uncharted territory and Miles had been through so many options in his head. Some of the guys had suggested Auld Lang Syne, for the sake of this being a celebration of the first night of 2007 in the pub. There had been a lot of requests for the live version of Meatloaf's Bat Out of Hell, because it was the longest song anyone could think of, at just over ten minutes and also, at the opposite end of the musical spectrum, Don McLean's American Pie, for the same reason. They knew that Tim wouldn't have the nerve to turn down the volume, because then it would show that he cared and Tim liked to give the air that he wasn't bothered, especially when he was.

Finally, Miles had decided. Although it was probably one of the most obvious songs for an occasion such as they had, it could not be more perfect and ticked almost every box of inappropriateness that he could project from Tim. It had enough cheese, enough dated quality and enough contrast to Tim's usual musical tastes to be a fitting tribute, which meant that it was the opposite of a tribute to Tim. He would love it and hate it. In equal measures, or perhaps slightly more hatred, thought Miles, as he waited for a quiet moment in the bar. Having chosen his moment, he turned the volume as high as he could and dropped his money into the machine. He punched the selection number for Michael Jackson's Thriller.

The bar had been waiting for this moment and there's something about a mix of around 200 zombies and evil kittens, jacked up on Aftershock in a warm London bar, going crazy to a song that is a sight that could never be boring. The usual gender boundaries that you would expect from the theme hadn't really been adhered to and so, you had big, hairy kittens as well as demure and glamorous zombies. But that kind of crowd, spontaneously breaking into a unison dance and having the time of their lives to Thriller, takes it to another level of legendary. Of course, for many it is the zombie anthem and could be seen as a bit predictable, but for Miles he was lucky that there had been enough strong alcohol and that the jukebox carried the full 13 minute music video version to play to the cult crowd. Indeed, many of the zombies could recognise the song from the heavy breathing at the start and the sound of crickets, to the low hum of a car engine, before the song even started.

It was Tim's reaction that was the most legendary. His face twitched, there was a slight shoulder slump and he gently placed the glass down, that he was drying with a tea towel. Apart from that, there was no visible surprise. It was almost as if he had expected this to be the song choice, something he would later claim and always stand by. He then calmly walked the full length of the bar – taking his time as he realised there were eyes on him. He took a bottle of Aftershock off the shelf, took a clean shot glass, filled it to the brim and having his first ever drink under the roof of his pub, elaborately downed it. He then walked back the full length of the bar, to where Miles was sheepishly standing and filled two more glasses. Miles and Tim saluted the bar and downed these as well. It was pure theatre and the whole place erupted. Tim closed the curtains and lined up the rest of the bottles of Aftershock on the bar and that night they drank every one, with the place remaining at capacity until the small hours, when lines of zombies and kittens respectfully filed out into the London night, to give some of the local take-aways the shock of their lives.

Tim shut the bolt of the pub, and they both slumped into one of the sofas and surveyed the bar around them. They both had the slight ringing in their ears that comes from sudden quiet following a sustained cacophony, but both of them were smiling and Tim had brought over a bottle of Grey Goose, of course straight from the freezer and in an ice bucket.

It was Miles who broke the silence. 'Why did you let me pick the song?' He asked.

Tim paused. 'Because sometimes, the small things are the big things,' he responded, 'and I knew you would make a good choice.'

Miles gave Tim an affectionate squeeze of the shoulder.

'I thought you would invite Sophie along tonight, seemed like a perfect evening for it?'

'Yeah,' said Miles, 'I did think about it, but she has her own stuff going on at the moment. Anyway, we're still talking a lot and I've registered for Facebook, so we're friends on that as well.'

'What now?' Tim raised a quizzical eyebrow. 'Are you social networking? Whatever next?' But he was smiling; although Miles was surprised that he had even heard of it. Miles himself had only found out through Sophie and had generated quite a few friends in the short time he had been registered. It was fun seeing what old and new friends were doing. There were friends that he had not seen for years, perhaps since primary school, and he was now able to see their lives, their families, and was shocked that some of them had teenage sons and daughters.

This access to their lives was something that was so stark in its simplicity, but at the same time such a leap forward, that sometimes Miles found himself spending hours looking up old friends and trying to find people that he hadn't heard from for a long time. He would start with a connection he had made and then work methodically through their connections and friends of friends. Suddenly, they would be there, smiling out of their profile picture, with an explanation of their job, their relationship status and a running commentary of their social lives. Someone he had not seen for decades, but in a few clicks, he could see where they were now living and back-fill their lives and loves.

He explained this to Tim, that when you talked about small things, Facebook had given you access to experience these online. The feeling when someone accepted a friend request, or you saw some new pictures from friends having fun – it gave you a lift in life and made you feel good. Sure, everyone always seemed to look happy, but he explained that he could imagine people, miles from friends and family, or alone in a flat and feeling down, could now express that on Facebook. If they changed their status to suggest they were sad, or that they were awake in the night, then their friends could immediately see this. Imagine, that you woke up in the night with a fear, you could change your status and immediately alert friends to your situation, and if they were also awake they could rally round and send you positive messages.

It also had the added bonus that, whenever he was feeling like he was missing Sophie, he could log onto her page and look at her profile picture, one that he had taken of her smiling over a hot chocolate. It was also a way he could check how she was doing. If he sensed that she needed a bit of a lift, he always made sure he dropped her a funny message, or send a link to a video that he thought would make her smile. It was usually cats, or more specifically kittens, but Sophie would always respond and in turn it would make him feel good, and feel connected to Sophie.

'So basically, you use it to stalk people?' Tim was enjoying this.

'Absolutely, one hundred per cent, yes, and with the other person being blissfully unaware. The perfect crime,' smiled Miles, allowing Tim his moment of revenge from the Thriller episode earlier that evening.

'You'll never find me getting involved in all that nonsense.' Tim poured another glass of vodka, clinking Miles' glass as he settled further back into the sofa and closed his eyes.

He had absolutely no idea how gloriously those words would come back to haunt him.

Chapter 18

Slam

February 14, 2007.

When Sophie got back from town and as she stood there in the doorway of their flat, the first thought she had was that everything was in place, apart from Smooth, who was definitely not where he was supposed to be.

She had managed to arrange their surprise Valentine's weekend without Smooth's knowledge and she had left him in bed that morning, to finalise the last items of shopping. Smooth knew that something was planned for Valentine's Day, but he had no idea that it included a trip to an airport and three nights exploring Prague and the Czech Republic.

She had chosen Prague because of the number of times it had appeared in the previous year's James Bond movie release, coupled with the number of times that she had been made to watch that movie by Smooth. He was full of useless facts about the city and the buildings, particularly, that Prague had been used a number of times in the filming to represent places as diverse as

Venice and Miami. He insisted on pointing these out in an academic fashion, even though she had no interest and had already committed them to heart by the fourth or fifth time. Ironically, these 'little-known' facts had taken her less than half an hour to comprehensively catalogue on the Internet and she had planned a walking and bus tour of the various exteriors and interiors.

It also included a trip outside of Prague to Karlovy Vary and a stay in the Grandhotel Pupp, another Bond landmark, which Sophie had originally thought was just an amusingly named hotel, until she saw photographs and instantly fell in love. The building and the town surrounding it, epitomised everything she imagined about the romance and splendour of the Czech Republic. The trip, and especially the Grandhotel Pupp, had made a small dent in the wedding fund, but for Sophie this felt like a last chance and she had put all of her energy into making sure the weekend was perfect. She was just not prepared to give up and this trip would give them the best chance of proving to each other that they could move past the arguments of the last two months. Although he would have to play his part as well and show her some form of effort and attention. She felt she deserved that.

Smooth had been given strict instructions to take the day off work and she had left breakfast out for him in the flat. She left him snoozing and let him know to lie in for as long as he wanted, but for when he came round, there was fresh coffee from Harrods to prepare as a special treat. She had also warmed up some part-baked croissants before she left, so that the sweet pastry smell would lure him out of bed to the luxury of posh coffee and fresh baked goods. This was bound to start the holiday in the right way. She had also left a note next to the coffee, telling him to pack enough warm clothes for four days, including a nice shirt, and also to make sure he had his passport, because they were going to Prague! With a smiley face, so it didn't appear too demanding or bossy.

Her second thought when she got back from town was that everything was in its place and that included the croissants, which remained untouched on the kitchen worktop where she had left them. Plus, the packet of coffee was unopened and lay next to the unopened envelope with their plans for the weekend. Sophie figured he must still be in bed and she tried to suppress a tug of annoyance, because it left them a bit tight on time for the airport. Then she quickly checked herself; he wasn't to know what was planned, so although it was a little selfish that he decided to stay in bed, nothing was going to ruin this weekend. She had worked so hard on it and of course, needed it to be perfect.

But there was also something else wrong that she couldn't put her finger on. The flat just seemed a bit… emptier than it should. A bit more quiet, with a hollow feel as she came in. It was one of those London flats that had been renovated from a town house and had an open plan kitchen and living area. So from where she was standing, she could see over the breakfast bar into the lounge and dining area, and that's when she realised. The TV was missing, plus one of the two-seater sofas from the open plan living area.

She wasn't sure how long she stood there, her mind whirring and trying to process the information, and rationalise the situation as a burglary. A burglary and Smooth had slept through the whole thing. Plus, a robbery where the burglars were not fans of French breakfast cuisine. She rationalised that Smooth would be in the bedroom, oblivious to what had happened in the living area. It now seemed silly to be annoyed that he had slept in, as at least he had not disturbed the burglars. It might delay them a little bit in getting to the airport, but at least he wasn't hurt. What they could do is just tell the police when they were in the taxi and then sort it out properly when they got back. They would tell the police that they had to go away on holiday and perhaps leave them a key under the mat, so they could carry out the necessary detective work and have it ready for them to review when they got back. It wasn't as if they could help in any way, the burglars must have been experts. They had waited for the right moment and seen her head into town – perhaps even tailing her to make sure she was away for a while. They had then managed to get out the flat with furniture, without any signs of forced entry and without waking the unwitting, sleeping Smooth just yards away.

She rationalised this scenario because she didn't want to face the more likely scenario that had started nagging behind her ears, but was now blaring like trumpets. Smooth had gone and he hadn't even said goodbye.

Just like that, with that one thought, the panic set in, like a bubble bursting. The panic was like it was on New Year's Eve, but this time it was a blind rush rather than a gradual crescendo over several hours. She started to charge from room to room, looking for signs that she was wrong and that it was all a bad dream. She tore at the duvets, as if he would be hiding underneath them after all, threw open the wardrobes and the drawers, looking for his clothes, but they had all gone. All that was left in the wardrobe was empty hangers and in the

225

drawers bare chipboard, and the sad and colourful fanfare of flowery drawer liners.

He had done a good job of it as well, there was barely a trace of him. It was even as if his smell had also checked out. He must have done it all in one go and hadn't left any boxes behind, the whole thing was like a military operation. One lamp had gone from his side of the bed, the bedding had gone from the spare room, there was just enough ring-marked spaces in the cupboard where they kept drinking glasses, to say that he had planned it and tried to apply some kind of fairness to what he took. If she thought that she had made an effort planning their escape to Prague for the weekend, then he had planned his escape from their life together with equal aplomb.

Sophie collapsed into the sofa, staring at the space where the TV used to be. He had taken the TV and it wasn't even a good one. In the time when TV sets were getting slimmer and flatter, they had doggedly clung onto their old bulky cathode ray. They would reward themselves with a flat-screen once they were married, they had said. They had talked about that just the other day, when he must have known he was going to do this. She had been a bit preoccupied with the Valentine's weekend, but she hadn't noticed any distractions for Smooth. He had just moped around in the evenings as normal. So when had he decided this? Had he been planning it for months and been making a fool out of her for all that time? Thinking they could get away from the flat for a few days and fix everything. Then another wave hit her – the trip to Prague. She glanced at the clock on the wall, but there was just a space where it used to be. He had taken the wall clock.

Perhaps she could just go on her own, she thought, just enjoy herself in the beautiful city. They had separate tickets, so she could do it and use the weekend to forget about what was happening. She could wander the cobbled streets, take in the waterfront and get up early for Charles Bridge to avoid the tourists on the way up to the castle. She could take lots of pictures of the Bond locations and post them on Facebook so that Smooth could see what he was missing, and maybe even be jealous of her having a good time. But then, would there not be shadows in every square and Smooth's face in every gargoyle? It might ruin Prague for her for life and she definitely wanted to go someday.

A check of her phone made her realise there was no time now, even to get to the airport, the plane was due to take off in fifteen minutes. Which had meant she had spent the last hour turning the flat upside down. Or had she? It didn't seem that long. She must have remained frozen at the front door for a long time. Or maybe she had been sitting on the sofa for a long time. She couldn't think straight and felt like history was repeating itself. Here she was again, on the sofa, trying to figure out where Smooth was and what he was doing. Last time, she had called him and texted him, but this time she didn't have the energy. Sophie went straight to the other, darker place from that particular evening, and although it was only ten o'clock in the morning, she headed back to the kitchen and made herself a gin and tonic, and then another. One after the other, she drank them wide-eyed and staring at the wall, with no idea what to do or what her next move should be.

She didn't know how many drinks she had before she started calling people. It was definitely getting dark outside now, and she definitely wasn't feeling very well.

But the shock of the day had given her stamina for gin that she didn't realise she had. At some point, she must have gone out for more, because as she opened the second bottle, she vaguely remembered them only having one in the cupboard that morning, and that Smooth had taken the vodka.

She started with calling her close friends, but given it was late afternoon, no-one was answering. They were not expecting her call, they all thought that she was in Prague and that it wasn't an emergency. Likewise, her work colleagues were not answering. She remembered there were important clients in her offices that day, so everyone must have still been in meetings or been entertaining. One person after another, and nothing. It was probably for the best, as apart from mumbling vaguely at the wall, she had not practised, nor had any idea, what to say.

Dejected, she stared at the half finished bottle of gin in her hand and felt a sudden wave of sadness. She felt so alone and the stab of sorrow was so intense that the sound of herself sobbing caught her by surprise. She suddenly had the desire to call Smooth, she suddenly felt an anger and a need for instant explanation. What had she done? She had been so understanding, had tried so hard. He didn't know about the trip, but he knew there was something going on. He knew it was important to her and she had been excited for them – teasing Smooth about it and occasionally making clumsy James Bond references as clues. So he knew he was due a surprise and that she was doing it for him, wasn't that important?

Her hand hovered over the dial, but then she gathered herself, she was not going to give him the satisfaction. Instead, she poured enough gin into her glass, so that the clear liquid was just millimetres off the brim, took a deep breath and drank it all in one go.

It felt good, so she snapped the seal on another bottle, and did it again.

Chapter 19

Awakening

February 14, 2007.

The next thing Sophie remembered, was a vague but persistent knocking on the inside of her skull, which wouldn't stop and just got louder and louder. It started as a dull thud and was almost a part of her dreams, which were as dark as they were colourful. In her dream, she was balanced on a ledge, in an enormous room. She could see nothing but darkness below, but the vertigo was making her knees weak and making the room spin. The thud seemed to be coming from below, but was getting nearer and nearer out of the darkness, coming up to meet her. She didn't want it to get to her, in case it knocked her off her ledge and she became consumed by the darkness. She pulled a cushion over her head to drown it out, but it just kept getting louder and louder. Eventually there was a crescendo to the sound, a different kind of knocking, more final and with a splintering, as if the knocking had broken through something, the final barrier before it got to her. There was a pause and she was suddenly brought out of the dream by hands on her, strong hands and a familiar smell of wool and after-shave.

'Dad?' She said unconsciously. 'Dad, is that you? What are you doing here?'

The voice swore and this time it sounded like her dad, but she felt so light-headed and she had also never heard her dad swear – he never swore.

'Potty mouth,' she said, and broke into a fit of giggles.

She felt like she was moving, but again it was like she was split in two. She could feel herself moving, but at the same time felt like she was watching herself from the sofa, as if her mind was lagging behind her eyes. Sophie tried to open her eyes, but her eyelids were so heavy and were not under her control. Now she was trying to run away from something, but her legs felt like lead, and although she wanted to open her eyes and see where she was going, she couldn't. She tried to use her legs, but they also wouldn't do what she was telling them to and she realised that she was also telling them out loud.

'Left, right, left, right,' she heard herself saying and that made her collapse into another fit of giggles.

Slowly, she felt the fantasy fade and was brought round by more familiar smells. The leather of a car seat and then Sophie felt a duvet being drawn up around her, that smelled of her parents' house, her parents' washing powder with a hint of wood-smoke. She tugged it around her chin, happy to feel the familiar, and felt herself relaxing and the world swirling, swirling into a deep plughole. She would occasionally feel movement and more than once, felt like she was being lifted up. She was sure it was her dad now and each time, she buried her face into the coarse warmth of his jumper, not knowing whether to sob with sadness, or relief. If she was with her family then she was safe and everything was going to be OK, even though it wasn't and she couldn't remember why.

She wasn't sure how long had passed, but when she woke up, she was aware that it was light outside and that the light was like needles in her eyes, so she shut them again. She was also aware that her mouth tasted of vomit and gin, and that there was also a vague smell of bleach in the air.

Her thoughts were so muddled, that at first she thought it was Christmas. Usually, there was one night every Christmas, that she would wake up in her bed at her parents' house, unsure how she got there. On those occasions, it would have been after a night catching up with old friends in the local pub and it was only the hit of fresh air at the end of the night that gave her that memory loss. On those occasions, she would be woken by the drifting smell of bacon and would head downstairs in her pyjamas and watch some rubbish TV. But the thought of bacon this time made her stomach turn and gave her the first sense that it definitely wasn't Christmas; it wasn't one of those occasions. There was a deep rooted sense of doom and depression in the pit of her stomach that told her it was something more serious, but she needed a few more minutes to figure out what it was. She groaned and rolled over, which seemed to trigger a flurry of movement in the room

'She's awake,' this time it was definitely her dad, and she opened her eyes to see him leaning over her, with a concerned look on his face and a flannel in his hand.

'Hi Dad,' she said, 'what's with the flannel?'

Her mum came into the room at almost a gallop, with the same concerned expression, then took one look at Sophie and burst into tears. Her dad then also collapsed, with great sobs and the three of them fell together into an embrace on Sophie's bed, as the pieces also started to fall together in Sophie's mind. She couldn't think of anything to say to express how grateful she was, so said the next thing that came into her head.

'Dad, did you kick my door in?'

It had turned out, that was exactly what had happened. Sophie had called them during the early evening the previous day and had been making no sense. At first, he had been angry and just thought she had been on a boozy lunch with work and had dialled them by accident. But he soon realised that what he heard was not some kind of drunk ramblings, heard through a coat pocket, but an actual attempt by Sophie to talk to him. He had started asking her questions, trying to work out what was going on and where Smooth was, but the questions just seemed to make her more confused, and each time he mentioned Smooth, she started repeating the same word over and over again, slurred but unmistakable: 'bastard, bastard, bastard'. He had tried to give her a verbal slap in the face and get some sense out of her, but it was getting worse and he was starting to get very concerned, until she seemed to drift in and out of even knowing who she was speaking to. In the end, she had hung up. He had tried to call her back, but got no answer. He knew that Sophie could look after herself, but something this time had been different, something had felt wrong.

He tried another few times to reach her and cursed that he didn't have the landline number, or Smooth's number. He had accepted that Smooth and Sophie were going to be together, but had not asked for his number, he had no desire to share conversations with the boy unless it was in a family situation. Sophie was his only daughter and he hadn't even asked his permission to marry her. He found he couldn't sit still and couldn't concentrate, so made a snap decision and made the trip to the city. A cry for help was a cry for help, he thought. He had been relieved to see that her car was outside the apartment complex, which at least made him think she was in the flat. But when there was no answer and he smelled the faint aroma of cooking on the landing he panicked. Perhaps she had cooked something and left the gas on? Or perhaps the boiler was pumping out carbon monoxide and had sent her into unconsciousness, like he had seen on all those dodgy landlord shows. So after a while, he gave up knocking and took a more dramatic route and put his shoulder to the door. On his second try, he knocked the door off its hinges. It actually felt pretty good, but that mild euphoria went away with the scene that met him.

Sophie was sprawled on the sofa, it was only five o'clock in the evening and she had, what looked like, four empty bottles of gin at her feet. The room smelled of alcohol and croissants, but mainly alcohol. He tried to wake her, but it seemed that she was unconscious. In fact, he had never seen her in this state before. Watching Sophie grow up he had always been a relaxed parent and had always understood that she liked a party; but he also knew that she was a sensible girl and would never take things too far. He remembered her once, stealing a traffic cone at university, having been pressured into it during Fresher's Week. The next day, she had repeatedly called home, terrified that the police were going to be after her, that there must have been some CCTV and right at that moment the net was closing in. She had got herself into such a state, that in the end she stayed up late the next night and replaced the cone under the cover of darkness, in the exact place she had stolen it. So it was not like her to go this far, not like her to go over the edge.

But he couldn't figure out what had happened. He took a look around the flat, which basically looked ransacked, to see if there was any sign of Smooth. He couldn't and given that it was Valentine's Day he couldn't work out where he might be and what they were up to. His wife, Sophie's mum, had hinted that Sophie had some big surprise planned, but he was sure getting drunk on her own was not it.

It was on his second sweep of the flat that he found Sophie's note and read it with a sinking feeling. They were not in Prague, that was for sure, and that made his heart ache for Sophie. This was not looking good, but even if things were not exactly as he was starting to think, he would certainly be having some words with that boy.

He went back to the bedroom, to try and look for more signs and it was then that he spotted a second letter, that was almost hidden under mounds of duvets on the bedroom floor. It looked like the duvets had been wrestled off the bed at some point and the letter must have got tangled up in the bedding. This one was also sealed, so he didn't think that Sophie had seen it. He didn't want to, but he felt that to get the full picture he needed to open and read the note, even though it was a breach of Sophie's privacy. He had to do it – there were two unopened letters, a drunk Sophie and no sign of Smooth. So he needed to know what was going on.

He hesitated for a beat and then slit the envelope open, there was no need to try and do it secretly given the predicament and as he read it, he was happy that he had and his sadness turned into anger. The contents confirmed what a coward Smooth was and explained why he didn't have the courage to ask for his daughter's hand in marriage. He clearly had no moral fibre and although it was not enjoyable, he was sure this would be best for his daughter. Now he actually regretted not knowing Smooth's number, or his whereabouts for that matter, but this was not the time. All that was left was to gently lift Sophie to the car, call the landlord's number from a list of contacts in the communal hallway to explain the shattered door hinges, and head back to their family home. The best place for Sophie was at home, although he didn't know how to talk to her when she woke up.

Sophie listened to this trail of events in silence and with wide eyes, she felt so sick that it couldn't really affect her any more. So there had been another letter, but in her panic and haste she must have missed it. She needed to see it, even if she could guess from her parents' expressions what it was. Her dad looked grey and had clearly had no sleep the previous night. The chair in the corner of her room had pillows and a blanket next to it, he must have spent the whole night with her, making sure she was OK. The bleach smell must have also meant that things had got nasty, but there was no sign of vomit on her clothes, in her hair or in the bed, so they must have taken care of that as well. At that moment, as well as the dread she felt, she could not have loved her parents more.

With a concerned glance to Sophie's mother, her dad reluctantly handed over the letter and Sophie's mum just squeezed her hand harder. She read it noiselessly and then read it again. Her parents were looking at her, trying to anticipate what was going to happen next, poised and braced for Sophie's reaction. But she just smiled, the weary smile of someone who had given everything, but was not surprised at the final outcome.

At least she knew now. The mysterious 'E' stood for Emily.

Chapter 20

Viral

.

February 24, 2007.

Cause and effect is what drives life. Cause and effect, decisions and implications. It is a metronome in the background, moving us forwards and backwards, sometimes sideways. We wrap it up as chance, or fate, but in the end, chance and fate are just sequences of events, perhaps the most wonderful or devastating sequences of all. What if I stayed at home that day? What if I had chosen to do something different in that moment? Would it all be different? A small nudge on a particular morning, the butterfly flaps its wings in a different direction and someone else gets the hurricane.

Tim was standing behind Miles, as Miles navigated the Internet on Tim's ancient laptop. They were in the upstairs rooms of the pub, which were loosely known as Tim's accommodation, although he only seemed to live in half of the available space.

The pub took up the ground floor of the building and the upper two floors were sold with the building as living space. It included a generous three bedrooms, with the typical high ceilings and dark-stained oak floors that you would expect from that part of London. They were rooms that were expected to echo with the footsteps of the landlord's family, the scratching and thumping of the family cat or the pub dog. That was once the case, but the furniture was gone now, scuffed scars on the floor the only sign of where beds and sofas, tables and chairs, had once been. On the walls, painted masonry nails and smudges in the paint were the last signs of family portraits.

In addition to the bedrooms, there was a dining room, two bathrooms, several reception rooms and a cavernous kitchen, complete with an ancient wood-stove. The stove was responsible for heating the upper floors of the building and was also responsible for the main soundtrack to the apartment – a rhythmic thumping in the walls, as the back-boiler heated up the network of pipes, hidden deep in the brickwork and fed the gigantic cast-iron radiators. Radiators that reminded Miles of school, a feeling amplified by his own footsteps on the bare wood and in the empty rooms and hallways.

Tim used one of the reception rooms for most of his needs, which outside of pub hours, were mainly eating and writing. His tidiness in the apartment was as meticulous as it was in the pub. If you were generous, you would call it minimalist, but probably a better word was sparse. Outside of a sofa and a small table and chairs, there were approximately three categories of item in the living room: comics, books and video games. One entire wall, from floor to ceiling, was given up to alphabetised racks of publications, editions, releases – arranged so carefully that the comics gave the impression of a wall of red, the video games black, and then the books giving the only variation in colour and style, from the spines. Tim was obsessed with the wall and would constantly check the temperature of the room on a thermometer he had stuck to the painted brickwork on the wall, at the side of the shelves. Climate control, he called it. The reality was, that there was no predictable way of controlling the climate of the room, apart from him constantly fiddling with the window, opening and closing it so that you were alternately freezing cold or boiling hot, given that the main hot water pipes ran under the floor directly below the shelves.

Upstairs, the room that Miles and Tim currently occupied was the only other room, other than Tim's bedroom, that was furnished. At one time, it would have been the spare bedroom, complete with a more recent en suite bathroom conversion, one that Tim rarely used on account of the fact that it had been renovated at the opposite end of the house to any waste outlet piping. For Tim, all he could think of whenever he used it was that anything that was flushed had to travel approximately twenty feet, underneath the whole footprint of the building, before it exited into the drains. He preferred to use the family bathroom, at least it had a window.

The room itself, contrary to the living room downstairs, was a mecca to technology. It was a bit like the movies, where the nerve centre of a secret agency was always hidden behind some bare brickwork, or in the innocuous lobby of a bus station or cement factory. It was here that Tim kept his video game equipment that partnered the games downstairs, and the kind of home cinema that pummels your senses and shakes the plaster from the walls. Here, he could play games, or watch TV without any other distractions. There wasn't even a picture on the wall, or an item of furniture, that wasn't dedicated to enhancing the experience. There was just one enormous sofa, custom made, standing against a wall like an enormous marshmallow, and a brown leather Jacobson Egg chair stood nearer the TV, Tim's gaming chair. The sofa was perfectly positioned at the apex of the speakers and the gaming chair was a feature that could be moved close to the enormous TV screen, to ensure the best reaction times whilst playing online with kids and adults from all continents. Miles didn't need to ask whether the chair was an original, you just had to sink into it and hear it sigh in welcome.

That's where Miles sat, with the laptop open on his knee and Tim hovering behind him. Always a man of contrasts, Tim's laptop was old, slow and heavy. Tim would embrace video games, but not the Internet. He had every TV channel that existed, but would generally toggle between sports and The History Channel. So Miles was having trouble opening the video that he was desperate to show Tim and although he wasn't sure how long it was taking to buffer, he had definitely finished a beer whilst they were waiting. Tim was hopping from one foot to the other, like a child being made to wait for a fairground ride, so Miles sent him down to the fridge for more drinks and to distract him, he had a feeling they were going to need them.

Miles had first been alerted to what was happening that afternoon, in an email message from one of the biggest fans and followers of the *Misunderstood* circuit. This particular avid member of the community had attended at least five of the shows in the UK and had partied with them in Edinburgh the previous summer, during the festival. He had emailed Miles with a link that he himself had received from another zombie fan.

But this is where the story got strange. Coming from the *Misunderstood* community, you would have expected the link to be something to do with the play. But the link had come from the zombie circuit in North America, where the play was known to no one outside of a few of Tim's friends and the video games designer Tim had met in India that winter. According to Eyeball_Popping, which was the email nickname of his contact, the 'something strange' had started happening that morning, starting around the time that the West Coast of America awoke, when the link began to be passed through the community like wildfire. He signed off by saying that Miles *had* to watch it, because it was related to *Misunderstood*, and then to call him immediately. That was also strange, as apart from socialising at the performances and that one time in Edinburgh, he didn't consider them to be on calling-each-other terms. Who was he supposed to ask for anyway? Eyeball? Mr Popping? He couldn't remember his proper name.

He couldn't figure out how something related to *Misunderstood* would cause ripples and be in a format that could be emailed. It was clearly a link to a video clip, as he recognised the format from Sophie's blog. But they didn't video the performances and also asked others not to do so, until they could do it in the most professional way possible. The play, in their minds, was still rough and was still performed in pubs with temporary stage lighting. When they had tried to take a few clips for posterity, they also found that small parts of the play didn't get the message across properly. Even the finale, when filmed on a hand-held camera, looked a bit like the videos you saw from proud parents of their child's nativity play. A bit grainy and only recognisable or entertaining if you knew the context. Miles had seen enough B-movies to know that even the best stories can be ruined if short-cuts were made. Creativity, he believed in, but short-cuts he did not.

They had deliberately, therefore, taken care to not film it themselves, or have anything leaked out from the audience. They had an idea for a trailer for the play and when they had enough funding, they were going to hire and staff a studio and make it professionally, with proper scripting and direction. He hoped the video was not a copycat version of the play being produced in America. He hoped the zombie community would have more respect than that. Tim had told him all about the fake cheese incident, but with *Misunderstood* they must understand this was different, this was bigger than just a cool pus effect. So Miles dismissed that from his mind and trusted in his fellow zombie fans. Whatever it was, he was sure it was just some kind of new hype or fact about zombies and Eyeball was sending it to him as a plot idea or as a gesture as a fan of the play.

Given that assumption, Miles had gone about his business as usual and not given the email a second thought. He hadn't had time to open the link as he was just leaving for his evening shift and would have plenty of time later to check, given that they were not planning to write after the pub shut that night. So Miles wrapped himself up and shut the door to his little flat behind him. As he pulled his scarf closer around his ears, in the cold February air and headed over to the pub, he had no idea that something was happening. It was something that had a cause and an effect, and although they would later describe it as fate, it could be traced back to one accidental and spontaneous moment. One action, so simple and fleeting, that Miles could never have considered it; because it had nothing, and everything, to do with *Misunderstood*. The butterfly had flapped its wings and a chain of events had begun, which was going to change their lives forever.

Miles had a routine when he finished his shift at the pub. He was allowed one free beer from the pumps once the bar was closed and he always saved it until he had finished tidying up and cleaning down all the equipment. He would pour his beer, then take it over to the corner of the bar, where there was a small table that was rarely used. It had a small, riveted bar stool and a hammered copper bar table, which Miles would polish daily. He would always smile when people headed over and sat there, as he knew the type as soon as he served them. They were looking for a retreat and that is how he would use it after his shift. He would retreat once he was happy that his job was done, savouring the weight off his feet and the cold beer on his lips. He would use that time to read the evening's papers, listen to any sports updates on the transistor radio that Tim had behind the bar, and catch up on any text messages that he had received over the course of his shift. He liked to get all his luxuries at once and was even known to sneak a few packets of Monster Munch into the pub. On those days, it was always Guinness – Guinness and pickled onion Monster Munch.

That night started like no other, as he settled onto his stool and arranged the newspaper in front of him. The radio was discussing the Six Nations rugby, as Ireland had just demolished England in the day's fixture, the first and emotional meeting of the two sides at the historic Croke Park. The radio was talking about emotion, history and passion, all the things that Miles loved about sport. Miles felt content, the night had been a pleasant one, albeit a bit quiet for a Saturday, but the folk who had been in the pub had been in good spirits. Quiet, but that was fine for Miles, it was turning out to be a gentle start to 2007 and that was absolutely fine by him too.

He flipped open his phone, hoping for a text from Sophie. He had sent her a Valentine's present and unusually, had not heard back. The days where this would send him into a blind panic were over, but he had to admit that he had a funny feeling about it. He could also see that she had gone very quiet on Facebook and this usually signalled that things were not good that week between her and Smooth. He would usually react to that by sending her something to cheer her up, but this time something was stopping him and he couldn't figure out what it was. He knew her and he always thought he could feel her somehow. Something was telling him to leave it and allow her to get in touch when she wanted to.

When that happened, he was also looking forward to hearing what she said, because this year his present was a good one. The Killers were back on tour and had just finished the second stop in the UK, having come off sold-out legs as far and wide as Japan and South America. On their first leg in the UK, they had played one night in the Empress Ballroom in Blackpool, as a special gig for the radio. Miles had listened to it and it was majestic. The ballroom as a location, was just so perfect for a band visiting from Las Vegas and he wanted to find some memorabilia that Sophie might like. The gig had been small and the tickets had been very exclusive, but Miles had managed to find and buy some official tour photography on the Internet. The photo he had selected (showing the full line up at maximum energy, against the opulent backdrop of the ballroom, with its vaulted ceiling and Blackpool glitz), gave Miles the chills and he thought it was something of an iconic shot of the band. So he had bought it, had it framed and sent over to Sophie's apartment, with a note to say they should check out the band again that summer at one of the festivals. This year, he promised to hang out for the whole weekend, he had said – with a winking smiley-face.

But there was no text from Sophie on his phone, or at least not at first glance at the screen and Miles had to shut his phone and open it a few times, because it was obviously malfunctioning. Where there was usually the notification of text messages and the caller-ID of the sender, it just said that there were 23 text messages in his inbox waiting for him. Below that, was a notification that he had over 50 missed calls in his call log. All within the last five hours since he started his shift. He opened the text function and the texts were from people he knew, unknown numbers, but all had the same theme – the link that Eyeball_Popping had alerted him to earlier in the day. What was going on? He didn't know what to do, but he needed to find Tim and open that link immediately and he stopped off to get Tim a drink on his way. They were probably both going to need it.

He had headed to the back of the pub and there he had found Tim, who was sat in the lounge of his accommodation, hunched over his phone and also staring blankly at the screen. He looked up as he heard footsteps approaching and Miles could see that he had gone pale.

'What's going on, Miles?'

That was all Tim could say. Miles knew that if he himself received five texts a day, then Tim probably received one text every five days. He had only got the phone under protest and had insisted on getting the most basic model. He also used it like an old person, shouting into it in public and starting, every time he received a text message. When he did receive a text, it tended to then take him two or three minutes to get from the home screen to the message itself, often with lots of huffing and puffing. For Miles, Tim should have been an example of how you should make technology easier, but then the easier you made it; the less he seemed to cope with it. So if he was seeing on his screen, what Miles had seen on his, this was going to be far too much to process. Miles had to take control, needed to find some words of inspiration or calm. This could be a big deal, a big happening in their life and so he needed to let Tim know it was OK, it was probably good news and they should at least check what was going on.

Instead, in a weird accent and with bravado that he didn't have, as if he was a public service announcer, he pointed into the distance and said, 'To the laptop!' But it seemed to do the trick, and they did.

The first thing that registered, when they opened the video file, was that it was familiar surroundings, but was definitely not a video of *Misunderstood*. Even on poor microphones and recording equipment, you could at least make out some of the music and words, but on this video it was just a cacophony of barely distinguishable shouting and singing. The camera was swinging wildly around and having difficulty focusing, so it sometimes showed blurred faces and sometimes the bright lights of the ceiling. But one thing was for sure and unmistakable to them, given the time they spent inside the four walls,

247

it was definitely the pub. Tim looked at him and Miles could see what was racing through his head. Tim was doing what everyone did on those occasions, he was suddenly inventing ways that they might have broken the law and ways that the pub might be taken off them. Miles looked at Tim and shook his head, a tiny movement that replaced so many words, but gave so much reassurance.

Gradually, the video came into focus, as whoever shot it had been moving around to find the best vantage point for their footage. You could now hear a male voice, with an American accent and that explained the origin of the emails. He was obviously holding the phone in his hand and trying to work out the best way to film whatever was going on. Gradually, the sounds stopped merging into each other and Miles and Tim both leaned in closer to try and work out what was playing and what was being said. Suddenly, they locked eyes, as they both connected the setting and the music and started to realise what the video was about and what was happening. Coming from the laptop video footage of the bar, were clearly the opening notes to Thriller, by Michael Jackson.

The conclusion they were both coming to, was that someone who was visiting as a tourist, had accompanied another guest to the Zombies and Kittens party and must have shot the video. You couldn't see his face, as the video was filming outwards the whole time, but he had managed to find an elevated position above the crowd, either by standing on a stool or on the shoulders of another zombie. It was hard to tell and neither Miles nor Tim could recall, as both things were happening quite a lot that night anyway, to the extent that they inexplicably, had to wash spilled drinks off some parts of the ceiling.

What it meant for the video, was that whoever had filmed it, had managed to capture the whole impromptu rendition of the song, from an almost perfect vantage point and captured perfectly, the un-choreographed, but well-known dance routine to the song, with both zombies and kittens swinging their arms in front of themselves in perfect unison. Neither of them could see on the night from their position behind the bar, but most of the bar had managed to arrange itself in a typical line-dance formation, facing in one direction. The video also managed to capture the whole song, face-on to the dance, with zombies and kittens slowly lurching towards the screen and then passing by to either side and below the camera angle in single waves. They had to admit, it looked awesome.

The video went on for about five minutes and then cut to black. It felt spontaneous and as a lot of the zombies were also seasoned Cosplay or Zombie Walk veterans, the make-up was on the right side of gruesome. The amount of Aftershock that had been drunk meant that faces were wide-eyed and manic, made up almost as professional as actors would be in *Misunderstood* itself. As the front row of the dancers passed below the camera, some of them had seen they were being filmed and so had acted up even more, drifting between camp and crazy. It also helped that some of the kittens were drop-dead gorgeous and given the audience that was likely to have viewed the video, that must have helped its success and sharing. The revellers lurched and gurned with some co-ordination, and some un-coordination, and despite the quality not being what they had the ambition to film in a studio, they could not have filmed a more fitting trailer for the play.

But Miles could still not understand how the video had been connected back to them, the pub and the play. Sure, they could tell where it was, but it wasn't like there were signs around the pub, or any signals to the viewer that it was the same amateurs who were responsible for *Misunderstood*.

Miles logged into his Facebook, to see what the reaction was there, and try and figure out more. His wall was full of comments and references to the video and it appeared that Facebook was also the way it had spread in the first place. It was starting to make sense and he flipped back to the video again to read the comments. Miles could trace it back and could see that initially the video was just posted because it was cool, but then soon, fans of the play had started to make the link between the party and the play. A lot of the people who were at the party were also connected to the zombie fan-base, so had started sharing what a great night they had and how the pub was getting a cult following as an underground theatre. It had started there, but now it appeared that the video had a life of its own, and had gone viral.

They both stared at the screen and Miles realised that he was grinning. Tim had come back into the room with a beer in each hand, just as the video started and had just stood frozen to the spot for the full five minutes, unable to move. His mouth was hanging open as the video had played and finished and he kept glancing from the screen to Miles, and back again, as if waiting for some explanation of what they had just seen. Slowly, Miles reached out and pointed to the laptop. Tim followed his gaze, but Miles was not pointing at the video itself, more at a small space below the video. Tim followed his gaze, and took in the title: AWESOME ZOMBIE FLASH MOB PARTY AT PUB!

But that wasn't what Miles was also trying to tell him, because once Miles had seen it he was also unable to speak. Tim's gaze then fell further and he realised what Miles was pointing at. Just below the title, in the bottom right corner of the screen, was the view counter, and neither of them could believe what they saw. The video had more than half a million views.

Tim was the first to move. Slowly and deliberately, and one at a time, he poured both beers straight over his head.

Chapter 21

Shipwreck

March 10, 2007.

'Two years?' Sophie asked.

'Two years.'

'Really?' She said.

'Really. We have known each now, for two years.'

Miles and Sophie were in South London, sat in a pub at the edge of the Common. What Miles liked about the pub, was that it had always been a pub. That was becoming quite rare in the area, which was beginning to fall into a cycle of demolition and regeneration. Old government or commercial buildings were becoming pubs and the pubs were being knocked down to make way for apartments. The residents of those apartments would then complain that there wasn't a decent pub in the neighbourhood. Miles wanted to make sure he contributed to avoiding this ironic cycle.

Sophie had been staying with her parents outside London, so it was convenient to make the trip into the south of the city to see Miles. She had not gone back to her apartment since her engagement with Smooth had come to such an ignominious end, and had no plan to. They were out of their fixed rental period, so she had handed in their notice and planned to let the lease expire, whilst finding somewhere else to start again. As far as she was aware, the empty bottles of gin still lay on the lounge floor from Valentine's Day, perhaps even the unmade bed was still there. Her dad had made friends with the building manager, after the unfortunate incident that led to him kicking the door in, so she also knew that Smooth had not been back, having assumed that removing half of the furniture was an unspoken agreement on the division of possessions. Her parents had agreed to go back towards the end of the lease, clear out Sophie's belongings, clean the place and hand it back. This had made Sophie cry again, which meant that her mum had cried again, then eventually her dad, followed by yet another family hug. That happened a lot lately.

She had told all of this to Smooth in an email after trying several times to reach him by phone. In the end, she had given up and returned the engagement ring to Smooth's parents, who were more welcoming, and infinitely more graceful, than Smooth. They understood how good Sophie was for the family, even if Smooth did not. Although they stopped short of condemning their son, they apologised for how the situation had unfolded, offered money in compensation for what had been spent already on the wedding, gave hugs and handled the situation with humility and poise. So just like that, ties were severed and lines were drawn. A promise had been broken and the seams of lives that had entwined over several years, took just a few days to unpick.

For Sophie, it was not only the first time she had been to London since they split, but also the first time she had been out of the house for weeks. Recently, she hadn't really been sulking, or tormenting, but at the same time Sophie had not looked forward to anything for weeks. She had eaten just enough, slept well and talked things through a lot with her family. The only thing that she dreaded and could not bear do, was go near a phone or a computer. The thought of connecting with her online world and the anticipated humiliation all over again, was causing her the most stress.

She had explained this to Miles, as they sipped on a beer on the pavement tables outside the pub. The weather had been as unsettled as Sophie, but was now starting to look like spring, if you didn't mind dodging the odd rain shower.

Sophie's point, and the reason for her fear, was very simple. Her break-up, which was something that would have once been private, now seemed to be happening in public. Thanks to social networks, everyone she knew would soon be aware that her relationship had collapsed, as she would have to declare it at some point in her personal information. She knew they would be supportive, but the visible nature of it was something she had not considered when she had been so generous with her updates and progress of wedding planning.

At the point that social networking had emerged, her life was at the exact pinnacle of positive and exciting. Her page was covered in congratulations messages, of smiling pictures at her engagement party, and of her and Smooth sipping champagne. How strange that would seem now, it was barely a month ago, but already these pictures and wishes were mournful echoes of the past.

They were ghosts of parties past, there to haunt her every time she logged on.

What had happened to the times when you just built a bonfire of these painful memories, lit a match and they were gone forever, turned into ash with the satisfying drama of a life turned round? There was no metaphorical waste-paper bin on social networks, nothing that you could toss lighter fuel on and ignite, and that was driving her mad. What happened to the time when friends-of-friends would rely on gossip to know what was going on in your life, rather than having easy access to your most painful headlines of the day? So much of it was out of your control. The footprint of their crumbled relationship was woven into some kind of digital fabric and unless you took it apart, thread by thread, then there would always be a surprise around the corner – a new hanging sword, waiting to bring your self-esteem crashing back down again.

Similarly, her video blog had stalled. It had been a commentary on her life and her community were waiting to see what was going to happen in her fairy-tale. They wanted to hear her observations on life, through the rosy lens of someone who was on the ascendancy, someone who saw life from a more elevated position, looking down at the mundane and the struggling, and offering advice. But now, she was the one who had failed and she didn't think she could come back from that. What was she supposed to do? She couldn't post anything now. No one wanted to see her, make-up smeared and wine in hand, screaming injustices into the camera. The glamorous and aspirational Sophie had gone, perhaps forever, and would be replaced in their lives by someone else in a heartbeat – someone more fabulous, and Sophie would stay a pioneer of video blogging, but in a footnote.

That said, and despite her mood, she was looking forward to seeing Miles. She had been thinking about it for days and was certainly hoping she got the new Miles, not the old Miles. The old Miles, out of everyone, she expected to be the most irritating about the situation, so just in case, she had deliberately texted him rather than call about her break-up, and tried to gently hint that she needed space. She wanted to give him time to digest the information and work his way through any immediate emotions. The old Miles, she anticipated, would over-compensate and not leave her alone, constantly trying to offer cheery solutions and 24-hour support. He would be texting her at three o'clock in the morning, to make sure that she wasn't awake and worrying. Or he would be smug and pompous, telling her that he never thought Smooth was good enough for her, leaving enormous, twin-sized, pregnant pauses, he hoped would scream that she should have chosen him.

To her mild relief and surprise, she got new Miles. He just texted back, to say that he was sorry to hear about it and when she was ready to talk, she should call and he would meet her, wherever, night or day.

That had made her cry, the second time he had unwittingly done that since she arrived back at her parents that night. The first time was his Valentine's gift, when her parents brought it back bundled with other post from the flat. The combination of his thoughtfulness and the timing of the situation was so unexpected, that for the first time she had felt a need to rush to him, just to sit opposite him. She could picture him, open-faced and without judgement, being bafflingly silly, but at the same time, so sensitive to her needs, making sure everything he said and did was to make her happier. She wanted Miles to be the sponge for her sadness and as she took the train up to London, she found she had butterflies about seeing him. Perhaps this day could be the start of the healing process and Miles could give her advice on how to fix the situation and how to move forward, because at the moment she couldn't see how to do it.

In her anticipation of support, she was dead right with Miles. From the moment he affectionately hugged her and looked into her eyes, she could see nothing but love and concern. He had bought Sophie a scarf, in case she hadn't cleared out her stuff from the apartment, or in case she hadn't anticipated the wind that whips across the exposed parkland of the Common. He had listened to her story without interruption and had barely taken his eyes off her or taken his hand out of hers across the table. He seemed to be drinking her in and squeezed her hand whenever she looked like she was going to cry, which helped her carry on.

But, when she finished, she was in for another mild surprise. Miles was more on the offensive than she expected with his advice, he didn't share Sophie's self-pity. He saw only an opportunity for Sophie to redefine her life and that didn't include hiding, or not facing the truth. For Miles, these situations were best faced head-on, by turning heartbreak into fuel. When Miles had made "The Decision", there was no such thing as social networking and he could see that the impact of it would amplify the feelings of embarrassment and soul-crushing insecurity. He reminded Sophie of the night they had met and how she had described him, verbatim, as being a 'bit like a puppy'. He then asked her to consider how she

257

felt about it, about him, as he knew that she had not found it attractive or productive. He wanted Sophie to imagine how he felt, then imagine it was a Polaroid picture, then look at him now and how he had changed. Sure, he was doing something different, but every change he made was for positive reasons, not negative. He gave stuff up, but it was the stuff that was dragging him down, and he replaced it with the green shoots of his future and now present. The moment that his life had turned around was the moment that he decided not to be a victim anymore and to ignore what people thought of him. That started when he quit his job, almost exactly two years ago to the day.

'Look where I am now, Sophie.' Miles explained. 'You were a big part of this. You made me embrace life. I had never met anyone like you before and I didn't know why, but I just thought … no, I think … you're amazing. It put me on this path and I have no regrets. I'm not saying you should copy me and I'm not saying what I am doing is better or worse than before, you made me understand that I needed to change the comparisons and benchmarks of my life. I used to think marriage and family was the success, but now I know that it is actually love. You were the muse. I used to think a career was the only way to gain experience in life – but my life now is richer and I love the experiences I am having, even if I am certainly poorer. A lot of this is down to you, Sophie, and so I won't hear you wallowing.'

'Woah,' said Sophie, 'nice try, but you said the coffees were on you.'

'I think that you making fun of me, means that you are feeling better and actually, I should make you pay. Call it counselling.'

'If you think about what you just said, Miles, you'll realise that if there was a counselling bill, then you probably already owe me a million dollars.'

'Fair point,' chuckled Miles, 'and well said. Let's say that this is the start of me paying you back and I guess my point is this. Change the way you think about the situation and focus on what is going to make you happy. Two years ago, I decided to do that and it has taken some time, but now I can honestly say, that I am happier than I have ever been. I walked out of my job and my career, and basically, everyone was saying I was an idiot. They were even claiming I had a breakdown.'

Sophie arched an eyebrow.

'OK – maybe I did have a little one and for that, people will talk. They will talk to each other and they will talk about you. But the people you love will talk to you and will stand by you in life. If you stand with them and listen to them, then over time you find that the people in your life polarise. You may have less friends in life than on The Facebook, but these will be better friends and I guarantee, you will take them to the grave. People who stay with you in bad times become blood and the bond is not easily broken. In the world we are now living, it's not just the people you can call on the phone. Remember that you have built your video blogging on giving people positive messages in life and that is why they follow you. We have to get used to the fact that your friends are not always going to be up the street, or across town from us anymore. You should speak to them through your blog, get that going again and if anything, speak to them more than before. What could be more positive than this: I have been knocked down, but I have got back up again and I am proud and unafraid of what is going to happen next…'

Miles sat back and for a few seconds he and Sophie looked at each other, unsure of what to say.

'You realise it not *The* Facebook?' Sophie said, finally. 'It's just Facebook, I'm pretty sure of that.'

Miles smiled. He had rehearsed very little of what he had said and this was an unexpected, spontaneous, situation for him, when it came to Sophie. Leading up to them getting together, he had spent several nights lying awake and thinking about her. She had said that she wanted some space and he wanted to respect that, but sometimes he just longed to know how she was and let her know he was there for her.

One night, he had even composed a text in the early hours of the morning. He had woken up unexpectedly, with the unnerving feeling that something was wrong. In the darkness, he had convinced himself that Sophie was also awake and was upset, and he felt the desire to text her to make sure she knew he was thinking of her. At worst, she would get it in the morning and everything was OK, but if his gnawing suspicions were true, then she would know she was not alone. He had composed the text over the space of the next hour and a half, deleting and re-writing bits of it. He had got up, and paced around the room, and checked the Internet for a quote. He thought that something uplifting and about friends being there for each other, would be a good quote to include. In the end, he decided on his own words, over the character allocation of five texts and had sent it.

It was only after he had pressed the green button that he realised his phone was out of credit and so the message did not send. This escalated his situation to another level, as now he was certain that this was something that Sophie had to read. He had resolved to find a 24-hour news store or garage that sold credit and had paced the neighbourhood for a further hour, with no luck. Eventually, at about five in the morning, he admitted defeat. The night passed and the moment passed. By the time he woke up the next morning, the shadow had passed and he realised that it was just one of those demons that comes at night. He would wait for Sophie.

He had saved up all his words until that day and Miles could tell from the light in Sophie's eyes that it had worked. There was just the faintest glow, the flickering of a candle, which meant to Miles that she was coming back and she would come back.

It was going to be OK.

Chapter 22

Pixels

March 10, 2007.

When Miles got back to the pub, Tim was waiting for him on the doorstep, hopping anxiously from foot to foot, but with a manic grin on his face. This was happening a lot recently.

Since the YouTube video of their Thriller performance had gone viral, it would be fair to say that Tim had embraced all forms of social communication. From zero social footprint and a high level of disengagement, he now had multiple social media pages, plus a website for the pub and the same for *Misunderstood*. He would check them all vigorously and with a regimented focus and documentation that you would of course expect.

His favourite by far, however, was the YouTube video and its associated statistics. This video was where it had all started for Tim and it attracted his particular attention because of that, and also because he could study the numbers. Miles would joke that, if they were cavemen, then Tim would be the one that could tell them the exact number of sticks that made a good fire and the exact optimum time of day and weather conditions to light it. He was meticulous and so, not only did he check their hits several times a day, but he had recorded the views-per-day and carefully graphed them since the first night they had been alerted to it a few weeks earlier.

Such was his distraction by it, sometimes Miles would realise mid-shift in the pub, that Tim was nowhere to be seen. That could even be at peak times, which were several times busier than they had used to be and when the queue at the bar could be three people deep and four drinks in; thirsty, vocal and impatient.

They had additional staff these days, but there were some particular zombie-themed cocktails that they had kept on their menu since the party, that took time and considerable effort to make. Given they were designed by Tim, each cocktail also had a particular preparation technique, that only he and Miles could achieve to the standard required. On these occasions, Miles would head into the back searching for Tim and find him hunched over his laptop, his wide eyes illuminated by the light from the screen.

The first time it had happened, Miles had stood still for what seemed like a good two minutes with an impatient look on his face in the doorway of the pub's first reception room, waiting for Tim to notice him. Of course he didn't, as his attention was rapt on the screen, the only movement noticeable was his eyes, as they flicked forwards and backwards across the screen, drinking in the information and turning over the details in his mind. Miles had given a little cough, just a polite 'ahem' to let Tim know he was there. This had got Tim's attention, but instead of the desired effect, which was an apology and a return to the bar, Tim had instead leapt up and bounded the two paces from the computer to Miles, with the look of an excited puppy on his face. He had grabbed Miles by both shoulders and shouted into his face, loud enough to leave a small trail of spit between his lip and Miles nose.

'Four million!'

This is how it went these days. Miles had got used to Tim running through the pub, shouting over and over again a particular number, whether it be how quickly the latest showing of *Misunderstood* had sold out, or a significant uptick in their YouTube views, over a particular few hours of the day. Miles had got used to recognising what particular statistic Tim was referring to, as he also knew them by heart, thanks to Tim's regular updates.

So when Tim was waiting for him on the doorstep of the pub, he was expecting another update of that sort.

As Miles got closer, however, it seemed this time it was a bit different. Over the months and years they had known each other, just like with Sophie, Miles had become finely tuned to Tim's body language and emotion. They had spent so much time in each other's company that Miles could pick up the slightest change in mood from Tim, like a draught on a candle flame. Although this opened them up to friendly ridicule, it did actually help them in the pub, especially during delicate moments with customers. Miles could spot the exact moment Tim was about to snap and explode into temper in front of a customer. Therefore, he knew the exact moment when it would be best for him to step in and quietly lead Tim aside and handle the situation himself.

With the growth in notoriety of the pub through *Misunderstood*, this was increasingly important to maintain the reputation of the bar, as a fun-loving, easy going, zombie-friendly hangout.

So, as he approached the pub and was within a hundred yards of it, he noted that the foot-hopping was definitely new and the look on Tim's face was a mixture of excitement and panic, so this didn't seem like an update he was about to like. Tim had also started to manically wave and beckon Miles from a distance, again something that he had never done before, and certainly was not cool. This step outside of the usual body language and signals seemed, to Miles, that a brand new piece of information had appeared – and a big one.

This set Miles' mind racing. Had there been another video released? They had not had another party, and so if that was the case then it could only have been a new angle on the previous video. Or perhaps something bad had happened? Had Michael Jackson's people been in touch and asked them to remove the video? Preposterous as it sounded, both Tim's body language and Miles' increasing numbness to surprise events, meant that nothing could be ruled out.

These thoughts all raced through Miles' head, but in addition, he was feeling a new emotion. He was elated from seeing Sophie, so there was the residue of that, and the fact that he couldn't wait to tell Tim all about it. There was also a new feeling that this corner of the city, the bar and the flat, had become home. With that, he realised just how invested he had become in his new life and how protective he had become of Tim. He immediately relaxed when he approached the familiar streets of this home, but a big part of that was the fact he knew he would see Tim. The transition from boss to friend had happened, for Miles, quite quickly, but he realised that it had got stronger since. They had been through a lot together and without ever having a long conversation, they had revealed a lot about their lives and feelings to each other. Sometimes it was just a throw-away comment, sometimes a story from the past, or occasionally an earnest debate, but with every new piece of information, Tim had become more and more part of Miles' routine, his life, but also his fabric.

With this, Miles found himself breaking into a half run, half walk. This sent Tim into even more exaggerated hops and he started shouting something across the street, that although Miles couldn't quite make out, it didn't exactly sound like a number. Miles shouted that he couldn't hear and this sent Tim into an excited skip across the road, arms windmilling and making them both look like they were about to celebrate the campest football goal in history.

'Pixels! Pixels! Pixels!' Miles heard, as he got within earshot.

This stopped Miles in his tracks and he bent over with his hands on his knees. Not because of what Tim was saying, as Miles had absolutely no idea what he was talking about. But with laughter, because if you have ever seen a grown man skipping across the road, shouting 'pixels' repeatedly and waving his arms around, then it is quite a sight. Think Julie Walters, on a hilltop, in *The Sound of Music*.

Tim was oblivious to this and seemed to be in his own zone. He reached the laughing Miles and started slapping him on the back, shaking Miles by the shoulders and continuing to shout about pixels and the pond and other words that made no sense to Miles. He had never seen him like this before and as Miles calmed down, he placed a soothing hand on Tim's arm and led him back into the pub, to try and get some sense. Tim was also calming down and by the time Miles had fetched them both a shot of vodka and set them up in the corner at the copper table, Tim had recovered enough to return to his normal colour and composure. He sat down across from Miles, nailed his shot and waved the empty glass across at the bar for a refill. The next thing he said hit Miles like a brick.

'Miles, they want to make a video game. Out of *Misunderstood*. In America.'

Miles didn't know what to say. Two hours ago, he had been talking with Sophie about life and about his own green shoots, but what he was hearing now was on a different scale. He had heard that people were starting to create opportunities for themselves, through the publicity that YouTube alone could create, but he never thought it would lead to this for *Misunderstood*. It was generally musicians who were starting to experience this kind of route to fame. Cute girls or chiselled guys, in a small American town, with a guitar and undiscovered song-writing talent. Not two out-of-shape guys in South London, with a play about zombies.

On the other hand, he also couldn't help the cynical feeling that this must be how people get caught out. He had also heard stories of shady businessmen taking advantage of vanity projects, pretending to spot talent and then asking for up-front investment that was never seen again. But the look on Tim's face was different and despite his relative naivety online, he knew that Tim could sniff out a con from 500 paces.

So he asked Tim to start at the beginning. As Tim explained the last twelve hours, Miles started to feel like he had left his body and was watching the conversation from the ceiling of the pub.

The story began that winter, when Tim was in Goa. As it turned out, the chance meeting that Tim had made was also a very fortuitous one. Tim reminded Miles about the night and the only person that Tim had really talked to on his trip – the animator, in the beach shack. The animator that Tim had met, it seemed, had been impressed with Tim's encyclopaedic knowledge of early pop culture and had also felt that their meeting was a kind of kismet. Apparently, he had not been having a great holiday and was constantly being distracted by work back in Los Angeles. So the evening that they had spent together, with the warm Indian Ocean breeze and the cold Indian lager, had been the highlight of his holiday.

As with many highly driven people, he still needed stimulation, albeit of a different kind to relax. Quiet days and long evenings, without anything but work to think about and no one to talk to, were just boring and led him back to calling the office for updates about the very things he was taking a break from. So far, all he had encountered were polite hotel and restaurant staff and friendly, yet placid, couples in their middle age. So an evening, spent talking about what he loved and not thinking too much about the mechanics of business, had made his holiday and also gave him the evening he needed to relax, and headspace to reflect on his business and his life.

This is important, as the main problem he was wrestling with was both financial and creative. His business was animation, but actually it was doing far better than he alluded to with Tim and better than he could have ever imagined. For some years, they had been working on the animation and special effects for Hollywood blockbusters. It had been the kind of effects that couldn't be achieved in real life, on the kind of movies and projects that were becoming an important part of the film industry. If you like, he was the go-to guy for elaborate explosions, or breathtaking fantasy landscapes. Or an elaborate explosion, in a fantasy landscape, in space.

Because of this, he was also involved in animation for video games and computer games, and had such success in this, that one of the biggest video game publishers in the world had offered to purchase his company, for a staggering amount of money. His company would become part of the publisher and he would be given almost unlimited access to even more money, to continue to develop animations of a better and better quality, and to be part of an industry that anyone could see was really starting to take off. He would be given free license to dream about what possibilities there were in the animation industry and then be given enough money to try and make them happen. The offer was also the kind of staggering amount of money, personally to him, that would have meant that he would never again need to work, or at least not in the same way anymore. This was something that filled him with dread, as much as excitement.

He had always pushed boundaries and this was the creative fuel that kept him going, but at heart he was a purist. He loved the animations he created, but he wanted to do them his way and for himself. He had built his business with the creative edge that only independent

269

studios are capable of, so considering being part of a corporation, was something that he was wrestling with, as a decision. Should he stay independent and take the risk of survival in an environment that was becoming more and more competitive? Or should he accept the offer and give himself the security that he never dreamed he would have, when he started his studio in his apartment, a short walk from Venice Beach and away from the campus complexes of the Hollywood studios, and the increasing number of tech parks that stretched from the airport, to Santa Monica. The pressure to commit was building, he was at the decision point and the president of the publishers was waiting for an answer.

It was at pretty much this exact moment, when he had met Tim. He had been poised to agree to the deal and was taking the night to sleep on it, before making the call in the morning. He had decided to take a walk on the beach, to take himself out of the whitewashed beachside hotel and to see if that made him change his view. It was something he had used to do in Venice when he had difficult decisions to make. It was almost as if feeling the sand on his bare feet grounded him and quietened his mind, but on this occasion it had not helped, so he had ducked into the beach shack, where Tim was nursing a beer.

Of course, Tim was not to know all this, mainly because he hadn't asked. Perhaps that was the point. For the first time, the animator had a connection with someone, who had actually offered to help him, not the other way round. For years, he had lived the LA lifestyle and lived on the trading of information, of favours and of relationships. But here was a guy that had never heard of him, which was refreshing given his picture was not exactly on the front page of every newspaper, but was certainly in the news and online enough to be familiar. Of course, what he wasn't to know, was that at that time, Tim wasn't really the kind of guy to keep up on Internet news.

Also, Tim had re-connected him with what he loved. Tim had re-connected him and reminded him, of his love of characters and love of creation. It re-connected him with the toil of trying to create something new and different and then the satisfaction of seeing it come to life in your way, without anyone trying to homogenise it or analyse it from a financial perspective. When you created something like that, the only benchmark you used was love and whether the idea moved you.

So, based on his night with Tim, he decided not to sell. Not only that, but it gave him an idea. His idea was to make video games of his own. Not big, blockbusting video games; but video games that would appeal to people who grew up like him, who looked at video games as an art form, not a movie franchise. Games for geeks like them.

Tim then went on to explain that the guy had seen their YouTube video, recognised Tim and after a while of racking his brain, had connected the two things together and again thought it was destiny. He decided that his first video game would be a zombie video game based on *Misunderstood*. He had called Tim that morning and they had apparently chatted like old friends. Tim had admitted that he was sceptical and whilst talking, had run an Internet search on the animator. Whereupon, in Tim's words, his balls had shrank to the size of peanuts.

The animator wanted Miles and Tim to go to Los Angeles to have more discussions and to meet him and work out a concept for the game. The basic premise was that you would play the role of the zombie, trying to fight your way to survival, in the face of scheming humans and evil cats. As simple as that, and the deal was equally simple, it was 50/50. A license of the *Misunderstood* IP, in return for investment in making the game. Although, as the creators of *Misunderstood*, of course Tim and Miles would have creative sign off, of anything that was done.

Tim paused and for the first time, Miles saw the vulnerability in his eyes. He knew that, for the first time since he knew him, Tim was out of his comfort zone and needed him. He needed his support, but also he needed Miles with him on this walk into the unknown. Tim had started this journey alone and this was his dream. But it was only since Miles had started working with him on it, that it began to take shape. Miles had been able to give him the things he didn't have and had kept them focused as they wrote the play, and as they took it on the road.

Granted, Tim also helped Miles along the way, especially as Miles had the tendency to get distracted, especially by Sophie. But he knew, that no matter how excited Tim was, he would only do it with Miles' blessing. Both of their lives had been turned upside down already by *Misunderstood*, in a good way. The corporate drop-out and the dead-end bar owner had taken the sum of their parts and had made it bigger. Now it had the potential to go even further. This was the lucky break that people talk about and it was happening to them. It would turn their lives upside down again, but they had both found that life can look better upside down and the wrong way round.

Just like the animator, they were on the cliff-edge of a big decision, but this time they had each other. If they took the leap, they had to do it together; they had to be all in. To make the decision without accepting that, would not reflect the honesty and the bond that Miles and Tim had made, over the time they had known each other.

Of course, there was also a risk. A once in a lifetime chance to get it right, also means a once in a lifetime chance to get it wrong. Miles could see the doubt in Tim's eyes and could read his mind. The last time that Miles had faced an important crossroads in his life and the last time someone had really asked Miles to commit to them, Miles had stepped away, and not got married. He had decided to step away from the cliff. He could see that Tim was sensing that past hesitation in Miles, he was scared that he would do it again and this was not a moment for hesitation. He could tell that Tim wanted to know now, he didn't want to hear that Miles would think about it, or wait, or speak to Sophie about it. He wanted to hear that Miles felt the same passion about *Misunderstood* and that it was unreserved. All those hours spent analysing the YouTube statistics were part of Tim's nature, but also, because he was watching his dreams unfold in front of him and he was captivated by it. Now here he was, sitting in front of Miles and knowing for the first time that the decision was not his alone, and that he couldn't do it alone. Months ago, Tim had talked about small decisions and the importance of paying attention to them. This was not one of those. This was a big decision and one where you realised if someone really had your back.

In the end, it took Miles about two seconds to decide. This was not two years ago, he was different and this was different. At that moment, he knew that every small decision he had made for the past two years, had all led to this moment of choice and he knew, in his heart, that this was the right thing. So much so, that he didn't even consider winding Tim up a bit about it, because he couldn't help the look that was spreading across his face.

'I'm in!' He shouted, and punched the air. 'I'm in, I'm in, I'm in!' He shouted again, and did a little dance, before hugging Tim across the table, who was now sobbing into his shoulder.

Over at the bar, the staff and regulars were looking at them in a very peculiar way. They both needed to work on their celebrations.

Chapter 23

Promenade

May 7, 2007.

Miles caught his reflection in the veranda doors, as they swung open in a blast of lobby chatter and air conditioning. The heat and sea air was suiting him well, he thought. He settled back in his chair, which gave a satisfying creak against the wooden decking and sipped his coffee. In front of him, from his position, one storey above street level, were 200 metres of palm-fringed sand and the magnificent Pacific Ocean. Tim had told him about his time in Los Angeles in the years before he opened the pub. He would talk about the wave of oranges and pinks that greeted the sunrise in the sky above the headland, as the coast swept past the Palisades, on its way to Malibu. Then the retreating purples in the evening, against the canvas of the ocean. But it was more stunning than he had ever imagined.

'Is this for real?' He said, almost to himself, adjusting his sunglasses and straightening his toes in his flip-flops. This was the kind of breakfast vibe he could get used to and it was a good time of the day, with a slight breeze to take the edge of the knife-sharp heat and before the advancing summer humidity took hold during the day, especially when they hit downtown to work on the video game. Breakfast time was also the only peaceful time they had managed to catch, such was the schedule of meetings and parties since they had arrived two weeks ago.

Tim, across from him at the table, was sipping on a Bloody Mary, and smiled in response.

'Do you mean the life, or the breakfast burrito?'

Miles patted his stomach, he had to admit that he had eaten his share of Mexican food for breakfast, but he had quickly realised it was the only proper meal they managed in any given day. Once the car arrived to take them to the studio, it was a grabbed salad, or a rainbow array of boxed doughnuts, that kept them going until they headed back late to the hotel and crashed, or until they headed out to a club, as they had the previous night. He didn't know how Tim managed it, as he seemed to live on a diet of sugar, caffeine and alcohol, although he had realised early in their relationship that Tim had anything but normal habits in anything. This morning, he was eyeing Tim's Bloody Mary with temptation and wondered if it might help his hangover, but he had never really been one for hair of the dog. He tended to stick to the old fashioned remedy of coffee, heavy food and a grumpy disposition.

They were also heading back that afternoon, at least for this trip, having made some good progress on designing some of the zombie characters and putting together the storyline of the video game with the development team. Miles was desperately trying to lose the nausea, before another ten hours on the plane, so that he could arrive back in the best shape he could. Sophie had agreed to meet him at the airport and he wanted to make sure he took full advantage of his sun-kissed hair and complexion. They had talked every day over the last two weeks, her waking him up with a text every morning from the UK and then him returning the favour late at night, when the sun was rising across the Atlantic. They had even developed a routine. They would send each other song titles and then the job of the other would be to dig it out of their collection, or look it up. It had become an unspoken connection, waking up to a song suggestion, and Miles could tell that Sophie enjoyed waking up to the text as much as he did. He was very excited to see her again.

The two weeks they had spent in Los Angeles had also been a very enjoyable experience. Seeing their characters come alive was such a strange and beautiful experience. Where, on the stage, they were restricted by make-up and human features, in the video game there were no such restrictions. The only limit was their own imagination and the seemingly endless imagination of the artists. Sometimes, Miles found himself laughing out loud at the incredulity of it and the bizarre debates they would have over blood colours, or number of pus-filled ulcers on each zombie. This is what it's like, he thought, when you are making decisions about something you really love – they are important decisions, because they will affect how good the game looked – but they were certainly not onerous to make. Only that kind of enjoyment can make you forget about meals, about it getting dark; or getting dark and then light again.

It's enjoyable to talk for hours about whether a particular zombie would have mangy hair on the right side of their head and rotting flesh on the left, or vice versa. It was all down to how they lay in the grave, was the conclusion.

Tim also seemed to be in his element, and had been very focused on making sure the storyline fit to the vision he had for *Misunderstood*. For him, it was very important that the zombies were loveable, as well as realistic. After all, he would say, the spark of imagination that spawned the play was one of fondness and affinity, not horror. He wanted to make sure that anyone who played the game, knew that the zombies were the good guys and the humans the bad guys. He wanted to make sure that the cats were realistic, but in their eyes was a hint of how evil they were, or could be. Together, they had made a great team, and they could tell that the artists in the studio were impressed with their creative vision and the way they were able to finish and improve each other's sentences and thoughts.

There had also been talk about what would happen once the game was finished. The animator, had already had meetings with some of his contacts, and overall the feeling was good about *Misunderstood*. It wasn't just the concept, but also the way that *Misunderstood* had been discovered that they loved. The way that Miles and Tim had come together, the way that *Misunderstood* had gone viral and the way that the animator also had his place in the story, from the beaches of India and his conversation with Tim, to the way that he had discovered the video of *Misunderstood*. This was all storyline gold to the growing, reporting and reviewing community around video games. It was a modern story of romance, of discovery and of chance. There had been offers to film "The Making of the Game", and pleas for exclusivity from individual bloggers and publications.

278

They had agreed to stay coy about that, but had decided that there should be an announcement party and a way of introducing *Misunderstood* to a wider group of publicity and the entertainment industry as a whole. The way they were going to do that was unanimous and clear and was obvious as soon as they started discussing it. There was only one thing to do. They would hire a theatre and put on a stage performance of *Misunderstood* in Los Angeles, with a specially invited audience. There was no other way that could be more perfect and fitting to introduce the play and the video game. "Old school" to announce the "new school".

This was, basically, the reason behind Tim's and Miles' hangover that morning. Tim took another sip of his Bloody Mary and looked at Miles over the top of his sunglasses.

'I've had an idea for *Misunderstood 2*,' he said.

They had discussed this before, in passing, and Miles knew that Tim was already formulating the story in his head.

'Go on,' he said.

'So,' started Tim, taking a big slug of his drink this time and wincing against the alcohol and the spice.

'It's going to be a rock and roll theme. I think we take it up a notch. All this hanging out in Los Angeles has got me thinking, with *Misunderstood* we make a video game, but with *Misunderstood 2* we go straight to a movie. Loosely, about how rock and roll saves the world.'

'Loosely about how rock and roll saves the world?' Miles asked. 'I'm not sure anything could be loose about that. But go on…'

'You're absolutely right,' said Tim, 'there needs to be no holding back on this one and it goes like this. Now that the zombies have discovered how the human governments have been keeping surveillance on them, they are no longer afraid and have decided to take on the humans. They are feeling confident. However, there is still a long way to go until they are in a position to really challenge the humans, because the zombies have all been confined to camps, in some of the most remote places on Earth. To be free, they must take a more radical step and find a way of organising themselves as a civilisation. They work towards co-ordinating an almighty global battle between the living and the undead, where the zombies are fighting for the right to be free and unprosecuted by the governments of the world and to be left alone, once and for all.'

'OK,' said Miles, 'but firstly, you do realise that is how terrorists do it? Plus, where is the link to rock and roll, apart from the fact that you would like to spend more time over here on the West Coast?'

'I'm glad you asked, Miles, because that is the genius of it all. To make sure that the zombies are seen in a positive way and not seen as terrorists – it is set here, in Los Angeles. All the head zombies have come and set up a zombie government. They choose here, to keep away from the cold and the damp, which plays havoc with their open sores and rotting flesh. California is full of the zombies of people who came here to find their dream when they were alive and have been given a second chance to make a difference. That is where rock and roll comes in, because the zombie army is made up of actors and musicians – proper LA folk. It also means we can bring in some famous zombies, who can be the representatives of the zombies on TV, to dispel the propaganda of the humans and show that anyone could be a zombie one day, even famous people.'

Miles was struggling for a reply. 'This is weird,' was the only response he could think of.

'Oh, Miles, you have not heard the weirdest thing of all. The cornerstone of the whole spectacle, in my head, is the General of the zombie army; the guy who brings the whole thing together and becomes the hero of the play. He is the guy who also sets the vibe of the whole show and also provides the soundtrack. Zombie Elvis.'

There was a pause, and Miles looked at Tim. He couldn't work out if he was serious or not. Tim was looking out to sea and seemed lost in his thoughts, but the look on his face was deadly serious. Firstly, he was deadly serious about a sequel, Miles could tell that much, and Miles was excited by the prospect. But zombie Elvis? Presumably an army of other notable zombie characters, all equally sacrilegious, such as zombie Lennon, or zombie Sinatra. Surely that was too much, even for Tim.

'Are you for real? Isn't that asking for trouble? Remember, there are still a lot of people who think that Elvis is alive.'

'Hmm,' said Tim, 'you're right, I hadn't thought about that. Although at least it means we could even try and lure Elvis, himself, out of hiding to play the lead.'

For a split second, Tim's gaze met Miles'. Unreadable, and then a huge smile spread across Tim's face, and he collapsed into laughter.

'Nah, you're probably right about the idea. But I do want to do a sequel, I want to do this forever.'

Miles chuckled to himself. He could imagine having this discussion in the dark pub of London and he probably would have stopped Tim on the idea, well before he introduced Elvis. But here, on the veranda of a beachside hotel in California, it seemed like the most normal thing in the world. It seemed that anything was possible and he agreed with Tim – he wanted to do this forever as well. He loved his life.

For the rest of the breakfast time, they sat in relative silence, reflecting on the time they had been there. It seemed that opportunities were opening up every day, and it almost seemed unreal that they were going back to the UK. But that said, in the meantime, they had a lot of work to do in getting the play ready to stage in Los Angeles and had already set a date for the show to take place in one month's time – which did not leave a lot of time to relax and they both agreed, that before they knew it, they would be back stateside.

The first thing they had to do when they returned to the UK, was to gather the current cast of the show and tell them the exciting news. They had agreed to use the UK cast for the main parts and it meant they could work quickly behind the scenes on the other parts. The zombie chorus would be made up of jobbing actors from Los Angeles and although the British based chorus would be disappointed, it wasn't always a set group of individuals and many of them were really just locals from various pubs they had performed in.

They had actually begun a serious discussion about using the full cast from the UK, but when that fact was pointed out (along with the fact that they didn't even have a full set of phone numbers for the chorus and couldn't vouch for sobriety and behaviour in front of influential figures from the entertainment industry), they quickly rethought the whole thing and moved on. It also expedited the rehearsals, as the existing main cast was well-versed in the script and the songs, so the casting in Los Angeles for the rest could happen much quicker, as Miles and Tim could return in a few weeks and finalise the line-up.

Also, the prospect of bringing the main cast from the UK (the guys who had believed with them since the start and had travelled around the UK with them in vans and cars, to pubs and bars), was going to be an amazing experience for all of them. Miles thought about their faces, many of them zombie-fans, when they told them that not only was there a video game being made, but they were all going out to perform an American premiere of the show. It was another thing that made all the toils of the past few years, worth it and even if it didn't work, it would be another memory that they could take with them.

That just left one thing, which Miles had been thinking hard about over the previous days. As much as he loved the guys from *Misunderstood* and loved Tim, he was starting to believe that he also needed someone else by his side. As much as breakfasts on the veranda and Tim's casual alcoholism, were things that he valued, he was starting to feel like he needed to share every moment with the one person who had been there from the very start of this incredible journey. He needed Sophie here with him from now on, to share this.

His mind had been drifting in this direction for a little while. At the start, he had enjoyed getting home from the bar after calls with the animator, or from their first few trips and telling her all about it. He had enjoyed feeling like he had a story to tell and to impress her with. They had enjoyed long nights, over wine, talking about the adventure that Miles was on and also continuing to talk about Sophie's new life without Smooth. She was back in London permanently now, in a flat much closer to Miles and had started to enjoy life again. The drama of their break up had calmed and as the full picture had emerged, more of their friends had taken Sophie's side.

It seemed that Smooth had been leading something of a double-life, not just with the mysterious E, who turned out to be a junior work colleague, but also with some other girls from his office. He had used his ability to source free tickets to gigs, to win friends and had in turn used that to have a series of clandestine relationships. He had been running this entirely behind Sophie's back by text-message, probably whilst she was busy planning the wedding or recording episodes of her blog. This of course, helped Sophie forget about Smooth and it also gave Miles and Sophie a lot to talk about. Each of them enjoyed the soap opera of the other's life.

However, after a while, this fuel for conversation was not needed to pass the time and they started to just genuinely enjoy each other's company. They would spend late nights watching movies, or sometimes in silence watching TV, rather than in bars and over wine, laughing and building the bond that comes through mutual fortune and misfortune.

It was on Miles' current trip to Los Angeles, after the first few days of exchanging texts, that the thought struck Miles, as he took an early morning walk on the beach. It struck him so suddenly that he felt it and almost called her straight away, despite it being past midnight in the UK. He wanted to share the moments with Sophie while they were happening, not as a boast or talking point weeks later. He realised he had moved on from being an individual, he now wanted to share his experiences as a duo, and he wanted the other half to be Sophie. Not even in the romantic, or desperate sense that perhaps had been the case a few months before. Now it was just a natural progression for them. Enough time had passed since "The Decision" for Sophie to be unable to hang onto the argument that she would be a rebound, or that it was too soon for him to think clearly. Likewise, it had been months now since Smooth had left and Sophie was back to her old self. She had even started thinking about blogging again and Miles knew that would be something they discussed when he got back to London the next morning.

But he had resisted calling her. He would first discuss the prospect of Sophie coming to Los Angeles with Tim, that was his right. He would start by asking if she could be his plus one at the play, or they could even include her in the cast, as she had seen enough performances now to at least have a fringe part. He turned to Tim, who had just received his second Bloody Mary and was stirring it thoughtfully with a piece of celery and staring intently at Miles.

Tim didn't break his gaze, he had read Miles' mind. Just as when he asked Miles to make this step and commit to *Misunderstood*, he knew this was also a big decision and one that meant more than just the words themselves.

'I know what you're going to ask, my friend,' he said. 'The answer is yes. Of course the answer is yes. Of course she should be here.'

Chapter 24

Arrivals

May 8, 2007.

Sophie had even made a little cardboard sign, which was totally unlike her.

She had made it out of an old cereal box and gone a bit crazy with the glitter pens, if she didn't mind saying so herself. At first, it had seemed a bit cheesy and perhaps a little bit desperate. But the more she used the glitter pens, the more she realised that it had gone way past cheesy, even way past desperate and was probably now ironic. Miles would appreciate that. Of course, the irony for Sophie was that she used some of the art supplies that she had originally bought for making wedding invitations. But this didn't make her cry any more. In fact it didn't even make her angry or sad. She would much rather be making a name sign for Miles and meeting him off his flight, than getting married to Smooth a hundred times.

That said, she had some very interesting thoughts running through her head, as she sipped on a hot chocolate in the arrivals hall of the airport. Thoughts, and also feelings. There was definitely a knot of excitement and nervousness in her stomach, which had arrived the night before and showed no hint of going away. If anything, it was just getting stronger and she could discount driving to the very airport that she and Smooth were supposed to have left for Prague from, and she could discount nervousness about generally driving in London traffic, or missing her alarm and missing the overnight arrival from Los Angeles. So it must be the prospect of meeting Miles, because every time the electronic board that gave arrival statuses of the morning flights refreshed, she got a little bit more of a knot. Then when it said that the flight had arrived and that he had landed, she actually felt like she might throw up.

She also thought that arrival halls of airports did no favours to your emotions. If there was ever a magnifying glass on meeting or leaving a loved one, then airports were pretty much the Hubble Telescope. Sure, there were business people and holidaymakers in groups and they were probably the exceptions for different reasons. But for every stony-faced businessman who was marching to catch their flight, or eyeing the other name boards for their taxi home, or for every group of giggling holidaymakers with their names on the back of their shirts, there were three or four moments of heart-wrenching separation, or touching reunifications. Couples with a mixture of good and bad crying-faces, grandparents scooping up charging grandchildren, or boyfriends trying to act cool but at the same time thrusting flowers at their partners with just a little bit too much enthusiasm. There was a reason that films and TV adverts often focused on this place. To bring emotion to their stories and here she was, right in the middle of it, feeling as nervous and confused as she ever had in her life.

The truth was that when Miles had left this time, she had been sadder than she expected. They had got used to each other and she had got used to him being around. But she hadn't realised how much they did together and shared together without actually noticing. Miles was definitely one of those people that affected you like that, which was the complete opposite to Smooth. With Smooth, if he made you a cup of tea, or recorded a TV show for you, then he basically expected a medal for it. He would make dramatic gestures, or ask you several times if you got his affectionate text message. Then, if you didn't give the appropriate thanks, or if you didn't show enough amazement at his ability to wipe a sink clean, then he would begin with passive aggressive comments, before trying to pick a fight on every word, or every move you made. If you brushed past him, he would take the opportunity to hop around on one leg, as if you had broken a toe. He would also accuse you of looking amorously at an actor, or even a cartoon character, on TV.

Miles on the other hand, just seemed to get things done without you noticing. He would always arrive at the flat, even just to watch TV, with some kind of perfect gift, be it a steaming take-away coffee in the morning, or a carton of microwave popcorn in the evening and he never asked for anything in return, because he also had the gift of getting you to do it anyway. You could spend the whole evening watching reality TV, laughing so hard that the wine came out of your nose and then before you knew it, you were halfway through the sports highlights and you didn't mind. There was an unspoken balance having him there. So this time when he left, for the first time, she felt it. They had crossed some kind of line that meant they needed each other and expected each other.

She had realised this when his first text had arrived, to say that he had arrived safely. It was the first time that she had been surprised by her feelings for Miles. It was his third or fourth trip to Los Angeles and the previous times she had been excited to hear about it when he came back, but this time it was different. It had been quite by accident that she had sent him the first song link. She had just been sitting at work and her mind had drifted to Miles; it was mid-afternoon in London and therefore early morning where he was. A Killers song had been playing on the radio and it reminded her of him, so she had texted and said it was his wake-up song. They had then just chatted normally by text through the day, but then when she woke the next morning, he had sent her a song back. She was curled up in bed and when that text arrived, she had missed him for the first time.

That's how it started. A daily routine that filled the gap in her life whilst he was away and meant that she knew he was thinking about her every day. She liked how that made her feel special and made her wonder if she'd ever felt that special before. She was so lost in her thoughts, that she didn't notice that the electronic sign had now changed to read that the baggage was waiting in the baggage hall.

Sophie panicked and realised that she hadn't done her pre-meeting preparation. Not only was the sign still packed away in her handbag, but she also hadn't checked how she looked and the bathroom was a good ten minute walk away, which gave no chance to get there and back before Miles emerged from the security gates. Not that she supposed that mattered – given that Miles had just flown across the Atlantic in a small seat, with no chance of a shower. Plus, he generally liked her just how she was, especially if it involved jeans. She cursed herself, having deliberately given herself an additional hour on top of general travel time and now she was late. There was only one thing for it. She would just have to spruce up here at the table, which meant that she maybe didn't look at the top-end of how she wanted, but at least she would have time to walk to the gate. She especially wanted to make sure that she was there with her sign, but didn't want to have to run and arrive all red and sweaty. She quickly used the plastic cover to the menu stand on her table to check her reflection, unconsciously tousled her hair and smiled at the result. What was she panicking for anyway, it was just Miles, and they were friends. She should pull herself together.

It was at that exact moment, as she looked up and got ready to leave her seat in the coffee shop, that she saw Miles striding towards her.

Striding, was the right word. He had a bounce in his step, which she had not noticed before. Now that the summer had arrived in California, he had a slight bleached look to his hair and depth to his tan that only the salty breeze of an ocean can provide. It caught her so much by surprise, that she didn't have time to collect her thoughts. She was so happy, but she could feel another thought in her head, fighting to get to the front, but it couldn't get through – It was being blocked by her surprise and happiness for seeing Miles. She stood and too late, the thought got through. Be cool, it said. Be cool. But it was too late.

'I got you a sign!' She shouted, and grabbed it out of her bag. It exploded with a shower of glitter and in her hurry to get up, she also knocked over her chair and spilled her half-finished hot chocolate all over the table and partly over the sign, making the 's' darker than the other letters and slightly smudged, as the liquid soaked into the cardboard.

Miles smirked and quickened his step, leaping over the fallen chair and lifting Sophie in the air.

'If I get you chocolate sprinkles on the next one,' he smiled, 'you'd better not chuck that on the floor as well.'

As Miles bought the new drinks, a double espresso for him and another hot chocolate for Sophie, she regained her composure and propped her now-stained sign up on the menu holder that she had been using as a mirror. Miles slid in across from her and took her in from the other side of the table.

'I love the sign,' he said, 'and I love even more, that you made it for me. With, what seems like, such gusto.'

Sophie smiled. They chatted for a while about the flight. It had seemed that Miles had managed to secure an upgrade, so had managed to catch a good portion of sleep, as well as a few decent movies that had not yet been on general release in the UK. He promised to take Sophie with him to see one of them when it came out. It seemed they had got back into the groove and Sophie had pulled herself back together. But it showed how quickly things change in a relationship. As little as two weeks ago, they were equals and seeing Miles was as natural as seeing any other friend. Granted, there was still that spark between them, but the only time it came close to anything else was on a very drunken night, or perhaps when Sophie felt very vulnerable.

There was an unspoken limit that neither of them expressed, but that both of them adhered to. Of course, before that, Sophie was definitely the one in control. But now here they were and although it had been hard to actually speak whilst Miles was away this time, the connection that had flowed between them over text, had swung the pendulum back in the other direction. Miles was now in control and Sophie was the one who was urging him to look at her and trying to read his every move. Who would have thought that, all those years ago when they had first met, at the Shepherds Bush Empire on a cold November night?

'Well,' said Sophie after a while. 'I have something to tell you.'

'Well,' said Miles. 'Me too, but you first.'

'I'm going back online. I have decided it's time.'

Until a few moments before, she had been uncertain about whether she would start blogging again, either soon or ever. She had even written a list of pros and cons, whilst she was waiting for Miles, but seeing him had given her the confidence to make the decision. It had been a long time since she had last posted a video and of course, it had been focused on her impending nuptials, before literal radio silence for over a year. After a few weeks, she had started getting quizzical emails from her community, asking why she had not posted for a while. Then a while after that, she started receiving sympathetic emails, as word spread about the implosion of her relationship. It started as a trickle, but as soon as she then changed her relationship status on her social networks, there was a flood of communication, which was overwhelming and upsetting at the same time. This slowed, but still from time-to-time, she would get a message, urging her to get going again. The blogging community was growing and she was one of the first, so needed to keep the momentum going, or be consigned to the blogging history books. Lifestyle was a popular topic, but her fans still said that she did it in a way that no one else could. They said she was stylish, yet accessible and had an easy manner that some of the newer and more enthusiastic bloggers did not. It felt like she was doing it for them, not for herself, and that is why people listened. They were still ready to listen.

The itch had also grown as she had seen how much Miles loved what he was doing. In life, seeing someone take an unconventional path and follow it with such passion, was a very infectious thing. We hold ourselves back through fear, Sophie thought, but if you have someone who can give you the validation and the support, it helps you take the leap. The only question that remained for her, was how she should re-announce herself. There was a part of her that thought she should explain what had happened in the last year, perhaps it would give others the inspiration to question themselves and make sure they are happy in their relationships and their lives. Her fear, however, was that it would just end up being counselling for herself and would just be irritating. Her community took inspiration from her, but positive inspiration; not self-pity or bitterness, and she couldn't guarantee there wouldn't be either of those things. On the other hand, just going back online and pretending nothing had happened, would also be a bit weird.

Both of these angles, also gave Smooth an opportunity to text her and either complain about his privacy, or complain that she wasn't upset enough. He had the habit of doing that, out of the blue, every now and again. Even though she had heard that he was actually now living with the mysterious E. No, she had to do something completely different.

Sophie explained this to Miles, who sipped on his coffee, but Sophie could also tell there was something on his mind. It was unusual for him to be like this, perhaps it was the flight, or the excitement of the video game. Usually, he would be rapt in what she had to say, but the eerie intensity that was sometimes in his dark eyes wasn't there. Instead, he looked excited and as if he couldn't wait for a gap in the conversation so he could tell her something. She hoped it was good, because at this exact moment, she was both opening up to him and asking for his support. If she was going to post again, then she needed some of Miles' advice and encouragement.

Miles reacted perfectly. He felt how raw Sophie was to his next reaction and so instead of exploding with excitement, he reached across the table and took her hands in his. His expression changed from light, back to the dark look that she knew and again she felt the knot in her stomach.

But then he paused and seemed to be working out what to say and this threw Sophie again. She hoped he wasn't going to say anything too heavy, she needed him to stay on-topic, because what she was talking about was important to her. It was the biggest decision she had made for over a year and she hoped he hadn't rehearsed some kind pledge to her on the plane, not now. She was feeling something different, it was true, but right now she couldn't get into a conversation about it. But she knew that look, it was the look of Miles, when he had something important to say and it scared her. It was the look of someone, who had spent a lot of the flight in the bathroom of the plane, practising into the mirror. She had seen it a lot when they first met, so she had come to recognise it. Right now, she was in a delicate place and this was a delicate moment, so the next words that came out of Miles' mouth were very important. She took a deep breath.

'Sophie, I have something to ask you.'

Sophie darkened, 'Miles, this is not the time…'

But Miles instead held up a hand, and Sophie paused. 'Please, Sophie. I have something to ask you and I have an idea.'

Miles then explained about putting on the stage show in Los Angeles and the offers they had to publicise the game, even though it was not quite finished. He explained how he wanted her to come with him and that whilst they were apart, he realised that it was important for him that she shared the experience with him. He explained that he was going to wait, but when he listened to her talk about blogging, he had an idea and realised that the two things were connected. She should come with him, not as his plus one, but as a partner in the show. She could announce her return to blogging in LA and explain that she has had a change in her life and that's it. A change. When people say that, they don't have to explain anything else, because the only thing that follows change is a full stop. I've changed. I've had a change. Full stop.

She could use the trip to talk about LA fashion or art, but also cover the launch of one of the most anticipated video games of the year. Or at least, that's what she could say. She covered pop culture and this was it, you couldn't get any closer to popular culture than video games and Los Angeles. They could be business partners!

Sophie stared at Miles for a second, processing what he had said. Usually, Miles gave her advice slowly and gently led her through the field of his thoughts. But this was like a blast of water in the face. It sounded perfect, and terrifying. But it did make sense. She felt the knot again, but this time it was loosening, so that must mean something. But then she felt something else, as the emotion of the last two weeks and the last half an hour came flooding out of her in great sobs. Miles looked at her, unsure what to do, but then she leapt up and threw her arms around him, trying to speak into his shoulder and thank him, although she wasn't sure what for. He stood still for a moment, but then accepted her embrace and laughed into her shoulder.

'Is that a yes?' He asked.

'Yes!' She sobbed into his shoulder. She carried on holding him until the sobs quietened down, but she didn't want to let go. She stared over his shoulder, watching as the hall filled with people – all fresh off the big, long-haul overnight flights. Somehow, when she leapt up to hug Miles, her sign had managed to spin across the floor and she could see the glitter and the colour amongst the crowds.

They could be business partners. Business partners, she thought. She rolled the thought around in her mind and with that, the knot in her stomach was back.

Chapter 25

Curtain Rise

June 11, 2007.

'You know when they say: it's just like the movies?' Said Sophie, dripping.

'Yup,' Miles knew what was coming next.

'Well, it *is* just like the movies!'

'I don't remember a movie, where the leading lady runs screaming into the sea and is ungraciously hit in the face by a wave!'

Miles only just evaded Sophie's playful slap, by rolling a few feet from her and curling into a ball. He felt the wood of the old pier creak under his weight and could hear the crash of the ocean through the gaps in the slats, amplified by the old wooden and steel structure, which kept them suspended above the water.

This was becoming a familiar routine for them at the end of an evening, an unspoken, but never broken, agreement. They would find a quiet spot and lie side-by-side, staring up at the sky and rebalancing their own personal worlds. Perhaps it had even started on the first night they met – that time on the bed in the hotel. Since then, they had slipped away at festivals and parties, and they would often wake up at dawn, having fallen asleep in mid-conversation wherever they lay.

This time, they were on the pier at Venice. Earlier in the evening Sophie had insisted that they walk the full promenade, from Santa Monica to Venice, as she hadn't had a chance since they arrived in Los Angeles for the publicity performance of *Misunderstood*. So they had walked, firstly amongst the fashionable joggers and skateboarders that frequented the Santa Monica end of the stretch, and then through the street sellers in Venice with their weathered faces and their throws, that displayed their wares on the concrete floor. Once colourful, but now faded and bleached by the sun and the salt. As they carried on and the crowds thinned out, Sophie had seen the pier, a more basic structure that forever lived in the shadow of the more opulent Santa Monica pier, and had fallen in love with it. So she had insisted further that she wanted to come back later that evening, so she could listen to the ocean some more.

The pre-party, the performance and the after-party that evening were all conveniently located close to each other and close to Venice Boulevard, so it was easy for them to take the short walk down to the beach and the pier. It was late by the time the after-party was winding down, but the air was still warm, with the city in the grip of the first heat wave of the year.

She hadn't intended to, but just as they reached the beach, she was overcome by a burst of excitement and had run headlong into the sea, fully clothed – which was why she was dripping wet. Of course, what she had not taken into account was the steep slope to the shallows and the waves, which had looked especially small from the top of the beach. Once she got closer, she realised that it was her that was small, certainly not the waves. Perhaps even the sheer size of the ocean was what masked the real size of the waves – stretching from horizon to horizon and with no other land, for what felt like an infinity of miles. She had managed to hurdle the first wave, with just one trailing foot skimming the breaker and sending a plume of foam in the air. But the second wave had taken her legs away at thigh level, so that the third wave hit her full in the face, with a power both exhilarating and frightening. The shock had made her scream and before she knew it, Miles was there next to her, holding her with his back to the tide and trying to shield her from the foamy crests as they broke one after another in a relentless beat.

They had half-carried each other back to the beach and then gradually made their way back up the sand and onto the pier, where they had collapsed in an exhausted, but happy heap. Sophie could feel the salt stinging her eyes and could feel her dress sticking to her, but she felt alive.

It had been an incredible evening and all the hard work of the past month had been worth it. They had been non-stop since the morning she had picked Miles up from the airport. Tim had arrived a few days later, to bring over the last of the UK-based cast and crew, who they had managed to contact and were needed for the performance. In the end, the majority of the group that had travelled with the performance in the UK had agreed to come with them, or even demanded it.

The fact they had managed to gather the group, was testament to the way that Tim had gone about announcing the Los Angeles show. He hadn't told them what was going on, but contacted them one-by-one and told them just that there was an important meeting in the pub about the future of the show. It took him a few days of solid phone calls, but he had figured, approaching it like that and by talking to each individual, rather than doing it on email or text, showed that he was fully committed. In turn, it would mean that those who really cared would turn up and those who did not, they knew were not fully committed and that was fine. In the end, they knew they would be able to replace them with American based cast and it would save them a few plane fares.

What they hadn't expected, is that every, single person they invited turned up. Tim had laid on free beers and sandwiches and let the group all get reacquainted with each other before making any announcement. Again, it showed they were committed, but they really needn't have done it – it was amazing how much of a family it had become. They had to wait for several hours before they could find a moment to break away from the group and set up the small stage. What was more, no one had even asked them what they were there for. Everyone was just happy to be back together and have the chance to get drunk with friends.

Tim, ever the dramatist, had been working hard during his last few days in Los Angeles on the previous trip. He had secured the theatre and also had managed to convince some of the video game artists to create a huge piece of *Misunderstood* art for him. They had painted it on a bed sheet, which he now hung in the pub, behind the stage. As he did so, it was this that first started people talking about what was going on and questioning why they were there. The bed sheet depicted characters from the game, but also had a vista of some of the most iconic sights of Los Angeles, merged with more familiar landmarks of London. The room went from the excited chatter of friends, to a gradual hush and then a buzz of excitement as people started to try and guess what was going on. It started to become clear to everyone that they were going on the road again. Some of the cast knew about the video game, but no one had the chance to put these things together, until Tim strode onto the stage to the tune of Thriller and made the announcement.

The rest of the night had ridden on the news and the energy had kept going until the sun rose the next day over South London. There were calls made to cancel work and holidays, with shrieks of excitement occasionally rising above the voices and the music, as people told their excited family and friends the news.

Misunderstood, was going to LA.

It seemed that since then, they hadn't stopped and hadn't slept. For Sophie, she was going to Los Angeles for the first time and as a video blogger again. There was scripting to write, along with contacts to make, so that the piece could be about Los Angeles fashion and lifestyle, as well as *Misunderstood*. The contacts at the video game developers had introduced her to some of the people who seemed to know and connect the whole city, by simply making a phone call and she spent her time arranging meetings and practising her words. It had been a while, so her focus was getting back to the relaxed, confident and connected tone she had previously and shake off the rustiness of the time she had spent in silence.

At the same time, Miles and Tim had been planning tweaks to the show, rehearsals and participating in evenings of endless conference calls to the studio and the theatre, whilst casting and organisation was made across the Atlantic. Tim's flat became a base and the three of them would take turns with the bed and the sofa, not even considering the time, but just sleeping whenever they needed. There were blankets and papers everywhere and once a day the staff from the pub would bring in a supply of take-away pizza, chicken and beers.

The trip itself had then just unfolded in a dream. They didn't have time to think, because as soon they touched down at LAX, they were met with sleek limousines and buses with blacked-out windows, that ferried the performers, plus Sophie, Tim and Miles to downtown and straight to the hotel. There were dress rehearsals by day, script meetings by night, guest lists to review and media training to slot into any gaps in the schedule. For the first time, they felt part of the pulsating entertainment machine and part of the throbbing engine that drives it. Even the most relaxed of the staff they had met before, were now transformed, their personalities fully the opposite of their previous, laid-back selves. This was game-time in Los Angeles and everyone knew their place and their role perfectly. There was no room for error, no room for a false promise or misquote. Every spontaneous comment had been carefully pre-planned and every chance meeting meticulously scheduled.

At the pre-party, both Miles and Tim had been whisked around the room, a professional hand on the elbow letting them know when their time was up in a particular conversation and enough pleasantries had been shared. Sophie was in-tow and was equally regimented in capturing video footage of the room and recording comments from the invited guests. They were, of course, thrilled to be there and waiting in anticipation for the show, because the developer was a "big deal" and they knew how to play the game. Around the foyer of the theatre, where the pre-party reception was being held, there were full sized posters of the video game and Sophie would watch in amazement as the staff would expertly position the guests who were being filmed, without their knowledge, in exactly the right place for Sophie to catch a smile, an affectionate arm on either Tim or Miles, and of course a full length shot of the video game logo in the background. Even so, occasionally Sophie gave herself a mild fright, as she caught sight of a rotting eye, or a dismembered arm through the crowd of well-dressed and beautiful people of Los Angeles – even in 2D they were quite an impressive sight.

Tim, having the most experience in this environment from his previous acting days, was of great help to both Sophie and Miles if they struggled with some of the pre-arranged phrases and briefing points they had needed to learn. He had a way of politely stepping in front of them and delivering the right line, that Miles found, again, alien to his normal persona, but at the same time, so impressive. In the years he had known Tim, this never ceased to amaze him. The way he held himself, even made his unkempt beard look like it was grown deliberately for that moment. He could see Tim as an actor, blending into any part and becoming someone else, with a simple change in wardrobe and a flash of a smile.

Tim also made sure, that just before the show was due to start and just before they took to the stage, that he gathered Miles and Sophie in a quiet corner, backstage.

Miles felt Tim's heavy hand on his arm and in turn he found Sophie's free hand and squeezed it tight.

'So, friends. Here we are,' started Tim and looked them both in the eye with his piercing gaze. 'We are just about to do something, that we probably never thought we would. Not only that, but we are about to do something that not many people get to do and that we have been working hard towards for a long time.' They squeezed each other harder.

'That's the thing about working hard towards something, especially a dream that you have had for a long time. You can get caught up in it, you can hold on too tight and you can forget to look around.' He paused, and took a deep breath, motioning also for Miles and Sophie to do the same.

'So remember this moment. Remember where you are and put everything into it. Imagine that it's the last time you may ever say the line, the last time that we may all be together in the *Misunderstood* family. But also enjoy it, because, actually, it might be the last time we're all together doing this. This might be *the* opportunity, *the* one story that you can take with you and tell everyone for the rest of your life. People often take these moments for granted, because they're thinking about what's next. Let's not do that – let's just think about what is happening *now*.'

Tim paused again, but he hadn't finished. 'The soccer player who reaches one FA Cup final and scores. Or the footballer that gets one Superbowl ring and scores a touchdown in the game. We sometimes look at them and feel sorry that they didn't win two cups, or that they didn't get to the Hall of Fame. But we shouldn't do that. Instead, we should look at them and say: they got there and they did it. Maybe they wanted to go back and do it again and maybe there were a hundred reasons why they didn't. But no one can take away that moment, when they stepped on the pitch. No one can take away that moment, when they heard the stadium roar. That's what it's all about – it's all about that moment. Sure, it's a drug and you want more. But pretend that it will never happen again and give it everything you've got. Always remember: we were here, we were together, we couldn't have done it without each other and for that, I love you guys.'

So they did. They gave it their all. Tim's words took away any of their nerves and woke them up from the trance they had been in through the weeks of preparation and rehearsals. It woke them up so they could be free and loose, and take the best of their training and the best of themselves and make it bigger than it had ever been before.

As the applause faded and the after-party pulsed with congratulations, cheers, hugs, claps, bright lights and laughter, they all knew they had taken everything up to the next level. There was more hard work ahead, but they knew they had taken *Misunderstood* up to the next level. If there had been any doubt in the minds of Tim, Miles or the cast, they were now all gone. The question about whether they could do it, was now about how far they could get and how high they could go together. With a subtle glance from Tim, they also knew when it was time to walk away from the night and let the entertainment machine take over again. The cast and crew, as one, walked away whilst the party was in full swing – because that is how you should remember it. *Misunderstood* left the building.

Tim made an excuse and drifted back to his hotel, whilst Sophie and Miles rode the euphoria down to the beach, into the sea and onto the pier.

'I love the waves.' Sophie was the first to break the silence. 'I always wanted to live by the sea and just listen to the melody of the waves crashing. I don't think anyone could have trouble relaxing or sleeping, if they can hear the sea.'

Miles rolled back across the boards to Sophie and let his eyes adjust to the stars. It was clear and the moon was just a sliver, allowing the North Star and the Little Dipper to be clearly visible in the night sky. The grey light from the moon was catching Sophie's wet hair, giving it a halo and he thought again how beautiful she was.

'I know what you mean. Coming from a city, you lose out on the seaside. I was a bit obsessed with beaches when I was on family holidays. I used to spend the days down there, sitting cross-legged and reading Steven King novels, thinking it was all romantic and cool, despite it being freezing cold. I must have stayed out all day, imagining what it must be like to be older and getting a bit freaked out, thinking about the future, the world, the sky and just how big and overwhelming everything was. I used to try and imagine myself coming back to the same beach when I was old and what I might have done in all that time. I certainly never thought I would ever come to actual America, It seemed such an unlikely thing for a boy who had only really been on caravanning and camping holidays his whole life. Part of me thought that I would just end up being a hippy and living in a caravan my whole life, so I didn't have to make any hard decisions.'

'I think that is possibly, the cutest thing I have ever heard,' said Sophie, 'and don't tell me – you used to listen to The Levellers?'

'Sophie,' Miles theatrically feigned offense and put his hand to his forehead, 'actually, you're right. I was trying to do everything differently; it was my way of trying to make an identity for myself. Everyone else was listening to Guns 'n' Roses or the Thompson Twins and I was listening to folk rock. That's why all the zombies in *Misunderstood* leave the stage to folk music. All those macabre novels and fiddles and tales of subversion, gave me the romantic vision that everyone should exit their life to a whimsical tune.'

'It's now gone from cute, to very dark, Miles,' although at the same time, her hand found Miles' against the warm wood. Miles enjoyed the feeling of Sophie's damp fingers on his. Her hands were cold and his were warm. 'But the thing is – I used to like train stations, for the same reason.'

Sophie smiled, and pulled out a hip-flask. She took a long sip and passed it over to Miles.

'It's the predictability. Trains come in and trains go out. They come in and then they leave. If my life was feeling a bit out of control, I used to head to the train station and watch the trains coming and going. Then I would watch people running to and from the trains. If you squint your eyes in a busy train station, you can pretend you are in one of those films – the ones where you are standing still and the world is going on around you at super speed. It made me feel like my world was in control, I could just stand there, I didn't have to take a train. In a way it centred me, made me feel like life was not so crazy after all.'

Miles nodded, almost invisible now in the dark. 'It's still a bit weird, but I think I understand. I always think that it was hard being a kid when we were growing up – but it's even harder now. Everything is just so stressful. The playground bully can now text you at home, or post about you on The Facebook.'

'Facebook,' corrected Sophie.

'Facebook,' Miles continued, '... and you used to have to compete with the coolest kids in the neighbourhood, who had the latest branded trainers and the latest Walkman or Action Man. But now you have to compete with the coolest kids on YouTube, or on the whole Internet. It's stressful.'

'True,' said Sophie, 'but it's also stressful being an adult and having to learn all that stuff in an adult world. Adults have the same monsters, except they're not physical; instead they're the monsters of fear, or worry that lurk around every corner. At least the kids these days will be used to how small the world is, but I still feel like I'm coming to terms with it. I mean, I'm happy right now, but also, we must be on a massive comedown and I love the way that the waves are grounding us. They were here this morning, ten years ago, a million years ago, and they will be here tomorrow. They're predictable, so although we have just been through the most incredible month, the waves remind us to stay in the present.'

'To be fair, Sophie, it's not just the last month we're on a comedown from. It's been quite a year for you, outside of all this,' he gestured vaguely to the beach, suddenly feeling self-conscious. He meant her break-up with Smooth, he supposed, and it was the first time he had thought about it for a while. He had continued to stay away from the Smooth topic of conversation, even in all the time they had spent together. It was easier, he supposed, for both of them.

Sophie sensed it and for once, Miles felt she was open to it. 'I think it has for us both, Miles,' she said. 'But at the same time, I think there have been nothing but good choices and positive choices, and good decisions for us both, over the last few months and years. I sometimes wonder what might have been, if we hadn't met each other. In life, it was just such a chance meeting, but life has that funny way of throwing people together in that way. Then, what you do with that opportunity to be in someone else's life, is your own choice. I know we're not both directly responsible for the other's decisions, but in some ways it all started back then, when we first met.'

Miles smiled and picked at a stray piece of seaweed that had made it onto the pier, attached in some way to one of them.

'Yeah. I might have kids right now if I had continued how I was going.'

'Don't forget, Miles, the chances would be, that right now I could be walking down the aisle with Smooth. I could be Mrs Smooth. Actual Mrs Smooth. We could have bought a mid-level sports car, probably red, and driven off into the sunset.'

Miles propped himself up on his elbow and Sophie did the same, so they were facing each other.

'Hi,' said Sophie.

'Hi back.' Miles said, because he couldn't think of anything else to say.

There was one thing on his mind that he couldn't shake and hearing Sophie talk about Smooth again, had just brought it back. It was a small thing, but to Miles it defined their relationship either one way, or another. He felt protective of Sophie and she knew that. She also knew that he would do anything for her and drop anything to help her. Of course, the feeling was mutual – Sophie had shown as such when he had been stranded in Edinburgh. He had taken that help without question and would do it again. But there was one moment, where Sophie had chosen not to ask for his help and he needed to know why. It was almost the last secret that they had from each other and the last question mark that hung over their relationship. In Miles' mind, knowing the answer would mean he knew where he stood.

'There is something that I have always wanted to know, Sophie,' he started.

'Mmmm,' she said, as if she could sense there was something coming.

'That night, with Smooth, when it all went wrong and you drank all that gin. Do you remember?'

'Oh, I remember,' said Sophie, 'or rather, I remember the first bit.' She smiled self-consciously.

'Why didn't you call me?'

This time, it was Sophie that couldn't think of what to say. She had occasionally wondered about it herself, especially recently. The conclusion she had come to, was not one that she found easy to express. So instead, she just looked at Miles and moved closer.

After two and a half years and so much between them, for the first time, Miles and Sophie kissed.

Chapter 26

Light bulb

June 16, 2007.

Relationships are just a ticking bomb, Sophie had decided and it doesn't matter what you do, or how much effort you put in, you can't diffuse the bomb. The bomb was going to go off eventually, right in your face. There was just so much to consider and so many distractions, that it was only a matter of time before you were let down, or disappointed.

Take texting, for example. Before you were together, texting was exciting. The anticipation and the way that a text made you smile. But then once you were together, didn't texting just give you the ability to lie to someone more effectively? Or did it just make you say things that you would never dream of saying to someone's face and did that make it all just a bit disingenuous? When you look someone in the eye, or even when you talk over the phone, you have so many more signals to pick up on, like tone, or body language. When you need to deliver good, or bad news, in person, or over the phone, you needed to be so much braver in your words and your actions.

Texting, however, put that distance between you. How did you even know if the person was exactly where they said they were? Your boyfriend could call you and tell you he is in Newcastle, when he is actually in Liverpool. Your girlfriend could text to tell you that she loves you, from her lover's bed. Hadn't Sophie found that out herself, with Smooth on New Year's Eve and goodness knows how many other occasions.

Then, after someone had texted you, you had no idea whether they had just texted four other people the same thing, or had just received three texts from other people, telling them about what colour underwear they were wearing. It was just so instant, so fast and so uncontrollable.

She was reflecting a lot, since her and Miles had kissed, on this particular topic. They had always texted each other as the main form of communication. Neither of them was that good at expressing themself face-to-face and it removed the social awkwardness or the unnecessary forced humour. But at the same time, Sophie was struggling to figure out how that could work in the long term. On the one hand, it had brought them together in moments where they were not. Sometimes she confused her memories because of that and felt like she had been to Los Angeles many times before, or had to convince herself that was wasn't in Edinburgh for New Year. Those moments had felt so real, even though they happened over text and mobile phone with Miles. But in the long-term, how did that work? They couldn't live forever through written mediums, at some point they had to step away from technology and just be together.

That said, the last few days in Los Angeles had been great. Miles had been busy finalising the video game and continuing to meet additional press about *Misunderstood*. But when he had time, they had hung out as if they were having a holiday romance. They had hiked above the city to look at the Hollywood sign, they had eaten breakfast and watched all the small dogs on Rodeo Drive, and had explored the corners of the city – from the pink-washed Beverley Hills Hotel to a drive along Sunset Boulevard. It was innocent and exciting, like a holiday romance. Nothing much more had happened since the night on the pier, but with them both being away from the familiar and in the sunshine of California, it had made it easy just to postpone any heavy discussions and just enjoy being together. Every night, they had then gone back to Venice Pier and spent hours, just laying side-by-side and talking. So in some ways, nothing had changed between them.

Except that everything had changed.

In terms of the event, from what she could gather from Miles and Tim, it had gone very well, or actually it had gone brilliantly. At least that is what she could assume from the whooping and sparkling eyes of both Tim and Miles and their over-use of the word 'brilliant'. They had spent the morning after the show absorbing the local events pages and although she was no expert, the sheer number of column inches, pictures and the superlatives, meant that the coverage was better than they could have ever expected. They had been warned that the video game business was just beginning to gain momentum and that in Los Angeles it especially played second place to the movie industry. They had been warned not to expect mainstream coverage in some of the larger publications, but it seemed that *Misunderstood*

313

had bucked this trend. In some way, the crossover between theatre and video games had helped, despite both of these genres being detached from the glamour of film. Perhaps the use of theatre had helped the press to understand the story of *Misunderstood* a little bit better and the video game had given the show that little bit of modern sparkle. Or perhaps it was just that it hadn't been done before.

For Sophie herself, her job was also just beginning. Perhaps that was also what was making her feel nervous and daunted by technology and speed. She was sat in the hotel, in front of her computer screen and with many hours of footage to edit and shape into her renaissance as a video-blogger. She had the day to finish the video, post it and then head to the airport to fly home. The timing was important, so that the post coincided with a couple of big interviews that Miles and Tim had given, that were due to go to print.

She and Miles were travelling separately, as he had another two day's worth of work to do, so they had agreed that she would post the entry without showing it to him first. That way, she could claim an element of neutrality in the content and be confident that Miles or Tim did not influence it, before it went live. It was in some ways exhilarating for Sophie to feel like this was her actual job and at the same time, a scary thought for both of them, but they had agreed it was for the best.

The room was littered with balled up pieces of paper, discarded sketches and ideas for the angle or the theme for the post. Her content was a mix of fashion, lifestyle and footage from the *Misunderstood* performance and launch party. This meant that she had everything from interviews, to non-specific atmospheric shots. For example, in the days when Miles and Tim had been holed up in the studio, she had taken to walking areas of the city and then settling into coffee shops to people-watch. During these moments, she had just let her camera roll and taken hours of video from the bustling tourist havens downtown, to the boardwalk at Venice in the early evening. She was finding it hard to create a theme, or spot a trend that she could hang her episode off. It seemed that the longer she stared at the screen, the more startling it had become how much had changed in a year and the last time she had commented on life and fashion. Life and fashion had seemed to accelerate to another gear, and everything had become – more individual.

Her struggle was also to link this mish-mash of fashion with zombies. How do you create a link, from something that was so current, with the undead? Uber cool hipsters, with comic book geeks? It was a real dichotomy, because although both had been around for a long time and were cool in their own rights – they were almost at opposite ends of the spectrum. Fashion was so current, whereas zombie enthusiasts and video games were rejecters of fashion, an anti-thesis to the cool crowd and the cool attitude, so much so that they had created an attitude of their own. It was no less attractive and no less self-conscious of who they were, but in a completely different way. For example, she had seen guys walking along the beach, who had matched their Converse to their sunglasses, instead of their belt. You would never get Miles matching like this, although you would see him ensure that he never mixed his *Star Wars* baseball cap, with his *Return of the Jedi* t-shirt.

With this individualism, she was also discovering an awareness that had not been there before, in both men and women. There was almost an awakening of adventurousness, which had blurred some boundaries and created an expression that was more unisex. Plus, she had to admit, there were sunglasses *everywhere*. This was California, granted, but at the same time there must be something in this. They were the one constant, the one piece of the uniform that everyone agreed on, it seemed. She was pretty certain, that the summer before in London, she had not seen so many men wearing sunglasses.

Sophie paused on this thought and realised, that right there – she had her theme. She had been obsessed with making the piece about fashion and therefore, was struggling also to show *Misunderstood* in a positive light, but with credibility. Yet this was where she was going wrong. She shouldn't be talking about fashion, because clearly zombies were not fashionable, per-se. There was something about them and the way that Miles and Tim had presented them, with their teams of designers and producers, that was cool, but not fashionable. Something that was hypnotic and wanted you to be part of it, something that made you want to identify with them and their video game. But it wasn't fashion. It was style. In that sense, it had everything to do with the girls rollerblading on the boardwalk and guys hanging out together in the skate parks. Style was timeless and that was her theme.

Relieved, she now started to work faster and was able to create links between the city and the theatre. A shot of the lobby of the theatre, with a connection to a pavement bar at sunset. They were both stylish places, with stylish people, in their own way. Through this, she was bringing the nerds into the mainstream and blurring the lines between video games and life. She liked where this was going, she paused the screen on a shot of Miles and found herself unconsciously talking to him.

'Yep, I think you'll like it too!' She said, her voice echoing around the large hotel room.

That was another strange thing about reviewing the footage. She spent a lot of time watching herself in the third person and a lot of time watching Miles. She watched him hanging back nervously in the pre-party and in contrast, how Tim glided through the crowds with an easy manner, ever the actor. But at the same time, she could see how Tim helped Miles, gently leading him by the shoulder into the fray and picking up conversations when Miles was left faltering and looking anxiously around. In these moments, she saw the Miles she had first met, slightly flushed and seeming uncomfortable in his own body. Handsome, but with no awareness of that fact and no awareness of when a journalist or waitress gave him a flirtatious signal. These moments made Sophie smile, but also she felt a small pang of jealousy that made her feel warm and annoyed at the same time.

Of course, she also saw how she was in the third person. It was not always Sophie doing the filming. Sometimes she would hand over the camera to a member of the cast, or one of the video game producers, so that she could interview people without distraction, or just so that she could give the appearance that she was also part of the party and therefore, give her eventual blog credibility that it was real and natural. In these moments, she felt self-conscious in the way that everyone does when they see themselves on film, but also, she liked the way she was when Miles was around. She seemed to instantly relax and become more natural in his company. She could see Miles' shoulders visibly unclench when he

317

caught sight of her across the room, or when she joined a conversation. For her, she smiled more when she was with Miles.

She shook the thought off and refocused on the task in hand. There would be plenty of time for her and Miles to talk about their future, she was sure of that. She had to let things develop naturally and also make sure that she was certain about what their future was. She had still not really answered his question. Why had she not called him, when she was in so much trouble that night? She knew why Miles had asked it, because it meant everything.

If they were friends, then she would have called him and asked him for help. She wouldn't have been ashamed to do that, because that's what friends were for. They drop things for each other and they support each other in their time of need. But if it was more than that, then she could be forgiven for not wanting him to see her in such a state, physically and emotionally. If it was more than friends, then she wouldn't want him to see her at the end of one relationship, for fear that it could ruin the start of the next one. But there was also a third option. It could be that Miles was just a superficial distraction. Someone that just made her feel good in this time in her life, where she had so many questions, about so many things. Perhaps she had just not even thought of Miles, perhaps he had just not entered her head in that time of need.

Sophie knew she had to decide and had an idea. It was an idea of a way that she could make a decision, or at least form an unbiased opinion of their relationship. A way of looking past the surface. On the surface, she had to admit, it seemed great and when she thought of him and saw them together at the party, her stomach flipped. But there were many more hours of footage that could give a different view, away from the party and in the more mundane moments. She decided that she would move all the sections of content that included her and Miles and put them in a separate folder, as an unedited b-roll of footage. Then, she could watch this footage and use that to help her decide and try to change her view of the world. Were they friends that made a mistake, or were they destined to be together? Or in other words, had the bomb already gone off, did they have some time to enjoy the countdown?

By the time the sun was losing its heat, Sophie felt she was done. She had edited, re-edited and reviewed the post. At a little over ten minutes long, it was probably the longest piece she had done, but the fact that it was a re-announcement of her blogging, meant that she didn't just have to create a topical entry, but also needed to include an explanation for her absence. Most of her community knew the reasons, but at the same time, she wanted to say it in her words. She stayed away from the specifics of her heartbreak, but at the same time made sure that she explained the journey she had been on and why she had ended up in Los Angeles. It was unavoidable to mention her allegiance to *Misunderstood* and to Miles, but this provided a good link to the show. She felt like she had kept that part of it factual and made it clear that she was in Los Angeles because of something she believed in, but also with an open mind.

Happy with the post, she saved it and started the upload. Sophie then turned her attention to the folder that she had used to store the clippings of her and Miles together. She had a few moments before she had to leave and it would also take a little while for the clip to upload to her blog. She decided to have a look at the unedited footage and at least start to think about things between them, before she got on the plane. She would have a further eleven hours to consider their future, on the way across the Atlantic and then a little while more, before they would see each other, given that Miles was going to be 24 hours behind her.

She turned her attention to the new folder and checked the time. She had about thirty minutes and that should be enough, before she had to take her taxi. But when she looked back to the screen, she started in surprise. There was almost two hours of footage of them together. She hadn't been paying attention when she was reviewing the footage and moving the small clips across, so it was only when she opened the folder that she saw the length of the video. Not only that, but it wasn't just footage they had taken for fun. There were shots of them messing around together, shots of Miles telling stories and recounting their days from coffee shops and bars, but also, there were shots of them together at the parties and events related to *Misunderstood,* which Sophie didn't remember. It was as if they had gravitated towards each other at every opportunity and their relationship had moved on from hanging around together, to simply being together. It was an unconscious transition, there was no mistaking it and no mistaking how they fit together. She had somehow edited Miles into her life.

The next surprise was that Sophie found herself crying. She didn't know when it started, she just suddenly realised that her face was wet, but she was smiling. She realised that she had been obsessing about the kiss, but in the end it was everything that was happening around the kiss that was important. She thought back to the conversations they often had, about the place where you could be yourself and finding a way to feel safe from a world that was getting faster and more difficult to control. But she realised for them, they had both found their peaceful places in each other. In the middle of California, or the middle of London, it didn't matter where. It was together that they would find peace, in their own bubble in the storm.

A sudden noise brought her back to the present and she realised that it was her blog, finishing its upload. She glanced at the clock on the screen and realised that also, she had to leave, she had a plane to catch. So she took a deep breath and closed down the video. She could watch the rest on the plane and then when she landed, she could also see the reaction of the community to her new blog. The two things together were pretty overwhelming, but at the same time Sophie felt excited. She realised that she didn't need to make a decision at all, it was already made and she needed Miles to know.

Without thinking, Sophie copied the b-roll footage of her and Miles to a memory stick. She placed it in the middle of a blank piece of hotel stationery and drew a heart around it. She was sure he would find it and know what it meant, but just in case, she also shot off a text to Miles to let him know that she had left him a present for his long trip back to the UK. Then Sophie left the hotel and she left California. As she boarded the plane, she thought about the memory stick on the table in the hotel. She glanced out the window and wondered when she would be back.

It was a calm night in Los Angeles and Sophie's mind was calm as she settled into her hoodie for the flight. But the butterfly had flapped its wings again and somewhere, in the corner of the world that belonged to Miles and Sophie, the hurricane was starting again.

Chapter 27

USB

June 17, 2007.

It was the end of something and the start of something else. There had been so many of those. Not too many to count, but enough that you could track in your mind where you were and what you were doing.

There was the very first Killers concert, which was also the very first time they had met, so really, it was just the start of something. Then there were the festivals and the heartbreak that had happened at Reading. The Killers had featured there as well, Brandon Flower as incendiary, as the end of the night was devastating for Miles. They were a part of their history, Miles supposed. Part of the good bits and part of the bad bits, like rock and roll should be.

Miles wondered if they would ever get the chance to visit Las Vegas, perhaps even go to Sam's Town Hotel and Gambling Hall, which had been the inspiration for the Killers' latest album title. He should probably take Sophie there one day, as a surprise - perhaps it could be the next time they came out to Los Angeles. They could hire a convertible sports car and take a road trip out there, spending the days driving from town to town, as the desert gradually took over and the temperature rose, before the desert then gave way to the neon oasis of lights and excess. Or perhaps they could fly there, first class, as a celebration when *Misunderstood* launched as a video game and he had made some money at last. Hours in the air, sipping champagne and watching movies together, or marvelling at the expanse of ocean and the tiny mountains beneath them.

So many of the times, over the years they had been together, had ended with regret and long periods of silences. But then there was now, this something. The something that had happened on the pier and the something that was happening every time they hung out over the days that followed.

Miles guessed that, if they wanted to, they could regret it. There were a lot of unanswered questions, a lot of things unsaid or not discussed. On a few occasions, he had woken up in the early hours in his hotel room and thought about it, even panicked a little bit and if he knew Sophie, then she would be doing the same, even though she would never admit it. He had almost texted her a few times, just to capture something he had remembered about the night, something he liked and to let her know that he was thinking of her. But then he had decided against it. He had got to know Sophie so well, that he knew this was a very delicate time and the best thing to do would be to bury the questions, at least until they were back home and find a natural occasion to bring it up.

They were not always in separate rooms. The day that Sophie was leaving for the UK, he had woken up early in his room, with Sophie next to him. They had been out late celebrating and as was customary, had come back together and fallen asleep, side-by-side. This time, Sophie had fallen asleep first and it had almost been in mid-giggle, although he couldn't remember what they were laughing about. It was the last time he was going to see her face and her eyes, before they were home, so he had stayed awake a bit longer and just watched her sleep.

The venue they had chosen to celebrate their last night, was in Malibu, where the Pacific Highway takes a sweeping turn along dramatic coastline. Although Malibu had the reputation as a spot for movie stars, they had a peaceful night relaxing on a beach terrace and watched the last of the surf crowd coming in for the evening. It felt like they could have been there thirty years ago and it wouldn't have been any different, with beautiful beaches giving way to cool hills. They had sipped cocktails and reminisced about the trip and how a few days had felt like a lifetime. The reviews for the show had been so good, that the whole day had felt like a dream. As a group, they had agreed beforehand how they would approach the next few weeks and months and had been set realistic expectations by the studio heads. If the coverage was average, then they would take note of the comments and re-work the game and the story accordingly. The trip and the event would be passed off as an experiment, or a test. They would then come back stronger, with another event and with the confidence of the learning they had taken from the show. The studio was geared up and they had no intention of cooling the intensity of production, no matter what the outcome. They were committed to the idea and would keep trying.

If the coverage was good, then they would push this even further. They would double down staff, work night and day, and capitalise on the good feeling to launch as soon as possible.

So, given the coverage was nothing short of spectacular, Miles and Tim were expecting some very busy times ahead.

That particular morning however, maybe it was because Sophie was leaving, Miles was feeling reflective. Recently, good things and good people just seemed to have fallen out of the sky and into his life. That is what had happened with Sophie and Tim and he felt so grateful. He supposed that, because of where he was in his own life at the time, he had taken this opportunity and embraced what was happening. He regretted nothing of what had happened over the last few years, because it had led to where he was now. But he couldn't shake the feeling that perhaps Sophie would start to regret anything happening between them. It wasn't even as if he had that feeling from Sophie, in fact, it seemed that she had finally accepted they should be in each other's lives.

It was just that it was so easy these days to regret things. Perhaps it was because you did so much that had the potential to be regretful. You could publish things online, that the whole world could see and instantly feel anxious about it. You could suddenly be emotional and goodness knows, Miles knew enough about that, and send an email or a text that you immediately regretted. Regretful moments no longer required you to have direct human interaction and didn't even need to be directed at people you knew. There was just a constant pressure there, a constant state of anxiety in the background, just waiting to push forward and take a grip of your brain. Miles knew that Sophie was most sensitive to that, having been through what she had with Smooth.

But for Miles, over the last few years he had learned that you needed more and more perspective in life. Most instant regrets can be fixed with actual interaction and a swallowing of pride, which again was something that Miles was very practised in. The real regrets in life for Miles, were the bands he never got to see, or the people that he had lost touch with.

In that sense, things between Sophie and him could never be a regret. It was something that had to happen, something real, not over text or the phone, just so they knew what it felt like. There had been such a tension between them, that they hadn't even noticed was building. It was a white noise, always there, but gradually the pressure had built and brought the noise forward, from the periphery and into their ears. If nothing else happened ever again, then he would be sad, but he could never regret it. Maybe it was just the things that you didn't do, that you ended up regretting.

These were the thoughts he had that morning and they stayed with him for a while after he had got up, showered and headed out to meet Tim for breakfast. Ahead of them, was the last day of this trip, but a lot of planning to do for the next one, so the lingering worries that Miles had woken up with, were soon pushed to the back of his mind.

Tim met him outside the hotel and as usual looked like he had slept in his clothes. He smiled and smoothed down his crumpled t-shirt in a dramatic gesture, reading

Miles' gaze. It was actually difficult to tell either way these days, whether they were the same clothes as the day before, as Tim had taken to a clothing method that he called 'simplifying the wardrobe'. He would pack only a few pairs of shorts and jeans and then buy the remainder of his clothes on arrival, usually from one of the discount stores. He would then leave the majority of these clothes at a charity store as he left the country, on the way back to the airport. It had happened so often now, that the charity store he tended to choose had got to know him and greeted him with a coffee and a smile, the former of which he appreciated on the remainder of the journey to LAX.

Invariably, this meant that Tim would either be dressed in a plain white t-shirt, or a grey tourist edition emblazoned with 'I HEART LA' or a pictorial ode to 'MUSCLE BEACH'.

Miles could not argue with the logic, as they were constantly shuttling between two countries and it meant that Tim could arrive with hand luggage only, whilst Miles was struggling with baggage and queues at the carousel. So many times, Miles had exited into the arrivals lounge and know where to find Tim - in the bar, on his second beer, but always with a fresh one for Miles.

That morning, it seemed that Tim also was in a reflective mood. Miles knew this, as it was always started the same way, when he had something important to say.

'Miles, my friend, here we are.'

Miles smiled and took the take-away coffee that Tim passed to him.

'Do you know, we have created something? Actually created something and people like it?'

Miles was not sure where this was going and given that he was just waking up from his own reflective mood, could only nod.

'Do you know what the thing about it is, Miles, my friend?'

Tim didn't wait for an answer and continued, 'There are a lot of people in this world, who have created things that no one likes, except them. Or maybe they haven't had that break, or a person who backs them up or understands their originality. Perhaps they were just a little bit ahead of their time, or talked to the wrong people at the wrong time and got discouraged. I have love for them, because creating things is the hardest thing to do in life and creating something original is even harder.'

Miles could only agree. He had never thought about it like that before. It was just something they did, something that was natural and instinctive. But Tim was right – they had created something.

'There are also a lot of people in this world, who make a very good living, talking about other people's ideas. Talking about them, critiquing them, maybe to the point that people give up and are convinced their idea is not a good one. But that's the difference between the creators and the critics, Miles, my friend. The fact is, it's actually quite easy to find problems with other people's work and quite easy to comment on it. Creating it is hard, critiquing it is easy and we are one of the creators, we are the good guys. But for us, we have created something that people love. Loved, endorsed it and tried to make it theirs, by saying they were the first to discover it, or that they had already seen the play in the UK, even if they haven't really seen it. We are part of the chosen few, Miles, the chosen few in life who have created something that has captured the imagination of everyone who has seen it. I realised this last night and it has given me even more energy for *Misunderstood*. I realised, that if everyone who had said they had seen *Misunderstood*, in its original form in the UK had actually seen it, then we would have been playing stadiums, not pubs!'

Tim let out an energetic laugh and clapped Miles so hard on the back, that he spilled his coffee on his jeans.

Miles found his mood uplifting and instead of worrying, cast a thought back to Sophie, in his hotel room. She would probably be getting up about now and starting on her blog. Miles knew that she had to finish it that day, before she went back to the airport and was quite excited to see it. However, they had agreed that Sophie would write it and post it, without showing it to anyone – not Miles and not Tim. It had to be impartial and it had to be credible. Miles also knew it was important for Sophie. This was her first one for a long time, so she had to be able to do it alone, to know that she could; Miles respected that. He thought about texting her and even got out his phone, but thought better of it. They were now arriving at the studio, which meant that if he texted her, he would be rushed and he didn't want that. There would be time later to text her, then before he knew it, he would be back in London and they could figure things out together.

Being home was also something that he couldn't wait for. He loved Los Angeles, but when you wanted quiet times, it was a place that was hard to be. There was the temptation of the beach and the temptation to always be outside, to feel the breeze. Bars invited you in, with the vibe of a bottled beer, condensation soaking the napkin. In London, spaces could be more oppressive and the weather encouraged you to find a base, a haven that he could use to do the opposite – shut out the world and just be snug, insular and cosy. Los Angeles never gave you the feeling that you needed a cosy base, instead it gave you the feeling that all you needed was a bed and an open window, so you could hear the ocean. That said, perhaps he could find something of that base in this city. Perhaps next time, he and Tim should find an apartment rather than a hotel, even rent one for a few months if they were going to be that busy. He felt a ripple of excitement, as the taxi pulled up outside the glass-fronted studio.

The next two days, were a blur of meetings and conversation. It was the first time they had been with their investor since before the show. Miles added him to the list of people who had just fallen out of the sky, into a bar, on a beach in India, that Tim happened to be in that very night.

They had analysed the press coverage they had created from the show and compared that to other video games that had launched, with their various levels of success. What was clear, was that the coverage received from *Misunderstood*, was bigger in number of articles and better in terms of acclaim, than any project that the studio had been involved in. He was understandably excited and had so many ideas and visions for the following months. But one thing was clear, they were going to have to push everyone really hard and also extend the good feeling that the event had gained in the United States, across into Europe. In the US, the

331

coverage had been good, due to the invited guests and the event, but it was clear that a similar event was required in either London or Paris. Or perhaps somewhere else, somewhere more gothic, where you could imagine being infested with zombies. Prague was even mentioned, which gave Miles a flash of Sophie. He couldn't wait to tell her that.

They talked about *Misunderstood 2*, the themes of which had now grown from a seed of an idea and was starting to take shape. It had kept the ambitious nature that Tim had talked so frivolously about, but they had found a way to create something more believable and less fantastic. Tim had been talked down from a movie, back to the creation of another video game – at least first of all. But it was definitely a big project and would take even more time and money, than the first game. They felt it was starting to take the form of a story, rather than a collection of ideas. They could see how the video game could follow from *Misunderstood 2*, just as it had from the original.

It was strange talking about it before the first game had even launched, but this was the nature of the industry. The investor had enough experience, he said, to know that the first game was going to be a success and they couldn't afford to let that momentum slip. They needed to start putting the agreements and contacts in place, so that they could move seamlessly from one title to the next.

On the second day, they left the studio exhausted, with enough time to take a stop at the hotel, gather their belongings and head to the airport. They had spent the previous night at the studio, bunked down in one of the meeting rooms, so that they were available for the animators and the story-writers if required. The team was now pretty much working 24-hours a day, to get the game finished and it would be a few weeks before Tim and Miles could get out to Los Angeles again.

Because of that, Miles had almost forgotten about the text that Sophie had sent the previous night. He had received it in the middle of a meeting, so had shot back his love and best wishes for the flight. He had also done the same when she texted to say that she had landed safely, this time they had also both talked about how excited they were to see each other. He was excited for the present she had left, but hadn't been back to the hotel yet, having spent the previous night on sofas at the studio. But if it was something she had left, then he was sure he was going to enjoy it. He also asked her about the blog, apologising that he had not yet had the chance to view it. She just said that she understood and that the views had started slowly, which was understandable given she had been offline for so long. But she said that views were picking up and that everyone seemed happy to have her back.

When Miles got to his room, it still smelled of Sophie. She had been gone for a day, but she was the last person to shower in there. Miles took in a lungful and headed over to the desk. There he found the paper and smiled to himself. At first, he assumed the USB was the blog, but then he realised the blog was already live and would have been when Sophie left for the airport. He wondered aloud what it might be and was half-considering watching it, when at that moment there was a knock at the door and a muffled shout from Tim that their car was outside for the airport. So Miles scooped up the paper and the USB and zipped it into his hand luggage.

There it stayed; all the way to the airport and onto the plane. Just as Sophie had done the previous day, Miles settled into his seat and texted Sophie, letting her know that he would watch whatever was on the USB whilst he was in the air and that he was intrigued as to the content. He then let the wave of tiredness from the trip wash over him. Before the plane had even left the runway, Miles was asleep and dreaming.

He was dreaming about Sophie, dreaming about Vegas and dreaming about the future. A future with Tim. A future with *Misunderstood* and a future with Sophie.

Chapter 28

Heart

June 18, 2007.

Being madly in love, is still madness. It makes you act irrationally and changes the perception of you, by the people around you. But in your own torment, and even if they don't realise at the time, it makes others act differently and sometimes unexpectedly. Those who know about love will stand by you, strangers may smile at you and it creates bonds between friends. You never forget someone who stood by you when you were mad, because they saw through it; through the irrationality, and just saw love in all its breathtaking glory.

For those who have experienced this madness, it is intoxicating and addictive, and although you may have moments of clarity, it is a brief surfacing. People will tell you that it subsides and becomes a deeper love, something that is rational and shared. Perhaps this is true, but then how do you explain how a smell, or a touch can change your mood, so many years later? Couples who hold hands after being together for 50 years, might not think they feel exactly the same as they did in the first moment, but they still do it, they still hold hands and for that brief moment, they are mad once more.

Miles often thought about this when he reflected on the time he had known Sophie, he was pretty sure there had been a little bit of madness. As the plane descended into London, he couldn't catch his breath and he thought about it again. Every second seemed to last forever and he was almost willing the plane to land quicker, so that he could see her. Everything around him was amplified, the whine of the engine, the smell of the seats, the crisp breeze of the air conditioning.

Of course, it was the video that had caused his euphoria. He had woken refreshed, with three hours still to go in the flight. As soon as he woke, his mind immediately drifted to the video, but he decided to wash his face and have a snack before he settled into it. He wanted to feel good and properly awake when he watched whatever it was, although as he impatiently waited for a bathroom cubicle to be free, it was almost as if the USB was burning a hole in his mind, as well as his bag. He couldn't wait to see what it was, but at the same time he was nervous. Something about the way that Sophie left it, told him that what he was about to see was big. She didn't make gestures like that often and in fact, the last one he could remember was the cardboard sign at the airport. This made Miles unsure what was going to happen. Considering she had been working on the blog at the time, Miles could only assume it had something to do with that, but there, his speculation ended.

With a shaking hand, he had tried to slide the USB into its slot. Then turned it upside down and inserted it the other way, of course. He double clicked on the content.

Some miles away, back in her flat in London, Sophie was thinking about Miles and thinking that he must be entering UK air-space soon. She pictured the little map and the blinking plane image on the TV screens, hovering above Ireland.

Sophie was experiencing something of a surprising morning herself, given what had started happening overnight, around the time that Miles must have been getting on the plane. She didn't usually log onto her laptop before bed, but something that previous night had made her take a look. It was probably just to get a last look at Miles' face and to feel connected to him, now that she knew he was out of reach for the eleven hour flight back from Los Angeles. She took the laptop to her room and logged on from under the duvet.

When she first looked at the blog, there was not too much untoward. There had been a bit of a spike in views, which was very pleasing for her. It showed that, slowly, the community was passing around the link and that was good for her, as she re-established herself as a video blogger. There were also some familiar names reappearing, for example she noticed that SuperSuperLove was back and that made her feel good in the way that the familiar always does. There was also more comments than usual – although she guessed this would probably be the case, as she had been offline for so long. A lot of her community had some pent-up wishes to give her and forthright views on Smooth. The majority of them were supportive and were expressing joy and love that she was back, and back with such a great piece. The consensus was that she had not lost her touch and that her community was looking forward to much more of this from now on.

But every now and again, there was a comment specifically about a part of the video and specifically the parts that featured her and Miles. Her community was giving her a message. It was a comment from SuperSuperLove that first caught Sophie's attention.

'So, you and Miles. Damn! ☺'

Sophie smiled. Trust SuperSuperLove to comment on that. To be honest, she had always assumed that he was a he, because of his profile picture and some of the comments he made. But at the same time, who's to know? But whether boy or girl, it was very kind of them to notice the chemistry between them and it gave Sophie a warm feeling, as she closed the lid of the computer and turned over to sleep.

She wasn't sure if it was that comment, or just the anticipation of seeing Miles, but Sophie didn't sleep well that night and found herself up early. It was probably around the time that Miles woke up on the plane, because she could just see the first thread of dawn starting to reach above the city horizon.

Of course, she was not to know that, at that exact time, Miles was watching her video and realising that she was in love with him. But whenever she thought about and looked back to that day and that moment, she always liked to think they were connected in some way As she woke, she noticed her laptop on her bedside table, where she had left it, so decided to take another look at the blog.

As she read and absorbed what was happening, she remembered the story that Miles and Tim told her, about when the video of *Misunderstood* took off. Of course, being Miles and Tim, Sophie had been rapt as she watched them fight for the best one-liner and cut the air with wild gesticulations, but at the same time she had found it hard to comprehend. How you post something from a flat in London and it's viewed by several million people across all continents. She understood the concept of having a few people in different countries who viewed your videos. There were people like that everywhere – small pockets of extremely enthusiastic Internet viewers, who would surf for hours from video to video. But millions? To a generation who had not grown up with the Internet as children, she just couldn't picture that.

They say that experience brings wisdom and for Sophie, wisdom was about to hit her hard, because it was all about to change for her that morning.

Sophie had expected something to happen, when she blogged about *Misunderstood*. She had seen and experienced how powerful the reaction to the show had been and had experienced the coverage that the show had received first hand. So she did expect part of the increase in her views to have come from this fact and also the Zombie community, which she knew was very tight and one that loved to share.

But what she hadn't expected, were the comments specifically about her and Miles. From everywhere.

From zombie fans and her regular fans. There were comments from her own friends and even from journalists, who had referenced the article and placed a link in their own articles of the day. It seemed that everyone had seen what she had seen and felt, even though she had moved most of the more obvious clips to the separate video, which Miles was currently viewing at

35,000 feet. Everyone could see the chemistry between them and everyone could see that they were in love. Madly in love, as Miles would probably say.

Plus, it was not just a few comments. Overnight there had been pages and pages of posts and links. She started reading them, but realised that it wasn't something she could do from her bed. She needed to shower and wake up properly, to try and comprehend what was going on. She needed coffee and she needed Miles to be here with her. This was something that she should share with him, because it underlined everything that she had meant when she left the USB for him. On the USB it was suggested and it was subtle. A clip of a look that passed between them, or a clip of a light touch. But the community had seen through all this subtlety, as only strangers can. The theme was very simple and clear. Their theme was focused on one thing only; that Sophie was back, but also, that there was no Sophie without Miles.

At the airport, Miles had landed and he was busy trying to disentangle himself from the plane, whilst at the same time shooting Sophie a text, to let her know that he was on his way, he had watched the video and that he couldn't wait to see her. He was in such a daze, that he almost unconsciously told her that he loved her. Be cool Miles, he thought to himself. Not yet.

Being cool, of course, was not easy to accomplish under the circumstances. His body and his mind, were fighting with the comedown from the time he had just spent in Los Angeles and then what lay ahead of him in London. He was used to feeling desperation towards Sophie, but usually he was desperate in what he said and desperate to be with her, but not in this way. This time, there was a chance it was going to actually work between them, so it was desperation to find that out and he knew that a text or a call could not answer that. He navigated through the crowds and immigration, almost on autopilot, never taking his eyes off his phone. He was willing Sophie to text back and at least confirm what he thought and what the video was. It was a declaration and this time there was nothing to spoil it, no one else in their lives to get in the way. Miles felt like this was their chance and there was no way that he was going to let it slip.

It took until he was in the baggage hall for his phone to buzz and Miles felt his heart leap. He glanced down, but it was Tim, wondering where he was. In his delirium, Miles had completely forgotten to wait for him. They had sat separately on the plane, which was another of Tim's rules. He didn't like his friends to see him asleep, he said that it was the one piece of mystery that he still wanted to keep from a world that seemed to want to photograph and film everything these days.

Miles expected that it was more likely to be because of excessive drooling, but hadn't ever been bothered to try and find out. He had realised very quickly in their relationship to respect the boundaries that Tim set, so he went along with it. Only once, on a previous trip, he had taken a wander to the back of the plane to try and catch a glimpse of Tim. What he had found, had given him as much ammunition to mock him, as seeing Tim with his mouth open, or snoring loud enough to disturb fellow passengers. At first, actually, he couldn't find him and had to check from seat to seat, to try and identify where Tim was sitting. When he eventually found him, he was not surprised that he didn't recognise him. Tim had pulled his hoodie up and over his face and used the toggles to lock it in place so that only his eyes and nose would be visible anyway. He had then covered his eyes with a regular eye mask, the kind that is handed out on long plane journeys. That was also normal enough, but then Tim had also wrapped a scarf around his face, so that the only skin showing were two nostrils, presumably so that he did not suffocate in mid-flight.

Miles shot a text back to Tim, explaining that he would see him later at the pub and that he had pressing business to attend to. They had arranged to take a taxi together, but Miles explained in his text that he was going to take the train straight to Sophie's house. He added that he hoped that Tim would understand and that he would explain everything tomorrow.

Back at Sophie's house, she was in the middle of her breakfast, when Miles texted. It surprised her, in the silence of the flat and snapped her out of her own thoughtful trance. He had landed and she was so happy, but it had been quite a morning. She had so much to say to him and couldn't wait to explain how she felt about him and show him the comments on her blog. Since that morning, the views of the video had increased even more, her phone had also started ringing. Mainly it was friends, who she hadn't connected with for months, since she broke up with Smooth. She had tried not to answer a lot of them, it was more her nature to hide on these occasions. But given that this was the age of the Internet and the mobile phone, rather than a landline and a doorbell, she had given up and taken some calls, at least to give her the chance to start to rationalise what was happening. From her friends' perspective, she had suddenly been to Los Angeles, she was blogging again and was in love. Her friends had so many excited questions, as all this seemed to have happened in the space of just a few weeks.

Maybe that is how she would explain to Miles; because in reality, it wasn't just a few weeks. Hadn't it really started when she met him for the first time, at The Killers gig at Shepherds Bush? If it had been up to Miles, they would have got together that very night. Was it not Sophie, herself, that had complicated things since then? She was the one in a relationship to start with. Then she was the one who had pushed him away at every opportunity since then, with a reason, or an excuse. It was her, who had also drunk herself into a coma in her flat and not called Miles for support. She knew in her heart, that every decision she had made felt right at the time and that if they had got together then it wouldn't have lasted. But should she have given it a go to find out, rather than just trying to avoid it?

It was then her, who had started to let Miles in, slowly at first, but when she did, she found that only good things happened. He had made her night, that first time. She had been stood up and if she hadn't stumbled into Miles, then she would have spent a miserable night on her own, or perhaps with someone who was equally as unsuitable as Smooth. He had given her some of the best times, he had made her laugh when they partied at festivals, it was him with whom she had exchanged thousands of texts and messages, and when she had bared everything to him over coffee, he listened and gave her some of the best and honest advice that anyone could give.

Then there was New Year's Eve, when everything started to fall apart with Smooth. He had given up his night to be with her on the phone. Granted, he was having his own personal nightmare, but that didn't really matter, he stuck with her and she stuck with him. Now, with *Misunderstood*, that was another level. It could be the beginning of something huge for both of them. But none of this would have happened, without Miles' relentless conviction that they should be together and his perseverance with her, in the face of so much adversity.

When they didn't speak, it was her that had pushed Miles away, even when it was for the right reasons at the time. For so long, it had never seemed like the right time and it was always her that said the words. But when you cut through all the complications and all the excuses, hadn't he now been a part of her life, since that very first moment? Wasn't that really the best and most important spontaneous moment in either of their lives, despite what had happened since, to both of them? That was really the night, where the course of her world changed. It was the night when she first started looking inside herself and thinking about who she was and how to be happy. She was happy, all because of that night, just like Miles had said then and always since. It was only fear that had held her back. Fear that once she was involved with him, there was no turning back – they had to be together forever, or never speak again.

She didn't know how to put it into a text and she didn't want to call him, but she needed him to know something, now that he had watched the video. She knew what he would be thinking and although he didn't say it in his text, she knew that the silence was just anticipation. Sophie picked up her phone and chose her words carefully as she typed.

At the station at Heathrow, Miles was going crazy that Sophie hadn't texted back yet. But then, just as he was getting on the train, his phone buzzed. He pulled it out of his pocket, his hands shaking so much that he almost dropped it onto the tracks. He only had to read it once to know what it meant.

IT IS WHAT YOU THINK. COME HERE, NOW...
X

Perhaps it was thinking about this text that distracted Miles. Part of him couldn't believe this was happening, but at the same time, it was down to the choices he had made. He had chosen to walk away from things that had not made him happy and run towards the things that did. He had learned to live in the moment, but with that rare ability to know where he wanted the next moment to be and whom he wanted it to be with. It had all started when he met Sophie, when she had bumped into him and given him the first of her many put-downs. It began when he chose not to give up on her and on them. He chose it because he could see something in how they were together. She gave him clarity of thinking, he knew how to be with her and how to help her. Through this he also got a clearer understanding of who he was. She gave him the confidence to be who he was and not be ashamed, because if she loved it and if she loved being with him, then no one else mattered. For most of the train journey, he kept checking those eight words and smiling.

In the end, that is what some of the people on the train recalled. Whenever they did, it made Sophie smile. Of course, they were always strangers, as Sophie didn't actually know anyone on the train that day and at the time, the strangers didn't know it was 'that' Miles, or 'that' Sophie, until the news broke on social media. But even strangers remember the look of true love, when they see it, even on another stranger.

Perhaps it was the video, the pictures of them together that had made his attention wander. The time when he was not checking his phone, he was watching the content from the USB. He was watching the looks they shared and how they fit together. They were so easy in each other's company and along with Tim, they could read each other completely. He caught himself wondering, if this was what it was going to be like when they were older, perhaps when they were working on *Misunderstood 8*, or perhaps when Sophie was the most-viewed video blogger in the world. The world was changing, but the video showed how much in life is unspoken and physical, communicated by a movement of the eyes, or the head. A hand on the small of your back, a casual nudge of the shoulder.

It might even have been the card that Miles had tucked away in his pocket. He had made sure he grabbed it before he left the airport and had written the first thing that he thought of in it. He couldn't really express what he was feeling in his own words, but he had remembered every song that they sent to each other whilst they were apart and texting in the mornings. One of them was his particular favourite and he had copied some lyrics carefully, whilst he was waiting for the take-away coffee that he hoped would give him the pep and the energy he needed to get across town. Whilst he was writing it, Miles found himself wondering, whether poets came first, or musicians. These days, they were the same – musicians were the new poets and video games were the new TV.

As he got off the train and through the barriers, into the sunlight of the June afternoon, he checked once more that he had everything; wallet, card, mobile phone, keys, computer. He wondered if he had chosen the right song and whether he should turn up with himself and his own words. Greeting cards were part of the old Miles, the Miles that he had left behind, the night that Sophie had fallen from the sky and into his life. The song had been going round and round in his head since he had written the lyrics.

Perhaps it was this that distracted him, or perhaps it was as simple as the bright June sun and the fact that he was tired, having just got off a long flight. Afterwards, some people who were nearby, swore that Miles stepped into the road and that he wasn't looking, but that wasn't like him. Despite everything, he was as careful in himself as he was caring in others.

Others said that it came around the corner too quickly and was too close to the kerb. They weren't going that fast, just fast enough, but then Tim always said it was often the small things that were important. Just fast enough.

Miles did not deserve for his luck to run out, right at that moment. A second earlier, or later, then it would have missed him and their worlds would have been very different.

He didn't deserve it and Sophie didn't deserve to lose him. For the first time since she had known Miles, it felt she had made the right choice by him. She had finally decided to commit. Now he was gone.

But that is what happened.

Chapter 29

Love

November 13, 2004.

There is no etiquette for the moment that you enter someone else's hotel room.

If you know them well, it is probably easier. But if you have met that same night, then it's one of the most awkward moments that you'll ever experience. Forget about the chances of stray underwear, or heaven forbid the lingering aroma of a bowel movement, just focus on the fact that you have to find somewhere to sit in what is effectively a bedroom.

In Miles' room, there were also no frills. Miles had been acutely aware of this, all the way back from Shepherds Bush. You basically had a bed and a sofa, the kind of multi-coloured two-seater that is probably multi-coloured to give some camouflage to equally multi-coloured stains. Where Sophie chose to sit, either on the bed or the sofa, would give him an impression of where she thought the night might lead.

He was also pretty certain there was a bit of a smell of damp, but he guessed that none of these factors were his fault. He never left the hotel room in a state, which was mainly down to the fact that he had become uniquely attached to the strangest places as "home" since "The Decision" and had become more fiercely house-proud then he ever was when he had an actual house. In fact, for a few days he had been able to successfully wash, change and heat a decent meal in a Volkswagen Golf, with only the cigarette lighter for power supply.

So, as he stood in the doorway and as this thought process and protocols of the room cycled through Miles' mind, he was surprised to hear a yell behind him.

'SMACK DOOOOWN...'

Sophie came hurling past him, took two strides and a full swan dive, entering the bed space at the foot of the bed and landing squarely in the middle, taking one bounce and coming to rest noisily at the headboard. It was even noisier than it could have been, because the mattress was as well-sprung as it was worn, so her bounce basically flipped her over and she landed in an ungracious heap of arms and legs – the latter taking out the pillows in different directions and almost putting a hole in the ornate plywood.

Good heavens, thought Miles, I've just met her, but I think I love this girl.

Pulling himself together, he slumped on the bed next to Sophie, who had collected herself, taken her shoes off and was busy trying to rearrange her sweater, which had twisted around so the hood was covering her face. This gave Miles another chance to take her in and although he was pretty drunk, he had to admit, she was probably one of the most naturally beautiful girls he had ever met, despite her attitude. She had been downright mean all night, but with such a playful look in her grey eyes that he couldn't help but think that underneath it all really, she had enjoyed hanging out. Some people just had different ways and she was still here, so it couldn't have been all bad. Plus, she was interested enough to come back to his room.

'I'm drunk, that was an ace night,' said Sophie when she had seemingly turned the hoodie inside out and back to front before finally getting it back as it was supposed to be. 'Where are we? Who are you?'

Miles laughed nervously, smiled self-consciously and blushed. He wanted to respond, but couldn't find any words. He really needed to work on his one-liners, if he was going to get anywhere with this girl.

For Sophie, for the first time since Miles and her had met earlier in the evening, she felt her stomach do a little flip at his shyness. He wasn't exactly her type, but he was handsome, even though he was clearly a damaged person. Initially, she had only talked to him because she felt bad for being mean about the first thing she said to him. It wasn't his fault that she had been stood up and once they had cleared up the misunderstanding and that she hadn't stolen his drink, he had perked up considerably. It was true, he was terrible at chatting up girls, but that just made it safe for her and meant that she could spend the evening chatting and not feeling under pressure to be the life of the party. Plus, he had a nice smile.

But then there was the dancing. Oh my, the dancing. Initially, he was obsessed with staying rooted to the spot by the bar, where she had met him, but gradually, as they got more drunk, she managed to convince him down to the actual stalls. Not into the crowd, but frustratingly, just on the edge of it. Get involved, she had said, and eventually he did.

As the night carried on, she found him very easy to talk to and found themselves both relaxing. Considering how badly her night had started, he had her smiling and then laughing, within a few minutes of meeting him. He had a self-depreciating humour that was part serious and partly, she knew, was designed to make her feel good. He kept telling her that his street-cred was seriously improving by hanging out with her, at which point she reminded him that by just using the words 'street-cred', he automatically lost any points on that account he had built up, but actually, it made her feel good in a way she hadn't felt for a while. Like she was the cool one in the relationship and that Miles appreciated just being around her, and even though she was just in jeans and a hoodie, she was attractive. It felt good, so she just decided to go with it.

She also had the whisper of another feeling, something she couldn't describe. Her rational mind was telling her that this guy wasn't right for her, that he wasn't handsome enough or cool enough. But there was another emotion fighting to get to the surface, there was something that made her want to be with him. Whenever he drifted off to the bar, or stepped out of the crowd, she was afraid he was leaving and she would never see him again. It was a tug that she couldn't explain and a tug to be with him. As for Smooth, she hadn't even switched her phone back on and was frankly not bothered what he was up to.

They were now lying side-by-side on the bed at Miles' hotel, surrounded by fried chicken boxes and staring at the ceiling. Miles stared straight ahead; because he felt like if he looked at her then she might leave. It felt like something was happening and he felt that they had a connection. Something behind the surface of the eyes, a thin thread that kept them connected for the evening, stopping either of them walking away, or making an excuse, or wanting the night to end.

He really wanted to tell her that. He wanted Sophie to know that he wasn't bothered about being cool, or saying the right thing, because he wanted to see her again. It was absolutely the wrong time for him to fall in love and he was trying desperately not to, but there was something in the way their steps fell instantly in time. He had fallen in love with Sophie that night and he needed to tell her.

But as much as it takes an instant for those threads to entwine, they are fragile and easily broken. Miles knew that, so he didn't say all that and instead, just said,

'Best night ever…'

Somehow, Sophie knew what he meant. Her stomach did a little flip again. She was definitely drunk and this was probably a bad idea, but she decided she was going to give him an actual compliment. What could go wrong? He didn't know her number, or her address. He didn't even have an actual address. If something happened, she could just slip away and get lost with the other ten million people in London, and never have to see him again.

She had spent her whole life, she decided, letting people come to her. Letting guys ask her out, letting her friends organise things, never putting herself out there. Why not take a risk? Maybe it was meant to be.

But as she did, as she ordered the words in her mind, struggling through the fug of lager, but feeling more excited and sober than she had for a long time… she realised that Miles was already asleep. She knew that, because he had just started snoring. She knew from the volume of the snoring, that if she stayed then she was unlikely to get a wink of sleep. But she wanted to stay anyway. She wanted to be there when he woke up.

Chapter 30

Permanent

July 1, 2007.

They were a long way from where they started, was what a lot of people were telling Sophie. It wasn't her fault, was another one. He was so happy when he was with her, was a third.

For Sophie, she had none of these feelings, as she sat on the edge of her bed, trying to figure out if she was strong enough to go to the funeral. Tim was in the next room and he was using none of this rhetoric. Tim was just waiting, just being there and that is what she needed.

The people who were telling her all these things, were virtual strangers. It brought it all into focus, the time that she and Miles had together. Their time together was not enough, not long enough, not deep enough. Seeing all the people that had known Miles for decades, when she had only known him for a few years, made her angry and jealous. Many of them she had never met before, which means that Miles hadn't seen them either for some years, so how could that be? If she had her way, she would go back in time to when they first met and spend every minute of the day with Miles. In fact, if she could go back in time, then actually she would go back even further – to when he was a little boy. She would find the little-boy Miles and spend every minute of the day with him. She would tell him what a special person he was at every opportunity and how he didn't need to be awkward, or ashamed of who he was. She would make sure that he wouldn't have to wait until the third decade of his life to realise that and have to do it all by himself.

Sophie knew that everyone meant well and that what she was thinking was unreasonable, especially given that for them, she was also a stranger. She guessed that was just the way the world was becoming these days. So much was done electronically, that for many of Miles' family and friends, she was just words on a text, or a sentiment in an email. She could tell that he had spoken fondly of her, otherwise they wouldn't have been so welcoming at the few gatherings that had happened ahead of today, they wouldn't have taken the time to let her know the details of the memorial service and wouldn't have asked her to do a reading.

But she had never actually met them, never stood next to Miles and shaken a hand, or kissed a cheek. Never shared a lunch, or a walk, or woken up in the morning and shared a coffee with any of these people. In a world where everything was starting to happen so quickly, it seemed that we had taken the opposite approach to human contact. We were no longer in a hurry to call someone, or spend an evening together, because we could get the bare bones of an update actively through a text, or passively through a social network posting. For most of us, relationships were becoming based on remote affection, and the eponymous greeting: how are you?

Once you could answer that through social networks, whether it be genuine or not, then what was left? You no longer needed to call someone, or take that step to spend real time to find that out. What was lost as a by-product of that? How much richness came after the first inquisition on their health and wellbeing? For her and Miles, the real richness of the conversation might come after that had laid in silence for minutes. Immediacy, had become the enemy of intimacy.

In terms of whose fault it was, who knows? Maybe it was her fault, for keeping him at arm's length for so long and then suddenly deciding that they should be together. Perhaps, by forcing them both to bottle-up so many feelings for so long, then she had created a situation that was always going to be explosive in some way. But as much as that moment may have been because of what Miles was doing and where he was in that exact, terrible second, the creating of Miles had been a long journey.

Years of low confidence had made him sensitive and years of knocks had made him emotional about the good things in his life. So, if he was so happy, then that was Sophie's fault, but she would never feel any guilt for it, because he couldn't have said that too many times in his life. It was all their faults. They had created a complicated, fragile, beautiful person, who was just trying to find a path in life and who it turned out, was perfectly suited to the place that the world was becoming. A place of computer animated zombies, a bigger place where you could always find someone, somewhere, to identify with, even if it was on a different continent. A place that took him away, just when he was discovering it, realising his own worth and finding his own calm, in the middle of the storm.

Tim had come in now and was sitting next to her on the bed. She could tell in his eyes that it was time to go and she knew that he was dreading it as much as she was. She knew that they were about to be with Miles, even if they wouldn't see him, and that it would bring his face to mind, without them being able to control it. Their only saving grace recently, had been that they didn't need to see, speak or think about Miles, when they didn't want to or couldn't control it. In the lucid moments, when they felt reflective and thankful, they had mentioned him and talked about it. But in the low points, both of them knew that it was best just to avoid the topic.

People always said that it was at the strangest times that you grieved and for Sophie, it was the moments when she was forced to think about Miles when she was not ready. When she found something of his by surprise, or she walked past somewhere that they had coffee together and laughed together. She always tried to take routes to places that were new, so that it didn't happen, but they had been to so many places that sometimes she forgot, turned a corner and caught a glimpse of a pub sign, or the pattern of an outdoor tablecloth. For that reason, neither herself or Tim, had been able to go back to the pub just yet. Miles was definitely there, reflected in every glass, his ghost was on every stool. They knew it would change and get better, but for now it was too early, too surprising, too uncontrollable.

The service, was due to take place somewhere local to where Miles had grown up, which in some way had helped both Sophie and Tim. Here, there were no echoes of Miles for them. At these times, they could just let life pass them by for a little while; let it pass in a blur. If they just didn't think about the fact that they were a three, not a two, then it would be OK. Every now and again, Tim would feel Sophie tense a little bit and would just place his hand over hers in the back of the car. They were getting a lift over from one of the main cast of *Misunderstood*, who had all turned out for Miles. They were his people, they had said.

Sophie and Tim had deliberately arrived early, so they didn't have to talk to anyone and could just find their place in the chapel, but when they pulled up, there was already a small group gathering. There were older people, who were clearly family, and then small groups of others, of various ages, who could be university friends, or ex-colleagues, she didn't know. Sophie could place a few of them from the last few weeks and was embraced warmly by Miles' parents. Others, she recognised from photographs as friends and relatives and touchingly, there were also some of the pub regulars there as well, looking completely out of place in smart suits rather than skinny jeans and scruffy t-shirts. The same could probably be said for Tim, although he had worn a pair of old Converse with a tailored suit that he had bought especially for the occasion.

Miles always wanted to see him in a suit, he had said. Ever since he had berated them in their first performance of *Misunderstood*, where Tim had introduced the new play to the audience in a beer-stained apron, Miles had chided him that he was missing an opportunity, because he would have cut a fine silhouette in a suit and there may have been eligible ladies out there. The Converse were Miles' favourite, he had said, and also a recognition that Miles would have expected him to ruin the look, somehow.

Mixed in with the pub regulars, was then a surprising few faces from both Los Angeles and from the zombie community. Sophie and Tim had put word out to the *Misunderstood* cast, but it was a touching sight to see that a few of the wider community had come along as well – especially some of the video game development crew from California. They must have found out through speaking with the cast, Sophie thought. For them to make the effort to come halfway across the world was incredible. For the rest of them, even getting them out of the city just showed how popular Miles had become. She took time to greet them all wordlessly, hoping that her face showed how thankful she was and that she didn't have to say anything. She then headed into the church, with Tim hanging back for a few minutes to chat with the guys, but thankfully not for too long.

When Tim came in, he settled beside Sophie and spoke to her, for what seemed like the first time for days. He had always been there, but they had almost had a wordless relationship. Perhaps it had been that way even since Tim had turned up on her doorstep, to let her know that the police had just been to the pub and that something terrible had happened.

He told her that some of the zombie guys, had only really found out late the previous night, so had rallied as many people as they could through the forums. They had shared lifts, co-ordinated taxis and created meeting points along the way. There were the staunch supporters, but also those who only remembered Miles and Tim by face, but had followed their story online and felt like they should come and pay their respects.

They felt they were all connected to the story somehow, either through having seen the play, or by having been a face in the crowd on the YouTube video that had gone viral and turned the rollercoaster into a rocket ship for Miles and Tim. The group had agreed between them, that they would stay outside and not interrupt the ceremony, but they just wanted to be there and they knew there were people who couldn't make it, who would appreciate their representation. Tim also said he had met a few people who had claimed to be followers of Sophie's video blog, although he said it wasn't hard to miss some of them, just because of their wacky fashion sense that was making for a strange sight against the black and grey of the zombie fans, as the two communities mixed. He also said, a few of them introduced themselves in broken English, as some very strange names. He assumed that it was their Internet identities, he said, but their accents were very strong.

Sophie smiled and made a mental note to see them afterwards. Right now, she was only focused on getting through the next hour of her life and the reading that she had promised to do. She had asked to do it right at the end, so that family and long-time friends had the opportunity to go first. Then perhaps she could close the service, even after the casket had gone, so that she didn't have to look at it, or in some way feel like she was speaking to Miles. The family had agreed, which made Sophie feel better, because then she knew that if she couldn't manage it, then it didn't interrupt the proceedings in any way. She had never experienced anything like this before, so she had no idea how it was going to go. She had visions of herself throwing up on the lectern, or over a close relative, and she didn't want that to happen.

As the service went on, Sophie felt herself calming. The atmosphere was crackling with emotion, but it seemed like a happy emotion. She thought about the people outside and how they had come so far for this final moment for Miles', she knew how important moments were for him. If he was here, he would probably be saying that this was what life was about, it was about physical gatherings of people, not virtual ones, despite the fact that it was the virtual in the end that he was so good at. He would say that in the storm that life was becoming, having everyone here together and at peace, represented the calm and that the calm moments were the ones that were most real. Where a minute felt like a minute and you spent longer than two minutes just sitting and enjoying the silence. He would say that it was ironic, that it took something so dramatic to bring everyone together and got them to be quiet and just enjoy each other's company. Perhaps, also, he would then say that the silence was actually making him nervous and that they needed music, so could someone put Hot Fuss on.

Perhaps it was these thoughts, or the public place, but both Tim and Sophie managed to hold it together, through all the words and the hymns. They managed to keep it together when the curtains closed and Miles disappeared from their lives. For Sophie, she had felt that Miles had left her the moment she had found out and part of her didn't need this final goodbye, to a box, not a face. She also didn't want this as a memory, she didn't want to build it up into that.

She wanted to remember the smiling Miles, the songs he enthusiastically texted her, even the song that he had written down for her, the day he died. She wanted to remember Miles at the festivals, with his geek bag that seemed to give a never-ending supply of beer. She wanted to remember the smell of the wood on the pier in Santa Monica, and how familiar the smell of his flat, and of Miles himself, had become. She wanted to remember the first time she met him and the last time she saw him. This was Miles and these were the thoughts that were in Sophie's head when she took the lectern, with the words she had written. Some of them were hers and some belonged to other people, the poets they had shared their lives with over the last few years.

But then she remembered, in one of his most nauseating moments, that he had told her that love was an ocean. An ocean, he said, sometimes calm and tranquil, sometimes raging and exciting. When you find true love, you are then in the deepest part of the ocean, and perhaps you have been crossing the ocean for decades and endured its storms, its currents and its tides. True love is to look at the clear and calm waters and feel the same excitement that you felt on the first day when you started the journey together, when the waters were shallow and fast moving. You only have a limited time in life, so to spend it loving, and sharing it with the person you love, can never be a waste, or convenient, or selfish. You might not have new things to learn about each other, but you can laugh about the shared stories as you re-live them, or laugh together as you crack the same joke for the 500th time.

You face the storms together, because you know you can get through them, together. The refuge is the arms of your love and the eyes, which are still the same deep pools of excitement and safety, that you fell in love with in that first, breathtaking moment in the water. She thought about this and she was angry, because she wouldn't have this with Miles.

She needed these people to know that, she thought as she took to the lectern, and not just some practised kind words, that meant nothing. Happiness and anger, jealousy and fortune, she felt it all, and all at the same time.

'I feel lucky, because I had more of Miles than I should have had ...' started Sophie, but then she could go no further. The words just wouldn't come. Sophie stood in silence, just looking out into the audience, at faces that she didn't know. As she stared, she wished that just one of them would be Miles. She wished he would just suddenly be there and that this was just a joke, or a weird dream and that she hadn't just lost something that had just begun. Someone who had just started to make her see the world a little bit differently. She was still for a few seconds, but it felt like hours, trying to calm her breathing to continue. She felt Tim appear at her elbow and it helped her to get control over herself. He laid a hand gently on her arm, as if to encourage her to leave the lectern, but she resisted. She wasn't ready to give up yet and so took a deep breath, meaning to continue, waiting for the words on the paper in front of her to stop swimming with grief and tears.

Just as she was about to continue, something caught her attention. At first she thought she had imagined it, as she looked in the direction where it came from, searching for the source. Tim looked at her quizzically, but then his expression changed, as he could hear it as well. It was just a faint sound, but as they focused on it and it got louder, they could tell it was unmistakably music, coming from outside the church. It was unmistakably the song that Miles had hurriedly scribbled the lyrics to, inside the card that he had intended to give to Sophie. Tim and Sophie exchanged a glance and this time, Sophie allowed Tim to lead her away from the lectern and towards the sound.

As they passed the first of the pews, the door to the church opened and light flooded in from the bright summer's day it had become. Both Tim and Sophie strained to see the shapes, but as their eyes adjusted, they met the happy faces of some of their friends from the *Misunderstood* community and other, more colourful people, that Sophie could only assume were fans of her video blog, as they filed past her and into the church, each holding candles and swaying to the sound of music. Smiling faces, that when they had arrived had numbered tens, and now seemed to number hundreds.

As they got nearer to the doorway, they could now hear the music more clearly, but also the sea of people that had gathered in the grounds outside. There were now too many to count, everyone with a candle, quietly sharing the time with Miles and now celebrating him with a song. It had seemed that the word had spread through the channels and more and more of their friends had made the trip from near and far, to say goodbye to Miles and share a moment with him. People, that until a few months ago, wouldn't have known Miles, but who had got to know him through the play. People, who would have only maybe met him once, but had been touched by his infectious spirit and who wanted to say goodbye. As Tim and Sophie passed through the crowd, Sophie felt her sadness melt away for now and they began to dance.

They danced to the music, but they also danced to the last song that Miles had thought about, the last words that he had written and they remembered how happy he was. There would much more time for sadness to come, but right now, they were remembering the good times and why the small moments counted. They were promising to carry that on and make sure that one person can make a change, if they choose to.

As for Sophie, she knew that she was going to be OK. Miles would be permanently with her, because permanence does not always come in the physical presence of someone. It comes in what they give to you and what you give back to them. Sophie had given Miles the confidence to live and believe in himself. Miles had taught Sophie to dream and that dreams built on love, are built to last. They had almost done it. They had almost found the calm in the eye of the storm and had almost managed to control the world that was raging around them. They almost found each other, maybe their fingertips just touched, before Miles was taken back into the storm.

As Sophie danced, she looked at the sky and smiled. Even at the end, Miles had got his wish and exited to a whimsical tune.